JULIE ANNE LONG

My Season of Scandal

THE PALACE OF ROGUES

AVON

An Imprint of HarperCollinsPublishers

MY SEASON OF SCANDAL. Copyright © 2024 by Julie Anne Long. All rights reserved. Printed in the United States of America. No part of this book may be used or reproduced in any manner whatsoever without written permission except in the case of brief quotations embodied in critical articles and reviews. For information, address HarperCollins Publishers, 195 Broadway, New York, NY 10007.

First Avon Books mass market printing: April 2024

Print Edition ISBN: 978-0-06-328095-3
Digital Edition ISBN: 978-0-06-328116-5

Cover design by Amy Halperin
Cover illustration by Kirk DouPonce, FictionArtist.com
Author photograph by Stephanie Herzer

Avon, Avon & logo, and Avon Books & logo are registered trademarks of HarperCollins Publishers in the United States of America and other countries.

HarperCollins is a registered trademark of HarperCollins Publishers in the United States of America and other countries.

FIRST EDITION

24 25 26 27 28 BVGM   10 9 8 7 6 5 4 3 2 1

My Season of Scandal

As the carriage bumped along, beneath his hands her ribs rose and dropped with her breath, which fell softly on his chin.

He heard a rustle as she shifted slightly in his arms. Suddenly his chin no longer rested against her hair.

And then he felt her fingertips, light as a moth landing, on his jaw.

Then skim along the curve of his bottom lip.

He could feel his heart beating in his throat.

His breath came in shreds now.

He opened his eyes to find her gazing up at him from the crook of his arms. Her pupils were large. Her expression, solemn.

Their lips were so close he could feel her breath against his.

When she kissed him—a whisper-soft bump of her lips against his—it could easily be construed as an accident of proximity. If either of them chose.

He closed his eyes against the exultation that roared through him. It was laced through with danger and a lust he could taste in his throat.

It felt like a question.

It felt like permission.

His will crumbled into dust.

Also by Julie Anne Long

The Palace of Rogues series

LADY DERRING TAKES A LOVER
ANGEL IN A DEVIL'S ARMS
I'M ONLY WICKED WITH YOU
AFTER DARK WITH THE DUKE
YOU WERE MADE TO BE MINE
HOW TO TAME A WILD ROGUE

The Pennyroyal Green series

THE PERILS OF PLEASURE
LIKE NO OTHER LOVER
SINCE THE SURRENDER
I KISSED AN EARL
WHAT I DID FOR A DUKE
HOW THE MARQUESS WAS WON
A NOTORIOUS COUNTESS CONFESSES
IT HAPPENED ONE MIDNIGHT
BETWEEN THE DEVIL AND IAN EVERSEA
IT STARTED WITH A SCANDAL
THE LEGEND OF LYON REDMOND

ATTENTION: ORGANIZATIONS AND CORPORATIONS
HarperCollins books may be purchased for educational, business, or sales promotional use. For information, please e-mail the Special Markets Department at SPsales@harpercollins.com.

To you, yes you, the person holding this book in your sweet hands or listening to it with your sweet ears: thank you. May something wonderful happen to you shortly after you finish reading this sentence.

Acknowledgments

∾

M<small>Y</small> DEEPEST gratitude to my splendid editor, May Chen, and the talented staff at Avon; to my stalwart agent, Steven Axelrod, and his marvelous staff; and to my beloved readers, particularly my Street Team, and the delightful, warm, enthusiastic communities at The Pig & Thistle After Dark Facebook Group and Instagram—you make me feel blessed every single day.

My Season of Scandal

Chapter One

‹‹‹◦◦◦›››

CATHERINE KEATING knew she was giddier than she ought to be for eleven o'clock at night on a Thursday evening, but she'd ordered a cup of tea anyway, just because she could, just for the delightful novelty of having it brought right to the door of her boardinghouse room on a tray by a maid named Dot.

Go to London and make all the young men fall in love with you, her father had said.

Catherine frankly liked her chances.

Her dresses might be two seasons old, but she had new handkerchiefs, new gloves, and, thanks to the skillful social maneuverings of a certain Lady Wisterberg, more than a half dozen or so invitations to the season's balls and assemblies. And while she might not have much of a dowry, she did have her lucky necklace that had once been her mother's—a single pearl on a gold chain—and her mother's eyes—wide spaced, sky blue. What more did a girl need?

The plan had been impulsively hatched at a Lancashire house party a few months prior by Lady Wisterberg and Cat's Aunt Keating, who had been delighted when Catherine and Lucy Morrow, Lady Wisterberg's goddaughter, had got on famously. As Lucy had been staying with Lady Wisterberg in her crowded-with-relatives London town house, Catherine and her aunt had written to arrange for a pair of rooms at The Grand Palace on the Thames, a boardinghouse described by their village vicar, Mr. Bellingham, as Elysium by the London docks. *The food! The company! The chandelier!* he'd rhapsodized.

But much like the thrilling plot twist in *The Ghost in the Attic,* the story fellow guest Mrs. Pariseau had read aloud to the others in the boardinghouse sitting room this evening, at the very last minute Cat's great-aunt badly sprained her ankle and couldn't make the journey. Cat had reconciled herself to staying home.

Her father had insisted she go anyway. *I'd like to see you settled, Cat. I won't be here for forever.*

It wasn't a platitude. Her father was a physician, intimately familiar with the tricky intricacies of the human body and the infinite variety of ways in which it could fail, and his was failing. They both knew there was a reason he now needed to pause on the landing to get his breath as he went up the stairs, and why he struggled to travel miles in the dead of night to deliver a baby or sit by a dying man's bed. It was his heart. He and everyone who knew him had long taken for granted that his was as roomy, battered but indestructible as the old leather bag he carried with him when he went to his patients. But they'd buried her mother five years ago—she'd died after a short illness. And Cat suspected her mother had been half the reason her father's heart beat at all.

At the time, it had felt as though her own young heart had been hurled irretrievably into a deep well. Into every life, she supposed, came an event to which one must simply surrender and live through.

Bloom and decay, birth and death—nothing instilled pragmatism and awareness of the rhythms of life more than growing up in a small town in

Northumberland as the only child of the only doctor for miles and miles. Cat wasn't inclined to self-pity. They were far from wealthy—her father had a habit of accepting things like dandelion wine or a piglet for payment when his patients were short of shillings—but there was little she'd ever truly wanted that she couldn't have, unless it was for people and animals she loved to live forever. She'd learned that everything beautiful and beloved was merely on loan. The gift in knowing this was that every moment now seemed as precious as currency, and every rare pleasure pierced.

And for these reasons, as much as she'd yearned for the excitement of a London trip, she'd balked at leaving her father behind for an entire month. They could only just afford it, besides.

I forbid you to worry about me, he'd said sternly. *I'm not going to expire tomorrow, child, and I can do without you for a month or so. I've Mrs. Cartwright to persecute, er, look after me.* Mrs. Cartwright was their beloved housekeeper. He'd said this within her earshot so she could squawk in happy outrage.

Cat was clever and her parents had seen to it that she was well-read and well-spoken, and her aunt and Lady Wisterberg asserted she was more likely to meet a similarly clever, educated, and well-spoken young man—who also had an independent income, and maybe even (thrillingly!) a title—in London than in Lancashire. The notion of this jostled her heart pleasantly.

The flare of a young man's pupils when a step in a quadrille brought their faces flirtatiously closer, the hitch in her breath when a strapping young fellow effortlessly hurled her trunk up onto the mail coach, the startling lunge and shock of lips on her skin when an inebriated Henry Thatcher had been overcome by ardor and kissed her on the cheek when they were both eighteen—all hinted at a world of sensual discovery awaiting her. All called to something earthy and restless in her nature.

And yet. While a few young men had tried to court her, none had yet infiltrated her imagination. She did not lie awake at night pining for any of them.

She did not yet know how shortened breath or a pupil flare evolved into love. She knew what love ought to look like: her father standing behind her mother, arms wrapped around her, watching the sunset in softly absorbed silent communication beyond conversation. He had courted her mother assiduously, and won her, or so went the story they always told; there had never been anyone else for him.

Surely she would know love by how it felt?

So in the end, she and her trunk had come in on the mail coach, accompanied by an older, widowed neighbor who had a few days' worth of business in London and would be abiding with her relatives near Covent Garden. Mr. Bellingham had assured both her and her father that the boardinghouse proprietresses, Mrs. Hardy and Mrs. Durand, were ladies through and through, and would look after her as well as her aunt would. Lady Wisterberg would look after her the rest of the time.

The notion that she needed looking after amused Cat. She was twenty-two years old. She'd once helped her father sew the tip of a man's finger back on. She'd once assisted in delivering a lamb. When his assistant had gone home for the day, she sometimes handed him bandages or ointments or lent an ear to any suffering patients who arrived after hours, and she regularly strode or rode alone around the countryside to neighbors' houses or into town—but only safe distances, familiar ones, because her head was about as level as a girl's head could be without being flat as a table. Nevertheless, she understood that if a young man wanted to meet her, he would need to ask Lady Wisterberg for an introduction. She would be the bulwark between Catherine and any whiff of impropriety, and quite possibly the sentry at the gate between Cat and her own moment of watching the sunset with a man's—perhaps even a *titled* man's—arms wrapped around her.

So Cat could foresee only delights while she was in London: she was looking forward to seeing Lucy again, as they had laughed a good deal together during the fortnight of the house party. Lucy was forthright and kind and enjoyed horrid novels and archery and vigorous walking about to see the sights. Her embroidery was exquisite and her watercolors abysmal, and for Catherine it was the other way around. Lucy had brought a tantalizing whiff of London sophistication into the country, as she'd often stayed there with her godmother, Lady Wisterberg, in her town house.

And as for The Grand Palace on the Thames, she'd seldom had a more congenial evening. Mrs. Hardy and Mrs. Durand were everything that was charming and kind. All the guests had been given a little glass of sherry after a delicious dinner of fish stew and a tart for dessert. And after Mrs. Pariseau had read aloud a chapter of *The Ghost in the Attic*, a story that fair had her nibbling on her nails in suspense (even though she wasn't certain she believed in ghosts) a funny man named Mr. Delacorte had gotten in the mood for singing. "Oh, I know what we should sing! I'll teach it to you, Miss Keating," he'd said. "It's a bloody good song. It has a clap in it, where you're supposed to say 'arse'!"

This had caused an abrupt and reproachful silence. Whereupon Mr. Delacorte proceeded, red-faced and contrite, to an Epithet Jar and dropped in a penny. Everyone had been very understanding and murmured condolences and magnanimously blamed the sherry, as apparently, he'd gone for forty entire days without uttering an epithet in front of everybody else. To make him feel better about it, they'd all (with great reluctance, she noted, on the part of Mrs. Hardy and Mrs. Durand) sung the song he chose.

And it *was* a bloody good song, Cat thought to herself, mischievously. No wonder he'd been so enthusiastic about it. It was naughty, too. She'd been loudly and merrily singing it ever since she'd returned to her room a half hour ago.

Truthfully, neither "bloody" nor "arse" shocked her much; her father was known to passionately expostulate now and again. She knew better than to say them in company, however.

"Oh, I'm a man of great valor and honor, at least that's what he said before he climbed on 'er!" she sang as she pulled her night rail from the clothing press.

She was wholly delighted by her room, in fact.

Behind her, a veritable cloud disguised as a bed—she'd tested it with a bounce—was crowned with two equally decadent pillows and draped in a pink knitted coverlet. Perched on the little writing desk was a porcelain vase into which a fluff of white blossoms had been stuffed. The entire room smelled of spring, which meant it also smelled like hope. The blossoms had likely been plucked from the tiny, perfect park encircled by a wrought iron fence in front of the building.

The first of the London balls, at Lord and Lady Clayton's, was tomorrow night. Her heart took up a frisky tempo at the thought. With whom would she dance first?

She impulsively seized her pelisse to use as a partner and waltzed it around the room, singing: "'Have pity,' he said, 'have patience, I pray, I've a stick up me CLAP and gray in me hair!' La la la la—OH! Ow! Oh *no*—"

She'd spun herself and her pelisse partner into the desk chair.

Which teetered drunkenly, then toppled onto its back with a mighty crash that made her flinch.

She dropped her partner on the bed and crouched, rubbing her shin. "Good heavens, sir. It looks as though you may have imbibed too much this evening. Let me help you up," she said to amuse herself as she righted the chair.

A moment later she whirled again at a vigorous rapping on her door.

Lovely! Dot had arrived with her tea!

Beaming, she flung the door open.

And beheld a man.

He was coatless. His cravat dangled as if he'd been interrupted in the act of clawing it off, his striped waistcoat hung open, and his thick, black hair was dashed into peaks, very like he'd plowed two tormented hands through it. A shocking, tiny little V of bare skin was visible at his throat. He also had the shoulders of someone who could effortlessly hurl a trunk up onto a mail coach, and the sculpted cheekbones normally sported by statues of deities.

She wasn't proud of it, but these last three things were what made her close the door only most of the way instead of slamming it.

"I came as quickly as I could, madam. Shall I send for a doctor?" His voice was a rumbling bass she could feel in her sternum. His tone was all urgent, hushed sympathy.

"I—I beg your pardon, sir?"

"Surely one only caterwauls past midnight if one has suffered the loss of a limb, or has inadvertently run oneself through with a fireplace poker."

He sounded so earnest, and his Welsh accent was so beautiful—the "s's" caressed, the "r's" gently rolled—it was a full three seconds before she realized this was a grave insult, not a benediction. He'd made the word "caterwaul" sound like a poem.

She was mute with astonishment.

Through the crack of the door, his fierce dark eyes seemed as endless as the universe.

"I—I'm terribly sorry if I disturbed you, sir. You see, I'm new to London and—"

He held up a hand. "Ah. Say no more. You hail from a place where you can freely wail the song of your people to the hills, like a wolf. Mere walls cannot contain your exuberance. Sleep is as nothing when you are filled with song. One simply *must* twirl."

Her stomach contracted against the sardonic onslaught. He was so beautiful and colorfully *mean*. Despite herself, she was perversely thrilled. He was an entirely new creature to her experience, and she'd come to London for new experiences.

He gazed back at her, radiating enough impatience for the entire human race.

"How did you know about the twirl?" She almost whispered it.

"*Something* caused the crash. I suspect cavorting."

Oh no. "You heard the crash, too?" Her cheeks were fully aflame now.

"The building juddered like a ship in a storm." He explained this slowly, as if to a child.

They regarded each other through the four inches of open door while a series of eloquent and scathing little rejoinders sparked and died in her mind. He was rude. She was no coward.

But her sense of fairness was powerful. However ignorant she was of the thickness of the walls, it was no excuse; she was in the wrong. And this man appeared to be under some sort of duress.

She cleared her throat. "Well," she said humbly. "I am abashed. I apologize. I was unaware of your proximity, sir. Thank you for calling it to my attention. I shall endeavor to be quiet."

"If you would be so kind." These last words were briskly, exasperatedly delivered.

His point unforgettably made, he spun and vanished from the doorway as if he'd never been.

She stared, blinking, into the space he'd left, her ears ringing as if he'd been a cymbal clash, instead of a man.

Presently she heard a clinking and rattling, which turned out to be Dot proceeding at a stately, cautious pace down the hall, bearing a tray of tea.

"Dot . . . who was that man?"

Dot glanced stealthily over her shoulder. "Lord Kirke." She said it very quietly. "He arrived late this evening."

Cat was stunned. "*The* Lord Kirke?"

Dot nodded slowly.

An eloquent look passed between them as Cat took the tray.

"Mr. Pike let him in," Dot told her with a certain grim satisfaction, as if this explained everything.

Chapter Two

❧⊙❧

ONE NIGHT after feasting a little too enthusiastically on Helga's apple tart, Dot had dreamed she was swimming in a vat of treacle. No matter how hard she'd tried, she'd never been able to move her limbs fast enough to get to the edge and climb out.

The moment she saw Mr. Pike, the footman, striding across the foyer to open the door was just like that.

She'd been at the top of the landing. And if she could have, she would have skipped the last three steps and hurdled the banister into the foyer, as she'd once seen Captain Hardy do. Or perhaps she might have yanked off her shoe and whipped it into Pike's path, on the off chance he'd stumble over it. Or aimed it square for that place between his regrettably vast shoulders. She could be surprisingly fierce when it came to protecting things she loved, and of all her responsibilities at The Grand Palace on the Thames, opening the door was her very favorite. For her, it was emblematic of both the place itself, which she loved with all her heart, and her role in the world. She'd always been the first to *ever* see any potential guest who appeared.

But no matter what she did, she still wouldn't get to the door in time.

So she was forced to watch Pike stride across the checked marble of the foyer.

Pass beneath their beloved chandelier . . .
Open the peep hatch . . .
Then, God help her, for the first time ever . . .
Open the door.

THE MAN PIKE had let in had stood perfectly still beneath the chandelier. He was at least as tall as Pike, but a good decade older, she'd warrant. He had black hair and black eyes and his face was composed of stern, handsome planes. He'd looked tired. He'd eyed her with baleful amusement, as if a maid hurtling down the stairs, cap askew, mouth and eyes perfect O's of outrage, was only to be expected. He betrayed not one shred of surprise.

Dot knew Mrs. Hardy and Mrs. Durand wanted a large man to open the door at least at night, on the theory that nights were more dangerous than days. This was a fair assumption at the London Docks, a part of the city where one was just slightly more likely to be stabbed than other parts.

"It's the full moon on a Wednesday, Dot," Pike said, his voice lowered. "Remember? Just like you said in the kitchen when you knocked me down a few months ago."

She didn't reply. It was *very* ungentlemanly of him to remind her of that moment in the kitchen. That episode had been at least half his fault. But she still felt truly terrible about it.

They stared each other down.

Pike was gray of eye, square of jaw, and sober of demeanor. Dot had both a fierce sense of propriety and a profound appreciation for handsome men—which Pike unfortunately was, by anyone's definition—and these two qualities existed more or less harmoniously when the man in question wasn't so frequently underfoot. When he was, the friction was like a pebble in her shoe. It was a test of character and made her feel somewhat martyred and, given that she was the heroine in her own story, she admittedly took a frisson of pleasure in her suffering. She understood how much Mrs. Hardy and Mrs. Durand valued and cared for her, which never ceased feeling like a lovely miracle. But Mr. Pike had been the result of a long, daunting, and often bizarre search for a footman willing to work at the docks for a modest salary while being willing to perform a variety of tasks in addition to the usual footman duties, such as repairing the roof, or thumping an intruder on the jaw, or firing a gun if necessary. He was after a fashion a prize, while Dot had more or less come along with Delilah when Delilah had been Lady Derring, like a valise.

Mr. Pike was always all that was proper and respectful to everyone, the maids included. His manners were impeccable. But the maids were all on their best behavior around him lest he be taken away from them.

"It is indeed the full moon, so it is," she said cagily, precisely as if she'd remembered it and actually meant what she'd said at the time: that maybe she would allow him to open the door on that day. She hadn't considered that he would remember it so specifically.

Pike had already taken the man's greatcoat. She eyed it covetously. Before Pike, Dot had always taken away the coats and wraps of their guests, and their wraps told her so much about the person. She could see that this one had at least three capes. "And what you said in the kitchen that night? You're right," Pike said. "I *thoroughly* enjoyed opening the door. It's like opening a present, a gift, as you said. You never know who might be on the other side."

He looked her square in the eye with a determined glint as he said it.

She had a feeling that now that he'd gotten a taste of it, he wasn't going to give it up without a fight.

"I'll talk to our new person and find out what he needs," Dot said, on a low, fierce whisper, while their guest waited, gazing around the place, wearing a bemused expression now, as most guests did once they got a look at things. "And go and tell Mrs. Hardy and Mrs. Durand that he's here. You can take his greatcoat away."

There was a tense little pause.

"Very well," Pike said pleasantly, with the air of a man who knows he's won this round and intends to win many more.

"I FEEL LIKE a castaway in my own bed lately," Delilah mourned. "It feels so vast."

Angelique Durand and Delilah Hardy liked to end their days in the sitting room at the top of the stairs, where they would review the events of the day, plan the next, and do a little mending. They were reminiscing about their husbands. Which, granted, seemed silly to both of them, since Captain Hardy and Lord Bolt had only been away for a little more than a week and were due home in a day or so.

"I know what you mean." Angelique sighed. "I have to sleep with twice as many blankets without Lucien." Lucien liked to sleep naked and he was like her own personal furnace.

"I do wish Mr. Delacorte wasn't so very attached to that song," Angelique added dryly. "I'd rather like to contain it, like the plague, if we can, before we hear it sung all over London."

"If only it wasn't so insidiously catchy," Delilah agreed. It had been composed on the spot by their former guest, Miss Mariana Wylde, as a not-so-subtle dig at another of their guests, the Duke of Valkirk.

"We'll just have to somehow write another one to supplant it in his affections. Perhaps something cheerful about donkey racing."

They both laughed.

"This is Lucien's favorite waistcoat," Angelique said wistfully, extracting it from the mending pile and smoothing it as if her husband was inside of it at the moment. It was a dark plum color, and one of the silver buttons was loose.

Captain Tristan Hardy, Delilah's husband, a legendary former blockade captain, and Lucien, Lord Bolt, formerly-infamous-now-somewhat-respectable bastard son of a duke, were partners in the Triton Group, an import and export endeavor. They had gone up the coast to a shipyard to see about repairs to their beloved ship *The Zephyr*, which, after weeks of harrowing uncertainty, had limped into port well after she was expected, late, storm damaged, and dismasted. She was still sea-worthy, but only just. They were also seeing to out-fitting a new ship in what they hoped would one day be a fleet of ships—*The Rogue*, it was called, after the man who owned it, who was now also their partner. They were on the brink of a thrilling, and risky, but potentially immensely enriching new chapter in all of their lives.

Meanwhile, finances remained a trifle snug. And though the suites at The Grand Palace on the

Thames had been taken for the last half of the season, they were currently experiencing a bit of a lull in guests. Ebb and flow was ever thus at the boardinghouse. They had learned to love the unpredictability the way they had learned to appreciate the changes in weather.

So they both looked up alertly at the unmistakable sound of Dot bounding up the stairs. And winced when she tripped on the second to last one.

"A gentleman has arrived and he would like a room," she announced in a rush.

It was just a few minutes before curfew, the time at which all guests must be safely inside. The arrival of potential guests at this hour often heralded dramatic episodes at The Grand Palace on the Thames.

"Take a breath, Dot, and tell us what he's like." Angelique stood and reached over and righted Dot's askew cap with a finger.

"His shoulders are at least as wide as Mr. Pike's."

The moment the words were out of her mouth, a scarlet blush scrolled from her collarbone to the ruffle of her bright white cap. Taken with her blue eyes, the effect was unexpectedly patriotic, like a Union Jack.

They stared at her, nonplussed.

Dot looked stricken and a little amazed that the words had escaped her.

Granted, the three of them had created the small wonder that was The Grand Palace on the Thames from the tumbledown building Delilah inherited from her perfidious first husband, and the habit of assessing every man they met based on whether they were tall enough to reach the sconces in order to light the candles died hard.

The use of Pike as a standard against which to compare broad shoulders was new, however.

"I can almost picture him, Dot," Delilah replied gravely. Angelique bit her lip against a laugh. "Did you happen to observe anything else about him?"

"The silver cup with the words engraved on it—the one that the king sent to you and Captain Hardy as a wedding present?"

Delilah and Angelique waited with somewhat martyred patience. Sometimes—it helped to have had a sherry—one could almost follow Dot's cognitive leaps, which often resembled the floppy meanderings of a butterfly. Her mind was an enigmatic place, and surely she found much within it absorbing, as she often bumped into, tripped over, or dropped things as a result of roaming around up in its rafters rather than paying attention to what she was doing—for example, in several memorable instances, carrying a tea tray. But she had proved to be a savant when it came to describing their guests.

"Yes?" Delilah prompted.

"His voice is like that. Very deep and elegant and precise and perhaps a bit chilly."

"Mmm. Intriguing," Angelique approved.

"His boots are Hoby, I'd warrant, and the buttons on his waistcoat are silver, and his greatcoat had three capes." She might have once been the world's worst lady's maid, but she did know clothes, and her gentlemen from the not-gentlemen, and she could detect it in a heartbeat. Both gentlemen and not-gentlemen were welcome at The Grand Palace on the Thames, as long as they passed the interview and Delilah and Angelique agreed he would likely get on nicely with the rest of their guests. They had vowed to admit only people they liked.

They had realized this was a bit *aspirational* when the rooms were empty. They were pragmatic, too.

"Mmm. So an actual gentleman, then." Delilah began untying her apron in preparation for meeting him.

"But here and here"—Dot gestured to the little hollows beneath her eyes—"it's dark. Like he hasn't slept."

"Poor soul," Delilah said absently. She never slept as well when Tristan was away.

"And he smells as though he's been cooking over a fire," Dot concluded.

They froze in removing their aprons.

"Are you certain it's not just cheroot or cigar smoke?" Angelique finally asked.

"I know how gentlemen ought to smell," Dot said loftily, causing Delilah's and Angelique's eyebrows to leap in tandem.

"From taking their coats," she expounded, to their profound relief. "They smell like their coats."

They did. And for an instant, Angelique and Delilah simultaneously experienced fits of yearning for their husbands and the smell of their coats.

They puzzled over all of this for a moment. There had been a time or two where Dot had described a potential guest and they had immediately asked her to go back down and send them on their way. Usually it was a guest who had come bearing a yellowed menu of prurient services once offered by the building's former incarnation, which haunted the sign hanging over the door in the form of the very faint word "rogue" visible behind its elegant lettering.

And then Dot lowered her voice conspiratorially to deliver her coup de grâce. "I think he might be someone *important*."

"Or believes he is," Angelique was amused. In their collective experience, most gentlemen considered themselves important. At least more important than any woman in the vicinity.

But Dot had an eye for this, too.

"Once under our roof, all of our guests are equally important," Delilah reminded Dot diplomatically, with a quick wry glance at Angelique. While it was fundamentally true—and they had indeed received a number of "important" guests, including a duke, and very briefly, His Majesty the actual king—they knew in their heart of hearts that if circumstances involved a shipwreck, room in their lifeboat for one more person, and a choice between their longtime guest Mr. Delacorte and the monarch, well, England would probably need to go searching for a new ruler. They hoped they were never tested.

"Except he only wanted a regular room, not a suite."

This was interesting, too: usually the important people liked to emphasize their importance by taking a suite.

"And when I said, as you taught me, Mrs. Durand, 'Whom may I say is calling?'" *Nothing* made Dot feel more sophisticated than the word "whom." Angelique, a former governess, had recently taught it to her and she might as well have given Dot a tiara. "He said 'KIRKE.' Just like that. Sharp as a handclap." She demonstrated by bringing her hands together. "He's altogether impatient. I told him that we were an exclusive establishment and that you would need to speak to him first, he gave a laugh, like this—HA!" She imitated a short, wildly ironic laugh that made both of them jump a little. "And then he sighed and said, 'Oh, by all means, do go and tell them I'm here.'"

"He sounds like a joy," Angelique said dryly.

They were still a moment. Bemused.

In the end, curiosity, and the currently empty rooms, won.

"Let's go and meet him," Delilah said. "Will you make tea, Dot?"

Dot gave a little hop because bringing tea to new guests was her other favorite thing to do. And so far, there seemed no chance that Pike would ever be asked to do it, but one never knew.

DOT WAS RIGHT on all counts.

As it turned out, their guest was one of the people Mr. Delacorte referred to as a "The." For instance, *the* Duke of Valkirk had come to stay with them, and *the* King of England had briefly parked his majestic behind on the settee, and *the* Earl of Vaughn and his family had once taken a suite, and *the* Lord Bolt had reappeared from the alleged dead (and married Angelique). And though he had ultimately taken to all of those men—he liked nearly everyone, and eventually, everyone was given no choice but to like him in return—he was always more comfortable with the likes of Mr. Bellingham, a vicar who shared his love for donkey races and to whom he'd introduced the joys of singing bawdy songs in a pub while drunk. He felt he was becoming more refined by the minute, thanks to the marvelously civilizing powers of Mrs. Hardy and Mrs. Durand. But the "The" guests reminded him that he was a work in progress, and he always felt with them at first the way he did when his waistcoat buttons were just a little too tight.

The Lord Dominic Kirke's house had caught on fire. Something to do with a lamp. Hence his smokey aroma. He'd escaped just in time, with a few of his belongings.

They learned this straightaway because, as it turned out, Lord Kirke was every bit as . . . well, bracingly direct as Dot described.

Angelique and Delilah knew what to do with testy, tired, impatient, wild-eyed men whose houses had just burned nearly all the way down: they clucked over his shocking news, spoke in soothing tones, tucked him into a comfortable room, ferried away his smokey things to be aired and brushed, sent him up some drinking chocolate and a scone, and took his money.

And if he was a bit notorious . . . well, they had a good deal of experience with that, too.

"He's going to want to orate, isn't he?" Mr. Delacorte said somewhat grimly, when they delivered the news of their new guest as he was heading up to his room for the night. For Lord Kirke's fiery, eloquent speeches in the House of Commons were legendary, and frequently printed in the newspaper.

"Perhaps not," Delilah soothed. "After all, it's his job. Nobody wants to do their job all the time. Perhaps he'll want to quietly sit and listen to a story. Perhaps he'll enjoy a game of chess."

"*I* happily want to do my job all the time," Mr. Delacorte pointed out.

This was true. While he was a partner with Captain Hardy and Lord Bolt in the Triton Group, he was also an importer of remedies from the Orient made up of herbs and ingredients and what he referred to as "ground up bits and bobs, horns and testicles and whatnot," some of which worked a treat. He sold them to surgeons and apothecaries up and down England. It was how he'd made unlikely friends everywhere. He never missed an opportunity to make a sale.

"If he does orate, Mrs. Pariseau will be in heaven." Their guest Mrs. Pariseau was in her middle years and was thoroughly enjoying her relatively monied widowhood. And while she had no interest at all in ever marrying again, she loved few things more than handsome men and arcane debate.

And not even men like Lord Kirke, whose name regularly appeared on the front pages of the newspaper and the dripping-with-innuendo gossip pages that Dot read to the rapt maids in the kitchen, would be exempt from the rules. And that included gathering in the sitting room four nights a week with all the other guests.

"Does Tristan vote Tory?" Angelique wondered, on a yawn, as they tidied the sitting room for the night. Their new guest was a Whig.

"I don't know how he votes, to be honest. Except that he's exhibited an independent streak when it comes to voting against *The Ghost in the Attic*."

"Ah. About that. I think Mrs. Pariseau is actually plotting a rebellion," Angelique said cryptically, and they headed for their rooms. "Perhaps she'll recruit him and make a revolutionary of Captain Hardy yet."

Laughing at this notion, they made for their bedrooms.

Chapter Three

❧❧❧❧❧

CATHERINE FIXED her eyes on the plume merrily bobbing atop Lady Wisterberg's big, handsome head as they navigated the river of humans—London's finest—filing into Lord and Lady Clayton's grand Grosvenor Square house. Lucy, in lavender figured satin, was just ahead of her, spirals of brown hair bouncing at her temples with her every step. But Catherine had scarcely been able to do more than exchange compliments and greetings and smiles with Lucy: delighted to have a captive audience and full of high spirits, Lady Wisterberg had chattered about Lady this and Lord that, so many people and places Catherine didn't know the whole of the way there in the hack. She remembered none of it. Nerves melted all of her chaperone's words like snowflakes before they could settle into her brain.

At last, the crowd inside the ballroom came into view like jewels spilled from a pirate's chest. Splendor assailed her: bunting swooped from the ceiling, flowers and ferns exploded from urns, silk and satin gleamed on the women, and voices tumbled all over each other in shouts and laughter, competing with the sounds of a fine little orchestra.

Cat's heart fluttered like a trapped bird with excitement.

Lady Wisterberg expertly marched her charges

forth through the throng, yodeling greetings and waggling her be-gloved, beringed fingers to people who turned to waggle theirs at her. It was already sultry with heat from all the bodies. Catherine was happy to have a chance to use her best silk fan, painted with a Northumberland scene.

At last they emerged into a clearing of sorts, spanned by a long table bearing enormous bowls of ratafia and rows of cups.

Lady Wisterberg made certain the three of them were served. Then: "Cheers!" she said, and tossed the whole of her cup back in a gulp.

Catherine blinked.

Lady Wisterberg filled another one. "I find it's always best to begin as you mean to go on!" She winked. And apparently she meant drinking, because she drained that one in only two gulps.

Catherine cautiously sipped at hers. Tasty enough, but nose-crinklingly strong. She knew better than to drink it quickly. She'd been too full of jittery, delighted anticipation to do much more than poke at dinner, and she'd decadently slept through breakfast, awaking to coffee and a scone surely fresh from the ovens of heaven. Thankfully Lord Kirke had not been about to further abrade her nerves; he'd clearly been off somewhere being important. He wasn't at dinner, nor had she heard him rustling about upstairs. But at intervals throughout the day she'd amused herself by muttering under her breath, *I suspected cavorting*, in a Welsh accent.

Lucy sipped hers, too. They shared a wry glance.

"Oh look, Lucy, isn't that Mr. Hargrove and Miss Seaver?" Lady Wisterberg waved at a young man and woman. "Such fine young people. They're your age, Miss Keating, I'll warrant you'll . . ."

She trailed off and went as rigid as a hunting dog flushing game.

A startling, raw yearning skittered across her expression.

Catherine whipped her head wildly about to see if anyone was watching Lady Wisterberg with similarly restrained passion.

"She heard the pop of a faro box," Lucy stage-whispered to Catherine.

"Goodness." Catherine wasn't certain what expression she ought to wear in response to this news. She tried to look supportive.

It seemed the room adjacent was scattered with little game tables. People wearing rapt expressions were collected around them.

"My dears." Lady Wisterberg's voice was tense and abstracted. Catherine realized her body had been ever so slowly rotating away from them, like a spring coiling. "I'll . . . I'll just be . . . a moment . . ."

And in a blur of ruby silk she bolted to the game room.

"That's the last we'll see of her this evening," Lucy said matter-of-factly.

"Oh no!" Catherine reeled.

"I'm so sorry," Lucy said, somewhat desperately. "I didn't know how to warn you! I think it would have been different if your aunt were here. They would keep each other company. But, ah, allow me to introduce Miss Bernadette Seaver and Mr. Hargrove." Her two friends had come to join them. "Come and meet my friend Miss Catherine Keating, who is visiting London from Northumberland."

Dizzied by Lady Wisterberg's potentially catastrophic defection, Cat nevertheless managed to curtsy. "How do you do?"

Miss Seaver was fair-haired and lissome in pearl-colored silk overlaid with bead-studded net; her features were as small and neat as a painted doll's. The tall Mr. Hargrove sported a swoop of chestnut hair and matching, sparkling eyes. Silver buttons winked on his waistcoat.

Something about the way Lucy and Miss Seaver at once arranged themselves around Mr. Hargrove—their bodies angled in his direction, their faces slightly tipped up—suggested they both felt a bit proprietary about him.

"The color of your dress is divine, Miss Keating." The word "divine" seemed to last a century, so elegant was Miss Seaver's drawl. Cat imagined describing it later for her father over the breakfast table when she returned home: "Papa, don't these eggs look diviiiine?"

"Thank you," she said shyly. "Your dress is so beautiful, Miss Seaver. You look like you're emerging from a mist."

This for some reason caused a surprised silence.

"What a charming thing to say," Mr. Hargrove said fervently, and smiled at her so warmly Catherine blushed.

"Yes," Lucy said almost suspiciously. As if this was a quality Cat had been deliberately disguising.

There ensued an odd little pause.

"Very daring of you to pair that color with those sleeves, Miss Keating," Miss Seaver said finally, speculatively. "Are you perhaps making a point that we ought not to have left mancherons behind in 1818?"

This sentence seemed perilous. It was as oblique as an intercepted coded message from an enemy spy. Cat had no idea what it meant.

"Thank you," she ventured, deciding to claim it as a compliment. "I suppose it might be daring," she added cautiously. "I have always thought them dashing." Mancherons were essentially little epaulet details on sleeves, and all the rage, at least at one time. Flattering to the silhouette. Or so she thought.

Perhaps they were daring? Would she be perceived as an Original in this ballroom full of slashed and puffed sleeves, which were the kind of sleeves that both Lucy and Miss Seaver were wearing? Was this a good thing? Or would people be mocking her behind their fans when she danced by? She'd thought her dress was pretty. It had two entire flounces.

She was embarrassed to ask the young ladies present for clarification, lest the depths of the things she didn't know be revealed and she find herself hurled bodily into the street amid cries of "Interloper! Fraud!"

Miss Seaver's gaze on her now seemed as cool and sharp as scissors. Lucy's was watchful, where it had been warm enough earlier.

She glanced uncertainly out over the sea of gorgeously attired people, and suddenly it seemed there were as many eyes as there were crystals in the chandelier above. Some of those eyes were aimed at her. Perhaps they thought the blue of her dress was diviiiine. Perhaps they found her sleeves shocking. Perhaps they were simply curious about her. Butterflies, some velvety, some spiky, began circulating in her stomach. In truth, she rather loved the notion of being new, after being known by everyone in her small town for so long. But she understood that people were often uncertain of newness.

Possibly many people here were nervous, just like she was. This notion cheered her.

She accidentally intercepted the gaze of a strapping young man topped in blond curls. He appeared to be gazing about the room, too. He offered a swift little smile full of white teeth before he turned away. Her heart gave a leap.

It was mortifying to think that Mr. Curly Blond would need to track a foxed Lady Wisterberg down at the game table if he decided he'd like an introduction.

Unless they somehow shared a mutual acquaintance. Lucy, for instance.

In short, she was at the absolute mercy of Lucy at the moment.

"I understand there will be Dance Espagnole this evening," Lucy said.

"Oh my. I haven't yet danced it, but I'm certain I could learn," she offered eagerly.

"It's not much more than a fancy quadrille," Mr. Hargrove assured her.

"My first two dances are taken—I promised them to Mr. Wallace and Lord Cutler when we were riding in the Row yesterday," Miss Seaver volunteered.

"As are mine, and the first waltz. The waltz is for Mr. Hargrove." Lucy smiled up at the young man, then darted a glance at Miss Seaver.

Who looked startled.

It was becoming increasingly, distressingly clear to Catherine that she would be unpartnered for the first two dances. At the very least.

And utterly alone in a crowded ballroom.

Her stomach muscles tightened.

She supposed she could always join Lady Wisterberg at the gaming table. Imagine if the silver lining of being a reluctant wallflower turned out to be gambling her way to wealth.

But, like saying "bloody," singing bawdy songs in public, smoking cigars, and marching up to young men to ask them to dance, gambling was yet another thing young, unmarried ladies weren't supposed to do.

"Miss Keating, if I may be so bold . . . if you haven't yet a partner for the third reel, I should be honored if you would stand up with me," Mr. Hargrove said.

Lucy's and Miss Seaver's heads whipped toward him.

Cat's heart lifted. Lovely! She was going to dance with a handsome young gentleman she'd only just met. She could hardly refuse; moreover, she wouldn't dream of it, even if her presence seemed to complicate somewhat a story already in progress involving Miss Seaver and Lucy. She didn't feel as though her season in London would begin officially until she danced.

"I should be honored, Mr. Hargrove, thank you."

Moments later, her three companions were compelled to the floor by the start of the music for the first quadrille.

"I'm so sorry," Lucy mouthed over her shoulder as her partner collected her, and she did look sorry. But not sorry enough to take pity on her and forego the dance. "I'll find you here after this dance?"

Catherine nodded. And even though her stomach knotted, she honestly couldn't blame Lucy one bit, and would not have dreamed of asking her to stay by her side.

Well.

She was not yet prepared to call the night a disaster. After all, one could not always predict the outcome of a story from a single event.

Nevertheless, it was undeniably disorienting to feel so alone when hundreds of people were milling about. She supposed it was yet another new experience, like encountering a sardonically furious, disheveled Whig politician in the hallway of her boardinghouse.

For a mad moment, it occurred to her that this—alone in a huge crowd—was what the world would feel like when the people who knew and loved her best were no longer in it. Everyone a stranger.

Tiny, icy fingers flicked her heart.

She took a bracing breath and scorned the impulse to hide. But she could hardly stand about alone, like a looby.

Several pots of lush ferns propped up on pillars formed a sort of grotto in the corner, behind which a cluster of staid, important-looking older gentlemen were talking amongst themselves. They seemed unlikely to notice her. Something about the green, growing things made her feel more at home. It was like finding a little bit of countryside in the middle of a ballroom.

So that's where she tucked herself: in among the ferns.

She settled in to find things to enjoy about the dancing—the dresses, the music, the movement—until her reverie was interrupted by a voice: the same beautiful, resonant timbre that had nearly singed her eyebrows off with disapproval last night because he'd suspected cavorting.

"It's just that it's rather stirring to see him out of the corner of one's eye in a crowded room," Lady

Clayton had explained to her husband, who was fortunately secure in her affections, when she was compiling her guest list for the ball. "Like the Alps. He hasn't an unappealing angle."

(And one rather wanted to climb him, too, despite the risks, but she was wise enough not to say that aloud to her husband.)

Nor could Lord Kirke's manners generally be faulted; after all, he'd learned them with the meticulousness with which one might learn another language. But one got the sense that he would swiftly strip out of them like a suit of clothes if it served his purposes. In fact, Lord Dominic Kirke always brought with him into the ballroom the faintest whiff of danger, the way one carried the scent of a stormy night in with them on their coat when they came in from the cold. He had not been raised among them. He had done things and gone places their blue-blooded friends would shudder to do or go. His mere presence was often enough to raise blushes in women and hackles in men, and in conversation, he was as likely to captivate as he was to unsettle. But he did it with a panache that even his enemies begrudgingly admired.

And if rumors were his constant invisible entourage—well, he was a veritable fortress of discretion. He did not engage in frivolous flirtations. There was not, in fact, a frivolous bone in his body. His liaisons were initiated with a carnal frankness and conducted with the same single-minded conviction with which he conducted everything else. They ended much the same way. And perhaps for that reason, not always well. Or quietly.

And he'd only shot the one man that one time. But then, he'd been challenged.

He was the frisson of delicious notoriety every aristocratic hostess wanted at her event and nowhere near their young daughters.

Which was fine, as everyone knew Lord Dominic Kirke never danced at balls.

Oh, but I've done that, he'd say, charmingly, self-deprecatingly, when asked about it. As though it was a rite of passage that could never be repeated, like going to Eton, or losing one's virginity.

Tonight he stood on the periphery of the ballroom while that bloodthirsty mating ritual known as The Season played out on the dance floor. He held a snifter of brandy just to hold it. His smoldering mood required only a little prod to burst into flames. Too little sleep, and too much thinking, and the uncharacteristically unexceptional speech he'd managed to give on the floor of the Commons—despite these impediments and the general shambles of his life—had left him feeling as though a cue ball was lodged between his eyes.

He'd left his temporary boardinghouse home before anyone but the maids were stirring this morning and he hadn't yet returned. He'd brought his evening clothes with him to the Commons. He'd only just remembered he needed to return by the eleven o'clock curfew. Last night he'd been handed a card featuring seven little commandments for living at the boardinghouse, and while he would have agreed to anything last night, he'd looked at them again this morning with more than a little alarm.

The curfew struck him as both ridiculous and, perversely, not unwelcome. As though it was the penance he deserved.

He was thinking about the unobjectionably excellent pillow in his little room at The Grand Palace on the Thames and hoping the female in the room below him wouldn't take it into her head to warble tonight when Lord Farquar, who was very drunk, said, "Heard your speech today, Kirke. About the sad urchins. Wasn't quite the Freedom Speech, was it?"

Farquar, who owed his fortune in part to the orphans he harvested from workhouses and deceived into working near to death in his textile mills, was part of the circle of a half dozen or so fellow MPs with whom Dominic stood. They were somewhat obscured by large pots of riotously healthy ferns supported on pillars. None of the others had been present for his speech. It was a surprise to learn that Farquar had been.

Farquar was lazy and afraid of many things, chiefly change and thinking. As change and thinking were famously Kirke's favorite things, Kirke scared him witless.

And what Dominic wanted to do was pass a law that would in essence deprive Farquar of his favorite cheap labor.

People were forever quoting his damned Freedom Speech at him. He'd given it a decade ago.

"It warms my heart that you've paid enough attention to my speeches to rank them, Farquar."

He sensed what was coming, and realized it was precisely the raw, red meat his feral mood craved.

"Doesn't look as though your lot will ever get the votes." Farquar shook his head with mock sympathy. "Your lot" meant the Whigs. "Don't you feel like the chap from Greek myth who pushes a rock up the hill over and over and never gets anywhere? Shishyfuss?"

The name exited Farquar's mouth on a fine,

brandy-scented spray, a droplet of which landed on Dominic's cheek.

He stared at Farquar long enough for Farquar's amused smile to fade.

Then he delicately, slowly, and pointedly wiped his cheek with the tip of his forefinger.

"You must feel like Sisyphus every time you attempt to utter a word comprising more than two syllables, Farquar." He said this on a sympathetic hush.

The ensuing rustle of chuckles from the men around them turned Farquar's face a blotchy maroon.

"You'll get there eventually, old boy," Dominic added, with hatefully tender encouragement. "If there's anything you know I know, it's that I never, ever give up."

They stared at each other.

All of that would madden Farquar, particularly "old boy." Kirke, a baron of absolutely no pedigree, common as dirt, had been raised to the peerage by the king for years of exceptional public service. Farquar, a viscount, was the result of centuries of aristocrats with empty heads and bloated coffers mating with each other until the empathy was bred right out of them.

"Reminded me of that madman who roams Covent Garden shouting out lines from *Hamlet*. Blathers on and on," Farquar pressed on. "No one pays much attention to him, either." His gloating little smile was back. "Because he's mad, you see," he explained to the rest of the men. "Only a madman would do the same thing over and over with no result."

Pointing out that Farquar had clearly paid attention to his speech today was too easy. "I'll wager five pounds you can't say the word 'soliloquy' right now," he said, taking pains to sound bored.

More laughter and calls for "Try it, Farkie! I could use a fiver!" And "Go easy on him, Kirke! We all know 's's' are hard!"

Farquar said nothing. With his mouth, anyway. His eyes shot poison darts.

Dominic sighed and shifted his weight to his other leg. "You know, I am aware you have a point, Farkie." So conciliatory was his tone that Farquar's demeanor relaxed by about three notches. "I do have a tendency to go on. At least I'm in relatively distinguished company when it comes to that. After all, no one was inclined to indulge the king about his divorce. And no one listened to Joseph Utley."

There were more good-natured chuckles. "If wives were that easy to get rid of, we'd all swap them out twice a year," someone mumbled.

"Who the devil is Joseph Utley?" Pangborne was smiling.

"The nine-year-old boy who died of an infection after he was whipped bloody by the foreman of Farquar's cotton mill for working too slowly."

Kirke said it almost conversationally.

Oh, how he loved precarious, loaded, dense silences. The delicious, shocked, abrupt stillness of men who had, for one moment, collectively stopped breathing. He could toy with them to his own ends. Lighten them, if he chose. Turn them into teetering monoliths that threatened to crash down upon them. Tighten the screws on the awkwardness.

He'd become an expert at disrupting complacency. It was the only thing that worked to chip away at the layers and layers of it.

His secret weapon was that he was perfectly

comfortable with discomfort, his and theirs. Being common as dirt meant he knew how to, and was willing to, fight like a snarling dog in the street—both metaphorically, and quite literally—for those who didn't have a voice. But he'd learned thousands of better tactics since his more hotheaded years. Including a nearly impeccable sense of timing.

Those who crossed him often came away with the impression that he was—to quote the mistress who had hurled a lit lamp at him a day ago and nearly burned his house down—"a cold, ruthless bastard." But those who had come to know him—inasmuch as he allowed himself to be known—understood it was seldom personal. Much the way glaciers inexorably gouged out valleys and sculpted mountains over epochs, Kirke was uniquely designed—by dint of the sheer bloody-mindedness bred into him by brutal poverty, his Welsh parents, and living with his six semi-feral brothers and sisters—to reshape the English political landscape in favor of justice. He was an absolutely unstoppable force.

The so-called common people knew it. It was why he'd been elected again and again, and why they'd largely stood by him, even as the gossip pages did their best to undermine him and formidable forces were often arrayed against him.

A decade. That's how long he'd worked with like-minded others (many of whom had worked much longer than that) before they had finally passed the first laws abolishing the slave trade in 1810.

A decade. A grain of sand in the hourglass of time. A mere eyeblink for a glacier.

Farquar hadn't a prayer against him.

The skin of Pangborne's face had gone peculiarly tight. One of the men finally shifted uneasily. All of them, in their tension, had visibly, unconsciously recoiled from Farquar.

Who was *seething*.

"No one listened to Joseph, either, when he sobbed for mercy," Dominic added, politely. As if the silence was a request for clarification.

He saw Pangborne's throat move in a swallow.

Several of the lords with whom he stood bothered to vote so rarely they were actually fined during the king's attempted divorce for not appearing in Parliament for the proceedings. Life was comfortable for them, whether they voted for anything or not. They didn't need to care. He genuinely liked very few of them. He didn't much care if they liked him. Liking was often beside the point in politics.

But most of them had consciences, at least a modicum of intelligence, and children. He might not ever be able to move Farquar. But he could bloody well use Farquar to move the rest of them.

It was so quiet in their little group that they could hear Farquar's audibly swift breath, sucked in and blown out of his sculpted nostrils.

"Funny," Farquar finally said, his voice pitched strangely high, "that you should show more concern for that guttersnipe than you do for your own by-blow, Kirke."

When he looked back on that moment later, Dominic was confident he didn't so much as blink.

But he went briefly as sick and airless as though he'd taken a fist to the ribs.

The blood flashed away from his skin, leaving him ice-cold.

And then nourishing, hot fury flooded in.

Suddenly the eyes of the men were fixed on him with avid curiosity.

"I'm afraid you must have confused me with someone else, Farkie," he said gently. "Or were you perhaps crossing in front of a mirror when the word 'bastard' sprang to mind?"

Some instinct made him swiftly sidestep, and this was how he avoided taking Farquar's fist full in the mouth.

The part of him, which, of course, was causing Farkie all the upset.

But his head snapped back from the glancing blow, and all the men surged forward swiftly to seize Farquar's arms, restraining him, soothing him before he could cause a ruckus that would upset any nearby ladies.

They were prepared to restrain Kirke, too, but he held up his hand and shook his head: no need.

He touched his fingers to his mouth absently. He backed away.

And he fixed Farquar with the kind of black stare guaranteed to cause the man many, many sleepless nights wondering when he might hear from Kirke's seconds.

"If you'll excuse me, gentlemen?" he said mildly.

Chapter Four

࿔࿓࿔

I SURE HOPE Lord Kirke ducks in time, Catherine had thought, guiltily enjoying every second of listening to him walk that awful, bloviating man into a trap. Because much like *The Ghost in the Attic,* she was pretty certain she knew how the story was going to end.

Well, he hadn't.

When men got too full of themselves and liquor, it was best to just get out of the way of the flailing—she'd learned this from living in a town where everyone happily frequented the only pub. Goodness knew her father had matter-of-factly stitched a lip or two after a brawl.

She abandoned the shelter of the ferns, darted swiftly past the oblivious, promenading dancers until she was out of the ballroom, then wove through little clusters of people shouting and gesticulating at each other in cheerfully inebriated conversation. A few curious heads turned as she swept past and she offered what she hoped was a confident, I-belong-here smile.

She considered retreating to the ladies' withdrawing room, where at least she'd have some company and might meet a nice person or two, or have a chat with a lady's maid. But suddenly she felt shy about her sleeves, and was worried someone else might point them out.

So when she came upon the flight of stairs to the rest of the house, she impulsively dashed up, and with every step the music and the voices below grew fainter.

Presently she found herself in a marble-floored passage lined with gilt-framed portraits of what were likely relatives of the host and hostess— women and men in Elizabethan ruffs posing with narrow-faced dogs and solemn-eyed children.

A surprising hint of a breeze beckoned like a crooked finger.

She followed it to a pair of French doors opened partly onto a little verandah. Upon it were arranged a pair of benches surrounded by fluffy green trees and shrubbery in urns. Once again, she made for the green things with relief.

She sat down hard on the little bench, released a breath so gusty it fluttered the curls at her temples, then closed her eyes and agitated her fan beneath her chin. The marble was pleasantly cool on her bum through the silk. But behind her eyelids the ballroom colors still spun, as though she'd stared too long at the sun.

The palette of her life in the country was on the whole muted, softer, more limited, she realized now. The pace of life, though full, was leisurely as a sigh. She was unaccustomed to light bouncing from everyone and everything at once—from the silks and jewels and chandeliers and marble and tiaras— and to voices and music ricocheting and echoing off shiny, hard surfaces. She already felt a little queasy, like a child who'd glutted on a buffet of sweets. Her head was muzzy from her one delicious cup of rata-fia. She thought of the soft, rosy warmth of the sit-ting room at The Grand Palace on the Thames and she momentarily wished herself there instead. But that seemed like a failure of nerve.

She felt undeniably a little melancholy, but it was also a bit dreamlike and delicious to be completely alone in a strange place. As if she was floating unmoored through space. As if anything could happen at any time.

She froze in her fan flapping when she heard the sound of brisk footsteps on marble. They paused.

She leaned forward to peer through the windows.

Then jerked back behind the plant, her heart jolting.

Lord Kirke was standing alone in the passage.

She leaned forward again and, through the greenery, surreptitiously studied him as though she'd stumbled across a centaur pacing in a clearing.

For someone who had just been hit in the face, he seemed remarkably composed. One would have thought it happened to him every day. She had no trouble at all imagining that it did.

He seemed such a frightening man. Brilliant, certainly, but in the way the edge of a knife is brilliant. And yet she was grateful that someone so formidable was on the side of the vulnerable people of England. Her father had more than once patched up a child or a woman who had been at the mercy of the tempers of the men who controlled their lives: fathers, husbands, employers. Afterward, his mood was always grim and low.

She wondered if Kirke had sought a refuge from the crowd, too, to think about his choices.

He touched his fingers to his lip, then examined them. Scowled faintly. Patted his person a bit with his other hand. She knew the signs: he was looking for a handkerchief, and not finding one.

Indecision racked her. She really didn't want to risk speaking to him.

But the man might be bleeding. And she was a doctor's daughter, after all.

Finally, she quietly retrieved her own handkerchief from her reticule, drew in a fortifying breath, and stood.

Gingerly but resolutely, she took a step forward.

Then another.

He glanced up and went rigid. His eyes were wide. Understandably he was a trifle wary of the woman inching toward him from the dark as though he were a beast caught in a trap, a handkerchief trembling in her outstretched hand.

He glanced from her face to the handkerchief, bemused.

Finally, as slowly and gingerly as she'd extended it, he took it.

"Thank you," he said cautiously. "Mine seems to have gone missing."

"Perhaps it's still being laundered from the last time you were hi . . ."

She sucked in a breath and her hand flew to cover her mouth.

It was too late. The amazement dawning over his features told her he knew full well that the last part of her sentence was going to be "hit in the face."

Her own expression had doubtless confirmed this.

If she hadn't been held fast in the clutches of her own horror, she might have seized her skirts in her hands and bolted back down the stairs.

His face seemed peculiarly taut.

"Does my face strike you as eminently hittable, then?" he said finally, as politely and formally as a butler, on a hush that struck her as ominous.

"No! That is . . ." she stammered. "It's just . . . I'm new to London . . . I'm not very familiar with current ballroom . . . customs."

No undertaker had ever dug a deeper hole than the one she was digging for herself now.

His eyes widened. "'Ballroom . . . customs,'" he repeated dazedly.

And suddenly, before her eyes, his face went incandescent with wicked glee. Which was when she realized his taut face had been suppressing hilarity all along.

"*Imagine* if every quadrille was punctuated by a pair of hearty slaps," he crooned. "I'd never forget the steps. If we all stood about in a circle and ritually smacked each other to music once in a while there might forever be peace in our land."

She exhaled a shocked laugh, delighted and scandalized. "And the reels would be—"

She stopped herself. Uncertain.

"No. Out with it," he ordered. As if he were her confessor. As if she were cruelly depriving him of delights.

"Imagine how the reels would be. Everyone waiting patiently for a turn to grapple and punch down the center. Then patiently waiting . . ."

". . . to do it all over again. Ha ha!"

His laugh was a lovely echoing boom in the passage.

Good heavens. It was the strangest sensation. Knee-buckling relief and as though she'd been handed a guinea.

He sighed. "But then that would make every ball just like a typical day in the House of Lords."

Her smile wavered. For all she knew, it would. Men were confounding creatures, declaring eternal drunken fealty to each other one minute, challenging each other to duels the next. Sometimes both in one night.

"You witnessed the face hitting, I gather?" he asked, after a moment. Somewhat diffidently.

She considered lying. Something told her he'd know at once if she did. "I did," she admitted.

He merely nodded shortly. Then he touched her handkerchief to his lip and turned his head toward the corridor. "I'm sorry you were forced to see it." He paused at length. "I feel that some things need to be said, regardless of the potential consequences. I always calculate the return on my investment, and I knew this was worth it."

He said this somewhat abstractedly. Fortunately, he seemed to be speaking mostly to himself, because she hadn't the faintest idea how to respond. She was entirely out of her depth.

"It happens," she said, finally. Somewhat inanely. "Men will do that now and again. My . . . my . . . father is a doctor. I have seen a *lot* of things."

He turned his head to look at her again, somewhat surprised, amusement flickering in his eyes.

And slowly, subtly, he straightened to his considerable full height and went still.

Whereupon she had an epiphany: upon first meeting, most men seemed to preen or posture, smolder or fidget or gently condescend, all in the name of emphasizing that they were male and she was not.

But the very quality of Lord Kirke's stillness launched a primal thrill up her spine. It called to mind a swift object in motion come to abrupt rest—a hurled javelin, for instance, or an arrow—on its target.

It was intoxicating and unsettling. For this, too,

she knew about men: he wouldn't linger here one more moment if he didn't want to, manners be damned. Men did what they wanted to do, generally.

Her heart was now beating double time.

She probably ought to demurely lower her eyes but it seemed foolish to forego the opportunity to study the splendid geometry of his face. One day she would be able to tell her grandchildren about how the infamous Lord Kirke's thick brows drew closer together the time he scrutinized her at a ball. How there was the faintest frost of silver at each of his temples and how his eyes, the darkest and most alive eyes she'd ever seen, were ringed in faint shadows.

"You seem to know who I am, but I fear I'm at a disadvantage," he said finally. "And yet you seem familiar, Miss . . . Mrs. . . . Lady . . ."

Hell's teeth. If he didn't remember it, she was none too eager to remind him of their door-crack conversation.

"Keating. Miss Catherine Keating, sir. We haven't been formally introduced but"—she cleared her throat—"we spoke last night."

Not one glimmer of recognition flickered in his eyes. This both abraded her vanity and surprised her not at all.

"At The Grand Palace on the Thames," she admitted resignedly, finally. "Through . . . through the door."

His head went back, then came down in a nod. "Ah. You're the singer. 'New to London.'"

Irony fair shimmered about those last five words. But his eyes were filled with teasing glints.

She felt the heat rush to her complexion again. "I'm afraid so."

He hesitated.

"I fear I'm insufferable the night before I need to give a speech in the Commons." He paused. With a rueful ghost of a smile he added, "And at most times in between."

She suspected this was his version of an apology. And was in all likelihood true.

She thankfully managed not to say this out loud.

"Well. Goodness knows I deserved to be thoroughly castigated for singing," she replied humbly.

He fixed her with an amused, speculative look, clearly aware she was taking the piss.

"'Castigated,'" he repeated, approvingly, as if she'd just handed him a glass of wine of a surprisingly good vintage.

She couldn't help it: she smiled again. And so did he.

"So, Keating. Why are you out here instead of inside dancing and gossiping?"

"Keating," not "Miss Keating." As if she were a fellow MP whose back he might chummily pat. A coconspirator. Like everything about this man so far, "Keating" irritated her and she liked it almost too much.

But the question rendered her mute. The concerns milling about in her head like sheep without a dog would no doubt bore him. She was hardly a raconteur.

But there he was waiting, his hopes no doubt pinned on her ability to divert him again, and the notion of seeing disappointment flicker in his eyes for some reason made her palms sweat.

"I—it's—it seems my dress is wrong."

Of all the thoughts to escape from her mouth. She felt like an utter cake.

His eyes flared warily. His brows met in confusion.

Her face went warm.

He swept her person with an information-seeking glance that seemed to have nothing of prurience in it, and then returned an unreadable gaze to hers. She was mordantly amused he didn't attempt to disabuse her of the notion. Oddly, it made him seem more trustworthy.

"Someone said something that led you to this conclusion," he guessed finally.

She cleared her throat. "A somewhat offhand remark was made about my sleeves and . . . I inferred. I confess it didn't occur to me that it would matter very much. This dress is only two years old." She absently smoothed her palms along her skirt. "I hadn't time to get new ones before the season, as the opportunity came on rather suddenly, and I hadn't the budget for it . . . I've always been assured that . . . that blue is my color," she concluded, rather absurdly. She could feel her blush traveling. Surely her entire torso was pink by now.

"Mmm." He nodded, sympathetically. "I suspect there's a shortage of French modistes in Upper Sheep's Teat, Northumberland, or wherever it is you hail from."

She didn't even blink. She was getting a sense of him now.

"It's Nether Sheep's Teat, but please don't be embarrassed, Lord Kirke. Everyone always confuses the two."

He smiled again. She was beginning to feel a bit like Icarus, taking that fatal mad leap again and again in order to see that smile. This conversation seemed to hold equal potential for disaster and rewards.

"It's called Little Bramble," she expounded, somewhat meekly. "My town."

"Of course it is," he humored.

Lord Kirke, it was clear, was a conversational fencer: always feinting, disarming, distracting, testing. It was probably a quick and efficient way to uncover liars and fools. Not necessarily the best way to make friends or keep from getting punched. But she found it hopelessly compelling. One wanted to pass his tests.

"How did you know I was born in Northumberland?"

"It haunts your vowels," was all he said, cryptically.

This was fascinatingly specific, and yet again ranked among the most interesting things ever said to her by a man.

"And you, sir . . . are Welsh?" She realized this was like saying, "And you, sky, are blue?"

"Ah, indeed I am Welsh, Keating," he replied indulgently. "All the way from Satan's Arse Crack, a little town near Cardiff."

Not even in her wildest dreams had she ever thought she'd hear the words "Satan's arse crack" so exquisitely enunciated.

She began to wonder if he was a lot drunker than he seemed.

"It sounds lovely," she decided to say. "And explains a good deal."

When he smiled, slowly and fully, those charming parentheses deepened about the corners of his mouth and his eyes lit like dark stars. It made him look like Pan, willing to use his unimaginable powers to perpetrate dangerous mischief.

Then he winced and touched a quick finger to the corner of his mouth. She winced along with him.

"I think you've stopped bleeding," she volunteered.

He glanced ruefully down at the handkerchief in his hand. It was pristine, apart from a few drops of blood.

"Keep it. I have another." She'd always wanted to say something grandly magnanimous like that. She might not have the right dresses, but her new handkerchiefs were unimpeachable.

He arched a brow and tucked it into his coat. "Very generous of you. My thanks."

This would be the appropriate moment for either of them to discreetly melt away.

She was pleased that neither of them seemed inclined to do it.

"So, Keating. Is that the reason you're out here alone on a bench in the shadows—nursing hurt feelings about your sleeves?"

"Oh no. Not really. That is, I don't suppose my feelings are hurt. She doesn't know me, and they're just words, aren't they? I can't be hurt by someone who doesn't truly know me."

"Can't you?" he remarked neutrally.

"I shouldn't think it was a comment on my character, was it? It's just a dress." She looked up at him worriedly and smoothed the front of it again, then rushed on, because why on earth should a man like him care? "I suppose it has simply given me something to think about. Green things feel a bit like family members, as I'm from the country. And I suppose I'm just a bit . . . winded." She brushed her hand against her cheek self-consciously.

He frowned very faintly. "From the dancing?"

She gave a little embarrassed laugh. "From the newness. London and ballrooms and the like. It's my very first season and it's quite a lot to take in but I like it very much," she reassured him earnestly, lest he think she was insulting his milieu. "The people at The Grand Palace on the Thames are lovely, aren't they? I love it there. Everyone at this ball looks so beautiful and the music is the finest I've ever heard! And some of the dances are a bit unfamiliar to me but I'm excited to become better at them. I shall wade back into the ballroom presently for I'm to dance a reel with Mr. Hargrove. I expect in no time at all I shall learn who the kind people are by what they say and make friends of them."

For a man clearly possessed of little patience, he'd listened to all this with apparent, even flattering, unblinking attentiveness.

But he said nothing for such a long while that it occurred to her that his thoughts might have simply drifted away toward something he considered more worthy of his attention, fights and speeches and the like, and he hadn't even realized she'd finished speaking.

Finally, casually, he leaned against the wall and bent a knee, as though he was settling in.

"You're walking through a jungle on your way to a pressing engagement." His cadence made it sound like the beginning of a story. "This engagement is a matter of life or death. And blocking your path is a body of water teeming with hungry crocodiles. There's no bridge, no vines upon which to swing. No trees. You've no tools. You're wearing what you're wearing now, your allegedly wrong dress. Some crocodiles are sleepier than the others. Some are more vicious. You're desperate. They're desperate. How do you get across?"

Somehow it seemed only fitting that this odd conversation would eventually include a riddle. Perhaps they were a tradition in Satan's Arse Crack.

"I suppose I could . . . wait until they fall asleep, because they have to sleep some time, dash through the shallowest—"

"Wrong. Congratulations, now you're crocodile food."

She gave a start.

"You'll need to swim across. And in order to swim with the crocodiles, one must become a crocodile. Or at least don a convincing crocodile disguise. And everyone in there, Keating"—he jerked his chin in the direction of the ballroom—"is a crocodile. Particularly during mating season."

She was speechless. And fascinated.

"Speaking of which. What are you doing wandering about, without your"—he spiraled a finger in the air, as if paging through an invisible dictionary for a word—"minder?"

"My *minder*?" She was startled. As if she were a donkey.

"Usually some formidable woman of middle years charged with trailing young women to protect them from straying into the hinterlands of houses and launching into conversations with scandalous personages like me. Your chaperone. Your companion. Your Reputation Protector. Whatever the ton has decided to call it this year. Who is she, where is she, and why are you alone?"

This sudden transition from riddle to inquisition rattled her. She thought of Lady Wisterberg. She couldn't bring herself to say she was at the gaming table.

"Are you scandalous?" she whispered finally. Her heart sank.

He flicked his eyes skyward briefly. "Crocodile food," he muttered, to no one specifically.

He reached into his coat and produced what appeared to be a cheroot, which he idly rolled between his fingers.

He didn't light it. His expression had gone serious.

"Or . . ." He narrowed his eyes thoughtfully. "Perhaps, whoever she is sent you out here hoping to orchestrate a compromising situation, the sort that would make me, through misguided honor, fall upon that sword known as matrimony. Perhaps she thought I'd be reflecting upon my mortality after having been hit in the face, and eager for a life of quiet domesticity. It's been tried more than once, Keating, and all have failed," he warned darkly. "It can't be done."

She was once again speechless. She clamped her teeth to keep her jaw from dropping.

The astounding cheek of him!

Or . . . was he teasing her again?

This seemed likely. But now she was curious. What would this entrapment entail? A swoon in his proximity, a spy waiting in the wings to dart out to catch him with a woman in his arms and threaten ruination? What kind of woman would lay a trap for such a man? Did people actually do that sort of thing?

Perhaps a crocodile would.

She could well imagine the covetousness he inspired—all beautiful things, from dresses to people—seemed to stir varying degrees of turmoil in onlookers. But for heaven's sake. He seemed such a difficult man. Half imp, half satyr. All wrapped up in an intimidating mantel of notoriety. He'd be no more appropriate as a husband than the King of the Fairies would be.

She suspected being married to him would be

like forever yearning for something even while it was clutched in your fist.

"Well. That is disappointing to hear, indeed," she humored gently. Ever so slightly dryly.

He didn't reply. But after a moment the corners of his mouth deepened, and a devastatingly soft, wholly unguarded amused warmth gathered in his eyes. She could feel that warmth in her solar plexus; it spread softly through her limbs. And then he gave his head a slight, wondering shake.

For one mad instant she felt as though she'd been given a peek beyond his drawbridge right into the burning heart of the man.

The moment was over too soon, and left her breathless and restless.

"It's Lady Wisterberg," she confessed. Her voice was faint. "My aunt turned her ankle and couldn't come to London."

She did not like one bit the cynical, knowing light that flashed in his eyes when he heard the name.

But he said nothing. He pushed himself away from the wall briskly. "I'm going to do you a favor and vanish like an apparition because heaven forfend you're seen chatting merrily and alone with the likes of me. But I'll leave you with a bit of wisdom. If someone spent a precious breath insulting your sleeves, it likely meant she perceived you as a rival, which is useful to know. Sometimes insults are more valuable than compliments, and sometimes what seems like kindness is a sort of chess move. Good luck with your season."

His bow was swift and graceful, and just before he vanished around the corner he turned around and walked backward two steps and flashed a final grin. "And by the way, Keating, blue is, indeed, your color."

LADY WISTERBERG, HE thought wryly. *That* was almost funny. God help the girl.

Confident Farquar would have been piled into a carriage by now, Kirke strode back the way he'd come up the stairs, past all those Clayton ancestral portraits, their chins engulfed in ruffs, their hairlines plucked so that their foreheads looked vast. All, no doubt, wearing the correct, stylish sleeves for the era. *Imagine* wanting to decorate your walls with your relatives, he thought. Apart from his great-uncle—who'd had money and had seen something in young Dominic, and had sent him to school—his own would be a gallery of rogues, ruffians, and ne'er-do-wells. A row of proud sneers and square chins.

The only painted image he had of any relative was Leo.

The thought of him made Kirke tense as if he'd brushed up against a wound.

What the bloody hell did Farquar know, if anything? And how did he know it?

As he did with many things, Kirke had a contrary relationship with crowds. Like a porpoise surfacing for air, he invariably needed a moment or two of solitude during people-packed soirees, whether or not he'd just been hit in the face. He'd in fact only reached adulthood with his sanity arguably intact thanks to a refuge he'd found near his teeming-with-humanity family home: a secret, secluded patch of clover-blanketed hillside shadowed by a boulder. He supposed that made him a bit like

Keating, who found comfort next to green things. It was in all likelihood the only thing they had in common.

He half smiled to himself. Given a chance, the young men of the ton were going to enjoy discovering Keating. And she them. She had eyes like the view out a window on a spring day and a flatteringly direct gaze, and the lines of her body could make a less jaded man forget his name.

But he was thirty-five years old now. His own appetites and interests did not run to innocents, or to women who wanted anything more from him than a few hours or so of naked oblivion. Innocence was a language he could no longer speak.

Thoughts of naked oblivion and inappropriate sleeves called to mind the perfidious Marie-Claude, who had found time before she'd nearly burned his house down (and who had either fled or planned to flee across the Channel, or so he'd heard today) to order and charge to him something ridiculously expensive in blue silk which had not yet been retrieved from the modiste's. His man of affairs had only just meticulously accommodated one recent shock to his bank account only to confront another one—the burned house—and was none too pleased to present him with an outrageous dressmaker's bill on top of all of that. Kirke would of course grit his teeth and pay for it because it wasn't the hardworking Madame Marceau's fault.

Though theirs had been a business arrangement— initiated by her—Marie-Claude had ultimately wanted something from him she could not quite articulate, but which manifested in a restless torrent of demands. And while it was no hardship to now and again indulge a beautiful woman, it became clear the requests would never stop. Whereupon he'd bluntly called an end to things.

At which point the lamp had become a projectile.

He was ardent, but remote. He'd come to understand that this drove some women mad. More than one had sensed that some part of him would never be known to them, and he supposed it was merely human nature to want what one could never reach, on the assumption that the struggle to get it made it worth having.

He would *definitely* quibble with this.

Only he knew the truth: before the age of twenty he'd felt nearly everything a man could feel, in gruesome proportions. Soaring love and searing shame. Passion and joy, terror and struggle. Gutting loss. The whole bloody lot had dug such brutally deep channels through him that little he felt in the aftermath was capable of shaking him or leaving a mark. Nearly every emotion he'd felt since had seemed a mere echo by comparison.

For a long time he'd allowed himself to believe that this was the source of his strength. His tireless attempts to right injustices took him to dire places, workhouses and mills and slums, places so desperate they might have broken another man. And while he cared passionately, they never brought him to his knees.

But his hands had shaken when he'd read the letter from Anna a little over a month ago. She'd sent it along with the miniature.

And everything he thought he could never again feel revealed that it had simply been lying in the underbrush to ambush him.

He'd once done something unforgivable. And through a blinding epiphany he'd understood there could never truly be atonement, only a reckoning.

He passed a painting of a woman in a blue dress, which reminded him of Keating. In normal circumstances, their paths would never cross. The two of them occupied two entirely different worlds. An innocent from the country; a jade from London. Her life was quiet; his was a tumult. Her future was an open road, a shiny, hopeful blank slate; his present was a snarl at best and his past had just come flapping out at him like an opened Pandora's box and his future would *always* be uncertain and complicated.

And yet they apparently both found refuge near plants.

When he came upon a footman relighting a sconce, he slowed.

Then stopped.

He was indecisively motionless for so long the footman looked up and gave a start. "Lord Kirke, sir." He bowed.

Kirke reached his hand into his pocket, and felt about. When he miraculously found a shilling, he approached the footman almost as gingerly as Keating had approached him earlier with her handkerchief.

He lowered his voice. "My good man. At 10:25 p.m., no later, if you would be so kind as to find Lady Wisterberg and tell her that she is needed at once—at *once*—to escort the young lady for whom she is responsible tonight back to her lodgings? Please say nothing more than that. I know you will not mention my name. Do not give up until she is away from the table. Do you understand?"

The footman eyed the shilling glinting between

Kirke's fingers. After an understandable hesitation—on one hand, a shilling was a handsome sum for a footman; on the other, it was a pittance for the battle he might have on his hands—he accepted it, and his mission. "Very good sir. If ten twenty-five o'clock it must be, then ten twenty-five o'clock it is."

They exchanged knowing looks. Everyone in the ton knew that once the dowager started in at faro, little short of Armageddon would shift her out of her seat before the sun rose.

It would of course be wildly inappropriate for Kirke alone to escort Keating back to the boarding-house.

He wasn't certain why he bothered to intervene. But the notion of the rare light in the girl's face dimming if she discovered she'd been abandoned and forgotten by her chaperone disturbed him, as though she were the last of her species and ought to be protected. She seemed openhearted and hopeful without being flighty, and kind without being dull, and these were the sorts of people the ton liked to grind into smithereens.

Good luck, Keating, he thought. He doubted she'd last the month in London.

Chapter Five

~⚬⚭⚬~

AN HOUR or so after dinner the following evening, Mrs. Hardy led Lord Kirke into the sitting room with an air of cautious ceremony, as if he were a falcon resting on her gloved hand. He was carrying a book, clearly intending to read while the socializing took place all around him. He seemed altogether tense and restive. Present on sufferance, as the rules of the house required, prepared to either be polite or to bite as the mood took him.

Catherine's pulse skittered.

She'd spent her own day reading in the park in front of the building—she'd fetched a book from the little library Mrs. Hardy and Mrs. Durand had set aside in a room in the annex. It had been a pleasant enough day—the blue sky gauzed with clouds, blossoms nodding all around her in the briny breeze frisking off the Thames, Gordon the cat lacing between her ankles and purring—but being at loose ends was yet another new sensation. She'd been meant to go to the Montmorency Museum today with Lady Wisterberg and Lucy, but Lady Wisterberg had sent over a note with a footman:

Dear Miss Keating,

I'm terribly sorry to report that I am indisposed this morning and will be unable to accompany you and Lucy to the museum today. I am quite bedridden with a mal de tête. There is a drummer in my head! I look forward to seeing you again for the Tillbury affair tomorrow!

Yrs,

Lady Wisterberg

She could imagine it. It had required two cups of strong coffee and a scone to vanquish the tympani in her own head, and she'd only had two glasses of ratafia. Goodness knows how many Lady Wisterberg had downed by the end of the evening.

Catherine only danced once the whole of the previous night, with Mr. Hargrove. And at no point during this dance did her heart accelerate, stop, or jolt, all of which it had done in the space of a conversation with Lord Kirke. She began to understand how difficult men could become an acquired taste, enjoyable in limited quantities, like espresso, or violent thunderstorms.

But Lord Kirke's face now seemed so forbiddingly cool it seemed to her miraculous that she'd ever had the nerve to approach him at all. Perhaps he erected that expression like a fortress to protect all of his weighty, profound thoughts.

The coolness evolved into a sort of bemusement as he took in the sitting room, his eyes lighting on the chess set, the pianoforte, the mismatched furniture which nevertheless seemed to belong together, just like all the people in the room. He'd laughed last night, but she struggled to picture him planting his hands on his hips and throwing his head back to release a deafening baritone. À la Mr. Delacorte, or gleefully clapping instead of singing out "arse."

Everyone had respectfully risen from their chairs to greet him and bow and curtsy.

Lord Bolt, who had returned that morning to The Grand Palace on the Thames with Captain Hardy, was the first to speak. "Welcome to our home, Kirke. Have you yet met Captain Hardy?"

"Bolt." Lord Kirke sounded pleased. Catherine was unsurprised; lords always seemed to know each other, as one species recognizes another. "A pleasure to see you. Thank you. You've an enviable home. I'm grateful for the shelter, even if the circumstances that led me here are a bit regrettable. And it's an honor to make your acquaintance, Captain Hardy. I know you by your formidable reputation, of course."

"Likewise, sir." Captain Hardy sounded a trifle dryly amused.

A wry smile played at the corners of Lord Kirke's mouth. As though he relished every aspect of his reputation, and every gradation of the word "formidable."

The proprietresses' husbands had welcomed her very graciously at dinner. Catherine considered both quite handsome—Captain Hardy was chiseled and stern, with close cropped hair and silvery eyes; Lord Bolt's face was long and elegant, his hair darker and longer, his eyes green. And it was a subtle thing, but it seemed to her as though the very building had collectively exhaled with their arrival. Mrs. Hardy and Mrs. Durand were welcoming and charming, but now they seemed easier and more joyful, and this joy infused the very room. She understood: all these people were all, after a fashion, a family, and she knew full well that when a member was away, the absence was a little disorienting and the balance of life felt a little askew, like wearing a shoe that was a bit too big. And the reminder of her own diminished family briefly twinged the breath from her.

"We've a smoking room if you're in the mood for a cheroot later, Kirke." Lord Bolt gestured with his chin to some place over his shoulder. "Although, one could hardly blame you if you happened to be holding a grudge against smoke of any kind at the moment."

This puzzled Catherine, but Lord Kirke gave a short laugh. "Since I generally subscribe to a hair-of-the-dog-that-bit-you philosophy, I'm all but required to join you for smoking when the time comes. Thank you."

Mr. Delacorte cleared his throat. "If you prefer not to smoke, sir," he ventured, "I've something in my case of medicines that might distract you from your troubles. It was meant to be a headache powder, but the last person who took it reported a vision of Lord Castlereagh soaring through the night sky while seated on the back of a winged horse. He said it was so majestically beautiful he'd forgotten he'd ever had a headache at all."

Everyone slowly turned to stare in bemusement at Mr. Delacorte.

Lord Castlereagh was the Tory leader of the House of Commons, and not currently a popular man in England, for numerous reasons.

Lord Kirke seemed to be considering his words. "Forgive my hesitation, Mister . . ."

"Delacorte. Stanton Delacorte."

"Mr. Delacorte. Better the night sky on a winged

horse for Castlereagh than the Commons, but I think I'll begin with cheroots and see how the evening goes. I wonder if you would mind expounding on the 'little case of medicines' bit?"

Mr. Delacorte beamed. "I import remedies from the Orient to sell to apothecaries and surgeons up and down the coast, herbs and other concoctions, some of which work a treat. And I'm a partner in the Triton Group with Lord Bolt and Captain Hardy."

"Is that so?" Lord Kirke sounded genuinely interested. "Have you anything in your case of remedies that would make the entire Commons hallucinate that they're Whigs instead of Tories?"

"I'm a purveyor of remedies, not miracles," Mr. Delacorte said in all seriousness.

Everyone laughed while Delilah and Angelique exchanged silent, eloquent glances, wondering if they needed to make "Whig" and "Tory" Epithet Jar words while Lord Kirke was in residence. Just in case "spirited" became a little too spirited.

"I haven't read your speeches," Mr. Delacorte added, somewhat challengingly. "But I've had them quoted at me in pubs. Usually the bit about the intoxication—"

"LET THE INTOXICATION OF VICTORY LEAD TO THE SOBRIETY OF A COMPASSIONATE PEACE," everyone in the room quoted in unison.

Lord Kirke didn't so much as blink. He nodded once at the tribute, slowly, a rueful smile lifting the corner of his mouth. This probably happened to him all the time.

"I see. Fear not, Mr. Delacorte, I'm bound to give a few more speeches while I'm here. I feel it's my sacred duty to make sure every Englishman experiences one." His eyes gleamed wickedly.

Mr. Delacorte's expression flickered between stricken and abject hope that Kirke was jesting.

"Now that you've met Mr. Delacorte," Delilah interjected somewhat dryly, "I should like to present Mrs. Pariseau. We very much enjoy her erudition and intellectual adventurousness and she admires your work enormously."

Mrs. Pariseau's curtsy was graceful. "A great honor to meet you, sir. I suppose I *am* rather an Intellectual Adventuress. I, in particular, admired your speech about supporting our prisoners of war! 'Are we *all* not prisoners of complacency?'" she intoned. "So stirring! And your Freedom Speech! 'No man is free whose liberty requires the enslavement of another.' Myyy goodness."

The almost vixenish appreciation Mrs. Pariseau radiated at Lord Kirke startled Catherine. *Imagine* having the freedom and confidence to overtly flirt with an MP in a sitting room full of people. Just one of the many benefits of widowhood, apparently. Mrs. Pariseau had claimed the night before that she'd enjoyed being married but had never wanted another husband after hers expired some years ago. It was beginning to seem as though some man had to die in order for a woman to really begin enjoying her life. Surely that couldn't be right?

Lord Kirke offered a patient little smile. "A pleasure, Mrs. Pariseau. Thank you for your kind words. I look forward to spirited discourse, as per the bylaws of The Grand Palace on the Thames."

This made Mrs. Pariseau clap a thrilled hand to her bosom.

He had not so much as glanced at Catherine yet.

Which, paradoxically, suggested to her that he was profoundly aware of her presence.

Her heart was thudding oddly now. She wondered if he would go still again when he looked at her, as he had last night. She had taken the memory out to ponder more than once today. The sensation had seemed akin to stepping a little too close to something beautiful and possibly dangerous, perhaps a wolf, in order to get a better view.

Delilah turned to her. "And Lord Kirke, I don't believe you've yet met our guest, Miss Catherine Keating. Miss Keating told us over breakfast this morning that she enjoys your speeches." She shot a swift, mildly remonstrating glance at Mr. Delacorte when she said this. Like every good hostess, Mrs. Hardy clearly knew that often the easiest way to make a man comfortable was to flatter him.

Catherine and Lord Kirke exchanged a bow and curtsy each. They both knew better than to let on they'd already had a conversation on a semidark verandah. At least she hoped he did.

Her breath snagged when their eyes met, as surely as though she'd been dropped a few inches from a height. The force of his personality was so *undiluted* in his gaze. Perhaps one would need to learn to build up a tolerance to it, as with ratafia, or anything else that inebriated a little

"How do you do, Miss Keating. I'm pleased to hear that you enjoy my speeches in the newspapers. I understand some people spread them under their puppies and in their birdcages."

She smiled. "My father reads them aloud at the breakfast table in a very deep voice—he imagines you as very stentorian, and says you have 'nerve.'"

"Oh, that I do, Miss Keating." A little smile played at the corners of his mouth.

"I find some of them rather stirring as well," she confessed.

"Only some of them? I fear you have set me a challenge," he said softly.

Warmth crept into her cheeks. She was suddenly without words.

"Miss Keating hails from Northumberland, and her father is a physician," Mrs. Hardy prompted helpfully. "She's here for the season and we're looking after her at The Grand Palace on the Thames."

"Ah. I imagine as the daughter of a doctor from Northumberland, you have seen a lot, Miss Keating."

Lord Kirke said this with every evidence of gravity. But Catherine was touched that he'd remembered their previous conversation, and by the hint at their shared secret. She smiled at him.

"Miss Keating told us that she helped her father sew the tip of a man's finger back on," Mr. Delacorte volunteered. "And once helped deliver a lamb."

Now she was a little embarrassed. She *had* gotten a bit garrulous the night she'd arrived, thanks to the sherry.

But Lord Kirke's eyebrows gratifyingly shot up. "How brave and interesting, Miss Keating."

He sounded sincere. It was astonishing to think that someone like him would find her the least bit brave or interesting. "It is kind of you to say so," she said somewhat shyly. "But that's just everyday life in my town."

He smiled as though she'd said something singularly charming.

"Lord Kirke," Mrs. Pariseau ventured, "you're Welsh, is that not so? Do you hail from mining stock?"

He turned to regard Mrs. Pariseau in silent bemusement for a tick. "Mining stock," he repeated
thoughtfully. "Is that what miners are simmered in?"

His little smile suggested he might be amused.
And also might not be.

"Lord Kirke has had an eventful week," Mrs.
Hardy interjected swiftly and gently. "We can press
him for his autobiography later. I'm sure we'll come
to know him better as the days go by. I see you've
brought a book down with you, Lord Kirke, and
you're welcome to quietly read. But I don't suppose
you'd enjoy a game of chess, would you? Mr. Delacorte is our resident champion."

"Is that so?" Lord Kirke said speculatively, turning to Mr. Delacorte. "You have the look of a man
who can put up a good, dirty fight."

"*Have* I?" Mr. Delacorte, about whom such a thing
had likely never been said, was tickled.

"No. Not in the least. Prove me wrong, Mr. Delacorte."

"Oh, HO!" Mr. Delacorte, always delighted to be
teased, gestured with a hand to the table, and they
settled in.

Chapter Six

cᴒᴓᴒᴓ

Mʀ. Dᴇʟᴀᴄᴏʀᴛᴇ, who was roughly the shape of an egg and had a broad, friendly face and surprisingly lovely blue eyes, was, in fact, a gratifyingly aggressive and wily chess player. He'd trapped Kirke's queen with alacrity. Kirke was pleased. He loved when people upended his expectations, and he loathed limply played chess.

Kirke maneuvered out of that and cornered Delacorte's queen a few moves later.

While Delacorte mulled this new predicament, Kirke could feel the little sitting room lapping at his senses seductively, as if it were a warm bath. Or as if he were a cliff it was determined to erode. A certain crafty genius was evident in its design, he thought dryly. The lovely Mrs. Hardy and Mrs. Durand were not just proprietresses. They had a calling.

They were so committed to this calling that they'd commemorated it in the second of their seven house rules:

All guests must gather in the drawing room after dinner for at least an hour at least four times per week. We feel it fosters a sense of friendship and the warm, familial, congenial atmosphere we strive to create here at The Grand Palace on the Thames.

The atmosphere in which he'd been raised could
best be described as "a pack of starving wolves,"
so the notion of a "warm, familial, congenial atmosphere" was as foreign to him as London apparently was to Keating. It was strangely disorienting
and odd that all that seemed required of him in this
room was his presence. His work had taken him into
nearly every imaginable milieu—the wretchedness
of the workhouses at Bethnal Green and the slums
of St. Giles, glittering ballrooms, hushed libraries
where the only sound was the glug of expensive
brandy into snifters, the smokey male luxury of
White's, the austere dormitories of the University
of Edinburgh—but his reasons for being in each of
those places were rooted in purpose and duty. His
own, currently somewhat charred home, he'd fur-
nished for utility. He was in it only to sleep, usually.

It seemed to him the primary point of everything in The Grand Palace on the Thames was
to . . . comfort. He could not quite say why. He
didn't think he would have necessarily elected to
stuff blossoms in a vase in his room, for instance,
but the damned blossoms suited him, which made
him feel as though his soul had been clandestinely
rifled through to determine his secrets. He absurdly resented it a little. He was not one to give up
anything easily.

Nor could he object to the company. Bolt and
Hardy were the sort of men he liked: both of colorful pedigree—Bolt the bastard son of a duke, Hardy
born God knows where, perhaps he'd been born already *in* the navy, so renowned were his ruthless
smuggler-catching skills—singular of personality,
characters shaped by hard work and hard-won authority.

And over in the corner the conversation between the ladies had become very animated. Possibly even heated.

He thought he heard the word "ghost."

Bloody hell. He was curious despite himself.

As Mr. Delacorte sucked on his bottom lip in contemplation, Kirke discovered that Keating's profile was within his line of sight, and he noted that the lush curve of her bottom lip was the color of the blossoms in the vase upstairs.

At once, an involuntary primal awareness settled over him like a net of little cinders and his stomach muscles tightened.

He suddenly felt like a lecher. She was a young woman whose woefully inadequate chaperone left her vulnerable in Gomorrah, also known as London. Not one of the forthright seasoned widows and matrons who often issued unmistakable innuendo-cloaked invitations to him.

He turned his head.

The little kerfuffle in the corner was growing in volume.

"But I *promise* you, Dot, you'll enjoy this one, too." Mrs. Pariseau's eyes were glinting with a determination. "It might even become a new favorite."

With a flourish, she produced a book she'd been holding behind her back and held it up so that everyone could read the title: *The Arabian Nights' Entertainments.*

"*The Arabian Nights' Entertainments*?" Dot was stubbornly suspicious. "But nights are ordinary! They happen every night! The year is filled with nights! Is there even a ghost?"

"Not as such," Mrs. Pariseau admitted.

"A love story?" Dot demanded.

"Well . . ." Mrs. Pariseau hedged.

"It's a story about how women are smarter than men," Kirke said idly.

Plink. Silence fell like a dome, so abruptly it was nearly audible.

Alarm and titillation ricocheted between everyone present: it seemed the controversial Lord Kirke was wasting no time in being controversial, right there in the sitting room.

Lucien's eyebrows went up. The words, "I hope you're enjoying the Whig you allowed to stay, Angelique and Delilah," practically pulsed in the air above his head.

"Are we really smarter?" Dot whispered finally to Angelique, who was closest.

"Yes," Angelique replied.

Her husband whipped his head toward her.

Angelique bit her lip against a laugh. "Sometimes," she amended on a whisper, with a wink at Lucien.

Captain Hardy's lips were pressed together. He was eyeing Kirke patiently and steadily, with a certain dry amusement and a bit of a warning, as if he was braced for all manner of anarchy.

Kirke continued easily. "To clarify, I do believe that's one of the fundamental themes running through a story about a king who murders all of his wives until he finds one who doesn't bore him. This version, by the way, is a translation of the French version called *1001 Nights.*"

Dot gasped and her hand flew to cover her heart. "Good *heavens*, Mrs. Pariseau!" she remonstrated. "Is that really what it's about?"

This was mostly dramatics, on her part; there wasn't a soul in the room who wasn't intrigued by that description.

Dot in fact adored being terrified in the safety of the sitting room.

"Who among us has never been tempted to murder a boring person?" Kirke pressed brightly.

Keating stifled a laugh.

"Or decapitate a spouse?" Mrs. Pariseau added supportively.

Everyone turned to her, startled.

She shrugged with one shoulder.

"Her name is Scheherazade," Kirke added helpfully. "The wife who doesn't bore him."

"Her name alone would take a thousand and one nights to spell," Delacorte marveled. "No *wonder* he was interested."

"How does he murder them?" Dot ventured after a moment, on a whisper. She couldn't resist.

"Chops their heads right off, I'm afraid," Lord Kirke said matter-of-factly. "Just as Mrs. Pariseau implied."

English history was unfortunately filled with all manner of bloody mayhem and, while appalled, Dot was less shocked than she could have been.

"Do they become ghosts?" was her next, perhaps inevitable, question.

"You would think," he said. "Though I don't know if the sultan has an attic. Or why a ghost would consider an attic their only option for eternity."

"Perhaps they don't want to stay in the attic, but they can't help it. Maybe they've no choice. They're compelled to drift right up there, like steam from tea," Keating suggested.

He turned to stare at her in surprise. For some reason he was almost *transcendently* amused by this. For such a soft-looking person Keating's wit had surprising angles and edges. There was almost nothing he loved more than angles and edges. They were the means by which puzzles were put together.

She smiled back at him, like a coconspirator.

He decided he liked her expressive brows.

"I find I cannot object to your hypothesis, Lord Kirke," Mrs. Pariseau, never one to shy away from the "spirited" part of spirited discourse, made all the men in the room apart from Kirke shift a little in their seats when she said this. "I wonder if you would explain your assertion about the superior intelligence of women?"

He was fully aware that his proprietresses—and their husbands—were poised for possible philosophical mayhem. Kirke knew how to foment mayhem; he also knew how to soothe it. He thought he might enjoy doing a little of both tonight. That would teach them to make him obediently sit in their diabolically comfortable sitting room.

He was also aware that Keating was now watching him as though he was a mad genius. He felt a ridiculous rare urge to impress for the sake of impressing.

"Well, Scheherazade was an extraordinarily brave and resourceful woman. The story begins when the *first* woman the sultan married was allegedly unfaithful—I know this is difficult to believe, given how charming the man clearly is." He paused for chuckles. "So he had her put to death. In fact, he was *so* incensed by her infidelity that he married a new woman every day, and on every wedding night he'd bid an executioner wait outside the door of his chamber. Each morning he'd send his new wife out to the chopping block. Literally cut a swath right through the young women in his kingdom. The whole thing was almost as bloodthirsty as the London season."

Keating smiled at this, too. Which gratified him, as he'd said it for her benefit.

Dot was pale and thrilled. "What a *terrible* man!" she breathed.

"Indeed. And you'll notice that the House of Lords has made it difficult for the king to simply divorce the queen here in England. You're welcome," he said to the gathered, ironically. "Thankfully, beheading them has gone out of style. So along comes Scheherazade, a brave, clever girl with a plan. She volunteered to marry the sultan so that no other women would die. And then night after night—*one thousand and one* nights, mind you, and I am a writer of all sorts of things so I can attest to the gruesome challenge of this task—she told stories that so enthralled him, that left him in such suspense at the end of each night, that were infinitely more compelling than *The Ghost in the Attic*, if you can imagine such a thing, Dot—until the day came that he forgot to tell the executioner to return. And that was the end of the killing."

There was silence in the room as the audience absorbed this summary in a thrall that was equal parts fascinated and appalled.

"And they all lived happily ever after," Keating said.

Dominic gave a laugh, then turned the laugh into a cough.

It was clear that despite her fealty to *The Ghost in the Attic*, the potential for a fresh influx of drama, gore, and romance was proving difficult for Dot to resist. Her struggle was written all over her face.

"To your question, Mrs. Pariseau—the sultan indulged a fit of pique and solved his problems by chopping them away. A lazy man's solution. Scheherazade, to save her life and the lives of other women, used her wit, wiles, courage, and resourcefulness. And often, these are the qualities that come to the fore when you have no power at all. And those who have no power at all are the most vulnerable among us, usually children and women. Abusing power simply because you can is despicable."

Everyone in the room was raptly quiet, absorbing the words.

"Is that why you wanted to become an MP?" Keating asked shyly. "To change the laws?"

Her eyes had gone a little starry, which made him wary. He was always quick to curtail budding urges in young women to view him as anything like a hero.

"I wanted to be an MP because I like a good fight. And I wanted to finally make enough money so that I could always sleep in my own bed instead of with any of my six siblings, because I never wanted to smell my brothers' feet ever again."

Everyone laughed.

He'd in fact been a lawyer at Lincoln's Inn before he was an MP, but the day he'd bought an excellent mattress with his very own money indeed was embossed on his memory.

"How many brothers and sisters have you, Lord Kirke?" Mr. Delacorte asked.

"There were seven of us children, and we all slept arse to toe, all crammed into one bed, except for the baby in the cradle."

A silence dropped instantly.

The ladies were watching him with eyes limpid with regret, heads tipped. The men were amused.

Comprehension set in.

He lifted a hand in resigned acknowledgment.

"Do forgive me." He stood, reached into his coat, found and gamely flung a penny into the Epithet Jar.

"It's harder than it seems, ain't it?" Mr. Delacorte sympathized. "But it's good for a man's character, I think. Like cod liver oil for the soul."

"Well said, my brother in profanity." Lord Kirke reached out and Mr. Delacorte shook his proffered hand. "I am living proof that you can only civilize a man so much."

"You should have heard me when I first arrived. I am improving by the day!" Mr. Delacorte declared.

"And so is that what you are intending to do, is that not so? Pass a law preventing the abuse of children in mills and the like?" Keating pressed urgently. As if this were some magic he could perform. As if he were a genie from a lamp.

"In essence, yes," he said carefully. "I expect we'll get there in increments, not all at once. For example, we'll perhaps achieve stricter enforcement of the weak laws already in place, which has been woefully neglected."

"Doesn't it get exhausting to try and try and not win?" Delacorte wondered.

Kirke looked genuinely surprised into momentary speechlessness. "The winning is in the fighting."

He said this as though he'd thought this would be obvious to everyone.

There was a silence as everyone absorbed this.

Catherine's heart contracted. It struck her as so valiant. *The winning is in the fighting.* She admired it so much she could scarcely breathe.

"Like chess," Delacorte ventured hopefully.

"No, with chess the winning is in the winning," Kirke said wickedly.

Delacorte deflated a little in his chair. He knew he was about to lose.

"You only start losing when you stop fighting. If you were, for instance, buried by an avalanche and you see a pocket of air, would you stop digging? I don't pause to wallow in disappointment or fantasize about outcomes. You dig until there's daylight. You never stop. You explore every avenue. And, well, you know I come from mining stock. I can hardly stop digging."

He winked at Mrs. Pariseau, to her absolute delight.

"How do you make a law?" Dot asked.

Delacorte hissed in an involuntary warning breath, clearly worried that she'd just opened the floodgates to orating.

Kirke was thoroughly undeterred. "Well, it works a little like this. Let's say, for instance, you live at The Grand Palace on the Thames and feel oppressed by the fact that you can't curse a blue streak in the sitting room. You might campaign for that particular rule to be struck from The Grand Palace on the Thames's rules. You would have to persuade everyone here that it's a good idea. You might have to give a speech. Maybe many speeches. Form a political party. Perhaps you could call it the Blue Streak party. And then you would hold a vote."

"This is *hypothetical*," Angelique hastened to add. "It is merely an *example*. We will not be doing this."

"What if we vote to clap instead of using a curse word?" Mr. Delacorte wondered.

Catherine laughed.

"What if we wanted to add a law that says only one certain person is in charge of answering the door?" Dot asked innocently.

"You would need to persuade everyone that this is a good idea," Delilah said dryly. "And I can tell you what your chances of that will be."

"Mind you," Lord Kirke added, "what I've just said is *quite* a simplification."

"Do you think women ought to be able to vote the way men are able to vote, Lord Kirke?" Mrs. Pariseau asked.

Catherine's breath stopped. It seemed to her a question so daring it plucked her nerves to hear it aloud.

She understood that some women who owned property—usually inherited—were allowed to vote, but usually through an appointed male proxy. Women were at the mercy of men in nearly every way, until, apparently, they were widows. But she in truth knew very little about it.

"Yes. I do. One day they will." Lord Kirke said it as casually as "would you please pass the peas?"

There fell another loaded little silence.

She knew men in her village would immediately push such talk away as "daft" or "lunacy" or even "heresy." She could imagine the mutterings about it in the pub now. People said those kinds of things out of fear of change, and always had dozens of reasons why things should remain the same. She wasn't even certain whether her father would agree. It was so easy to dismiss anything that hadn't been done the same way for hundreds of years.

But when Lord Kirke said it, she *knew* everyone in this room could picture it. Such was his presence and conviction. One would have to be mad or utterly fearless or some combination to say such things, let alone attempt to lead a populace toward

them. She supposed they were fortunate he had
chosen to use his powers on behalf of the weakest
among them.

She was momentarily held fast by awe. It suddenly seemed outlandish that she'd ever had the
nerve to speak to him, because history—the sort
recorded in books—was made by people like him.
Statues were often made of this sort of person.

"Those who have the power are loathe to relin-
quish or share it," he continued. "And they fight to
keep it out of fear—fear of the loss of power. This has
been true throughout human history. Fortunately,
every generation, a few mad bast"—Delacorte
cleared his throat noisily, and Dominic nodded his
thanks. "A pigheaded few like me are born, and we
attempt to push the whole of the world closer to
justice for all humans. I firmly believe we all suffer
when the weakest among us suffer. Oh, women voting probably won't happen, not in our lifetimes. But
one day. Mark my words."

Kirke looked over at Captain Hardy and Lord
Bolt and raised his brows at them in a "Well?" sort
of way. It was, after a fashion, a dare.

Bolt and Hardy were amused, and yet not, at his
capriciously stirring potential uproar in their sitting
room, and of putting them on the spot. But it was
only what was to be expected.

Captain Hardy sighed heavily and leaned back
in his chair. "Very well. Bolt, Delacorte, and I are
partners in our own business, the Triton Group.
Our wives own The Grand Palace on the Thames
and make the decisions about everything and everyone in it, and they run it beautifully," Captain
Hardy said. "You can see for yourself the results of

it. If only our country were run so well. I cannot think of a single reason women ought not to vote."

"And they were clever enough to marry men who were happy to leave them to it," Bolt added.

Cat thought she was witnessing a different sort of politics, the kind men learn when they're married.

Delilah and Angelique were both wearing contented, approving expressions, as if they'd known this all along about their husbands.

"If only the world were run like The Grand Palace on the Thames," Delacorte added, "with an enormous Epithet Jar to fund things like . . . road improvements."

"A room full of revolutionaries," Lord Kirke said on a hush. "Who would have guessed? I won't let on."

"We vote every night here," Dot told him shyly. "I'm good at it."

"Do you, now? And does your candidate win, Dot?" Lord Kirke asked.

"Well, it usually does. My candidate is *The Ghost in the Attic.*" She said this somewhat defiantly. She was loyal, Dot was.

"I see. Are there other worthy candidates?"

"That brings us back to *The Arabian Nights' Entertainments,*" Mrs. Pariseau said. "We have read and enjoyed *The Ghost in the Attic* countless times. We'd like to propose a temporary moratorium on *The Ghost in the Attic* and read *The Arabian Nights' Entertainments* instead for the next month."

Dot looked suspicious. "What is a morta—"

"An end," Mrs. Pariseau said bluntly.

Dot uttered an inarticulate cry of protest. "Does *everyone* want a mortatory?"

"It's time, Dot," Captain Hardy said gravely.

Lord Kirke leaned toward Dot, his hands clasped, and fixed her somberly with the full force of his dark eyes until she blushed. "You enjoy ghost stories, is that so?" he asked her. "Supernatural beings?"

She nodded.

"Dot, in one of the stories Scheherazade tells, a genie, which is a sort of magic being, emerges from a lamp and grants wishes. When the lamp is rubbed."

Dot's fingers curled tight on the arms of her chair. "Never say a magic lamp," she said faintly. She looked almost ill with hope.

"I wouldn't lie about something so marvelous," Lord Kirke said somberly. "More marvelous than Castlereagh riding a winged horse."

The tension in the room was palpable.

"Perhaps we should read a few pages of it," Dot said, with attempted casualness. Magnanimously.

The tension gathered into something like excitement.

"Shall we vote?" Mrs. Pariseau suggested gently. "Everyone who would like me to read from *The Arabian Nights' Entertainments* tonight, please raise your hand."

Every hand, including Kirke's, shot up for the vote.

Chapter Seven

❧❧❧

LIKE so many of the young ladies present, Catherine wore white muslin to the Tillbury ball. Her bodice was scattered with little embroidered blue flowers and a wide blue ribbon wrapped beneath her bosom and tied behind. Three rows of ribbon of the same color traced her hem and trimmed her short sleeves.

The dress was pretty but surely unremarkable— the sleeves were not puffed, they were not fancy at all—but perhaps that would also be a problem? She hoped no one would tell her whether they were.

She wore her pearl necklace, too. She touched it, for luck and reassurance.

Lady Wisterberg had once again delivered Lucy and Catherine to the refreshment table, tossed back two glasses of ratafia, and melted away, heeding the siren song of the faro box.

Leaving the two of them alone.

The somewhat fraught mission of the season—to get themselves husbands—had introduced an unexpected note of tension between Lucy and Catherine. Neither of them overtly acknowledged it, but they both tacitly understood and regretted it. They were compensating by being too nice to each other. But Catherine suspected Lucy would be crushed if Mr. Hargrove transferred any particle of his attention to Catherine, and they both remained in suspense about whether he would ask Catherine to dance again.

And Lucy was terribly embarrassed about her godmother, Lady Wisterberg.

"I'm so sorry, Catherine, truly. She's only like this at balls where a gaming room has been arranged."

Neither said that it seemed likely that every ball would feature a gaming room, because what else would one do with all the adults who weren't dancing?

"Somehow it will all come right," she'd reassured Lucy, which was the kind thing to say. She almost even believed it. "But the onus shouldn't be on you to make introductions, and I do not hold it against you one bit."

"Good evening, ladies. You both look lovely this evening."

Lucy and Catherine turned toward Miss Seaver, who also seemed to begin her evenings next to the ratafia. Her chaperone—her mother—was clustered with other matrons on the opposite side of the room.

Instead of Mr. Hargrove, this time she had brought with her the pretty young Lady Hackworth, whose husband was a viscount. Introductions and curtsies were exchanged.

Catherine wistfully eyed the tiara perched on Lady Hackworth's complicated yellow-gold coiffure. Her own wavy hair was pinned up rather simply, and strands of it spiraled at her cheekbones.

"There are to be two waltzes this evening!" Miss Seaver announced. "And I'm dancing the first *wiiiith . . .*"

She widened her eyes playfully.

The dramatic pause was clearly designed to torture poor Lucy, who had not yet been asked to dance tonight by Mr. Hargrove. Catherine was tempted to accidentally-on-purpose trod hard on Miss Seaver's instep.

". . . Mr. Richards," Miss Seaver finally said brightly.

Both Lucy and Catherine disguised exhales.

"I'm looking forward to the first quadrille," Catherine contributed.

Thanks to Lucy, Catherine had, indeed, met a few young men in the past thirty minutes. They had drifted oh so casually over to greet Lucy and had seemed quite pleased to meet her appealing new friend. Two of those young men had been anyone's definition of very attractive and the third—well, he seemed cheerful enough. Her dance card now sported *three* entire names. None of them were waltzes. Perhaps her season would improve just like this, in increments, the way Lord Kirke had said laws protecting children would be made.

She hadn't seen him at all today at The Grand Palace on the Thames—he was such an early riser!—but he'd been a low hum in her thoughts for much of the day. While *The Arabian Nights' Entertainments* had gotten off to a stirring start in the sitting room last night—Mrs. Pariseau even did the voices when she read, which was quite entertaining—it was Lord Kirke's earlier, bold, inspiring words that ran like a river through her mind as she drifted off to sleep. The soft rumble with which he'd delivered the word "vulnerable," the crisp metallic precision of the word "pique"—the choices he made about cadences and emphases reminded her of an orchestra conductor, except his instruments were words. It was impossible not to get swept up in the flow of them, the way one might be helpless not to tap a foot while listening to a waltz. It was the first time she'd understood how speaking could indeed be a gift, and how easily he could hold the House of Commons in thrall.

But he'd also said "arse" in the sitting room, and this delighted her almost more than his little speech.

Suddenly, as if she'd conjured him, through the milling ballroom crowd the man himself appeared.

The four of them stopped talking at once.

He deftly maneuvered through a clot of matrons blocking his path, then vanished again into another room.

His expression was remote and abstracted. He didn't look their way at all.

Catherine slowly released her breath.

They all spent a moment of silent, almost reverent appreciation in the aftermath, as though they'd spotted a mythical beast.

Lady Hackworth leaned toward the other young ladies confidingly. "I heard Lady Clayton say that she wanted to *climb* Kirke."

Catherine nearly reared back. Lady Hackworth's nose was turned up at the tip, which made her look as though she was literally sniffing out gossip. Her eyes were a startling shade of near turquoise.

She didn't know what "climbing him" meant, precisely, but it sounded as though it had something to do with sex and her cheeks went hot.

She was hardly completely naive about those matters. She knew which body parts were inserted where during sexual congress when it came down to it. But she was indignant on Lord Kirke's behalf. It was the first time anyone she'd known personally had been so shockingly, cavalierly discussed and she was surprised at her impulse to throw herself, metaphorically, bodily in front of him. Especially since she barely knew him, and she was absolutely certain the man had no trouble protecting himself. Furthermore, he'd outright told her he was scandalous.

"She wants to climb him because he's tall, like a tree?" she said, furrowing her brow. She wanted to see how far Lady Hackworth would go to explain herself.

Lady Hackworth laughed merrily. "Oh, my dear! You are too, too much."

"Perhaps you shouldn't repeat that sort of thing," Lucy bravely suggested, confirming to Catherine that she, too, thought it was about sex. They exchanged a swift glance of solidarity.

"Oh, my little gooses," Lady Hackworth, who wasn't much older than the two of them, soothed, sounding genuinely contrite. "I didn't mean to upset the two of you. It's just something silly I heard and I was making conversation. And it's a compliment to the man, truly. *One* day, if you're lucky—as lucky as I am—you'll understand."

There was little Catherine loathed more than this sort of condescension.

"He hasn't danced at a ball in a decade. What I wouldn't give to waltz with him! But it's probably also a mercy. I think a girl might crumble into ash." Lady Hackworth gave a theatrical little shiver. "When he looks at you, it's hard to know whether to cross yourself or lie back and hike your skirts. Perhaps both," she mused. "I've heard he's *very* good."

Argh! Appalling! Were these words actually emerging from Lady Hackworth's mouth? Did everyone in the ton talk like this? To young women?

Was . . . this the collective opinion of him?

Catherine didn't dare ask.

And yet . . . upon consideration, perhaps this did actually go a long way toward explaining how one felt in his presence.

She could hardly vociferously defend his honor without betraying some special knowledge or acquaintance. And she knew much better than to reveal they were staying in the same boardinghouse.

"*Has* he looked at you, then, Lady Hackworth?" Catherine said, instead. Feigning innocence again.

"How could he resist?" Lady Hackworth said airily, lightly, and waved her fan beneath her chin. She smiled to imply she was jesting.

Catherine couldn't object to her insouciant confidence. But her stomach was unsettled now.

"It's indeed a struggle to imagine how he could," she said politely, just a little dryly, which endeared her to Lady Hackworth and made Lucy shoot her a mischievous glance.

RATAFIA WAS THE sort of liquid nonsense he normally avoided, but Kirke had been later than usual to arrive at the Tillbury crush—he'd had a long day of constituents and builders—and he'd arrived thirsty.

He regretted his impulse to taste it at once. Some fool had laced it with whiskey. The whole bowl needed dumping, or the Tillbury ball was going to be remembered for brawls, possibly between young ladies. The footman charged with serving the stuff had probably gone off to relieve himself, leaving it unattended.

He took a few steps into the adjacent game room to see if any other servants were in evidence and observed about two dozen people clustered at tables, happily popping faro boxes or inspecting the hands dealt them in five-card loo or whist.

He saw Lord Farquar's wife, a small, solemn woman to whom he was apparently genuinely devoted, next to Lady Wisterberg, who was wearing an expression so rapt it was clear that nothing else in the world existed for her in that moment but her hand of cards.

Kirke absently felt in his coat pocket for the shilling he'd made certain to tuck there earlier today. Just in case.

"Kirke. You must be bored indeed if you're contemplating gambling." Pangborne was suddenly at his elbow. "How is your mouth, by the way?"

"Still capable of forming words, I'm sure Farquar will be happy to hear," Kirke said, ironically. "Thank you for asking."

Pangborne laughed. "Just thought I'd tell you that I've spoken to representatives of the Printer's Guild regarding apprenticeships for at least twenty boys from Bethnal Green," Pangborne finally said.

Kirke took this in wordlessly, with some surprise.

Pangborne was a Tory. And he hadn't been persuaded to do this as a result of witnessing one ridiculous drunken episode at a ball. Likely he'd been thinking about it for some time because, in his way, Kirke just would not relent.

It's how they did it until they could actually pass a law: they eroded the edges of the problem. Came at it from different angles. Attempted to cut off the sad, endless supply of orphans available for exploitation by placing them in apprenticeships that would pay them a fair wage and feed them properly instead of the indentured near enslavement of the textile mills. Instilling awareness and shame and a sense of responsibility into the voting and business-owning populace, until by the time the law was passed the notion of exploiting children for gain would be distasteful at best, very out of fashion at the least, and God only knew the ton loved its fashion.

"Very good to hear it," he said simply. "It's an excellent start."

Kirke liked to think the previous ball was the straw that tipped the balance. Which was why Pangborne was telling him now.

And no doubt there was something else in it for Pangborne, too. An exchange of favors, a promise of votes. It didn't matter. It was simply how their world worked.

Kirke suddenly recalled Pangborne had a son.

He hesitated, then ventured, "How old is your son now? Theodore, isn't it? How is he?"

"Seventeen." Pangborne sounded surprised. And a little touched that Kirke remembered.

"Do you recall what you liked to read at that age?"

Pangborne's eyebrows flicked, and then he gave a short laugh. "I tried to avoid reading. It was a bit of a struggle for me, frankly. I liked riding and shooting. I was a thoroughly unexceptional young man. Typical in most ways. But my son is a reader. He likes to read novels, God help me. *Robinson Crusoe. Rob Roy.* He's a fine but not excellent shot. Won an archery competition, however."

"You must be proud. A gentleman can never go wrong by perfecting one's aim. Something Farkie ought to have spent more time doing."

Pangborne laughed. And then he was quiet a moment.

Kirke decided to be direct. "You've got something else on your mind, Pangborne."

Pangborne twisted his mouth wryly, then sighed. "I've been trying to decide whether to tell you what I've heard. You may already know, anyway. Bertram Rowley is thinking of running for your seat. The plan is to, ah, emphasize the moral differences between the two of you. As of course Rowley is pious as the day is long, and so forth. Allegedly spotless of character."

"Ah," Kirke said ironically. "And it's alleged I'm none of those wonderful things." He paused. "I must admit, it's not a bad approach."

Pangborne grimaced. "He's a first-rate prig."

In other words: the strategy would be to imply that someone who was as allegedly scandalous as Kirke could hardly get the job done, so busy was he with seduction and so forth.

It had been tried before.

The difference this time was that Bertram Rowley was outrageously wealthy, thanks in part to investments in textile mills. He could finance a campaign entirely on his own. He could all but buy his parliamentary seat, if enough voters could be persuaded.

Kirke mulled this new development darkly, and with a certain relish. Anyone who wanted to come for him was welcome to it.

But damned if he wasn't a little bloody tired of *developments*.

"I'm not concerned," he said easily. Which wasn't entirely true. "If I may ask—why are you telling me this?"

Pangborne paused to consider this. "Better the devil you know? Things would be dull without you, Kirke. We'll accomplish less. And Rowley is, in fact, an idiot."

Kirke nodded. This was merely true.

"Perhaps now would be a good time to give a particularly spectacular speech."

Kirke stifled a sigh. "Thank you, Pangborne. The notion hadn't occurred to me."

Kirke told Pangborne he'd see him in the library later, and slipped out of the game room. He presently found a footman who was willing to do two things: dump the ratafia, and wrestle Lady Wisterberg away from the game table in time to get Keating back to the boardinghouse by curfew.

He might not ever write another speech, he thought dryly, but damned if that wasn't a satisfying night's work.

He slipped up the marble stairs and turned left at the top. He passed three doors in the hallway, heading for the alcove near a window where he knew he could sneak a cheroot and contemplate the vexing vicissitudes of his life in peace.

He stopped abruptly, assailed by a surge of irritation.

His destination—a bench in that alcove next to an enormous, frilly potted plant—was occupied. By a woman.

His first swift impression of her—a delicate profile, the generous swell of breasts outlined against a muslin bodice, the creamy skin of her throat revealed by her dark uplifted hair—rushed his senses and tightened the bands of muscle across his stomach. He could not recall the last time a woman had stolen his breath.

A second later he realized it was Keating.

He went motionless. Stupid with surprise.

More than a little disconcerted.

He was blankly still a moment, then a strange,

quiet anger seeped in on her behalf. His chest felt tight. He didn't know why he should find uncomfortably poignant a pretty young woman taking refuge alone near a plant at a ball. It just seemed . . . such a bloody pity. An unconscionable waste. She ought to be dancing and reveling in the music and her beauty and the newness of London.

He pivoted a half step to leave her with her thoughts just as she turned and saw him.

Her lovely face was at once ablaze with delight and surprise.

He stopped. And then found himself moving toward that light.

He did so slowly.

"Good evening, Keating." He gestured to the plant. "I see you're with family again."

"Oh. Yes. Good evening, Lord Kirke. I am a bit abashed that you have found me again near green things." She flushed.

"Am I intruding upon your solitude?"

"No. But thank you for inquiring. Were you looking for some solitude and found me here instead?" She stood and smoothed her skirts. "I apologize, and I will find another place, if so. It's just . . . that it's peculiar to feel alone in a ballroom absolutely crowded with people. I am a bit nervous, and I felt very conspicuous, although every third woman here tonight is in white muslin."

"While that may indeed be true, your sleeves strike me as exceptional."

Her lips curved in a somewhat rueful smile. "I'm beginning to feel quite foolish about hiding near plants, to tell you the truth." The pink in her cheeks had darkened.

Sympathy panged him with surprising force.

He hesitated. "If it will make you feel any better . . . I confess it's a habit of mine to find a moment alone when I'm obliged to spend hours in a crowd. Especially before or after a speech. I have a favorite bench in a little park just outside the Commons. It's tucked between two scowling lion statues. Passersby can scarcely tell the three of us apart."

He'd never, ever confessed this to another soul.

In revealing this he felt strangely as though he'd just inappropriately removed an article of clothing. It occurred to him that he seldom shared the minutiae of his life with anyone. And yet thousands of people all over England thought they knew him. The anonymity at the eye of fame had long suited him. .

But he was pleased when she smiled. She absently waved her fan beneath her chin and studied him, her eyes soft and sympathetic and curious.

"Are you ever nervous before you give a speech?"

"I'm often deadly nervous." He'd never confessed this to another soul, either. He doubted anyone even suspected. "But the nervousness seems to evaporate once I get started, and then once I've momentum, it's almost better than—well, it's tremendously satisfying."

She pulled in a deep breath, then exhaled at length. As if she'd found relief in his words.

It seemed absurd to view his weaknesses as strengths simply because she'd found comfort in them. To suddenly be grateful to have something to offer her.

"It strikes me as a very brave thing," she ventured, eyes starry, "to stand up before so many people to speak, even when you're so nervous."

He wasn't prepared to concede he was brave

in any sense of the word. Nor did he particularly want to encourage adulation. But it was difficult not to bask a little in the admiring light in her eyes. "Perhaps."

The ensuing pause was the perfect moment for him to make his bow and take his leave.

Somehow this intention failed to communicate itself to his legs.

"Lord Kirke?" she ventured. "I've something a bit delicate to ask of you."

He stiffened warily. Hell's teeth. He should have obeyed his instinct to bolt.

Her face lit with amusement. "My goodness. Your expression! I apologize for putting it that way. It's just . . . I know that Lady Wisterberg is not a suitable chaperone . . ."

"Good manners prevent me from outright agreeing, Keating," he said dryly. "But I suspect you have guessed my views on the matter."

She cleared her throat. "I'd hoped . . . I'd hoped you would not mention it to anyone. Her . . . ah . . . delinquency, that is."

"Because you'd be obliged to leave London as you are essentially unchaperoned at balls."

"Yes."

"Very well, then. I promise I will not report it to the magistrate in charge of monitoring maidens."

She gave a soft laugh. "Thank you. It's just . . . I find that I do not want to leave London just yet. Not until I've . . . well, I'd like to see it through. I should like to give the season my very best effort."

"I approve of your ambition, Keating. And in light of your aspiration, I likewise feel compelled to advise you that you should not reveal that I am currently living one floor above you."

She paused. "I gathered that," she replied gently.

The pause was interesting. This made him wonder, ironically, which rumors she'd heard about him. And whether what she'd heard had repelled or intrigued her.

On the whole, it was probably for the best that she not take to thinking of him as her pet MP.

"But please do have a care about wandering off alone. Not every man is as harmless as I am."

She studied him in silence for a moment.

"Harmless," she repeated thoughtfully, and so quietly it was nearly a caress. "Ha."

It was also almost a question.

He offered her a patient, enigmatic smile and did not reply.

A little silence stretched.

She cleared her throat. "Will . . . will you be dancing tonight?" she asked, somewhat shyly.

"Good God, no, Keating. In my view, dancing is for the spouse seekers, the inebriated, the terminally cheerful, and the very young. And I am none of those things. I never dance at balls."

Her smile gradually grew wider as his list went on. "Surely you're not very old."

"I'm thirty-five."

"Oh. Well. I stand corrected, then."

He smiled, and shook his head slowly.

"But . . . then . . . why *do* you go to balls?" Her brow furrowed. "If I may be so bold?"

"To make friends," he said.

She laughed. Which delighted him.

"Ah, but you wound me, Keating. In truth, men will often let down their guards when surrounded by pretty women and loud music and free liquor. Alliances are born, confessions are made, and all sorts of useful knowledge can be gathered. It's as valuable as a night at White's. Sometimes more so. Relationships of all sorts are the most important part of my job."

She listened to this solemnly. "Is that why you didn't duck in time when Lord Farquar swung for you? Because your guard was down?"

Her sky blue eyes were wide with faux innocence.

"If blue was not so decidedly your color, Keating, I would call you out for such insolence."

She merely smiled happily, basking in his feigned outrage. "Duels. Just one of the many, many things that only men are allowed to do."

He snorted. "Yes, it's desperately unfair that young women can't go about challenging each other to duels. Think of the carnage over sleeves."

"I imagine you're right. But poisonous subtlety as a weapon has its limits. And I've no practice at that, either. So far, I'm a failure as a crocodile."

"The possibility of a duel is admittedly a useful sort of option for a man to carry about in his masculine quiver, so to speak."

"The threat of sudden death?" she said lightly. "I imagine it would be."

"Mainly because Farquar knows that I would shoot him if I called him out for hitting me. And now he's on his back foot, which is precisely where I like my political opponents. Uncertain and beholden to me."

He supposed he'd said it in order to make certain she did not take to viewing him as anything like cuddly or benevolent or benign. He also—and this surprised him—was trying once again to impress her, as he had last night, because she was clever, and he realized with some surprise that he considered her worth impressing.

She took this in, her face ever so faintly troubled and thoroughly fascinated. He was accustomed to seeing this expression on women.

"Would you, indeed? Shoot him, that is?"

"Well, yes. If I'd agreed to duel him, certainly. The alternative is that he would shoot me, and we can't have that."

"Have you shot anyone before?"

"Don't ask questions you don't want the answers to, Keating."

She raised her eyebrows.

"Yes," he said evenly.

She was quiet.

"The man in question objected to the way I expressed my views on the way he'd been deceiving orphan children into working for his textile mill—they are promised things that never transpire, like adequate food and pay, and are tricked into agreeing to work for him until the age of eighteen. Admittedly, I was, ah, colorfully blunt and rather personal." He smiled ruefully. "I may have disparaged his parentage. And he called me out. I thought it was best to address this in a way that no one could misunderstand or forget. And this is how Farquar knows I'm just mad enough to perhaps do it, and that I am a very good shot. Shooting someone in order to kill them is one thing. Shooting to wound them in order to make a point is another." He smiled faintly. "That takes a special kind of skill."

"Well," she said uncertainly.

"I've only needed to do it once," he said. "Though funnily enough, there's something about me that people want to challenge."

"Funnily enough," she repeated after a pause of exquisitely perfect duration.

He found himself smiling at her again, and she was smiling at him, for the most peculiar instant he could not feel his feet against the floor.

"Will *you* be dancing this evening, Keating? Or should I assume your placement by the greenery is an indication of how your season is going?"

"I do have a few names on my dance card tonight," she said cheerily. "My friend Miss Lucy Morrow made the introductions. Lucy is dancing with Mr. Hargrove, a young man she's known for quite some time and I believe would like to marry. I believe it is the same man Miss Seaver would also like to marry. She has known him nearly as long."

He shook his head gravely. "I foresee pistols at dawn for all of them in the future, Keating."

She smiled at this, more fully this time.

"What about you?" he asked suddenly. "Will you be throwing your hat into Mr. Hargrove's ring?"

"I haven't yet decided. I've only danced with him once. I know a good deal about him, however, because he talked and talked about himself. He scarcely took a breath. He shot the most grouse at a house party a fortnight ago. His horse is named Benjamin. And so forth."

"Well, it helps to be armed with information about a person before you marry them. Thoughtful of him to supply you with it."

She quirked the corner of her mouth. "Thoughtfulness is a good quality in a man." She absently touched her necklace then. He noticed she did that now and again, as if to reassure herself it was still there.

A swift glance told him the pearl dangling from it had vanished into her cleavage.

Unbidden he imagined gently sliding a finger

into that shadow between her creamy breasts, looping a finger beneath the chain, and slowly, gently gliding the pearl out.

Momentarily his head emptied of thought as though blasted away by lightning and his groin tightened.

Shaken, he turned his head away from her abruptly.

Men, he thought, darkly, were simply base, there was no help for it.

He stared down the hall, the direction from which he'd come, for a few silent moments. Someone ought to look after Keating's welfare, and looking after her welfare meant maintaining propriety, and that meant the two of them ought not be alone.

He returned his gaze to her. Her eyelashes were thick and dark, and he could see the little shadows they lay against her cheek when she turned her head. He stared at them. And suddenly those shadows felt like the subtlest, softest of traps. He could not move away if he tried.

"I know nearly everyone in the ton. I might be able to help narrow your choices, in the name of efficiency," he offered casually.

He shoved to the back of his mind the little voice that told him this suggestion was not entirely altruistic. Because the truth was worrisome: he wanted an excuse to hear her thoughts. About nearly anything.

"Oh!" She looked up at him gratefully. "That might be helpful. Thank you."

She handed over her little dance card.

Chapter Eight

✎❦❧

CATHERINE WATCHED him peruse her dance card with every appearance of interest and knew a fresh wave of indignation that anyone should say unkind or prurient things about him. No doubt a man like him—a charismatic public figure—would always simply be a lightning rod for imaginations.

He looked up. "First of all, I think it would be helpful to know what sorts of qualities you are looking for in your ideal husband."

She blinked. Catherine had never thought about her husband search in terms of qualities one could list, as though she were going to market for ingredients for soup. She'd always imagined she would know when she met him by how he made her feel. But she supposed the season was referred to as the marriage mart for a reason.

"Well, I suppose I should like him to be friendly."

"Friendly," Lord Kirke repeated warily. He made the word sound like "scoundrel."

She nodded, very amused by this.

"Like a . . . spaniel?"

"Not *unlike* a spaniel," she clarified. "Pleasant. Cheerful. Loyal. Always happy to see me. Like that. I think that would be very pleasant."

"Comes when he's called, and can fetch you a pheasant you've shot, a face-licker, that sort of thing?"

"I hear nothing to object to in that list of things, though no one has ever licked my face. Perhaps I'd like it. I should hate to dismiss it out of hand. I've come to London for new experiences, after all."

Every time his eyes creased at the corners with amusement, she felt as though she'd won a prize.

"As admirable as your spirit of adventure is, Keating—a word of caution about saying such things candidly to your dancing partners. You're liable to open up regrettable conversational avenues. A London ballroom is *boiling* with hidden peccadillos."

"Is that so?" She was alarmed and intrigued. "Isn't it better to find out about them as soon as possible?"

"You'll want to save some mystery for marriage. A lifetime is a very long time."

"I suppose you ought to know, having lived most of your life already."

It was a risky joke. But he mimed being stabbed in the heart, to her delight.

"It's to do with London and obscene wealth," he explained. "People's habits mutate in unusual ways when they've no useful occupation."

"Nothing a little work in the mines wouldn't cure, I'm sure," she said.

He grinned, and her heart soared. "Precisely. Very well. You're looking for a friendly chap. What else? Should he have money?"

She flushed. "Well. That is. I should hope so. How will we feed the children otherwise?"

"No need to be coy about money, for God's sake, Keating. What other reason is there to marry?"

She was amused at this baldly unromantic notion of marriage. "Have you ever been married?"

She regretted asking at once. She was worried

her question had been insensitive or too bold. What if he was a widower, and his heart had been irreparably broken?

What if she simply disliked the answer, for . . . some odd reason?

She realized her breath was held and her heart had taken up an odd slamming rhythm.

But he just snorted softly. "No. Can you imagine the sort of husband I'd be?"

She studied him, attempting this as earnestly as if he'd made a literal request.

"It's not the easiest thing to do," she admitted, hesitantly.

His smile was difficult to interpret.

She found she simply could not quite slot him into one of her favorite cheerful images of a potential husband: passing the fried bread around the table while the sun poured through a kitchen window. Or standing quietly, his arms wrapped around her, as they watched the sun go down. Despite his fine manners and his title, he didn't seem the least bit domesticated. He wasn't at all like the merry, teasing young men she'd imagined courting her.

But she thought the top of her head would reach to just beneath his chin, and she could almost, even now, imagine how her cheek would feel pressed against the wool of his coat, and how his hands would feel on the flat of her back.

Her heart gave a startling, strange lurch.

"How many children will the two of you be wanting?" he asked.

Her composure took a moment to recongregate.

"Ah . . . well, I hope . . . there will be enough so that when we all laugh at a joke around the dinner table, it makes a happy sort of racket. And so that when we gather around the pianoforte we can sing harmony. Like at The Grand Palace on the Thames."

Something so fleetingly warm suffused his expression that she went still. As though he'd been hopelessly charmed. She could not imagine why.

"How many siblings have you now, Keating?"

"Well, I haven't any," she said almost apologetically. "There was just the three of us." She cleared her throat. "My father and mother and me. But now there's just the two of us. My mother passed away five years ago after an illness."

"I'm very sorry to hear it," he said gently.

"Thank you. That is a kind thing to say. We do miss her very much. Whereas you have many siblings?"

"Oh yes. There were seven of us. I'm in the middle. My parents are no longer with us. Five of us are still alive. We are all exactly as lovable as you might expect."

She smiled at that. "I expect it's why you would savor a little quiet time to yourself quite often, from living among so many people."

She had the sense she'd surprised him somehow.

"Perhaps," he admitted, shortly. The corner of his mouth lifted, somewhat ruefully, but his eyes were a bit guarded. As though she'd inadvertently uncovered a secret.

"Somewhere in the middle of two and seven children would be just about right, I think," she said.

"So you'll want a good income to feed your three and a half or so children," he said briskly. "This fellow, Mr. Gardner"—he pointed to a name on her dance card—"while by all accounts charming, and altogether fine company at White's if one is *desperate* for company, is hunting for an heiress because he bet an enormous sum that his high-flyer could beat Lord Ipswitch's in a race, and he lost."

"Oh my," she breathed, startled. "And he seemed pleasant enough. He has a very cheerful face. I'm not one of those. An heiress. I've a bit of a dowry, but not the sort that would make anyone's pulse race. I'm afraid a young man is going to have to like me rather a lot to make up for it."

"Laying aside *that* hurdle," he said matter-of-factly, which made her muffle a shout of laughter with her palms, "what about courtship habits? Do you go in for poetry? Chaps declaiming about blue eyes and flaxen hair and that rot, er, that sort of thing? I feel it only fair to warn you that I've heard Babcock"—he pointed to the second name on her card—"writes wagers in the form of poems in the betting books at White's. Though I suppose a chap has to do something to stand out in a crowd of admirers, and he's otherwise unobjectionable. Apart from the inadvisable wagers. He also laughs at his own jokes, which—and this is subjective of course—are not funny."

"If only I had a crowd of admirers! But I don't know why you should object to poems when *you* are so eloquent."

She'd said this a little too fervently, she realized, and was instantly abashed.

His slow smile tingled the back of her neck. "Am I, then, Keating?"

She cleared her throat. "That is, don't you write speeches for a living?"

"Speeches. Not poems. I don't stand before my fellow MPs there and spout rhymes, Keating. Eloquent, I'll humbly allow, when I'm at my best, but they're also practical and purposeful. I began life as a lawyer and I still think like one. Poetry is meant to diffuse and I feel it is best to be direct, to eliminate potential for confusion in matters of—in all matters."

She stared at him.

He'd stopped himself. He'd been about to say "in matters of romance" or something to that effect, she was certain of it.

She was almost *unbearably* intrigued.

What would this directness entail? Baldly issued invitations to climb him?

She shoved the image aside.

"Oh, I shouldn't think so, regarding poetry," she finally managed. "It would be a bit awkward, wouldn't it, if the poem isn't good? I think I would find it excruciating because I don't know if I'd be able to make the right grateful sounds as I'm not very good at pretending. I loathe to hurt anyone's feelings. But if it's someone I like very much I would be touched by the effort."

He listened to this with apparent solemn absorption. "In short, you think poetry best left to the professionals, like Byron."

"Perhaps I do! And oh my, aren't his poems lovely? Are you acquainted with him?" It seemed plausible. Lords all seemed to be acquainted.

"I have indeed met the man. And if anyone would be inclined to attempt face-licking, it's Byron."

She laughed, which tapered into a sigh. "Well. Thankfully my hair isn't flaxen, as I don't think anything rhymes with it."

"Waxen," he said at once, somewhat absently. "No, it's amber now, in the lamplight."

She immediately went mute from an almost violent rush of pleasure at his words.

She fought an urge to touch her hair, as if it was suddenly aglow like a candle flame. She felt, oddly, shyly, as though she'd been crowned. It wasn't poetry. And yet it was, to her.

It was probably the sort of thing he said all the time. Amber was just a color, after all. Just like flaxen.

They were watching each other, and for a moment doing only that. It seemed a strangely sufficient occupation. Her heart bumped once again almost painfully hard against her ribs, and then resumed its usual pattern at twice its usual speed. Perhaps all along he had been noticing the details of her the way she'd been noticing the details of him.

Clamber, she thought, *rhymes with amber.*

And "clamber" reminded her of climbing. As in Lady Clayton wanting to climb him.

Suddenly every inch of her skin felt warm.

She was overcome with confusion, and tempted to duck her head. But she refused to do it, lest she miss a second of the way in which he was regarding her: as if he'd never seen anything so worthy of his attention.

Cross herself or lift her skirts, was how Lady Hackworth had put it. One was for protection, the other was surrender. She supposed that they were the reflexive natural responses to anything so powerfully compelling it unnerved, something that one didn't quite understand . . . but wanted anyway.

He probably couldn't help the intensity of his gaze any more than, for instance, a falcon could. It was likely just his nature.

She recalled suddenly, and too vividly, how a small V of his chest had been exposed by his clawed-away cravat the night he'd moved into the room above her.

Her fingers hummed with the new, shocking, urgent compulsion to know the texture of his skin.

"That's just as well," she finally said, a trifle subdued. "As I don't believe anything about me is waxen."

"No, you've the healthy complexion of someone accustomed to striding about the hills and vales of Upper Sheep's Teat."

"Precisely," she said, with some relief at the jest. "Unlike that pallor you've acquired from carrying all that coal up from the mines."

When he grinned at that, happiness was a strange pressure in her chest, as though her heart had literally puffed up with it.

There was a little silence.

She cleared her throat. "And . . . and I also think I should like to admire him," she ventured, somewhat shyly.

His brows dove again. "Admire him. His pearly smile? His bank account? His title? His Richmond estate?"

She flushed. "His character. I should like to admire the way he conducts his life, and the things he believes in, and the way he treats people. His convictions. And his . . . his accomplishments."

There was a beat of silence. "Ah."

She could see at once that he knew why she'd said it, because she hadn't any practice being the least bit sly or subtle.

And now he was clearly a little wary. Oddly, she thought she saw something like regret or sadness flicker in his eyes. Maybe even pity.

Oh God. She was embarrassed.

"Like my father," she added hurriedly. "Who is a very fine man."

"I'm certain he is," he said gently. Carefully.

A moment or two passed where he seemed to be considering what to say. "I would only advise that even heroes are just men underneath the skin. And awe isn't what keeps your bed warm at night."

She blushed furiously and instantly like the veriest virgin. Which of course she was.

Lady Hackworth likely would have known something provocative to say in reply.

Catherine didn't have anything like that vocabulary. She was mute.

She wondered if he'd said it in an attempt to make her go quiet. To impose a distance.

Or was it to test her?

What did it say about her that all she thought about now was lying alongside him in a bed? Was that a test she had passed or failed?

For an instant it seemed as though he could read all of her thoughts clearly in her eyes, because his own flared so fleetingly hot that her knees all but turned to smoke and she felt an aching throb *right* at the join of her legs.

This was her first inkling that the things said about him might be grounded in some sort of truth. She understood viscerally then that there were very good reasons she ought not be alone with him.

And perhaps these were the same reasons, deep down, she wanted to be alone with him.

She could add this to her list of London season revelations. And new experiences.

His face went unreadable again. She could see he was poised to bolt.

"By the way," he said suddenly, "someone poured

whiskey into the ratafia. I've asked a footman to dump it and to tell his hosts. But you might want to wait a bit before tasting any."

"Very well. Thank you for steering me away from . . . iniquity."

She could administer tests, too.

She felt his little half smile as a delicious shiver along her spine. As if he sensed she was beginning to consider whether certain kinds of iniquity were appealing.

"Oh, it's entirely self-interest, Keating. I shouldn't want you to return to The Grand Palace on the Thames drunk and frolicsome and rob me of valuable sleep."

She laughed.

"There's the music for your dance. I'm off again. *Bon chance.*" He turned.

"Have you a handkerchief, for the punching portion of the evening?"

He threw her a wry parting glance and patted the pocket of his coat by way of reply and disappeared.

How she hated it every time he vanished from view.

Chapter Nine

❧

ALL GUESTS will eat dinner together at least four times per week was the very first rule printed on the little card handed to him when he'd taken a room, so clearly the proprietresses of The Grand Palace on the Thames took this seriously.

He'd survived the gathering in the sitting room.

The gathering had also more or less survived him.

So dinner was the next hurdle.

What had Keating called it? A cheerful racket. She'd enjoyed it so thoroughly she wanted to pattern the future dinners of her life upon it, and he found himself oddly curious to discover why. His own family dinners had been fraught, resentful affairs, as there often wasn't nearly enough to eat, his parents were irritable, and his siblings liked to kick each other beneath the table.

The word he would have chosen for the dinner at The Grand Palace on the Thames was "mild uproar."

But cheerful it definitely was, and as frank and frill-free as an occasion could possibly be, if a little merrily harrowing.

Hardy sat at one end of the table, Bolt at the other, and everyone else found chairs in between.

Platters and tureens heaped with fresh sliced bread, boiled and herbed potatoes, peas, gravy, and eel pie were passed around, and then passed around again, often nearly colliding on their way to their destinations amid chuckles and cries of "look out!" and "butter on its way!"

Kirke took a bite of eel pie.

Chewed.

Closed his eyes with wonder.

Opened them again and stared at Mrs. Hardy and Mrs. Durand.

"What manner of witchcraft is this?" he demanded.

Everyone beamed delightedly at him.

"Helga is better than a genie," Delacorte declared.

"Lord Kirke, if you would be so kind as to pass the peas, which are languishing by your elbow," Mrs. Pariseau requested.

"Miss Keating, careful with your sleeve, it's almost in the gravy," Dot urged. The gravy was en route to her via Lord Bolt's long arm.

"Oh my, thank you for the warning." Keating tucked her arm back.

"Butter, if you would, when you're finished with it, please," Captain Hardy said, and Angelique, who currently had custody of it, handed it over.

Next to him Mr. Delacorte ate with speed and efficiency and the utter trust that came from knowing he was never going to get a bad bite to eat here in this boardinghouse. He created gravy rivers among his potatoes. Across from him, his pleasant view was of Miss Keating, happily, neatly, and thoroughly demolishing her dinner.

This effect of the dining table was similar to that of the sitting room. It was subtle, but it was as if his spirit had been offered a chair after years and years of standing.

"We'll convey your compliments to Helga for you, Lord Kirke," Mrs. Hardy said.

"Thank you, please do," he said. "Will you please pass the eel pie, Miss Keating?" he asked to get into the spirit of things.

She handed it over to him, beaming.

"Gordon caught a mouse outside and brought it into the house!" He heard Dot marvel. "He ate it and only left behind one toe!"

"Maybe not at the dinner table, Dot," Delilah replied with great patience.

"Miss Keating, did you enjoy last night's ball?" Mrs. Pariseau wondered.

"Oh, it was grand. I danced with some pleasant young men. Although one of them laughed at all of his own jokes—which weren't very funny—and none of mine."

She flicked a surreptitious, mischievous glance across at Kirke.

He felt a surely outsized gratification at the acknowledgment that she'd agreed with him about her dance partner.

Mrs. Pariseau clucked in sympathy. "Oh, I know the sort! Not all men are like that, fortunately, dear."

"Why on earth wouldn't you laugh at all the jokes you possibly could, no matter who made them?" Mr. Delacorte wondered sincerely.

Kirke thought of all the children who were crammed into workhouses and orphanages. And now he understood why The Grand Palace on the Thames wanted to create a familial atmosphere. Mrs. Hardy and Mrs. Durand clearly understood that basic human need to belong, to feel a *part* of something. Wanted, welcomed, even needed. And they'd gathered around them people who felt like family.

"I understand you've just returned from the ship-builders," Kirke said to Hardy and Bolt. "Fruitful?"

"Yes, thank you. *The Zephyr* should be seaworthy again inside two months," Hardy told him.

"Do you think the builders could use a few very young apprentices to the trade they're willing to pay and board?"

Bolt and Hardy exchanged glances. "We will definitely ask, if you'd like. But yes, I imagine we can use our influence to find a few places for them."

With luck, a few more boys would soon have a place to belong, too.

AFTER DINNER MRS. Pariseau paused in reading a chapter of *The Arabian Nights' Entertainments* to her rapt audience in the sitting room to ask, "If you rubbed a lamp and a genie emerged, what would you do?"

As this seemed an earnest question, there ensued an obediently contemplative little silence.

"I think I would urinate all over myself," Mr. Delacorte concluded somberly.

Everyone slowly turned to stare at him. Unanimously bereft of words.

"Stone terrified," he clarified frankly, as if this was the reason for the gaping silence. "Is what I'd be, if I rubbed a lamp and an enormous man popped out."

Kirke nearly levitated from suppressed hilarity.

"Mr. Delacorte . . ." Delilah began, gingerly.

"I used the fancy word for it!" Delacorte swiveled his head wildly to stare at the Epithet Jar. He didn't want to lose another penny this week. "Didn't I?"

"I might equivocate about 'fancy,'" Mrs. Pariseau said tautly.

"Well, no one would believe you, either, would they, if you said, 'there's a man in my lamp'?" Mr. Delacorte was committed to his point. "You'd be taken straight to Bedlam. Bolt killed a pirate but I wager even he would faint dead away if he innocently rubbed a lamp and a man popped out."

"Hold on now." Lord Bolt was indignant. "You think *I'd* faint?"

"It's all well and good when you read about it in a book. Or dream about it after taking a headache powder," Delacorte insisted. "But the real thing? Does anyone really want that? A large man springing out of a small lamp?"

"Ah, but think about it, Bolt," Kirke said mischievously. "Mr. Delacorte has a point. You know what your enemies are. Meaning, you have the advantage of knowing a pirate has roughly the same number of limbs you have, and the same kinds of reflexes, and similar skills. You know they live on ships. Not in lamps. You know what their capacities are and you know what yours are. You'll make decisions accordingly. A genie, on the other hand, is an entirely unknown quantity. You might begin your defense with what you know and fail dismally against its powers."

Delacorte nodded vigorously, thrilled to be vindicated. "I don't think there's a sane man alive who wouldn't—you're the orator, Kirke. What's the fancier word for . . ." He leaned forward and whispered a word in Kirke's ear.

Kirke whispered helpfully in reply.

"—defecate on the spot if a man popped out of the lamp," Mr. Delacorte maintained earnestly.

Kirke had seldom had a better time in his life.

"It's true," Kirke contributed. "People always fight against the unknown—any kind of change, for instance—because they're afraid of it. People fight what they fear. It's the biggest hurdle in my job."

"And it's about the last thing you expect, isn't it, when you rub a lamp. Imagine if you're dusting one day in the sitting room and that happens," Mr. Delacorte said. "I think Hardy might faint dead away, too. Or get his pistol out."

"If I thought Delilah or anyone for whom I was responsible was in grave danger, yes, I would probably shoot it." Captain Hardy was exasperated. "For all the good it would do me. I've never fainted in my life, Delacorte. For God's sake."

"Because you've never seen a genie," Delacorte persisted.

Kirke never dreamed he'd be so entertained by hearing Bolt and Hardy defend their masculine honor against a fictional genie.

"What about you, Kirke?" Delacorte turned to him. "Do you think you'd faint, shoot, defe—"

"Mr. Delacorte," Angelique interjected with a sigh. "Lord Kirke. Gentlemen. Jar words dressed up in more syllables are still jar words."

She glanced uneasily at Catherine, who, as the youngest, was the one with the supposedly tenderest ears.

But Catherine looked absolutely delighted with the whole conversation.

"Is the genie handsome?" Dot wanted to know.

"Some of them are. Some of them aren't," Lord Bolt explained somberly. "And whether they're nice or not depends on how well you rub the lamp."

Angelique shot a wide-eyed quelling look at her husband.

All the men in the room were suddenly close to bursting from stifled hilarity.

In a matter of seconds things had tread very close to the edge of mayhem. Such was the exhilarating risk of spirited discourse.

"But, if you had a wish," Mrs. Pariseau asked, with great, great patience, raising her voice slightly, "what would you wish for? I suppose that was my point, and I take responsibility for phrasing it poorly. Would you wish for something like . . . a thousand wishes? Or immortality? Something else?"

"But if people lived forever, would love exist? Would there be any need for it?" Keating asked.

Kirke's lungs seized.

Another silence fell abruptly.

All eyes were on Keating in absolute astonishment.

"Oh no. Forgive me. I didn't mean to . . ." Keating flushed. "Oh my goodness, please forget what I said."

"No, do not apologize. I feel you have introduced a fascinating point, dear. Care to expound?" Mrs. Pariseau said gently.

"It's just . . . that is . . . I just . . . change is also the thing that makes things more precious, isn't it? Knowing that anything in life can end in a heartbeat, at any time for any reason, and that things may not always be the same? And if you know that you're going to live forever, and if someone you love lived forever, would you not then take them for granted? Do we love things and people because we know they're temporary? I . . . I just wondered."

At once, Captain Hardy and Delilah and Angelique and Lord Bolt exchanged glances, their way of reassuring themselves of each other's existence.

Kirke stared at Keating. He was amazed and oddly—reluctantly—spellbound. For it did not seem wise or safe to feel bound by her in any way at all.

But he knew these kinds of thoughts only originated from personal suffering. For these were the questions one asked when confronted with the mercilessness and unsolvable mysteries of life. As if there was comfort to be had in reasoning through it. For a certain kind of person, he supposed there was.

Others drank, or threw lanterns.

Bloody hell, but he loved a thinker. He felt one could *exhale* around a thinker, as though there was more room to simply exist.

His breath had gone oddly, painfully short at the thought of her struggling to find sweetness and sense in a world that had, and would again, take things she loved.

Her eyes were worried when they met his.

It suddenly seemed urgent to offer her something of value. But the truest thing he knew was that loving could be the most dangerous thing a human could do. She was right to question every single thing about it.

But he could not allow her to endure more silence in that room after she'd opened up her heart.

"I think . . ." he ventured slowly, for it was nothing he'd ever considered at length, and this he found more exhilarating by the moment. "If we lived forever . . . I have a feeling that we humans would instinctively create reasons for change, and separation. Rituals or rites of passage or seasons, like the one you're enduring now, Miss Keating." He smiled slightly. "For I believe we humans have learned that things like anticipation and longing and pleasures that are fleeting are the things that give life its dimension. Its poignancy. Its shadow and light."

She took this in. "So it's possible love could always exist." Keating sounded relieved. "Even if we lived forever."

He didn't take this up. The surest way to discover that someone had not yet been in love was how casually they wielded the word in conversation. They would have more respect for it if they understood that it possessed mad, dangerous power, like a magic spell, or a curse.

"I like to view these sorts of questions—the kinds we can never hope to definitively answer—as a bit like . . . undiscovered continents," he said. "We may not find precisely what we're looking for as we seek answers, but the search may reveal to us other useful or beautiful things about ourselves and our world. In that way, ignorance is the beginning of not just knowledge, but wisdom."

When she smiled at him, the tension left his body, as if he'd just performed a delicate rescue. He felt like a bloody sage.

"If we lived forever, things would get awfully crowded," Dot reflected. "Imagine going to market if everyone lived forever. We might never get the best eels."

"Perhaps people wouldn't begin mating until they were three hundred and twelve years old, or thereabouts," Mrs. Pariseau reflected.

Delilah and Angelique stirred at this observation, preparing to head things off if "mating" took the evening in yet another anatomical direction.

"One wish?" Mr. Delacorte mused. "I can't think of anything I want that I don't have, or expect I will have. Unless it's a slice of cheese right now."

"We can make your wish come true, Mr. Delacorte," Delilah told him warmly.

"*Better* than genies any day," Mr. Delacorte declared, gesturing to Angelique and Delilah, as if this proved some important point, and Captain Hardy and Lord Bolt nodded in agreement.

Dear Leo,

Your mother informs me that you enjoy reading. I am sending with this letter editions of Rob Roy and Robinson Crusoe, an entire set of Mr. Miles Redmond's tomes on the South Seas, and a book called The Ghost in the Attic, which I'm assured is "ever so thrilling."

Read everything you can get your hands on.

You will find that I have included half a guinea under the seal, so that you may pay for my letters.

KIRKE'S QUILL PAUSED there.

Today he'd purchased the books Pangborne had mentioned, and he would send them with the letter. But he wasn't certain he had the right to issue advice. Still, he wanted to throw himself in front of that young man and the world and its crocodiles. Failing that, books, and what they contained, could help Leo craft his own armor.

He wanted to say something more profound and true.

I am grateful to know you, and I look forward to becoming better acquainted in the years ahead.

True, yes. But that sounded like a letter to his bloody solicitor.

He could hardly burden a boy with the actual brutal truth, things he'd never possibly understand: you were created out of love and ecstasy and stupid, reckless selfishness. The aftermath of which was anguish and terror.

Oh, but there was joy, too. Fleetingly.

> *Dear Leo—I've lately realized I've constructed the whole of my life along the edge of the abyss into which you and your mother vanished.*

He wanted Leo to know that he had always mattered to him.

But perhaps this mattered little to a boy who currently thoroughly resented him.

But he could never tell him that he had, in fact, indirectly determined the entire shape of Dominic's destiny, even though he'd only just learned he truly existed.

Kirke himself was only coming to realize this.

He could feel the right words milling about in the murk of his mind, but they dodged away from him when he tried to grasp hold of them. As though they felt he'd long ago lost the right to use them.

The qualities that had come to define him, that had served him well—pride and arrogance and certainty, wit and stubborn ruthlessness—they suddenly felt as flimsy as so much tinsel camouflaging a hapless boy. None of those qualities were of use to him here. What was required was absolute humility.

After all of these years, it darkly amused him that he'd lost the knack for it.

> *Dear Leo—I sometimes still jerk awake from nightmares of your grandfather's musket pointed at my face—the first, but not the last time, someone has threatened to kill me. In case you're wondering what that feels like: I do believe my soul left my body for an instant. I lived on. Such is the pugnacious nature of the Kirkes. Here is the thing, Leo: I deserved it.*
>
> *I sometimes still wake up, sweaty, terrified, and freshly sick with grief, from a dream of wandering around and around in inky dark, fruitlessly searching for the two of you.*

Those were things he had never told a soul, not in so many words, and probably never would.

But he wasn't getting any further with a speech, either. There would be a vote soon on whether to tighten the enforcement of the already-in-place child labor laws, and decisions made about funding for apprenticeships with London guilds for children in the workhouse. He would be expected to string a series of magnificent words together before the end of the season and stand up and address the Commons and, thereby, the nation, and perhaps more importantly, he thought ruefully, the constituents who kept him employed. Usually he was *filled* with things he wanted to say.

Who was he without words? He rubbed his forehead, as if it was a magic lamp. Perhaps words would spring forth.

He smiled slightly when he became aware of

Keating quietly humming in her room below. He closed his eyes to listen to the sounds of her feathering her nighttime nest: pushing the chair back under the desk. The slight thump as she settled into bed.

He imagined her stretched out in a white night rail that draped the lovely curves of her body. Instantly, a ferocious *want* pulled his every muscle taut.

He breathed into his hands.

Then swiped them over his face and blew out a breath.

Christ.

How he wanted to be a better man. A moral man, a certain man. He knew how a better man would speak to a girl like Keating, the way he knew which fork to use at dinner.

And even though he could act the part of that well enough in the sitting room, before an audience—as he had tonight—he was also a man who had said "bed" to her last night when they were alone at the ball, because he knew how to light fires in a woman's imagination, not to mention a woman's loins.

And with a thrill he'd felt smack in his groin, he had seen it. He had seen her pupils go the size of pennies. He had planted a seed in her imagination, and his cursed ego quietly thrilled to this. He knew how to nurture that seed. He *wanted* to nurture that seed.

He really ought to go to the devil for it.

He'd said it because he'd suddenly had a stabbing premonition of how she would look at him if she knew the whole truth of him. Certainly not with that starry-eyed, shy adulation, or that frank, undisguised admiration for his manly physique. And he'd said it in part because something in him wanted to

demonstrate both to her and to himself what a fine
line there was between innocence and . . . whatever
he'd become. And how very, very easy it was to
stumble across that line. One little word like "bed"
at a time.

A hero would not have done that to ease his
own discomfort. A hero wouldn't want to protect a
woman as badly as he was tempted to corrupt her.

Then again, disliking himself was not a new
sensation. He was indeed a bit of a bastard. After
all, twice in as many days someone had hurled
something at him—a lamp, a fist—and it had not
escaped his ironic notice that the common denomi-
nator in both circumstances was him.

But he never lied to women. He never made
promises. There was a satisfying simplicity in this,
and a relief in knowing that the ending of his every
liaison—and they were hardly legion, regardless
of what the gossip sheets implied—was essentially
foregone the moment it began.

The trouble was, the pace here at this bloody
boardinghouse was gentle and rhythmic. He was
held fast in one place for the first time in as long
as he could remember. And this captive domesticity was blurring his sharp, hard edges. Today,
during a difficult meeting with a constituent he'd
caught himself calling to mind the way Keating's
face lit when she saw him the way another man
might reach for a shot of whiskey.

In her presence, he felt increasingly unfamiliar to
himself, which made him uneasy. Her naivete and
depth and her wit and her sweetness all wrapped in
her unconscious natural sensuality wreaked havoc
with his surefootedness. Shimmering somewhere
outside of the reach of his reason were memories

which seemed to hold the answers, but when his thoughts brushed too close to them, his chest tightened with an odd atavistic fear, the sort prey has for predators.

It would have shocked anyone who thought they knew him to discover he was afraid of anything.

He decided to abandon for the night his attempts to write anything better than what he'd already written. He'd send the package of books to Leo tomorrow.

He got into his nightshirt and climbed into the absurdly comfortable bed and surrendered his head to the bosomy pillow. He wasn't looking forward to a repeat of last night: he'd awakened with a start from a dream that his bed was on fire.

But he would rather let Farquar hit him again and again in front of a cheering audience than let anyone know that he sometimes still soothed himself to sleep by imagining he was a little boy in Wales again, stretched out on a cool, soft bed of clover, on a scrubby, unprepossessing hill, in the shelter of a boulder. The sun and breeze on his skin. Keating's quiet humming evolved into the hum of bees as sleep took him under.

Chapter Ten

⮞⮞⮞

AT THE Southam assembly—the Earl and Countess of Southam were their hosts—Catherine began to recognize the many people she had seen at previous balls and yet hadn't met, and the many men she hadn't yet danced with and might never. Perhaps all of these people never, never tired of each other's company. She certainly would love an opportunity to discover why, if that was so.

Instead, her social circle remained stubbornly unexpanded. She stood again with Lucy, Miss Bernadette Seaver, and Mr. Hargrove while Lady Wisterberg gambled a few rooms away. She hoped the dowager was at least winning, because someone ought to be.

Tonight Miss Seaver wore a dress of lilac satin, trimmed at the bodice with little satin roses. It was so pretty Catherine's heart ached.

"Oh my goodness. You look like the personification of spring," Catherine told her. "That color is so beautiful."

Mr. Hargrove, flatteringly and unfortunately, seemed enchanted by this assessment. He beamed at her. "The personification of spring! How magnificently put. Why, she does, indeed. You do have an interesting way of seeing, Miss Keating."

She smiled at him carefully, given that the other

two young women were watching her like hawks, their expressions tense.

"Thank you. That is very kind of you to say, Miss Keating," Miss Seaver replied. "Are you saving your nice dress for the Shillingford ball? I mean your nicest dress?"

Catherine stared at her for a full two seconds. For heaven's *sake*.

"I do plan to wear a nice dress to the Shillingford ball," she decided to say, with great, great patience.

Apparently the Shillingford ball was the event of the season.

It seemed improbable that she'd even be included on such a personage's invitation list, too, but, as Lady Wisterberg had said, complacently and intriguingly, *Even Earls and Countesses have need of fresh blood, dear, and I know a lot about everybody. They were happy to include you and Lucy.*

"Oh! I've something exciting to tell you, by the way, Miss Keating." Miss Seaver's eyes were alight with news. "That is, I hope you find it exciting. I wasn't certain whether I should say anything. But I heard from a friend . . . who heard from a friend . . . who heard from another friend . . . that Lord Vaughn said he would like to be introduced to you. Do you know who he is?"

Catherine's heart gave a little skip. My goodness, if this was true, her season was about to go off like a roman candle.

Because Lucy had indeed pointed Lord Vaughn out to her. He was remarkably handsome and artfully groomed. And while he seemed pleased with himself—he had every reason to be, she supposed, given that he was the heir to an earl, and given the face that looked back at him from the mirror—his general air did not seem to be too cool or haughty. One never knew, of course.

"Well," she managed to say casually. "How very gracious of him to say so."

"Do you recall what he said, precisely?" Lucy was eager to help, both for Catherine's sake, and likely for her own. Certainly the attentions of an earl-to-be would trump Mr. Hargrove's any day.

"I was told that he inquired about the 'pretty blue-eyed girl in green,'" Miss Seaver said. "And"— she lowered her voice and scrunched her nose sympathetically—"you are the only one in green tonight. So I drew my conclusions. But I loved that shade, too!" she hurried to reassure her. "In 1817."

Catherine almost sighed. That was three years ago. Her dress was only two years old.

She could not imagine wanting to see Miss Seaver ball after ball after ball. Why was Lucy friends with this person?

"Well, I thought it might be my only hope for being noticed in such a crowd of lovely girls," Catherine finally said somberly. And wholly ironically. "I'm glad to see my strategy worked."

Miss Seaver looked uncertain.

Lucy cast her a wry look.

"But . . ." Miss Seaver continued, "I told my friend to tell him that I didn't know where your chaperone might be." She delivered this with wide-eyed innocence and gave a little shrug.

Catherine's heart sank. "But . . . Lady Wisterberg is in the game room. And I thought . . ."

She was going to say, "I thought everyone knew that, and you certainly did, too," but it might have embarrassed Lucy.

"As it so happens, he sought me out for clarification, and I'm going to be dancing the waltz with Lord Vaughn tonight." This was Miss Seaver's coup de grâce. "I shall say kind things about you to him during it," she magnanimously lied to Catherine.

Catherine and Lucy stared at Miss Seaver, a bit awestruck.

If this was a chess game, they'd been roundly outplayed. Because now Mr. Hargrove looked a trifle jealous at the notion of Miss Seaver dancing with the young heir, and Lucy looked anxious about the fact that Mr. Hargrove was jealous, and Miss Seaver had snatched the attention of an heir from Catherine.

She recalled what Lord Kirke had said, about putting his enemy or rival Farquar on the back foot, which was where he'd wanted him. And this was what Miss Seaver was attempting to do: put Lucy and Catherine on the back foot.

On the one hand it was intriguing; on the other it was dispiriting. Catherine didn't think there was a chance in the world she could negotiate an entire season this way. Sincerity was her native language. She'd learned when she was much younger that lies were a drag on the spirit. She could just about trace this lesson to the day she'd sneaked a jar of jam from the kitchen, eaten nearly all of it, lied about it, lay upstairs with a stomachache—and then was compelled to eat dinner. She'd been casting her accounts for days.

She'd likely make a terrible politician, should the day come when women not only voted, but were elected.

Miss Seaver wouldn't dare say the things she was saying if he were standing here with them, she thought. He was *somebody*.

She was nobody.

She suddenly felt profoundly like a bumpkin in her two-year-old green dress. No, worse: as exposed as if she were naked. Before she could brace herself against it with anything like reason, desolation whistled through her and took her breath away.

What delusion had made her believe she'd been in any way prepared for London? She stood in the ballroom now, motionless, airless, and wondered if she knew herself at all.

No matter what, she was still without a partner for the next few dances.

And while Mr. Hargrove, Miss Seaver, and Lucy went off to dance their quadrille, she went in search of a comforting place to wait.

"COME, KIRKE. HELP me sell some newspapers." Thomas Barnes, editor of *The Times* exhaled his cheroot smoke, which joined the cloud wreathing the men in the Earl of Southam's library. "Go out there in the Commons and bang on about something patriotic to get English hearts pumping. You know—'The intoxication of victory! What man is free and et cetera!' You know, that thing you do."

Barnes actually did a creditable Welsh accent. Kirke was darkly amused.

The editor shook his head admiringly, wistfully, and added, "Now that was *some* speech."

But there was a hint of warning in it. A suggestion that everyone was prepared to be indulgent of Kirke the politician, with his quirks and secret scandals and penchant for pushing everyone toward change, as long as he continued to perform in ways that benefited and entertained them.

"I must thank you for the suggestion, Barnes," he

said evenly. "As it never would have occurred to me, otherwise."

Barnes, not without a sense of humor, hiked a brow and the corner of his mouth.

But Dominic could feel his inner barometer rising.

Across from Kirke, the odious Bertram Rowley—why was *he* invited?—was smirking.

"I'm looking forward to our contest next year, Kirke." Rowley's speaking voice called to mind a goat awakening from a rough night of debauchery.

Kirke smiled and tipped his head to study Rowley quizzically.

" 'Contest,' " he repeated affectionately. As though Rowley had said something adorable.

Around him, despite themselves, most of the men hid smiles.

Rowley's face went stony.

Kirke, however, had not been handily elected over and over by assuming getting elected would be effortless. He personally thought there would be a contest. As much as he loved a good fight, it was very witty of fate to decide to throw this new fight onto the tangled heap that was his current life.

A few moments later, under cover of smoke and laughter, he slipped out of the library and headed back down the stairs. He threaded past the dancers on the floor, his eyes running swiftly across them, before veering to casually peer into the game room. When he saw Lady Wisterberg, a white plume like a planted flag on top of her head, deep in play, his heart gave a single hard, odd bump.

He made at once for the stairs. This time he turned left, the opposite direction from the library, and made his way down a softly carpeted hall. From experience, he knew he would find an alcove.

He found her sitting alone on a bench next to an urn from which a froth of ferns and flowers spilled. She was somewhat camouflaged in a pale green dress.

Even he knew this wasn't this year's color.

He froze as two epiphanies struck:

He hadn't been so much seeking solitude just now as he'd been specifically seeking her.

After his little encounter with Barnes and Rowley, he'd wanted to see that light in her face the way he might want a breath of clean air.

He froze. She hadn't yet noticed him; it wasn't too late to turn around.

Suddenly she tipped her face into her palms.

It was so clearly a moment of private despair. It sliced right through him.

"Keating." The word was out of his mouth before he knew he could stop it. He said it almost urgently, as if he were warning her to step out of the path of a rushing carriage.

Her head shot up in surprise.

And her face brightened immediately when she saw him and that was better.

His heart was beating strangely quickly, as if some accident had been averted.

She slowly rose to her feet. They regarded each other for a tick or two of silence.

He wondered what she'd read in his face. He took pains to adopt a neutral expression.

She said cautiously, "Lord Kirke, I feel as though I'm forever intruding on your quiet places. You seem to know where they are in every town house."

It was almost another way of saying: "You seem to know where I am in every town house."

"I've had years of experience at the same parties. And I haven't a monopoly on quiet places. You are welcome to any and all of them. Do you feel unwell? Shall I go and fetch your chaperone?"

Every muscle in his body had tensed in preparation to act.

"Why would you . . . oh, you saw . . . Oh." She was flustered now. "No, thank you. You are too kind. I was just . . . resting my face for a moment."

"I see," he said both gently and dryly. "All that holding it up gets tiring after a time, I suppose."

Her mouth quirked at the corner. She turned away from him slightly, as if to hide her expression.

A wordless few moments passed during which he felt irrationally helpless because he couldn't fix whatever was wrong for her.

"Truthfully . . . I was just beginning to wonder whether I ought to go home." She gave a little laugh, to attempt to make her words sound wry. But they weren't.

"Back to The Grand Palace on the Thames?"

But he understood what she meant. He'd only said it because he knew, suddenly, with absolute conviction, that he didn't want her to leave.

"Back to my home in Northumberland. It's beginning to seem as though my London season is a farce. If it was a horse, it would have been shot for lameness before now." She gave a short, ironic laugh. "I would love to come to know the city, and I do not usually give up easily, but I am beginning to believe I might not be cut out for the place. I'm wondering if it's worth it, after all."

He remembered his prediction to himself days ago: she wouldn't last the month in London.

Two impulses warred in him: to encourage her to

go home, before London could take that light out of her face forever. It seemed to him that one never stopped needing to conquer London, freshly, again and again. At least this was true of the circles of London in which he was obliged to move. Perhaps it was why he felt so at home here—fighting was what he was born to do. She should go home, to the green fields and the kinder people. And away from people like him.

"Perhaps if you return next year?" he suggested carefully.

"I'm afraid I won't be able to afford it," she said frankly. "I'm twenty-two now. Not precisely on the shelf, of course. But there isn't enough money for another season. My father has a habit of accepting things like piglets instead of money for payment, and we are not wealthy. Mind you, we *like* piglets, and don't lack for anything we want." She looked up at him earnestly, assuring him of this. "But he would like to see me safely settled soon because . . . he's . . . well, it's his heart."

"His heart?"

"It isn't . . . it isn't what it used to be."

His heart isn't what it used to be. That rather described his own, too.

"His heart is . . . failing?" he guessed.

"He thinks so. He grows tired climbing the stairs, and he cannot travel to see patients the way he once could . . . well, he believes it might not be long for him now."

And it immediately put into context what she'd said last night in the sitting room. She'd already lost her mother. She hadn't any siblings. How the thought of losing him, too, must frighten her.

Kirke's chest tightened. He'd heard the warmth in her voice when she talked about her father.

"I see. I'm terribly sorry to hear it."

She searched his face. She could hear how sincerely he meant it and he saw that she was grateful for that. Her expression eased.

She nodded. But she didn't reply for some time, and he honored her with silence.

"But that's simply life, isn't it?" she said finally. "One can hardly predict it. None of us are exempt from its . . . caprices. I have been luckier than many, I know. I try to make the best of the moments I have. I'm not certain I'm making the best of the moments here in London," she added dryly.

She didn't think life owed her a thing. And this, he realized suddenly, was why it was so peaceful and easy to be in her presence. Loss and experience seemed to have taught her acceptance and given her depth and strength and rare maturity.

She didn't have to say: "And when my father dies, I'll be alone." But that was absolutely implicit.

It was immediately clear that this London season for her could mean the difference between a future of security and joy and ease, or a future of genteel poverty and loneliness.

He knew firsthand that life could cut you off at the knees, and you could still go on. That the human spirit could be almost stupidly, defiantly resilient and indestructible. It built up fortifications and strange adaptations to do it, granted. But the realities he'd witnessed had not made an optimist of him. Women had far fewer choices than men.

He ought to drag Lady Wisterberg away from the gaming table by her nape and get her to do her job. He could think of no way to directly approach her about Keating that wouldn't be construed as insulting or wildly inappropriate.

"Was it . . . are you worrying about your father at the moment? Or did something particularly daunting happen this evening to have you contemplating the sacrifice of Helga's magnificent scones at The Grand Palace on the Thames?"

"Oh, I am always a little worried about him. But our housekeeper is there with him and I know she'll take good care of him, and he insisted I go to London. To be honest, I wanted to go." She paused. "But something did happen tonight."

She looked at him uncertainly.

"Would you like to tell me?" he asked gently.

"Just a moment ago, I learned that Lord Vaughn was interested in an introduction to me. Do you know him?"

He went still. Lord St. John Vaughn was the young, very handsome, very wealthy heir to the Earl of Vaughn.

And just like that, before he could hurl his considerable powers of reason in front of it in defense, the most shocking, black jealousy came at him like boiling oil dumped from a turret.

He went airless. His thoughts snarled as though a grenade had been hurled right smack in the middle of them. He could not get out a word.

What. The bloody. Hell.

He was stunned. It was an absolutely primal reflex. He hadn't known he was capable of that sort of jealousy.

He breathed through it as he would through any new shock.

And the young heir was just about the best match he could imagine for Keating.

"Lord Vaughn is interested in meeting you?" He managed to sound neutrally interested.

"I was told that he inquired about the 'pretty blue-eyed girl in green.'" She cast a glance up at him, just a flicker of flirtation in it. "He told this as such to a friend of a friend of a friend of Miss Seaver, who told him she didn't know where my chaperone was. And . . . I know that she did know."

"Is Miss Seaver an eligible young lady this season, by any chance? Is she the one who also, er, carries a torch for Mr. Hargrove?" No one was more mordantly amused than he was that he knew these minutiae about the ton.

"She is." She paused. "Do you suppose it was a crocodile maneuver?"

She sounded so hopeful that it wasn't.

"I'm afraid so, Keating."

An inspiration was forming. Every now and then a bold and unexpected move in a chess game could throw off an opponent and snatch victory from the jaws of defeat. He reasoned that her season could hardly be going much worse. Without a decent chaperone to facilitate things, it wasn't likely to get any better. She deserved better.

But he could not sort his strategic motives from the unwise ones. They resisted parsing, and this was because the battle now was between his common sense and his senses. He was unaccustomed to searching his mind and confronting a sort of mocking wall behind which all the answers lay.

There was almost nothing he hated more than feeling like a fool. But his need to ascertain a particular something was running roughshod over his acquired wisdom and ironclad cynicism.

He felt as though he ought to be certain of his reasons before he opened his mouth and said the words, for her sake and for his own.

So he didn't say them yet. He would give himself until the moment the music began. And then decide.

"Are you acquainted with Lord Vaughn?" she asked.

"Yes. Lord Vaughn," he began carefully, evenly, as if the terrain was volatile, liable to shoot hot geysers at him if he put a foot wrong, "has very good manners. Respects his elders. He's uncontroversial, possesses the normal amount and type of vices, all within reason. He seems a decent, intelligent young man, if not particularly driven. His father is an earl, a good sort, and I don't say that lightly about anyone. You could do much, much worse than Lord Vaughn. I should say he's nearly perfect. And he clearly is a man of discernment, if he sought an introduction to you."

She regarded him somberly, fixedly, at him and a rosy flush moved into her cheeks.

How odd it was that his breath should go peculiarly short every time his eyes collided with hers.

"I've seen him. He's very handsome," she said offhandedly.

She was studying his face like a map.

"Yes," Lord Kirke agreed, darkly amused. "When you meet him, you should tell him that, in case it hasn't occurred to him."

She smiled.

He could not quite force his mouth to commit to a smile.

"He ought to be easy to fall in love with," he added, casually. "If indeed that's the sort of thing you want to do. I expect stranger things have happened in a ballroom during the season."

SHE STARED AT him. Catherine was fascinated by how the introduction of Lord Vaughn's name had changed the conversational weather. She wasn't entirely certain why, given that Lord Kirke had given the man his approval, something he no doubt never gave lightly.

One, however, would be forgiven for thinking the opposite was true, based on how rigid his posture had suddenly gone.

She was afraid, suddenly, of what this could possibly mean. Or was she actually excited? The two emotions braided, and momentarily she was breathless at the implications.

"Have you ever before been in love?" she asked him.

"Yes."

The word came down with the deadly swiftness of a guillotine and it was edged all around in ice and razors and "keep away" signs. She was as jarred as if she'd walked into an actual wall. She nearly took a step back, but she was made of sterner stuff than that.

She was reminded swiftly and simultaneously of two things. He could be a rather scary man. Not a man to cross. At all times, including now, he was likely simply indulging her and that could end.

He was also not the sort of man likely to indulge anyone lightly, without a reason. And he'd been indulging her for some time.

These two things seemed somewhat contradictory.

She didn't know what she'd been expecting, or how on earth she'd gotten bold enough to ask the question yet she didn't think she was sorry. But it was just as much of a window into him as that soft vanishing warmth she'd seen during their little chat on the verandah.

That answer meant he was protecting someone. Was it himself?

Was he in love with someone now?

Her heart contracted oddly at the notion, as if curling in on itself in defense against that thought.

She remembered the word "by-blow" the man had lobbed at him the other night. Such a vicious term for a child who had not asked to come into this world.

Was it true? Did he have a child?

Her cheeks went abruptly hot, as they generally did around him. And yet she had the oddest impulse to touch his arm. By way of comfort or apology, she wasn't certain.

By way of saying: "Don't leave me just yet."

All she knew was she felt frantic when his eyes went remote, as if he was retreating from her.

But he had just drawn a line. And somehow nothing had ever seemed more seductive than crossing it.

And suddenly the music for the waltz drifted up to them.

"Keating." He seemed to be considering what to say next. "I should be honored if you would dance with me."

The breath left her.

She stared at him, stunned.

His expression revealed nothing but calm expectation of an answer.

"But . . . you don't dance. Everyone knows you don't dance."

Everyone. Listen to her sounding as though she were actually a part of the ton.

He raised his eyebrows at the "everyone." "I dance well enough. I *seldom* dance. There is a difference."

She studied him a moment longer, then her eyes

flared. "Oh God. Don't do it because you pity me!" she breathed.

"Keating," he said so gruffly she blinked. "Do you really think I would stoop to anything so frivolous as pity? It's a strategy. A favor to a friend. Your season could hardly be going worse. This might be an opportunity to make it better. I feel it only fair to warn you, before you answer yea or nay, that it will have consequences. There is no chance at all that it will go unremarked. You will be noticed. This might be all to the good. It could be the opposite. It could be some piquant blend of the two."

"Surely you're not so scanda—"

"I never lie," he said patiently.

It also sounded very much like a warning.

No matter how intently she examined his face, he gave nothing away. And this was because he was hiding something, this much she was certain. It maddened her, this ability to disguise his thoughts.

Perhaps the fact that he wanted to dance with her as much as she wanted to dance with him. But why?

At the thought, her heart began to slam so hard she could hear it ringing in her ears.

"Thank you," she said gently. "I would be honored to dance with you."

Chapter Eleven

❦

"*I*'LL FIND you against the wall nearest the ratafia table," he told her.

And so, her heart all but galloping, she preceded him down the stairs. They could hardly be seen strolling together from an upstairs hideaway, after all.

A few moments later, he followed her, and found her, and bowed.

Then extended his arm and raised his eyebrows.

His smile was barely that: a lift at the corners of his mouth.

She realized then that every muscle of her body had always contracted ever so slightly at the sight of him, like a heart leaping.

And it did that now, at the prospect of touching for the first time.

His arm tensed a little beneath her hand, his muscles flexing as if he was preparing to lead her out over the backs of sleeping crocodiles.

Her heart a steady bass drum in her chest, thusly they promenaded together to join the other dancers.

She was conscious even then of heads turning toward them.

She curtsied to him, as prettily as she was able when she was nearly dizzy with nerves.

He bowed again.

After the minutest hesitation, as if he sensed it was an irrevocable act, he gently closed his fingers around her hand. When his other hand came to rest on her waist, it suddenly seemed like something essential that had long been missing from her.

And they merged with other dancers, as if they had done it dozens of times before.

She'd never danced with his sort of man before. The way he moved his body, his gaze, and the way he'd touched her—everything felt like intention. As though he never put his hands on anything or anyone without the determination to possess it wholly. The gravity of whoever he was and the things he knew seemed to communicate themselves to her body through his hands.

And just like that, her skin felt as if it was made of a thousand tiny lamps, all softly blazing. As if her every cell had raised a violin to its shoulder and drawn a bow.

Judging from the temperature of her face, she was likely a shade of raspberry. Her only consolation was that this likely looked well enough with the shade of green she was wearing.

And as they moved together in the familiar, graceful rhythms of the waltz, he wore a faint frown. His eyes were fixed on her and they burned as if his entire being was marshaled to the task of seeing her.

Heat rayed through her from the places their bodies touched: her hand at his back. His at her waist. Their linked hands. His mouth seemed strangely beautiful to her, long and fine, and she knew by this dance she would be able draw it with her eyes closed, anytime she wished. What she wanted was to trace his lips with a finger. To discover the textures of him. His hair, his skin. An odd ache began in her chest, and her eyes stung with some nearly overwhelming emotion she could not quite name. It felt like yearning. Inherent in yearning, she knew, what made it so enticing, so romantic, was the notion that it would never, ever be satisfied. That it was out of reach. Perhaps even wrong.

Surely he could feel it in the rise and fall of her ribs, just above where his hand rested at her waist. Or the kick of her pulse in her hand.

Oh, look at me now, Lady Hackworth and Miss Seaver, she exulted silently.

"You do dance passably well," she said finally. Because it seemed clear he was not going to speak. "Perhaps you should do it more often."

He finally smiled faintly. "Your effusiveness is going to make me blush, and then we really will have a scandal on our hands. This waltz only has value because it's rare, Keating. I allowed it to appreciate in value, like a priceless antique."

She laughed, breathlessly. "Thank you for spending it on me."

His reply was a subtle nod.

"Are they watching?" "They" being the ballroom at large.

"If you look up you can see Lady Sedgewick's molars. Her jaw has dropped."

She didn't want to look anywhere but at him.

She almost said it aloud.

She was certain her eyes said it for her.

And yet she began to feel it: the gradual shift in the attention of the room, as if the direction of a breeze had changed. Those not dancing were watching them. Those dancing were also watching them, or at least as best they could without colliding with each other. She thought she saw Lucy's wide eyes as she turned about in the arms of Mr. Hargrove, which was where Lucy wanted to be.

She exulted, which is how she knew she'd been suffering just a little more these past few days than she'd been willing to admit to herself. How glorious to be so thoroughly seen at last. Whatever the consequences. What a strange miracle that her benefactor was such a very noticeable man.

"It was very kind of you to interrupt your unbroken record of not dancing at balls," she said.

"Kindness had nothing to do with it."

His words were almost too brusque. But the closeness of his voice, the bald, definitive statement, was thrilling, because it suggested he was keeping something leashed.

"Something you'd do for any friend, no doubt," she said softly. It was inflected almost as a question.

He didn't respond, apart from a slight indenting at the corners of his mouth. It was an ironic smile, not entirely amused, acknowledging that he knew she was testing him.

Even now she could almost sense all of the things he was—the things that she'd only ever glimpsed that undershot his charm and attention and the soft warmth she sensed hidden at the very core of him. A cold ruthlessness that made it possible for him to do what he did as a politician. A brilliance that could lacerate. A pride and ferocity that boded ill for any enemy. And a core of mystery, the part of him he revealed to no one. Nobody would toy with him without consequences. She didn't know why she would be excepted. She really shouldn't tease him at all.

But she could see no benefit to him for dancing

with her. And if it was not a kindness, it was because he'd wanted an excuse to touch her. Perhaps he had thought about it for some time.

In much the same way she had wondered about him.

She didn't know why this should make her feel both frightened and protective, except that he was her friend. She was certain of it.

"Don't look now, but Lady Wisterberg has been flushed from her den. She is even now watching us. Someone must have gone to fetch her out of alarm," he said.

"What does she think you'll do to me?"

Her own daring unnerved her.

She knew this was a question to which he could not and would not reply.

But his eyes did it for him, with a flare of heat and that little unamused smile, and this time the smile was most definitely a warning. She was not going to get an answer.

The notion that she might never know suddenly panicked her. It seemed imperative to know.

She had never felt more exhilarated, or more confused.

The thing that they had been weaving between them over a series of days now was perhaps friendship, but it was also a sort of net. And down, down, down it sifted, until they were standing too close but somehow not close enough, and the music was over just in time and yet far, far too soon.

They did not step apart at once.

Mainly because neither seemed able to bring themselves to do it.

Finally, his shoulders moved when he took in a breath. He slowly led her from the floor, through a gauntlet of eyes, straight to Lady Wisterberg, who was standing on the periphery of the ballroom and not-quite-but-almost wringing her hands.

He bowed to both of them, and then without another word calmly strode off. She suspected he had gone to find some place to be alone.

ON HIS WAY back to rejoin the men gathered in the library, Kirke saw the plume on Lady Wisterberg's turban rising above a little cluster of the curious, like a victor's flag planted on a battlefield. He was relieved and gratified that she appeared to be dispensing introductions to Keating with alacrity. At last.

He tensed against a flock of other emotions fluttering on the periphery of his awareness, dark as crows. One of which was something like panic, as though his pocket had been picked of something shockingly valuable. Briefly something oddly akin to sorrow clutched his throat.

The thing to do was to not look, and to walk away, thereby scattering the emotions like birds attempting to settle on a field.

So he did.

But he knew that he had already walked himself into a trap of his own making. Because beautiful women abounded in London. It was easy to want a beautiful woman.

But alchemy was different. It was about ineffable things. The way someone's head went back when they laughed, or the set of their shoulders when they walked. A voice. An essence. The way the very gravity of a room seemed to change when someone was near.

It was two people, who, when combined, would ultimately combust.

He'd had to know.

Now he knew.

His enemies would reach out with both hands and greedily scrape the news of his waltz with a young woman toward them like coins they'd won in a card game, hoping it was a vulnerability they could exploit. The gossip sheets might try to imply he was attempting to corrupt her just because he could.

He was concerned for her sake. It would bear watching. But there was almost nothing he couldn't adroitly manage or endure. He wasn't going to dance with her ever again, and he would be keeping his distance from now on, so he would not be heaping kindling onto any nascent gossip.

Of infinitely greater concern to him was the fact that he'd seen a tiny gold birthmark shaped like a heart alongside her pearl necklace, right above the shadow of her cleavage.

And that. That was going to bloody haunt him.

It would be what he saw when he closed his eyes at night and he thought he might die if he never touched his tongue to it.

LADY WISTERBERG CRAVED the rush of a wager. Nothing made her feel more alive. So when it became clear she was suddenly in custody of a horse she could back—Miss Catherine Keating—she abandoned the gaming tables and became as efficient and brisk as a general. She skillfully fielded the sudden flurry of requests to meet Catherine that resulted from her waltz with Lord Kirke, and unabashedly reveled in the reflected glory.

When Catherine's dance card was nearly filled, Lady Wisterberg pulled her aside and launched into a lecture. "Oh, my dear, no. No. NO! Lord Kirke is a good-looking devil, and I'll grant you he has pretty manners but the main word is 'devil'—he's not looking for a wife, he's at least fifteen years older than you, and he's certainly inappropriate for a young woman to be dancing with! However did you happen to fall into his clutches?"

"I didn't 'fall into his clutches.' He was doing a kindness. I suppose I looked disappointed not to be dancing and he took pity."

Lady Wisterberg looked almost disdainfully skeptical. "My dear, men like him don't do 'kindnesses' for pretty young women out of charity."

This was probably meant to alarm her, but Catherine found it thrilling instead because she suspected it was true.

She also felt it would be imprudent to point out that she'd gotten into his clutches, so to speak, because Lady Wisterberg hadn't been there to put a stop to it. Lady Wisterberg knew this. Cat was also very careful not to note that she literally lived under the same roof with him, and that Lord Kirke's floor was currently her ceiling, as she suspected Lady Wisterberg would demand an end to this shocking arrangement immediately. Catherine liked the arrangement very much, indeed.

"Though I suppose it's flattering that he took notice of you at all," Lady Wisterberg added begrudgingly. "Men are conundrums at the best of times."

"What do you mean, men like him?" Because she suspected Lady Wisterberg was finally going to tell her.

"He has affairs, dear," she said bluntly. "Volatile affairs, from what I understand." This last sounded almost wistful. "This apparently suits him better than marriage, for various reasons."

This news jabbed Catherine right in the solar plexus. It jolted her heart into a sickeningly quick tempo.

"How do you know this?" Her voice had gone weak. She tried to sound more curious than demanding. Surely Lady Wisterberg wasn't Lord Kirke's confidante.

Lady Wisterberg waved a hand. "Women talk. And it's definitely not the sort of gossip a young unmarried woman ought to be hearing, but I thought it best to apprise you of your very close call."

For heaven's sake. As if he'd actually pounce upon her on the dance floor.

"Until I'm married, in which case I'll hear all of it."

"Precisely," Lady Wisterberg said without a shred of irony.

Catherine's head spun almost nauseatingly. She struggled to mold this unwanted—and what sounded like appallingly authoritative—view of Lord Kirke around the image of him to which she'd become attached: a challenging if surprisingly kind, admirable, devastatingly attractive man who had done her a good turn.

Then again . . . he had also said "bed" to her in a conversation.

And in the space of a waltz, he had somehow managed to set her whole being alight like a fuse.

She was breathing more swiftly now.

She might be the veriest virgin. But she wasn't entirely naive. And it seemed very clear to her that this alleged sexual adventurer found her riveting.

And as this realization solidified, her knees felt again like butter.

With whom did he have affairs, if he did? Who were these women available for carnal exploits?

And he'd admitted to being in love at *least* once. Was he in love now? Or was he in love every time he had one of these alleged affairs?

But he'd made that admission to her the way someone under attack might draw a sword.

"There's also some speculation about his income," Lady Wisterberg continued, relentlessly. "I have heard that he has declined to participate in a few excellent investment opportunities lately, the sort he normally would leap upon, and the whispers are that it's because he's been in some sort of financial difficulty. Perhaps because of lavishing women with gifts, who knows. Furthermore, his town house isn't even currently habitable, thanks to a fire. Though, granted, he owns it, which is no mean feat. But his fortune was never family money. Which means he must *work* for it." She'd lowered her voice for the word "work" as though it was an epithet worthy of the jar. "For all that he is a baron, he's a plebeian. Not far removed from peasants."

"So am I," Catherine nearly said, but refrained. Lady Wisterberg, in her zeal to lecture, had clearly forgotten.

"And . . ." She paused, seeming to consider whether she ought to go on. "All right. I'll say it." She cleared her throat. "There are rumors he has an illegitimate child." She said this sotto voce, though no one was listening but Catherine.

Catherine went mute with shock.

She could hardly say, "Well, yes, I've heard

them. The night he called a man a bastard and was punched in the face."

But this was increasingly chilling and sobering. "Where there's smoke, there's fire" was an adage for a reason.

Catherine held herself absolutely still. As if in so doing she could prevent this unwanted new information from sinking in.

In their parish alone she knew of several girls who had "gotten in trouble." It was considered a tragedy for all when this happened. People known as "rakes" were usually involved and for the most part suffered few consequences.

Had a man who was purportedly so concerned with the welfare of children created a fatherless child?

Nevertheless, it didn't mean it was true.

But it occurred to Catherine that she *had* been lucky. That if another man had discovered her alone on a verandah he might have responded to her very differently.

And surely this was a mark in Lord Kirke's favor? Surely this supported her own view of him as a fundamentally decent man, regardless of rumors?

Having clearly thoroughly subdued and thoroughly chastened her charge, Lady Wisterberg's tone shifted to more sympathetic.

"He might be a skillful politician, but when a pretty girl has only a modest dowry her reputation cannot withstand even a bit of tarnish. He is nearly the last man in the world you ought to dance with if you want a successful season. If you do it again, you'll definitely wind up in the gossip sheets and not in a nice way. Your waltz with him could easily have gone the *other* direction, my dear, if you were any less charming or obviously innocent. We can seize this moment, and turn the ton's aroused curiosity into new friendships. But your behavior must be impeccable—*impeccable!*—from now on. Do you understand?"

After a moment, Catherine nodded dazedly.

"I think we can find you a nice heir," Lady Wisterberg concluded confidently, and gave her shoulder a little pat. "Lord Vaughn seems just the thing." Her eyes gleamed shrewdly.

She had learned of Lord Vaughn's interest in Catherine from Lucy.

Lucy was startled by Catherine's sudden rise in fortunes and the means by which it occurred, but in the race for Mr. Hargrove's affections, it looked as though she was ahead by at least a nose by the end of the ball. If Lucy was a little envious, she had little to complain about, given that the sudden flurry of invitations they had come away with from the ball—to picnics, to an afternoon tea, to two more private assemblies—included her, too, at Lady Wisterberg's insistence.

And the rest of the night, until they departed in order to meet The Grand Palace on the Thames's curfew, Catherine had danced every dance. Six of them.

This was *exactly* what she'd dreamed of when she'd come to London. What she'd hoped to be able to report to her father when she returned home.

It was truly a pleasure to dance—she loved to dance!—and to such wonderful music, among such beautiful people, for the rest of the evening. But the names and faces of the young men blurred together. Kirke had somehow flooded her senses and her thoughts. None of the others could get much of a purchase in her imagination, which seemed ironic and unfair, since this was the moment she'd been waiting for all season.

And it seemed downright ungrateful to crave a moment alone in the ballroom when she'd yearned to be anything but since she'd arrived in London. But she wanted some privacy to tuck away in her soul, like keepsakes of certain sensations before they faded: the press of Lord Kirke's hand on her waist, the heat of his fingers wrapped around hers, and his eyes on her, hot, fixed, and enigmatic. So that she could pore over them again and attempt to conjure the powerful, inadvisable longing they kindled in her body—that simultaneous rush of power and weakness. Of fear and exultation. For she sensed she might never feel that way again.

Chapter Twelve

❧❧❧

ONCE LORD Kirke had set her season in motion like a spun roulette wheel, he'd receded from her life until he was merely scenery on the edge of it.

As the week went on, Catherine's flagging hopes were revived by a strategic flurry of teas, impromptu picnics, and turns about Rotten Row with Lucy in a carriage belonging to a friend of Lady Wisterberg, all arranged in the spirit of making sure everyone got a look at the first girl with whom Lord Kirke had danced in longer than anyone could remember (though Lady Wisterberg didn't put it that way). Lady Wisterberg even decided to hold a party at her town house a few weeks hence, which would of course benefit both her and Lucy. Invitations were sent out straightaway, and Lady Wisterberg had aimed *daringly* high—she'd invited young Lord Vaughn and his parents, the Earl and Countess of Vaughn, and many an unmarried heir under the age of thirty, and lots of the finest young ladies, too.

Such a party had never been held in Catherine's honor before. She was dizzied to learn that most of the invitations had been accepted within *days*. Days! From heirs! People with titles! Lady Wisterberg made it clear to her that this was an honor indeed. Catherine's heart now seemed in a perpetual state of racing.

Surely this social whirl was a harbinger of a

dazzling future? And even though she understood her popularity was rather of the manufactured sort, she was still prepared to enjoy it thoroughly and to take advantage of her opportunities. One did not look gift horses in the mouth. For while Lord Kirke had set it in motion, it really did seem as though people were prepared to like her, perhaps because she was prepared to like them.

And as Lady Wisterberg had warned, she had appeared in the gossip columns. But it was more amusing than alarming:

The season has suddenly been enlivened by the mysterious appearance of a certain captivating miss, who appeared from nowhere like an angel on high wearing last year's green dress to waltz with the devilish Lord K-- who hasn't danced at a ball for nearly a decade.

"Angel on high" was a bit much, though she didn't hate the notion of being found captivating. But the "devilish" bit worried her and made her furiously indignant on Lord Kirke's behalf. Did nobody know him at all? Surely he wasn't kind only to her? Was it necessary to hurt his feelings? For wouldn't it?

The "last year's dress" stung far more than she'd thought it might. She supposed if the same little wound was lashed again and again, it was bound to eventually throb.

And for heaven's sake, she thought acerbically. If whoever had written this was so very particular about fashion, they ought to have recognized that her dresses were from *two* years ago.

But if this little item was the extent of consequences of which Lord Kirke had warned, she expected she could cope very well.

If he'd noticed or read it, he'd said not a word to her.

For the past week, Lord Kirke had been present at dinners at The Grand Palace on the Thames four days per week as the rules required, and in the sitting room, where he and Mr. Delacorte took turns vanquishing each other at chess and gloating or muttering darkly in loss, as the case may be. He then retired to the mysterious smoking room with all the men of the boardinghouse, and who knew what went on in there apart from smoking.

Paradoxically, given her new popularity, the favorite part of her days were now the nights.

She would lie in her night rail beneath the soft blankets and listen to the house creaking and sighing as everyone settled into their beds. It was the coziest feeling to be surrounded by people she liked, all tucked into individual little cubbies.

Night was the only time she had Lord Kirke to herself anymore.

But only the sounds of him. She could sometimes hear him pacing across his room, or sliding his chair back. She imagined him plowing his hands through his hair in frustration, thinking his grand thoughts, writing a speech.

Getting out of his clothes.

His coat, first.

Unwinding his cravat.

Pulling his shirt off over his head.

Sliding off his trousers.

Pulling off his boots.

She imagined all of this in sequence, for the fascinating pleasure of shortening her own breath.

And then, at last, there always came the little *thunk* she now recognized as him settling into his bed.

Because the fuse he had lit when he'd touched her during the waltz had burned low, but constantly. It was disturbingly clearer and clearer that this wasn't the sort of fire that went out if left unattended.

If she paid it one glancing bit of attention—if she fed it the kindling of her imagination—it flared hotter.

Which beset her with an exquisite restlessness. When she thought of him, parts of her body would thrum for all the world like struck instruments.

This fuse—and therefore, he—had been ever with her over the past week, when she was riding in a carriage in the Row, and meant to be admiring the fine figures of young men riding on horseback alongside, and returning their smiles and tipped hats with nods; when she was taking tea with matrons, any one of whom could very well be the mother of her future husband; when she was attending a picnic with Lucy and more young men to which Lady Hackworth had also been invited. Lady Hackworth had invited her to a salon at her house, but had asked her not to tell Lucy. *I'm afraid we only invite people who intrigue us*, she'd said, under her breath.

Lady Hackworth made her uneasy. And yet, there was something seductive in being found intriguing enough to invite to an exclusive salon. She'd had no sense of herself before outside of the context of the country. She'd thought she'd known herself well. But was she *truly* singularly intriguing, and hadn't realized it? Was this why Lord Kirke had paid any attention to her at all?

And . . . was Lord Kirke conducting an affair during the hours she didn't see him?

She did not know why this possibility should be both a torment and a titillation. She could not reconcile this admittedly scandalous notion with the flash of aching panic she'd seen in his face when he'd caught her in a moment of despair. Just before the waltz.

Would a devilish man truly be concerned about her? For she thought he genuinely cared.

Because he was her friend. Wasn't he?

And yet.

In the dark, tossing fitfully enough to tangle her sheets, she had imagined his hands hot against her back, pulling her up against his body, and felt such a rush of blood to her head and to her nether regions she nearly swooned from it.

All of these sensations were new to her, but clearly not to him.

Had he delegated her to some far corner of his mind now that he had accomplished his allegedly altruistic mission of waltzing with her?

There were any number of logical reasons to believe this.

Except that not once—not once between the time she'd waltzed with him and now—had he met her gaze directly.

He had not even looked directly at her during dinner this evening, even when he'd politely passed the peas.

They were now all gathered in the sitting room, waiting for Mrs. Pariseau to return from dining out with a friend so they could resume reading *The Arabian Nights' Entertainments*, which she was thoroughly enjoying. Catherine, Dot, Angelique in one corner of the room. Captain Hardy and Lord Bolt sat nearby. Mr. Delacorte's back currently obscured her view of Lord Kirke. The two of them were at the chessboard.

Catherine gasped when Mrs. Pariseau at last swept into the sitting room. "Oh my goodness—your dress is so beautiful!"

"Thank you, Miss Keating." Miss Pariseau smiled and pirouetted, and the soft sitting room light danced over the purple silk of her dress, which was shot through with rose threads. It shimmered like a hummingbird's throat. The long, fitted sleeves and square neckline and the slim rows of quilting at the hem perfectly suited Mrs. Pariseau's generous curves and set off her dark hair. She looked marvelous. Everyone sighed and murmured in admiration.

And for a flashing instant, a potent envy, shot through like the silk with wistfulness, stole Catherine's breath. She was not in the habit of coveting anything. But it was almost inconceivable that she would ever own such a beautiful, expensive thing. She was ashamed that this abraded her heart.

Mrs. Pariseau settled gracefully into a chair near Delilah and Angelique. "I've not had a new dress in a year or so and when I saw this particular bolt of shot silk at Madame Marceau's . . . well, you know how it happens. It was a *coup de foudre*." She clapped her hand over her heart. "It spoke to me. I feel it makes me look like a hibiscus."

As it was unclear whether this was her hoped-for outcome, this declaration was greeted by a cautious silence. Mainly because at least half the people present didn't know what a hibiscus was.

"Is that anything like a proboscis?" Catherine touched her nose. Part of being a doctor's daughter was that she often looked at people and thought things like "clavicle" instead of collarbone, even if she'd never heard of Scheherazade until recently.

Mrs. Pariseau gave a happy shout of laughter. "Do forgive me—a hibiscus is a flower, my dear! A frilly pinkish tropical sort. I saw it in an orangery one day and didn't it make me daydream of warmer climes! I never forgot it. Though I love the idea of flowers shaped like noses."

"A flower that can smell you back," Catherine said, and everyone listening laughed.

"There might actually already be a nose-shaped flower, you know," Mr. Delacorte volunteered. "I've seen flowers like all sorts of unusual things. Like trumpets, for instance." He'd traveled all about the Orient, and he had seen quite a bit of interesting flora and fauna, some of which were incorporated into the various ground-up powders and pills he carried about in his case. "That might be the sort of flower I'd be. A trumpet flower."

"You might be interested to learn, Delacorte, that apparently there's a gigantic flower that blooms only once every few years in the forests of Indonesia and smells shockingly, unforgettably bad when it does," Lord Bolt volunteered. "I read about it in Mr. Miles Redmond's books."

Mr. Delacorte slapped the table happily, causing the chess pieces to rattle. "Yes! *That's* the flower I am." He loved being teased. And he mostly confined his flatulence to the smoking room, for which everyone was grateful. But no one at The Grand Palace on the Thames had been completely spared it.

"Oh yes, of course, that's perfect for you!" Mrs. Pariseau said excitedly. "It's known as *Amorphophallus titanum*, which is Latin for 'enormous misshapen phallus.'"

Shock sucked the sound from the room.

Mr. Delacorte's smile plummeted from his face.

He eyed Mrs. Pariseau balefully. Faintly wounded.

Catherine had never been happier that she knew what a phallus was, because she was now both delighted and scandalized.

"I thought we'd agreed that the fancy words for jar words are still jar words," Mr. Delacorte said indignantly. He was none too pleased to be compared to an enormous misshapen phallus.

"What is a phallus?" Dot whispered to Angelique, who reliably answered all of her vocabulary inquiries.

Angelique squeezed her eyes closed.

"If Mrs. Pariseau doesn't put a penny in the jar, I think I should be allowed to say the other version of that word out loud in the sitting room," Mr. Delacorte insisted. "The one that rhymes with clock."

He directed this appeal to Mrs. Durand and Mrs. Hardy.

Controversy crackled like lightning in the room.

Lord Bolt and Captain Hardy were smiling so broadly their eyes nearly vanished.

"I think a distinction can be made, Mr. Delacorte, between words that are used to expostulate and words that are used to elucidate," Mrs. Pariseau suggested, carefully.

Mr. Delacorte's expression made it clear he thought "expostulate" and "elucidate" should be jar words, too.

"Perhaps at the next Epithet Jar Congress you can further clarify the parameters," Lord Kirke suggested, and Catherine laughed, then coughed when Mr. Delacorte and Mrs. Pariseau swiveled their heads toward her.

It was no laughing matter, the Epithet Jar.

"While both of you have made excellent points," Delilah finally said, diplomatically, "if you feel overcome by the urge to mention anatomy, or if it seems critical to the discussion, I would like to suggest that a certain discretion ought to be employed. I feel we have gotten a bit too, ah, anatomical, in this room this week, and *surely* there are other topics we can explore."

Angelique looked relieved by this answer, as though she concurred.

Mrs. Pariseau could usually be counted on to graciously do the right thing after she'd inadvertently done the wrong thing, which had been more than once.

She sighed. "Yes. You're right of course. I understand. I'm terribly sorry. I do get carried away. You see, I attended a lecture called 'The Flora of the Indonesian Forest' and I found it all so fascinating that I just did not even think before I opened my mouth. I thought the flower's magnificent singularity was a good fit for Mr. Delacorte. He is one of a kind, is he not? I did not mean to imply that Mr. Delacorte has a . . . that his . . . ah, is . . ." She cleared her throat. "Forgive me, Mr. Delacorte?"

"Of course," he said graciously. "We all make the odd mistake, now and again. And my . . . well, it's not, by the way. Misshapen," he said with great dignity.

Everyone winced.

Since Mr. Delacorte was usually the one making mistakes, and Mrs. Pariseau was known for being right about everything, and she did not precisely feel she'd made a mistake, a minute little tension ensued.

But then she gamely went up to her room to fetch a penny to drop into the jar, and Catherine admired again the play of light over her skirts as she, with dignity, swished by.

"What sort of flowers would Mrs. Hardy or Mrs. Durand be?" Delacorte wondered. As if comparing people to flowers hadn't already proved to be a risky endeavor.

"Delilah's favorites are daisies," Captain Hardy said.

This earned him a melting look from his wife, who had told him this only once and he had never forgotten it. He had, in fact, remembered it on one of the most memorable days of both of their lives. "But I think pansies, too," he added a moment later, surprising her, judging from Delilah's questioning glance.

"Later," he promised her under his breath.

Captain Hardy would never be comfortable effusing in front of other people.

"Angelique is a rose." Lucien said this as if he'd decided this long ago. "A golden yellow rose, very soft with layers of ruffled petals, gone blush at the tips." Lord Bolt was a great reader of poetry and an unabashed user of metaphors.

Angelique smiled at him, and when she blushed, Catherine could see how easily he had come to this conclusion.

Her heart twinged, sweetly and painfully. How lovely it would be for someone to see and know her so well that he could compare her at once to a specific flower. Or know her favorites. She hadn't a favorite, unless, perhaps it was poppies because that shade of red stole her breath. She liked all of the flowers she saw, especially wildflowers, especially when they sprang up in unexpected places. Every year when things began to bloom after a winter, it never ceased feeling like a miracle.

"Dot would be bluebells, I think," Delilah suggested.

"Oh!" Dot breathed and clasped her hands, as though she'd been anointed.

"Or dandelions after they've puffed out and are ready to float away," Delacorte mused.

"Because you can wish on them?" Dot wanted to know.

"Yes, that's why," Delacorte said, after intercepting a warning glance from Delilah.

"What about you, Lord Kirke?" Mrs. Pariseau turned to him.

"I'm a horse chestnut," he said at once, without looking up from the chessboard. "Prickly and dangerous on the outside, hard on the inside. Sometimes poisonous."

He winked at the audience at large, so they would feel free to chuckle. Which they did, albeit a trifle uneasily.

"But chestnuts are rather nice when they're toasted in the fire, as you nearly were," Catherine said.

He lifted his head and turned it slowly toward her. Once again, she had the pleasure of watching his face go brilliant with glee before his lips curved.

"Good God," he said. "That was dark indeed." He paused. "Well done."

She smiled at him, and he smiled back, and when those little crescents about his mouth appeared it felt as though the sun had come out for the first time in days. Though it had, in fact, been a gloriously sunny week. Perfect weather for picnics and so forth.

Her neck muscles forgot how to turn, now that she had his eyes to herself again.

She became aware that the two of them had been looking at each other and not saying anything, but she couldn't tell for how long, because something odd had happened to time.

Finally he returned his attention to the chess game.

But she noticed that he remained absolutely still for a moment, as if he'd forgotten where he was or what he meant to do. He'd laid his hands flat on the table. Almost as if he didn't trust them and wanted to watch them.

She stared at them. She imagined so easily feeling the weight of his hand on her waist. That was all it took for heat to fan through her torso, pool between her legs, flush her cheeks.

She had come to understand that what she felt was lust.

She wondered if "lust" was considered a jar word.

The ease with which she was able to call it up to her body by just looking at him was fascinating and more than a little frightening. The consuming intensity was unexpected.

How unnerving it was to suspect that he might feel the same way about her.

Moreover . . . he knew what to do about it.

According to Lady Hackworth, Lord Kirke was allegedly "good."

Whatever that meant.

"And we're all grateful that you were not a toasted chestnut, Lord Kirke," Angelique soothed.

A scattering of chuckles greeted this.

"What flower is Miss Keating?" Mr. Delacorte asked.

Everyone contemplated her and Catherine held her breath, happily awaiting the verdict.

Lord Kirke looked up. "Clover." He said this quietly but definitively. Then returned his attention to the chessboard.

Catherine nearly recoiled.

It sounded much like that "Yes" he'd delivered

when she'd asked him if he'd ever been in love: The word arrived with a fence built all around it.

Clover. Food for cows and sheep. Nearly as common as dirt. Half of England was carpeted in the stuff. That's how he thought of her.

She felt scalded breathless.

Because she was a country girl? And could not possibly be a bright, complicated bloom, like Mrs. Pariseau? Or even Delacorte? What kinds of blooms were the other anonymous mythical London women with whom he allegedly had affairs?

He returned his attention to the chess game after having uttered those enigmatic two syllables as if he hadn't said anything at all.

Perhaps she'd simply been briefly novel for him the way everything in London had been novel for her, and now he was bored of her.

Perhaps he was embarrassed now to meet her gaze.

Perhaps the concerted way he refused to look at her was nothing more than embarrassment that he had danced with a bumpkin.

And yet he seemed helpless to look away when he finally did look.

This frustration and confusion were as new as all of her other sensations. All of them originating with him.

"Clovers have lovely blossoms. And make the nicest honey," Delilah approved.

If this had anything to do with his reasoning, Lord Kirke opted not to expound. "Checkmate," he said to Delacorte, instead.

Mr. Delacorte froze. His eyes bulged. "Wha . . ."

Then he shot to his feet. "BLOO—"

He clapped his mouth closed just in time and the rest of the expostulation swelled his cheeks as if he was blowing into a trumpet. It sounded like *"mmmmmfffhmph."*

He closed his eyes. Sucked in and blew out a few deep breaths.

Then lowered himself gingerly back into the chair and sagged in defeat.

Lord Kirke smiled at him beatifically.

"Miss Keating, if you like, I'll take you to Madame Marceau tomorrow morning to choose a new ribbon for your bonnet," Mrs. Pariseau volunteered. "I'm to collect a spencer they're tailoring for me."

During her garrulous first evening when they'd all been given a sherry, Catherine had indeed mentioned she would like a new ribbon for her bonnet.

"Oh, I would like that very much, Mrs. Pariseau, thank you."

She might not be able to have an entire new dress, but the prospect of a new ribbon was undeniably consoling.

FROM A COMFORTABLE position stretched out in bed, Captain Hardy watched Delilah plait her hair at her dressing table, as was his habit. He found it soothing. It was as if she were sewing up the day, putting a finishing touch on it.

She turned to him. "Do you think women are smarter than men, Tristan?"

"Yes," he said at once, yawning.

"Is that because you don't want to sleep on the settee tonight?"

He laughed. "Am I so transparent?"

She laughed, too, and climbed into bed next to him. He stretched luxuriously, crossing his arms behind his head, then gathered her up. She snuggled into his body and sighed.

"It's so much better when you're here," she said.

"You took the words right out of my mouth."

They were quiet a moment.

"Kirke is a politician to his bones," her husband said drowsily. "And a provocateur to his bones. He says things like that to jar people into thinking about something they wouldn't normally, or into thinking about things in a different light. *He* may not even believe it. But I don't know why intelligence ought to be apportioned according to gender. A man may start out in life believing that sort of thing because it's what he's taught, but sometimes I agree with him that the definition of wisdom is knowing definitively how much you really don't know. Admire him or revile him, I don't suppose Kirke is wrong about much. So far, anyway."

"How shocked his majesty would be to hear you sounding like a Whig," she teased.

"Whigs were His Majesty's dear friends while he was regent," he said dryly. "Shockingly, once he became king, he embraced the Tories and the divine right of kings and so forth."

"I think I'm glad he's here," Delilah said. "Kirke. Because from the looks of him, if ever a man needed to lay burdens down for a moment, it's that one."

"Any man who gets to sleep under this roof is a lucky one, Delilah. I'm the luckiest of them all."

"Now who's the politician?" she teased. "But so true," she murmured, against his smiling lips, and then he kissed her, long and slow.

"Why pansies?" she whispered after a moment.

And it was a long moment before he replied. "Because your eyes are as soft and dark as their centers." He ran a thumb across her bottom lip.

And just like that, he'd turned her insides molten.

He was not a man of many words; he was more accustomed to giving orders.

"Ah. But that's only when they're looking at you, my love," she whispered.

In the kitchen early the following morning, Delilah found Angelique and Dot sitting across from each other at their floured worktable. This wasn't unusual.

But Angelique's expression was as grave as a solicitor delivering bad news about a will. Her hands were clasped in front of her on the table.

Dot's expression was haunted and abstracted. Her eyes were lowered.

They both sported hot pink spots high on their cheekbones.

Delilah's head swiveled with alarm toward Helga, their cook, who was hovering behind Dot.

Helga's face was scarlet and her eyes were watering with what looked like suppressed hilarity. She held a finger to her lips.

". . . but . . . does that mean . . . that is . . . so they're not always misshapen?" Dot asked very quietly.

After a moment, Angelique shook her head slowly.

Dot took this in for a long moment. "Just the enormous ones, then?" So quietly it was nearly a (somewhat horrified) whisper.

A long, tortured silence ensued.

"Possibly," Angelique finally decided to say. It sounded somewhat strangled. "Sometimes."

"But . . . does that mean they all are *usually* the same shape and size?" Dot's brow was furrowed.

Behind Dot's back, Helga lifted a rolling pin, wagged her brows and pointed at it by way of asking whether Angelique wanted to use it as an illustrative prop.

Angelique cast her eyes up to Delilah with a "help me" expression.

"Dot, I think the flowers in the reception room vase need to be replaced. Will you go and do it at once, please?" Delilah said brightly.

Dot rose gingerly, as if her body was now unfamiliar to her, and progressed rapidly from the room, carefully avoiding everyone's eyes.

She had been given a good deal to ponder. They just prayed it didn't result in a dropped tea tray.

Angelique slumped. "Dear God. It was like quicksand. I felt we needed to answer her, ah, request for clarification from last night before she got her answer from someone else. Or inadvertently used the word incorrectly. And somehow, I just got sucked deeper and deeper in." She shivered. "I may never be the same."

Helga plunked a cup of tea in front of Angelique as though it was whiskey and Angelique gulped it gratefully.

"Thank you for undertaking that noble task. But surely she's not that naive about those things," Delilah said. "She's always seemed sensible about men."

"No, not entirely naive, as it turns out. It was the fancy word for it that caused the turmoil," Angelique said. "Phallus," she muttered darkly, under her breath.

"I'm sure you handled it well, Angelique," Delilah said. "Women are smarter than men, after all."

They all laughed.

"It's a risky game we play, all that discourse in the sitting room at night," Delilah said, with a happy sigh.

Helga placed a cup of tea in front of Delilah, too.

"Thank you, Helga."

The cook turned to begin delegating tasks to the kitchen maids and Angelique and Delilah sipped their tea.

"Angelique . . . the little gossip item about Lord Kirke in the newspaper the other morning . . ." Delilah lowered her voice. "I meant to mention this to you. But it occurred to me that it might be about our Miss Keating."

Angelique had been stung by the gossip sheets before she'd married Lucien (who had featured in them frequently when he was younger), and while Dot, for instance, was captivated by the glamorous life they captured, she remained cynical about them. "I considered that, too. She wore a green dress the other night. But would Lady Wisterberg allow her to dance with Lord Kirke? And surely that bit about him not dancing for a decade is an exaggeration?"

They both knew that was what the gossip sheets did: exaggerated. Find a particle of truth, distort it for maximum drama, embellish both the pleasant and the unpleasant: that was their mission.

"You know, it occurred to me, too. But our Miss Keating seems to have a level head on her shoulders."

"True. But how level is any woman's head when it comes to handsome men?"

Angelique gave a soft laugh. "Still. He has been all that is proper and respectful in the sitting room. He doesn't seem to pay *particular* attention to her . . . then again . . . a man of his age and stature and alleged experience would surely be discreet about that sort of thing. He seems to work very hard. And I don't recall anyone ever accusing him of corrupting young women."

"No, the gossip sheets just print coy nonsense about how Lady R rent her garments when Lord K ended it with her, or some such rot," Delilah agreed. "Not that I'm paying attention or know much about that world anymore. His affairs are . . . his affair, as far as I'm concerned. As long as he follows the rules while he's here, we won't have to . . ."

They were both thinking of the second to the last rule on the little card they handed guests:

> *If the proprietresses collectively decide that a transgression or series of transgressions warrants your eviction from The Grand Palace on the Thames, you will find your belongings neatly packed and placed near the front door. You will not be refunded the balance of your rent.*

"Well. If it was indeed Miss Keating, it sounds as though it was only one dance," Angelique concluded. "And Lady Wisterberg seems to have things well in hand, given how busy she's kept Miss Keating this week. And Miss Keating has been under our watchful eye in the sitting room. Hopefully we won't need to resort to evicting anyone."

But they were certainly prepared to do it, if it came to that. So far, they'd only needed to deploy that rule once to toss out a guest.

Then again, Delilah had gone on to marry the transgressor.

Chapter Thirteen

❧❧❧

"How do you do, Mrs. Pariseau. It's lovely to see you again. And I see you have brought a friend with you today!"

Lord Kirke had been correct when he'd surmised there was a shortage of modistes in her part of the world, especially the faux French sort, so meeting her was novel, indeed. Catherine liked Madame Marceau's long, regal face and her shrewdly sparkling brown eyes.

"It's a pleasure to see you again, Madame Marceau," Mrs. Pariseau said. "I'm here for my spencer, as you likely know. I've brought Miss Catherine Keating, who has decided upon a new ribbon."

Catherine gestured to the little spool of ribbon she'd chosen.

Madame studied Catherine fixedly for a full three seconds of silence, her face alight with pleasant and, it seemed, an unusually avid curiosity.

"How *delightful* to meet you, Miss Keating!" It sounded as though she meant it. "You've made a wonderful choice! That shade of pink is so subtle. It's the color of the roses in your cheeks, I should think."

"You are very kind, Madame Marceau, thank you. I admire your work immensely. Mrs. Pariseau's new dress is so beautiful."

The modiste nodded, graciously accepting the

compliment. "Speaking of beautiful things . . ." She pressed her lips together. "Well . . . forgive me if this is presumptuous, and a bit unorthodox . . . but we have here a beautiful blue silk ballgown that was made for a woman who decided she did not want it, after all. Can you *imagine*?" she clucked. "The extravagance! The waste! And as you appear to be about the same size . . . well . . . I wondered . . . would you like to have a look at it?"

Catherine's heart skipped.

"We can make alterations if it fits you," Madame Marceau added briskly.

"Oh my goodness . . . I . . . I don't know . . ."

Certainly there was no way she could afford an entire dress, let alone one made by seamstresses employed by the celebrated Madame Marceau.

"My dear, it wouldn't hurt to have a look. It might be serendipity," Mrs. Pariseau coaxed.

Catherine was tempted to say, "But it might hurt a *lot* if I love it and can't have it." Her feelings around dresses were increasingly raw.

But her season had so far featured quite a bit of serendipity. More would not diverge dramatically from the plot, she told herself.

TEN MINUTES LATER she stood in front of a mirror wearing a dress that was spun from her dreams.

Blue silk shot through with gold threads poured over her body in a smooth column to a hem trimmed in filigree embroidery and three vandyked rows. The low bodice was caught in the middle with a single bar of velvet ribbon in a way that fetchingly highlighted her fine long neck and excellent cleavage. The sleeves were short, puffed, gauzy affairs, scattered with tiny spangles and trimmed in more velvet. She looked . . . *queenly*. She looked like dawn coming up over the horizon of a day that promised to be sunny. She looked like the sort of girl who would make an excellent countess.

She quite fell in love with herself and could imagine other people doing it, too.

It was a little snug in some places and loose in others, but the general proportions suited her utterly and could easily be adjusted.

The two other women stood by and gazed at her with their hands clasped beneath their chins in delight.

"There was much competition over this particular bolt of shot silk. I know a number of other women wanted it before it was purchased and brought to me."

"It's easy to see why. It's so beautiful my heart hurts," Catherine sighed. "But I couldn't possibly . . . I'm certain it was shockingly dear. Surely you can reuse the fabric . . . the trim . . . the spangles . . ." She almost didn't feel worthy of touching it.

Catherine was an expert at taking apart dresses and turning the fabric to get more wear out of them. Her practical streak balked at the shocking notion of anyone *giving* such a masterpiece away. Then again, the thought of anyone dismantling this beautiful creation was like swallowing glass.

"But the craftsmanship, you see, is priceless, as is the time of the seamstresses, and taking it apart again might damage the fabric," Madame Marceau said regretfully. "Our customers tend to be a bit fussy about that, too—wearing something made for someone else, that is. So there's no charge, my dear."

Catherine's heart stopped. No charge? Surely this couldn't be true?

Her experience with dressmakers was that they drove hard bargains, and that was because they deserved to be paid well for their skilled, artful labor. And she couldn't imagine that even wealthy customers wouldn't want to brag about a bargain. It was one of life's little pleasures, after all.

But perhaps it really *was* different in London? So many things were.

She didn't know how Lord Kirke could look at her and think "clover" when she was wearing such a dress.

"You may think I am mad, Miss Keating, but I believe you will be a priceless walking advertisement for our exquisite garments," Madame Marceau persuaded. "I believe this with all my heart. We can make little alterations and deliver it to you as soon as tomorrow."

"Do you often give dresses away?" Catherine was still a little wary.

"It is a rare occurrence," Madame Marceau conceded smoothly.

She did not expound.

It was almost too much for Catherine to absorb: the sudden popularity, her social life roaring into life from a nearly complete standstill, and now a stunning dress. She was mute with wonder.

"Will the woman who originally ordered it be attending the Shillingford ball?" Catherine asked. This was of critical concern. Given what she knew of the ton, she was certain the original owner would waste no time in pointing out her rejected gown if Catherine happened to stroll in wearing it.

"Oh, I can assure you she will not. I believe she is, in fact, currently out of the country entirely. And no one has yet seen the dress but her and my staff."

"Well, then." Cat's voice trembled. The miracle of it made her as dizzy as if she'd bolted too much ratafia. "Thank you. I believe I will take it."

THE SMALL, ECCENTRIC, valiantly blooming little park in front of The Grand Palace on the Thames comprised a few blossoming trees and shrubs and was encircled by a wrought iron fence, through which flowers eagerly leaned their bright little heads. Kirke had become fond of it as he raced past it every morning, just after dawn. This morning he'd been out even earlier; he'd had an important assignment for his man of affairs.

He'd never seen the park in full daylight, but today he'd inadvertently left behind in his room some correspondence he'd meant to mail, and he'd rushed back in a hack midday to retrieve it and tuck it into his coat. He thundered up the stairs and then down them again.

He'd asked his hack driver to return for him in thirty minutes, so he could have time to take a tour of the little park.

When he emerged into daylight again, he stopped abruptly.

Keating was standing just inside the wrought iron fence, standing on her toes sniffing a blossom on a tree.

His heart stopped.

Then hurtled forward again, as a wayward exhilaration swept him.

He hadn't been alone with her since the night of the waltz.

Unless one counted the nights. Because he was excruciatingly aware that her bed was likely right below his. And as he listened to her settling in for sleep, he would lie very still. As if he remained so braced, none of those wicked, vivid notions hammering away at the iron walls of his will could ever get through.

She turned.

When she saw him, her face went brilliant.

Hell's teeth. This clanged his heart like it was a damned bell.

They regarded each other from that distance, in absolute silence. He could only hope she hadn't seen his expression before he'd settled it into a less incriminatingly rapt one.

"Good afternoon, Keating," he said politely.

"Good afternoon, Lord Kirke. I was just having a sniff of the blossoms. I like to read here in the park, when I can." She did indeed have a book in her hand.

"Any nose-shaped blooms yet?" he asked.

"No, alas. No enormous misshapen ones, either." She didn't say "phallus," but the word fair hovered silently in the air.

His lips curved in a small, wry but not entirely amused smile. The resulting hot rush along his nerve endings was inevitable and could not be helped.

He knew she had come to suspect her effect on him and was shyly dazzled by it. She was testing it, and testing him.

They were both much safer if he stood where he was.

He moved closer expressly so that he could witness that minute leap of her bodice when her breath caught. Better than a shot of whiskey, that leap.

She was wearing a white day dress. The wind whipped it about her legs and threw the ribbon of her bonnet like confetti.

It was a brutal test of his fortitude not to flick his eyes down to her cleavage, looking for the little heart-shaped birthmark.

They regarded each other wordlessly while the only sound was the wind moving through the greenery around them.

"I didn't think Mrs. Hardy and Mrs. Durand would mind that I plucked this. Here. Take this with you into battle today."

She extended a little pale pink sprig of blossom.

After an absurd hesitation, he gently took it from her.

Reflexively, he held it to his nose. His eyes closed fleetingly and involuntarily. It was so vulnerably soft it made his heart contract. It was indeed the color of her lips.

Which were, in all probability, exactly this soft.

His head went light.

He tucked it in his coat pocket. "Thank you," he said quietly.

When he could speak again.

There was a little silence, during which his feet refused to turn him around so he could leave.

"I just returned from visiting the modiste with Mrs. Pariseau a few moments ago. I thought I'd enjoy the rest of the day outside. Did you know the park is named for Lord Bolt's mother? It's rather sweet." She pointed to the bench.

Her visit to the modiste was, coincidentally, the reason he was up earlier than usual this morning. He'd directed his man of affairs to do something which may yet prove inadvisable. He had struggled with the decision, but in the end, he'd been unable to stop himself.

He read the little plaque on the bench, which

said *Helene Durand Memorial Park.* "I didn't know. That's lovely indeed. He must have cared for her very much."

"My mother is in the churchyard at home. I wondered if she would like a bench with her name on it, too. But it seems as though she's everywhere I look in our village, somehow, regardless. She might wonder why I decided on a bench, specifically." She gave a little laugh. "She never did like to sit still for long."

He was wordless, but his heart contracted almost painfully.

"Do you resemble her?" He hadn't known he'd intended to ask this question.

"I'm told I have her eyes."

And there were things he might have said then if he were someone else, and if she was someone else, too, someone less innocent, less vulnerable: *Your mother must have been devastating,* was one. *How hard your father must have fallen for her,* was another. Something torrid but wholly sincere. He knew how easy it would be to coax stars from her eyes and nurture the dangerous little flame between them, and he had no bloody business doing simply that because it was better than champagne as a distraction.

"Did you see the little gossip item in the newspaper?" she asked.

"I saw it," he said shortly.

"I thought it was unkind of them to refer to you as a devil."

He smiled slightly. "Don't call anyone out on my account, Keating. I've been called worse."

She smiled uncertainly at that. "And it was inaccurate to call me an angel."

If this was an innuendo, he wasn't going to take it up.

"Yes. Well. The gossip columns aren't known for their specificity. With luck, that one item will be the end of the matter."

The "end of the matter" rang with a certain implication. They both knew it.

She glanced away briefly, then returned her gaze to his. He had not moved his from her for one second.

"I have not yet had an opportunity to thank you. My season seems to be going very well at last. Lady Wisterberg will even be holding a party at her town house. Everyone invited is coming," she marveled.

"I'm glad," he said gently.

Neither one of them remarked on the fact that he was not invited.

She cleared her throat. "I wondered if you would be attending the soiree at Lord and Lady Hackworth's house this evening? I'm told it's after a fashion a salon." She gave the word "salon" a flourish.

He went still. It was a damned shame she'd somehow been introduced to the Hackworths, but he supposed not terribly surprising. The Hackworths were all about pursuing social power, and cultivating Keating, who now had a certain cachet, was naturally part of that. The Hackworths were also profligate spenders, in debt up to their sparkly eyes and lived decadently on credit—in other words, by taking advantage of unpaid working men and women. They never ceased inviting him to their events, however.

"I was indeed, but I'm afraid I won't be attending. And I don't think you should go, either, Keating. I can't imagine it would be any more stimulating than what goes on here in the sitting room at The Grand Palace on the Thames."

"But I thought you attended all of these events for the opportunity to 'make friends.'" She'd given the last two words an ironic emphasis, too, quoting him.

He smiled slightly. Not entirely amused. "I can tell you definitively that the Hackworths are awful people. Boring and bored and empty. They are all glitter on the surface and spiteful beneath. Indolent, but the cruel sort of indolence, not the content sort. They are like spiders. Always needing a new novelty to drain. And guess what you are, Keating."

It had been an almost cruelly undiluted assessment, even for him. It was his true self at his most unadulterated. Even he was shocked at himself. He had from the beginning been gentler with her than he was with most.

But she ought to fully understand this, too: he was not, on the whole, a man prone to delicacy.

He'd meant every word sincerely. He was alarmed that she might be pulled into their orbit.

"Lady Hackworth seems charming to me."

Her voice had gone somewhat faint. And a trifle defensive. It sounded like a dare for him to convince her otherwise. He'd unnerved her.

Keating was more astute than that about people, he'd thought.

He studied her for evidence of facetiousness.

"Yes. 'Seems' is the proper word for it. Have I been wrong about any of the people you've met so far? Perhaps we have different tastes in friends."

He suspected she was testing him, which irritated him. He usually quickly recognized and smacked down attempts to manipulate him. But it was clear she'd sensed he'd created a deliberate wall between them since the waltz. This was her way of trying to discover why.

He was unaccustomed to being readable. Or in any way vulnerable.

"No. You haven't been wrong," she admitted. More subdued.

"Was your friend Miss Morrow invited to the Hackworth soiree as well?" he guessed shrewdly.

She hesitated. "Lady Hackworth said it was rather an exclusive event and she could not invite everyone," she admitted, carefully.

This didn't surprise him a bit. These were the sort of games the Hackworths enjoyed. Dividing friendships. Playing people off of each other, fomenting rivalries, perpetrating, then feigning ignorance of, tiny slights.

"Who will be your chaperone for the evening?" He could not imagine Lady Wisterberg tolerating one of their soirees, either.

"It's in the early evening, and only for a few hours. Surely I can call upon them without one? For a few hours and come straight back to The Grand Palace on the Thames?"

He was a little angry now. And incredulous. "Come now. That doesn't sound like something you would do. Surely you know that isn't wise?"

"What harm could come to me?" She sounded a bit defiant.

That sounded like a dare, too.

He didn't honor that with a reply. She knew full well the harm. "And they will make you feel even lonelier, Keating," he wanted to say. "The Hackworths will."

"From what I understand, Lord Vaughn will be in attendance," she added idly.

He tensed. She'd somehow known that name in particular would jar him. He resented that he could be so easily riled. And so uncharacteristically clearly seen.

"I've told you what I think," he said tersely. "By all means, Keating, go, don't go. It's all the same to me."

Her face tightened against some flare of emotion. Likely hurt. She looked away briefly.

His heart felt scored by the line of her profile. The fine straight line of her nose, the soft, full swell of her lower lip. The slightly short chin.

She turned back to him. "Forgive me," she said stiffly. "I'm sorry to bother you about it. I think I see my mistake now. I didn't know."

"What didn't you know this time?" It was a stunningly unkind thing for him to say. If he worked hard enough, perhaps he would get her to dislike him, which seemed safer for both of them.

"That a man can care very much about *the* people while not actually caring very much about people."

It took a moment for her words to fully penetrate, but they somehow slid like a shiv beneath all of his clever armor and pierced him clean through.

He stared at her, stunned.

He was filled both with fury and breathless admiration for the accuracy of the strike.

What had she said that night he'd found her on the verandah? *She can't hurt me if she doesn't know me.*

He doubted she believed her own words. She'd said it because she knew it would hurt him.

He felt shamefully close to rank fear at being so seen.

"What rot," he said with idle contempt.

He arranged his features into an expression of boredom.

When she flinched, he felt it as surely as if someone had hurled a dart right into his chest.

But she wasn't a fool or a coward. She knew she'd hit her mark. This he admired so fiercely it was an ache. How he loved a fighter.

"No doubt it is. I suppose you would know, as you know so many things," she said politely.

They stared at each other from a distance that felt somehow unnatural. Since she'd touched him and he'd touched her, any moment during which they were not touching felt unnatural.

"I hope you enjoy your evening, Keating," he said politely, and stepped into the hack that came to take him away.

Chapter Fourteen

❦

"MISS KEATING'S father is a physician. Isn't that charming?" Lady Hackworth had taken Catherine gently by the elbow and steered her, like a tray of proffered sweetmeats, to a pair of beautiful people, a man and a woman with titles. She thought they might be a viscount and his wife. Lord and Lady Glossop?

They looked at her uncertainly—then back at Lady Hackworth—which darkly amused Catherine. They were probably wondering why they were being compelled to commune with a peasant wearing a two-year-old dress.

And she fought the urge to roll her eyes. Of all the things being a doctor was, charming was probably the least of them.

She would have loved for Lord Kirke to be wrong, except she'd known all along that he wasn't.

She had done, for the first time in her life, something she *knew* was reckless and foolish: she'd come without a chaperone, slipping out of The Grand Palace on the Thames to hail a surprised hack driver, who took her to St. James's Square and the Hackworth town house. Lord Kirke was right: she was not that sort of person.

As far as she knew, Lord Kirke hadn't been in when she'd left.

He hadn't been at dinner, either.

And the whole last hour or so had felt like walking barefoot over cut gems. Everyone was beautiful. But all of their edges were glitteringly sharp and uncomfortable to brush against. They were witty and quick but their accents were all drawled, London-y irony, as though they took nothing at all seriously. She thought about how Northumberland haunted her vowels. She knew she betrayed her otherness the moment she opened her mouth.

Lord Vaughn wasn't present. Perhaps he knew better than to associate with the Hackworths, too.

She felt she hadn't really anything to say to them—how could they find her life particularly interesting? And yet they seemed to be enjoying her anyway, the way they would enjoy a pantomime. She was aware that they saw her as both very pretty and quaint. She knew that to consider something quaint, one must feel superior to it, at least a little.

She knew that if she asked what they thought about Lord Kirke in the airy, insinuating, knowing sort of voice that Lady Hackworth used conversationally, they would likely tell her. And as much as she wanted to know—she was afraid to know.

"What is your favorite poem by Byron?" she asked Lady Glossop, when someone mentioned Keats. This was a salon, after all. She thought she might as well exhibit a little of her education.

There was a little silence. Followed by a sympathetic head tilt.

"Oh, my dear, we don't talk about him ever since that little to-do between him and Lord Hackworth over Lady Hackworth." She said it on an admiring hush. "Everyone *wants* her, you see."

Ugh.

"Tell me, Miss Keating," Lady Glossop pressed

on a hush. "You danced with him. You were close enough. What does he *smell* like? Lord Kirke? I've always wondered. We have a wager, you see."

Catherine stared at her. For God's *sake*.

But oh, she'd never been more sorely tempted. "Like sin and strawberries," she considered purring. Or "Like sulfur and brimstone and blossoms all rolled into one."

But she knew anything glib she said would be repeated, and possibly printed in the gossip sheets. She would never, never, never do that to him.

"My parents raised me not to sniff members of Parliament," she said gravely, instead.

"Oh," Lady Glossop said, bored with her again. "Why did he ask you to dance, do you suppose?"

"I don't know," Catherine said, and offered a blandly disingenuous expression.

They didn't seem to know how to respond to that.

Catherine stifled a sigh. She didn't particularly want to be anything other than who she was. But it was a strange, gray feeling to know there were people in the world who viewed her as a novelty. It was new, and she supposed it was valuable to know that such a viewpoint existed, and that she wanted none of it.

She liked the people at The Grand Palace on the Thames, which was where she properly fit. She wished she was there right now.

Well, it had been an experience, even if coming here was a mistake. She was sorry she'd come, because it was a reminder of how empty the world could feel when no one truly knew you. It seemed a foreshadowing of the loneliness that seemed to lie in wait for her if her London season was a failure, after all, and in a fit of superstition, it made her want to bolt.

And it seemed patently ridiculous, infuriatingly ridiculous, that a famous, scandalous politician—thirty-five years old, with a little gray in his hair and faint lines about his eyes, and the most fascinating face she'd ever seen—should suddenly feel like her best friend, when he could so easily do without her.

Surely this, too, was the fault of London. If she were to return home, perhaps every bit of this confusion would recede like a fever.

And yet. She'd somehow been certain he would appear here tonight anyway, despite his well-founded scorn for the Hackworths. Because she had seen the expression fleeing his face as she'd turned around in the little park today.

Raw hunger.

It had shaken her, and thrilled her nearly beyond bearing. Because something in her responded to it as powerfully as one wolf calling to another in the dark. She thought she might never be comfortable again.

"I don't feel well," she said abruptly to the Glossops.

And she quickly slipped away and went out the door to find a hack to take her back to The Grand Palace on the Thames.

"You've been quiet all night, Kirke."

White's was as lively as it ever was during the season. Dominic had joined some fellow Whigs for a game of five-card loo, brandy, and a discussion about developing apprenticeship programs for some of the children who were in the worst of the workhouses, like Bethnal Green.

He was, in fact, miserable. As restless as if he

were wearing a hair shirt. Nervy. Which was unlike him. He was beset with a guilt that he for a change probably didn't quite deserve.

"I can't tell if you're complaining or celebrating, Holmquist," he said finally.

"Can't it be both?" Holmquist said idly.

Dominic smiled.

"He's probably dreaming of ways to make Farquar uncomfortable."

Dominic didn't reply. The whole of his mind was elsewhere. He was playing badly which was also unlike him, and unfair to the other players. It took all the fun out of beating him.

He reached into the pocket of his coat and touched the blossom he'd tucked in there earlier. His fingers caressed the petals.

Finally, slowly, he laid down his cards.

"Gentlemen, I fear I must take an early leave of you. Try not to mourn."

He departed swiftly, leaving behind a ring of startled faces and a losing hand.

ON A TYPICAL night, hacks swarmed White's like gnats about a picnic, ready to ferry home drunk lords. Dominic hailed one straightaway, and gave him the directions to St. James's Square.

"Hurry, please, if you're able," he asked the driver as he boarded, and filled his palm with coins.

He didn't know why he should feel so anxious.

He leaned forward the whole of the way there, as if he could compel the horses to go faster.

As they pulled closer to the Hackworth resident, twilight had turned the tops of the buildings into shadows and the sky mauve. But there was enough remaining daylight that he knew, at once, the woman standing in front of the town house was Keating.

He knew it was her by the way she held herself, and the way the light glanced from her hair.

She was shivering, pulling her shawl tightly around the shoulders of her muslin dress. Her expression was hunted.

He tensed.

She appeared to be craning her head, looking for a hack.

"Why the devil is she . . ." he muttered.

Why had no one noticed that she had left the town house, and alone, to boot? This infuriated him as irrationally as the fact that he hadn't been there to see her out.

He thumped the roof of the carriage and the driver pulled it to a halt.

He pushed open the door and leaned out.

"Keating," he called. Quietly. Gruffly.

She halted and her head swiveled all about looking for the voice. She actually looked upward for a moment. The notion that she might think of his voice as the voice of a deity amused him. Or perhaps she thought it was instead the voice of a gargoyle lining the roof.

Finally she turned and saw him leaning partway out of the open carriage door.

She went abruptly still.

When their eyes met, he could feel the jolt of it in his body, as surely as he'd gone over a rut in the road.

They regarded each other across that short expanse of cobblestone.

He finally beckoned with a sideways tip of his head.

She hesitated.

Then her shoulders rose and fell in a sigh.

And resolutely, she crossed over to him.

She pretended not to see the hand he extended to help her up and climbed gracefully enough into the carriage, pulling the door shut behind her.

He thumped the ceiling again and the carriage lurched into motion.

Because "Didn't I tell you?" and "You were right, when aren't you?" hardly needed to be said aloud, they let the silence say it for them.

He took absolutely no satisfaction in that.

Nor did either of them mention the reason he just happened to be rolling through St. James's Square in a carriage when his plans hadn't involved a soiree at St. James's Square.

Or the reason she had been outside.

They both knew why.

She'd instinctively known he would not be able to stay away.

Dominic was nervous enough to want a cheroot.

Absurdly, his heart accelerated.

Finally, he shrugged out of his greatcoat. "Here," he said quietly.

She glanced over and up at him, then down at the coat. She tipped forward a little so he could gently settle it around her shoulders.

She carefully leaned back against the seat.

Something radiant swelled in his chest at the sight of her in his coat.

He felt peculiarly delicate and volatile, as if he were some substance that might spill over and ignite. He had come because he could not help himself. It somehow felt as though she'd won, and surely for her to have won must mean that he had lost. He'd gotten so used to thinking of his life in terms of battles. He hated losing.

He studied her profile. She was staring straight ahead into the twilight, subdued, but not defeated. Thoughtful. But he thought he detected a worried shadow across her brow. Why his throat should feel tight with emotion he didn't know.

He slid one arm gently behind her and wrapped the other about her waist the way he might exhale, instinctive and unconscious. He gathered her up.

She folded her arms atop his and settled, softly, back against his chest, as if, God help them, they'd done it just so a thousand times.

Her head rested right over the traitorous thud of his heart. Surely, she would feel it.

As the carriage rolled along, he just held her. It seemed all he had available to him by way of apology for the ton and the way it was. He wished it otherwise in that moment, even though he had mastered its thorns and battlefields and relished conquering them. If the world was different, would there be a point to him? He was who he was.

The point to him now seemed to be that he was the person against whom she leaned, and sighed in a sort of relief.

Imagine that. Imagine someone finding comfort in his arms.

His chin brushed her temple. He closed his eyes because her hair against his cheek was silky and he wanted, for one mad moment, to feel only this ever again. Every muscle in his body locked against a furious onslaught of longing.

His breathing went shallow.

And as the carriage bumped along, beneath his

hands her ribs rose and dropped with her breath, which fell softly on his chin.

He heard a rustle as she shifted slightly in his arms. Suddenly his chin no longer rested against her hair.

And then he felt her fingertips, light as a moth landing, on his jaw.

Then skim along the curve of his bottom lip.

He could feel his heart beating in his throat.

His breath came in shreds now.

He opened his eyes to find her gazing up at him from the crook of his arms. Her pupils were large. Her expression, solemn.

Their lips were so close he could feel her breath against his.

When she kissed him—a whisper-soft bump of her lips against his—it could easily be construed as an accident of proximity. If either of them chose.

He closed his eyes against the exultation that roared through him. It was laced through with danger and a lust he could taste in his throat.

It felt like a question.

It felt like permission.

His will crumbled into dust.

"Keating . . ." he whispered.

When he claimed her lips with his own, their vulnerable softness nearly broke him.

She sighed against his lingering, nearly chaste kiss, a skim of his mouth over hers, as her fingertips glided along the line of his jaw, traced his ear, twined in his hair. As though she had imagined long before how she would touch him. Had wanted to feed the knowledge of him to her senses.

He could not recall ever being touched with this

sort of reverence. As though he was being joyously discovered.

He felt absurd, as vulnerable as a clam without a shell. And yet some need he'd apparently kept chained in an inner dungeon yearned toward the tenderness like a whipped dog. It undid him, that she could so easily expose him. He was part fury, part wonder.

In the twilight of the hack, in this world apart from the world, it seemed safe to surrender to raw tenderness. His trembling fingertips trailed along the silky skin of her throat as his lips brushed her brow . . . then her temple . . . then lingered to savor the swift thump of her pulse in the hollow beneath her ear. The little jump of her rib cage beneath his hand and her sigh of pleasure when he touched his tongue to the whorls of her ear made him feel as powerful as Zeus hurling lightning bolts down from a mountaintop. This was magic: her body stirring and rippling with desire, coming alive with his touch.

Soon the gentleness ran parallel with tightly leashed savagery. His hard cock strained against the fall of his trousers. And when he returned to the miracle of her petal-soft lips, it was to part them with his so he could taste, then plunder, the sweetness and heat of her mouth. He groaned low in his throat.

She looped her arms around his neck to pull herself ever closer, as if she understood she was the source of his pleasure and torment. She was giving herself up to him to do what he would.

And only a fool or a saint wouldn't take and take. God help him, he was neither.

With each stroke of his tongue and glide of his

lips, he showed her how desire had strata, layers and layers that could be built and banked toward a glorious madness that only surrender could relieve.

She met him with instinct and abandon and fiery need.

When his palm glided over the lush curve of her arse to press her against his hard cock, she gasped and instinctively arched against him. Chasing her own pleasure.

He was shaking now from a desire that seemed anarchic enough to slip his control.

She slid his hand up from her waist to cup her breast, her head went back on a gasp. He looked down into the huge dark pupils. Her breath fell in short gusts against his chin. Her chest swayed with it.

Her hand rested against his jaw as he lowered his head and kissed her long and slowly and deeply, almost lasciviously, so he could feel the hitch of her breath, her moan of pleasure vibrate through his body when he circled his thumb over the hard peak of her nipple through the muslin of her bodice.

Lust drove a spike right through the top of his head.

Now was the time to lay her back, furl up her skirts, and guide his cock into the snug wetness between her legs. He imagined the two of them fucking like animals there in the rolling carriage. Her body pulsing around him as her first release came upon her.

In the state they were both in, he knew she would let him.

"Dominic?" she whispered against his mouth. Surrendered. Dazed with desire.

Her trust undid him.

"God," he rasped.

Like a man struggling up from the bottom of the volcano, he pulled gently away from her.

He dropped his forehead into his hands.

And his body heaved like a bellows.

CATHERINE'S SENSES RIOTED in protest at this abrupt abandonment. They wanted more of what they'd been given. If she touched her own skin now, she was certain she would feel her blood vibrating in her veins like a rough river.

Dizzily, she stared at him, but he was clearly overcome. His back heaving as he fought to recover his breath and his composure. Her own breath came in stormy gusts.

She had *felt* his desire for her humming in his body. She knew if she reached over and touched him now, she would feel it still.

She was awestruck by her own power.

By the need for him, thwarted, not yet receded.

She touched her fingers to her lips. They were swollen and tender. The taste of him lingered in her mouth, like a liquor she would never cease craving, and furious longing swelled in her anew.

Finally he turned his head.

They looked across at each other in a long moment of silence. It wasn't even full dark. There had been an eternity and mere moments involved in that kiss, and it was a shock to become aware of the world again. The sound of the wheels of a carriage over cobblestones seemed like something from a foreign land.

They would arrive at The Grand Palace on the Thames in mere minutes.

"Your hair," he said finally. His voice was quiet. "It's coming out of its pins."

"Oh. Will you . . . can you . . ." Her voice surprised her. It was hoarse, as if passion had scorched it away.

And small.

And uncertain now.

Very gently, so tenderly, he slid a pin free of her hair. He smoothed the wayward hair back in place, and with precise care, replaced the pin. Then did it with another.

His hands were trembling.

"There. Repaired," he said.

She managed a little smile.

He was watching her thoughtfully now, and she again resented fiercely his ability to hide his thoughts. But then, he was a lawyer and a politician, and had been alive longer, and had learned what she was learning: there were now and again very good reasons not to let anyone know what you felt. But she had a sense for what he was about to say.

"Don't apologize," she said.

"Keating . . ."

"You were going to. I refuse to hear it. I wanted to kiss you. You knew I wanted to kiss you. You wanted to kiss me. We kissed."

She hadn't known a kiss would have so many dimensions. He had also touched her breast, and all of this had been the revelation of a lifetime. All of it merely suggested to her that there was more to discover. She was terrified she would never learn it, and yet somehow relieved, too.

She knew they had both paced along a dangerous precipice.

He finally smiled, albeit faintly. "That is a fair summary of events."

"I do not consider that we are engaged. I do not consider myself compromised. I will not tell a soul. I do not consider myself ravished."

He took this in, wordlessly.

But she could hear his breathing, slower now. Why did it seem so precious, the sound of him recovering from passion? Just . . . the sound of him *living*. Why did it make her feel so tender?

Finally, his mouth tipped at the corner. "If you do not consider yourself ravished, perhaps I went about it the wrong way."

"I cannot say that I have anything to compare it to," she said carefully, slowly, "but I should like to say it felt as though you did everything perfectly."

Some fierce emotion suffused his face then—a blaze of raw longing, of vulnerability. So beautiful and bright her breath hitched.

It was gone before she could decide what it meant.

There was a little pause.

"So what you mean to say is that you were curious," he said carefully. "And it was a new experience."

It was a moment before she understood. He'd offered these words to her as a safe option, for both of them. Curiosity: that was all this feverish interlude was. It needn't be spun into a story. It needn't have ramifications. It needn't mean anything at all. It could be just another souvenir of her time in London.

And while this was a relief, it still somehow felt like a betrayal of both him and herself when she said, "Yes. I was curious. And my curiosity was satisfied. Thank you."

He nodded. Pulled in a long breath and released it slowly.

"You best go inside now. I'll wait here to make sure you're inside safely."

They both knew full well they could not enter the house together.

He'd used the word "home," which somehow didn't seem inappropriate, because if The Grand Palace on the Thames was anything, it was a home. And for a mad moment she wished it was, that he would be there and they could tumble from this carriage into a bed, and he could show her every other thing she knew he knew.

Chapter Fifteen

⤜⤐⤐⤐⤐⤐⤐⤐⤐⤐

Two days later ...

"*A* PENNY FOR your thoughts, Kirke," Delacorte said, as he blew a stream of smoke skyward.

He stared across at Delacorte in the smoking room. "Have you any pennies left or are they all in the Epithet Jar?"

Mr. Delacorte's week had been somewhat rough on account of losing to Kirke in chess more often than he was accustomed. Tonight he'd let fly with a quietly heartfelt "SHITE!" which had made all the ladies jerk in surprise, and Dot had accidentally stuck herself with the needle with which she was embroidering.

Granted, she accidentally stuck herself with a needle almost nightly, epithets or no epithets, and had once sewn her own sleeve to her embroidery.

But Delacorte had been mortified and contrite, and he had lost another penny.

"You're glaring at the wall opposite. I'm just grateful I'm not standing in front of you, or I expect my waistcoat would show scorch holes."

"This is just my usual face," Kirke said idly.

Hardy and Bolt, who had taken up the corners of the room with their cheroots, laughed.

Kirke was, in fact, idly, caustically imagining a special room for every vice. A compartment in which a man could privately succumb to his basest impulses, then exit with impunity back into the civilized world.

Like the inside of a dark carriage.

This smoking room was another genius design from the proprietresses. It was decorated in shades of brown and oxblood and cream. The chairs were deep and worn and comfortable, and the little table arranged before the settee was battered, perfect for supporting one's booted feet. The carpet and curtains were as thick and dark as the walls of a cave. It was the perfect room for men to regress to their primitive impulses, cursing, smoking, belching, and using bad grammar and the like. It suggested that women understood that men were little more than animals parading around in Weston-cut suits and Hoby boots, and if this could not ever be fully remedied then setting aside a room for them to misbehave was a compromise, the way one would set aside a box of wood shavings for a pet cat to defecate in.

He realized he had no one in which to confide his torment.

The truth was, he felt as though some scaffolding surrounding him had collapsed. He could not locate the ends of his composure to regather it. He had entirely been faking it for two days. He'd been undone by a kiss and he was appalled at himself.

He'd constructed the last nearly twenty years of his life in order to avoid ever again feeling this appalled at himself.

But every glancing thought of Keating made his muscles tense, as if preparing to pin her to a mattress. He'd meant to look out for her welfare. Instead he'd taken advantage of an innocent girl.

Yet . . . had he? It had not been calculated or strategic. It seemed to him that it could not have been helped.

This was what disturbed him the most.

He would be leaving London for two days to tour a textile factory for sale in Sussex. It was for the best. He knew she would be kept busy, now that her season was actually a season.

Unlike many men, he appreciated that women were often possessed of lusty natures and singular sexual preferences and he believed they were well entitled to them. He would never condemn Keating—or any woman—for seizing an opportunity for exploration.

Perhaps having had her new experience with a controversial baron, she could turn her attentions to the young heir to an earl. Which would be the best possible outcome.

Why did the notion of this clench every muscle in his body as if it was something beyond endurance?

"I shouldn't let the losing trouble you overmuch," he said to Delacorte, conciliatory. "You're just a nicer person than I am. I am simply too bloodthirsty to lose."

"Your day will come," Mr. Delacorte said sagely. "One wrong move will be your undoing, Kirke."

It felt a little too much like a prophecy.

THE DAY AFTER Lord Dominic Kirke had felt her breast in a carriage, Catherine and Lucy at last stood in front of an exhibit at the Montmorency Museum, escorted by Lady Wisterberg. They stared at the suit of another alleged rake. Lines had formed to see it.

It had been nearly an hour before they had been allowed inside.

It looked like an ordinary man's suit, albeit a nicely made one, and she thought perhaps that was the most poignant lesson: you can never tell from the outside what might be roiling inside any man. What secrets he might be hiding. No matter how handsome he was. So many titillating words had been written about Mr. Colin Eversea, the so-called Satan of Sussex, an alleged rake who had escaped from the gallows after being accused of murder and ultimately proven innocent. She and her father and her housekeeper had marveled over his exploits reported in the newspaper.

He was now, apparently, happily married and raising cows, the newspapers reported. He had donated his suit to the museum, elevating the museum's stature, rather the way waltzing with an allegedly scandalous man seemed to have, paradoxically, elevated her own.

Lord Kirke was to be away from The Grand Palace on the Thames for a few days—he had gone to visit a textile factory in Sussex, or so Mrs. Hardy reported—and at first, she was glad about it. She was inwardly stormy with thoughts, desires, confusions, and fears, and outwardly expected to take tea with fine ladies who could look her over and decide if she might be the sort their well-bred young sons and nephews should marry. She'd done this twice, once at Lady Wisterberg's, once at another matron's home. She thought she'd comported herself well enough. The next assembly, during which she could be expected to look beautiful and dance with young men, the sort she'd always imagined marrying, was a few days away. Plans for the party continued apace.

Her nights were wildly restless.

She wanted more than her next breath to feel the entirety of Lord Kirke's skin over hers.

It was the most wrong thing she'd ever wanted.

She longed to talk about how she felt with someone, but of course there was absolutely no one in which she could confide. She entertained herself by imagining the horrified gasps she would draw if she even so much as suggested she'd been alone at length with Lord Kirke, let alone kissed him.

How could she possibly explain? These things she knew to be true: life was short; it seemed a terrible sin not to seize extraordinary pleasures when offered them.

So why was it considered a sin to instead seize them? Why was society constructed in such a way to condemn this?

She might never have guessed that such glorious sensations could be coaxed forth from her body when touched by the right man, like a genie from a lamp. So she touched herself at night, exploring, and imagined her hands were Lord Kirke's, and discovered a few interesting things she might otherwise not have discovered.

At will, she could conjure the taste of him— liqueur and smoke and a rich, singular Essence of Kirke—and when she did, her knees nearly buckled and her groin pulsed with longing.

And then she tried to imagine the hands of other young men on her. For some reason her thoughts reeled away from this. The hands on her clearly needed to be the hands of a man she at least knew.

And trusted.

And wanted. Really, really wanted.

What if he was the only man she'd ever want in this way?

Her stomach tensed at this, too.

Because it seemed he no longer wanted her.

In the drawing room at The Grand Palace on the Thames, she surreptitiously studied Mrs. Hardy and Mrs. Durand and Captain Hardy and Lord Bolt, and wondered about their road to this domesticity—there Lord Bolt sat, holding yarn, while Mrs. Durand knitted, Captain Hardy quietly, intently listened to *The Arabian Nights' Entertainments* read by Mrs. Pariseau. Had their romances been paved with turmoil? Or passionate grappling?

"Well. Let that be a lesson to you," Lady Wisterberg said, after they had looked their fill at Colin Eversea's suit. "It is best to associate with men whose clothing does not end up in museums. Or whose names do not regularly appear in the gossip sheets."

Catherine and Lucy exchanged swift, droll glances and she led them out of the place to go and get ices.

WITHIN A FEW days of his return from Sussex, it had become very clear to Catherine that Lord Kirke had drawn a line between the two of them again. This one seemed absolutely impermeable.

He appeared in the sitting room at night, and he either played chess with Mr. Delacorte, or brought a book and quietly read it, or wrote letters or speeches and whatnot at a little table. He did no further orating.

He did not look her way or address her.

Not even once.

This omission seemed so violently apparent to her that she thought surely it was obvious to others, too. But no: the events in the sitting room at night were as peaceful, cheerful, and civilized as ever, with the clicking of knitting needles, the rustle of pages turning, the murmur of voices, the delighted commentary from listeners to the stories in *The Arabian Nights' Entertainments*. And this was so at odds with how she felt it seemed as though she was observing it all from within a dream.

Suddenly it seemed to her that she was on as much tenterhooks as poor Scheherazade, who had to wait night after night to see if she would get to keep her head.

She began to wonder if he had perhaps found the way she kissed unsatisfactory, though all signs at the time had pointed to otherwise. Perhaps he thought of her as a mere country girl, unsophisticated, not worthy of additional time or attention, after he'd satisfied his curiosity. He'd compared her to clover, after all.

Or perhaps—and this made her stomach turn over in sick misery—she had vacated his mind completely, the way one wouldn't continuously reminisce about or yearn for a perfectly ordinary meal.

She found it difficult to believe any of this was true. But what did she know?

It was as though he was afraid one look from him would feed her fevered imagination and hopes. Which was galling.

Her character clearly held unanticipated corridors, and she would never have known if she hadn't journeyed to London.

It seemed wildly unfair that she would be left to wonder, even as she knew it was sensible to let it be. If she were wise, she would simply follow his example.

A LULL IN entertainments left Catherine at loose ends the following afternoon, so she decided to visit the library room in the annex in search of a new book to read.

She froze in the doorway when she got there.

Her heart catapulted into her throat.

Lord Kirke was sitting at the little table. His coat was hung over the back of the chair, his shirt sleeves rolled up, leaving his forearms bare.

His quill was darting across a half sheet of foolscap, and around him on the table he had built a little fort of fanned-open books and papers and ink and sand.

She supposed this room offered him more space to spread out.

She stared at him in faint surprise, jarred into a realization. She so seldom saw him in the full blast of sunlight. And she'd been spending so much time of late with coltish boys and dewy young women that she was suddenly forcefully reminded Kirke was a mature Man, with a capital "M," and not a young one—the contrast seemed stark in this light. Everything about him seemed more distinct, imposing. Outside of his dark coat, the shoulders filling his white shirt seemed vast. His arms were corded with muscle and dusted with intimidatingly manly hair, dark as the hair on his head. In which a thread or two of silver glinted. His expression was absorbed and remote, and he seemed charged with fierce purpose. His fist had quite a passionate grip on his quill.

Suddenly confused and abashed, she hovered

in the doorway in an agony of indecision about whether to stay or go. It suddenly seemed outlandish that she knew how he tasted, or had ever had the nerve to kiss him first. Or that she knew how it felt when those strong, hairy arms tightened around her body as if she was the thing anchoring him to earth.

His head swiveled as if he'd heard a sound.

She could have sworn his breath stopped when he saw her. He was utterly still.

He rose slowly to his feet.

The only movement for the next few moments was the curtain at the window, languidly lifting in a breeze.

"Good afternoon, Keating," he said politely, finally.

"Good afternoon, Lord Kirke." Ridiculously, she curtsied reflexively.

There was a silence.

"Forgive my . . ." He gestured vaguely to his torso, apparently meaning his current somewhat ungentlemanly disarray.

"Oh! No need." She cleared her throat. "Forgive *me* for intruding. I just . . . I wanted to . . ." She stopped. "That is, I was going to . . ."

He waited with maddeningly inscrutable patience.

"Have I done something wrong?" she blurted.

At once, wariness screened his features. "Have you? Your sleeves today strike me as impeccable."

She remained mute because she hadn't known she would dare even blurt that question. She was unnerved, and embarrassed. It seemed to have emerged of its own volition.

His expression softened.

He briefly passed a hand over his eyes. Then brought it down forcefully, and sighed.

"No. I do not think you have done anything wrong," he said quietly.

He didn't pretend he didn't know to what she was referring.

Neither of them moved.

A moment later, very carefully very quietly, he asked, "Do you think that you have?"

She shook her head slowly.

She cleared her throat. "I'd . . . hoped that . . . despite . . . well, I hoped that we could still be friends." Her face was so warm now she could feel her eyes burning.

His eyebrows lifted in surprise. "Are we not?"

She was mute again, her stomach churning. This kindness—this *politeness*—felt well-nigh unendurable. She found, once more, she couldn't reply.

"Of course we are friends, Keating. My apologies if it seems to you that I've been preoccupied and not . . . friendly." He gave the word a hint of an ironic frisson. Teasing her a little, quoting from one of their earlier conversations. "My schedule is very full."

"I understand. It's just . . . you've never been so polite. It's awful. You're not yourself at all."

She felt once more like a complete cake.

She could see him struggling to maintain the detachment. His mouth finally curled up a little. "Well, that's an indictment."

"It just . . . it just feels as though you are avoiding me. And I don't think you've lied to me yet." She said it in a rush.

He froze warily. There was a scary little swift flare of impatience in his eyes.

How she hated the entreaty in her voice. She sounded like a child and she patently was not.

And yet, compared to him, and in his eyes, and compared to all the sophisticated women of the ton, no doubt she was.

She ought to leave him alone. She should leave it be.

He dropped his chin to his chest for a moment.

Then she watched his shoulders set as though he'd made some kind of decision.

He looked up and held her gaze fast. His voice was low and even. "What do you think will happen if we're alone together for any length of time? You're intelligent. And I know you won't lie to me, either. What is it you truly want? Be honest with yourself. And answer me truthfully."

She couldn't bring herself to say it out loud, but she was certain he read the answer in her face.

"Precisely," he said, as if her silence said it all. "It simply cannot happen again. Surely you understand this. I'm afraid we can't put this particular genie back in the lamp, Keating. This is for the best. It's for your own safety as well as mine. I think you know this. I'm sorry, but it's the truth."

She wished she could see a way in which it was not the truth. Because it meant she would lose his friendship. The notion of this caused a knot of panic in her stomach.

The day became dimmer somehow.

"It's . . ." She swallowed. "The season is . . . well, it's very lively now. I'm having a lovely time, for the most part. I've met many new people. But it's . . . it's somehow lonelier without you."

A soft surge of enormous emotion rushed his features again before he caught himself.

He was silent for a moment longer. The sun through the window slashed him in two, making his eyes brilliant, making the threads of silver glint in his hair, leaving the rest of him in shadow.

"Keating . . ." he said wearily, after a moment. "I'm an old debaucher."

"We both know you are neither of those things.

"Or at least not entirely," she added, a moment later.

He was unable to help himself: The corner of his mouth lifted. Rueful, ironically proud of her. Amused.

"And I'm a rake," he continued evenly, relentlessly.

"You say that as though it's an immutable quality, like being Welsh. What does it even mean? I've yet to witness you raking."

A long wordless moment later, something like resolve settled over his features.

There was a sort of weary finality to his expression that made the back of her neck tingle with portent that frightened her.

"Do you know how I came to be staying here at The Grand Palace on the Thames?"

She shook her head slowly.

"My mistress, in a fit of pique, threw a lit lamp at me while I lay in bed. It knocked over a brandy snifter, which helped ignite the counterpane and burned my town house part of the way down. I've builders crawling about the place now."

She felt as though a lamp had been hurled at her. Every single one of those words landed on her skin like fire. Her mind retreated from the shock, momentarily blank.

He waited with what seemed to her to be maddening patience after he'd said this extraordinary thing, which could not be unsaid or ever again unknown.

A well-bred girl ought to be appalled.

Well. She'd been warned.

His face was white. He seemed to be waiting, sto-ically, for a verdict, some reaction or rejection from her, like a man being fitted for a noose.

But instantly she thought of him in bed, naked.

And just like that, her breath came ever so slightly shorter, and her skin took up that sort of silent keen-ing. The air against it suddenly unbearably sensual.

She understood that this need lately uncovered in her was something that men addressed matter-of-factly, which was a luxury that women simply didn't have. She was neither stupid nor naive.

And yet, for her, it seemed tied to one man only. Never, never had she felt anything like this near any other man.

And so she stood, mutely entangled in an en-tirely inappropriate web of lust and black jealousy.

He waited.

"Is she still your mistress?" Her voice was hoarse.

"Absolutely not. I have it on decent authority that she fled across the Channel after assaulting me. And no, Keating. On my grave I swear that I would never have touched you if I was still involved with another woman."

None of this was comfortable to hear—that these circumstances were so commonplace in his world that he had developed a sort of code of be-havior for it. She didn't know whether it was hope-lessly sophisticated or debauched or neither. She didn't know whether she regretted losing her in-nocence—or was it ignorance? It had seemed like shelter. But perhaps it never had been.

"I shouldn't have touched you." His voice was a shred now.

She heard the apology and regret in it. Very nearly anguish.

"But why did . . . why did she throw . . ."

"She wanted two things from me that I was at that moment both unable and unwilling to provide. An emerald necklace, and my undivided attention. You would be safe in assuming it wasn't the first time she had a fit of pique." A ghost of an ironic smile here. "All in all, I don't believe she liked me very much."

"Perhaps that was why you found the arrangement comfortable," she said shortly.

He went still. A quick flame of anger flashed in his eyes, then wary respect settled in.

He didn't laugh. Nor did he have anything to say in response.

A silence stretched.

"I met her at a salon," he said quietly. "She eventually made a suggestion regarding a business arrangement which I found amenable at the time, and we came to an agreement. Which lasted for less than a year. I'm nearly thirty-six years old. She was not my first mistress. I find it excruciating to say these things aloud or to burden you with this information, but before you spend another moment of your life missing my company, you ought to better understand who I am."

He said all of this so evenly. Even as she saw the tension at the corners of his mouth. The tautness of his skin across his cheekbones.

Such formal, even-toned words to describe an arrangement in which he paid someone to be available for sex.

Her stomach roiled. This was not a conversation a well-bred young girl would ever have, in any other circumstance.

Her father would be horrified.

And she knew she ought to be more horrified, too. But a thousand feelings swarmed her, like stinging gnats, and one of the strongest of them was fascination. But it was too much, all at once.

"But is it who you are?" she ventured slowly. "Or is it simply something you've done?" Her voice was shaking.

It was both a serious question and a suggestion. She wanted to understand.

He took this in, and something like surprise, or respect, flickered in his eyes.

But then that resolve moved into his expression again.

He was determined to build a wall, and she could not fight against it.

"I know myself. I possess a healthy portion of self-contempt—that is, an accurate amount, the amount I deserve, as you might say. I am aware of my strengths and my considerable flaws and I have abided with them comfortably for nigh on four decades. I know what I do and do not want from life. But if I were to contribute to your ruin, Keating, if I were to prevent you somehow from having the future you want and deserve by making love to you, I honestly do not think I could live with myself. I think it would destroy me."

The words were raw and flatly, quietly, unequivocally delivered.

They nearly pressed the breath from her. Her eyes stung.

It seemed an admission of some enormity. She didn't quite understand why. But simmering about the hard, crisp edges of his words was something like desperation.

Almost a plea.

She could and should walk away now. She should leave it be. It was the sane thing to do. He was doing the right thing to try to brick the two of them apart from each other with words.

But she had left sanity behind in that carriage, when she had moaned pleasure against his lips.

"But you think about it." Her voice had gone hoarse. "Making love to me."

He gave a short unamused laugh and closed his eyes briefly.

When he opened them again, they were hunted. "I have secured my place in hell because it's all I think about, Keating."

It knocked the breath from her.

They stood in fraught silence.

"If you'll excuse me?" he said politely. Finally. Tersely.

She stood, frozen, as he got into his coat, methodically stacked his books, and gathered his papers.

He swept past her out of the room.

AND SHE WAITED, breathing in and out for the count of twenty, for him to leave, to be clear of the annex. Before she took herself swiftly back to her room. She'd forgotten the book she came for.

She lowered herself to the bed and pressed her fists against her hot cheeks and then against her chest, because that was where the emotion, the great hot, raging snarl of it, had lodged and now threatened to split her apart.

A mistress. How *cosmopolitan*.

She wondered if the whole of the ton knew.

It seemed as though Lady Wisterberg's gossip had been correct.

No wonder he thought of her as clover. Simple. Innocent. Ignorant.

Well, she wasn't any of that any longer, she supposed.

He shouldn't have told me, she thought angrily. He should have lied. He should have gone on being polite and remote. She'd liked her illusions and her ignorance. She'd pressed for truth, because she'd been simple enough to think that the truth was preferable at all times. Even the hard truths, about her father's failing heart, or her mother's illness and eventual death, were easier to take on; they were facts of existence and no humans were untouched by those.

She wasn't prepared to entertain these sorts of moral complexities. Or to so very much miss someone she had known for such a short time—someone who was apparently, as Lady Wisterberg had described, scandalous by the metric of polite society. Even as he was welcome into ballrooms and society, by virtue of being a lord and a politician, and, of course, so absurdly handsome.

So he'd been doing her a charity by keeping his distance.

But how was it that someone who could "ruin" her could also make her life feel immeasurably more vivid? How was it that he stood out from the rest of the world in a sort of stark relief? How was it that she paradoxically felt a strange sort of peace when she stood near him, despite the turmoil he inspired?

Did the admirable things he did offset the scandalous ones, or did one somehow support the other?

And most importantly: he shouldn't have told her that making love to her was all he thought about.

She felt—she *knew*—he'd done that deliberately.

Because when she ought to be dancing with bright-eyed boys who hadn't yet gotten around to making sexual business arrangements with women they'd met in salons, it was all she was going to be thinking about.

And no doubt he knew it.

The bastard.

Yes, she knew that word.

She wondered what she would do with the power this had conferred upon her.

Chapter Sixteen

❧❧❧

"**W**ELL, GOOD evening, you old Charred Ruins you. Ha ha!" Lord Coopersmith, a bluff and hearty Whig, handed Kirke a brandy as he maneuvered his way into the library.

"Very amusing." Kirke sardonically raised the glass to him.

It seemed everyone had read the gossip this morning:

> *Word in the Commons is that the reason Lord K's recent speech was significantly less fiery than usual was because his most recent affair de coeur went up in flames–literally. At this rate, Lord K's entire career will be in charred ruins by the time the next election rolls around– because the on-dit is that another young lady is already distracting him.*

All in all, quite a noxious little paragraph from start to finish, and a little closer to the bone than such items usually were. Every bloody word of it incensed him. The bit about the speech bothered him because, well—he agreed with it. And the implication that he might be distracted by another woman set his teeth on edge. It might have just been pointless blathering, and he hadn't gone near Keating in public since he'd danced with her, but he was prepared to draw blood if anyone dared insinuate anything about her directly. No one at all had mentioned her to his face since he'd danced with her. He knew better than to believe it was because everyone had forgotten.

And now it seemed clear that Marie-Claude had either *not* crossed the Channel as previously reported—or had managed to foment mischief before she did. How else would a connection be made between her and the fire at his house? The only person he'd told was Keating.

It occurred to him with an unwelcome jolt that she might be the only person he currently trusted as much as he trusted his man of affairs.

"An *affair de coeur* and another one in the wings." Farquar, who was standing in the opposite corner, drawled and shook his head to and fro wonderingly. "How *do* you do it, Kirke?"

"How do I do it? If your father didn't have the talk with you when you were a lad, Farkie, I fear I'm a bit too bashful to explain it to you. Does anyone here want to enlighten Farquar, and put his poor wife out of her misery?"

Much ribald laughter here and rude suggestions ensued. "Ask your wife, Farkie! She'll show you wear to put it!"

Farquar reddened. But curiously, his gaze didn't waver.

"I meant how do you have time to do your job, Kirke?" Farkie said evenly. "Seems like your constituents might start worrying about it."

Kirke thoughtfully regarded Farquar through the smoke in the library.

He seemed to be . . . gloating.

Suspicion prickled the back of his neck.

He sighed. "Oh very well. I'll tell you," he said mildly. He casually maneuvered through the crowd to Farquar, who tracked him the whole of the way, wearing a smug little smile.

He stopped mere inches from the man. And for the benefit of anyone who might be watching, he lightly, conciliatorily tapped his brandy glass against Farquar's and murmured, "How much did you pay Marie-Claude for information about me, Farkie?"

Farquar went rigid with shock.

His eyes darted back and forth like a trapped mouse between a cat's paws.

Kirke didn't so much as twitch a muscle. But he could feel a near transcendent fury spill into his veins.

Because this explained everything, including how Farkie had gotten any information about so-called by-blows. Marie-Claude must have somehow read his letter from Anna while he was sleeping.

Farquar turned away and swallowed.

"I guess an equally important question would be how your wife would feel about seeing your name in the gossip columns in connection with your new mistress," Kirke mused between clenched teeth.

Farkie blanched and his head whipped toward him. "You wouldn't—Marie-Claude is not—she won't—"

"Oh, *I* see how it is," he said with a slow, sympathetic little smile. "Marie-Claude might be greedy and perfidious, but she always did have excellent taste in men. A word from the wiser: once you give her something, she'll never stop asking for more."

He leaned in and murmured, "And I *know* you're fond of your wife, Farkie, so you'll want to keep the gossip sheets out of her hands from now on. I sell more newspapers than you do by merely existing, and I will. *Not*. Let. This. Go."

He backed away, and raised his voice a little. "And don't attempt to say 'perfidious' when you're drunk." He winked, and Farquar flinched as though hot water had been flicked in his face.

"Have you ever shot a man?"

As fate would have it, both Catherine and Lord Vaughn had been invited to Lord and Lady Coopersmith's private assembly. And if this question, asked as they were rotating in a waltz, surprised young Lord St. John Vaughn, it scarcely merited an eyebrow twitch. "I haven't. It strikes me as the sort of thing one can avoid if one really tries."

This was so dryly put that Catherine smiled. "I suppose if you were a soldier, you wouldn't be given much of a choice," she challenged.

"I suppose not. I'm aware that I'm exceedingly privileged."

It was the matter-of-fact tone with which he'd said it: it wasn't a brag—and she had indeed heard that sort of brag from more than one young man over the course of the past week, as several had taken pains to assure her that they were so wealthy and comfortable they would never be required to do anything so gauche as go to war.

She officially liked him. His wit was dry and he didn't natter on about himself. He didn't, in fact, natter at all. He had a tendency to attempt to smolder, which she was not immune to. She appreciated the effort. His features were sculpted and even, and his bottom lip had just enough sensual droop to be interesting. His hair was dark, his eyes blue. And he seemed a bit bemused by her. "I'm not terribly intriguing," she was wickedly tempted to tell him. "I just seem different because I'm from the *country*. That's what you're sensing."

"What if someone challenged you to a duel?" she pressed.

"That also seems like something one can avoid."

"People are unpredictable, Lord Vaughn. You never know when someone might take offense at something that seems perfectly harmless. Perhaps you might say, this cheese is delicious and they might reply, no, it isn't, sir. How dare you insult my taste. My seconds will call upon yours."

He listened to this madness, eyes alight with amusement.

She had quite uncharacteristically drunk nearly three cups of ratafia, which she suspected had been enhanced with something stronger. The waltz was making her dizzy, and not in a good way.

Lord Vaughn hadn't seemed to notice that she was foxed, thankfully.

"Then I would just apologize for offending him," he said simply. "Because I don't want anyone to shoot at me."

This was difficult to argue with, and yet seemed all wrong.

"Why the questions about shooting? Are you feeling in need of defense, Miss Keating?"

"Well, I do like to be prepared should my honor be besmirched."

"I see. Well, to reassure you, I'm a fair shot. However, I'm learning to play the violincello, and some men might prefer to die than hear me play, so I suppose I might retaliate that way."

She laughed. "Are you indeed? Can you play any recognizable tunes? I know a jolly one with clapping in it."

She was at once sorry she'd mentioned it. Because when she did, Kirke thundered into her mind as vividly and swiftly as the first night she'd seen him, when she'd summoned him by singing that song at the top of her lungs.

Her legs suddenly felt leaden.

Lord Vaughn eyed her as though he wasn't certain whether she was jesting. "Do you play the pianoforte, Miss Keating?"

"Well, yes. I do. I am not Mozart, but I can acquit myself passably well."

"I am attending a house party in Richmond a fortnight hence and I will have an invitation sent to you care of Lady Wisterberg, if you will agree to attempt a duet with me. I would be so pleased if you could join us."

Well!

Lady Wisterberg might very well need smelling salts when she told her this little bit of news.

Yet Lord Vaughn had not yet responded to his invitation to Lady Wisterberg's party. Perhaps he was busy that evening. Perhaps he was undecided.

Her newly invigorated chaperone had, in fact, been full of information about Lord Vaughn earlier.

"Lord Vaughn's parents would prefer him to marry someone with a title," Lady Wisterberg had told her frankly in the carriage on the way to the ball. "His sister, Lady Lillias, who was quite the belle of the ton at one time, apparently married an

American—an American! With no title!—and hied off to the wilds of New York. They are all putting a brave face on it and claim that they're pleased about it and that he's a very fine fellow. But it suggests to me that *should* his son fall madly in love with an untitled girl who has only a very modest dowry, the earl *might* be amenable to a match. They are a very good family. In other words, Lord Vaughn is not a waste of your time, and he has asked you to dance twice now. I should be my most charming self, if I were you."

Catherine wasn't certain what her most charming self was. Did Lady Wisterberg perhaps think she was keeping something in reserve? And she didn't love the mention of her "very modest dowry" any more than she loved the mention of her old dresses.

She couldn't wait until the ton saw her in that blue gown at the Shillingford ball—mere days away now.

"Although, granted, the on-dit is that Lord Vaughn has shown no inclination to marry at all," Lady Wisterberg had concluded, somewhat reluctantly. "See if you can change his mind."

Catherine was amused at the notion of changing any man's mind about anything.

She knew St. John Vaughn had never shot anyone—and he was right in that it did indeed, upon first consideration, seem avoidable for someone who wasn't a soldier—because he'd never been challenged. And he'd never been challenged because he'd never sought challenge, unless the violincello counted. Or put himself in the way of challenge. Would never, ever need to do it. And that he was so well-bred, so free of ragged edges or unexpected angles, that he'd likely maneuver his way out of a duel as easily as a china cup would slide out of wet hands. He would just apologize, and his honor wouldn't twinge and his reputation would suffer no nicks. And while he was very attractive, which came with its own perils and lots of attention, he was male and an heir and would likely suffer few consequences even if his name were to appear in the gossip pages.

His point of view was reasonable and seemed as peaceful to her as a walk down a country lane.

And didn't she enjoy country lanes?

There were more things she'd like to know about him.

But unlike "Have you ever shot a man?" she could hardly ask Lord Vaughn, "Have you ever traced a circle around a woman's nipple with your thumb?"

Unfortunately, she had liked that very much.

Lord Vaughn was a magnificent catch from any standpoint—Lord Kirke had even endorsed him, she thought with some bitter irony—and if she were to capture his affections, let alone a proposal, her father would probably consider it the gift of a lifetime. He would ultimately die a happy man, knowing she wouldn't be alone. Knowing that her life would be comfortable and safe and even luxurious.

She so very much wanted to be able to give her father this kind of peace of mind before she lost him.

Suddenly her throat was tight.

Mere days ago, if a soothsayer of some sort had revealed her destiny was to go to London and become some sort of lady, perhaps a countess, she would have been ecstatic. Well, and also a bit nervous. There wasn't much about being a doctor's daughter that prepared one for being a countess, but if she could do things like manage a household budget and help sew the tip of a man's finger back on, she was confident she could adapt.

Go to London and make all the young men fall in love with you, her father had said.

But she was afraid now. The things she thought she knew about love were warring with things she had never anticipated.

Like how it felt when a man drew trembling fingers along her throat as though he scarcely believed he had the right to touch her. As though, for that moment in time, she was the precious, beating heart of his universe.

Or a man's fleeting expression of pain when he'd come upon in a moment of despair, her face in her palms. As if her distress was his distress.

The ways he said her name: urgently, when he'd found her in distress.

And then with wonder . . . and surrender . . . against her lips in the carriage.

The way he'd gathered her up and laid his coat across her shoulders.

He not only wanted her.

He *cared*.

Didn't he?

Unlike Lord Vaughn, Lord Kirke had been willing to lay down his life for his beliefs in a duel.

He was willing to offend, he was willing to provoke, he was willing to stand up before the world and do it day after day even as the odds were against him. He was *made* of passion.

She had never anticipated how much her whole being craved it.

She might never have known if she hadn't met him, and this unnerved her, too.

But he had held her at a distance from the very

first, she was realizing. It was one of the reasons he called her by her last name only.

While she could indeed prepare a household budget, she could not reconcile all of these things in her mind: The lust and the tenderness. His fierceness and his flashes of vulnerability. Her exhilarating fear of him, and her desire to protect him, and the distance he was imposing, and all of the rumors that hovered about him. His intimidating worldliness that never devolved into condescension. The way he listened—with all of his being.

She didn't know that one person could make the rest of the world seem flat and false by comparison, like so much stage dressing. Perhaps she could put it all down to her own inexperience. Perhaps it meant little.

She had not anticipated coming to London for suffering.

Probably everyone looking at her tonight—and people did indeed seem to be looking at her a good deal, even though her goldenrod-colored silk dress was more than two years old—would think: *That young lady hasn't a care in the world! Look at her dancing with the heir to an earl! Her future is bright and assured.*

"I should love to go to your party," she told Lord Vaughn, who remained gratifyingly ignorant that her thoughts were spinning like the waltz. "Thank you so much for the invitation. I look forward to our duet."

He smiled at her with his beautiful teeth.

ON THE SECOND floor of the Coopersmith town house, near an arrangement of large green plants arrayed next to French doors, Kirke smoked and thought in relative quiet. Perverse man that he was, his mood had lightened just a little now that he knew who his enemy was, because Farkie simply wasn't very bright. He solved problems by throwing money at them.

The prospect of a fight or a problem to solve generally stirred his blood. The need to develop a strategy of any sort generally filled him with zeal. But he was still angry and disappointed with himself at a time when he felt he was fraying at the edges.

Seared on his memory was Keating's stunned, white face when he'd told her two days ago about his mistress and his house fire. He could not keep his mind from visiting this scene again and again. He still wasn't certain whether he'd told her more for her own good or his. But it was both.

It was just that he seemed unable to be anything other than baldly honest with her. She had the bravery born of innocence—she hadn't learned circumspection, or how to be afraid of answers to the questions she was asking—but she also had a fundamental, quiet integrity that was essentially the same as courage. He thought she could probably withstand anything.

And God. He hadn't realized how unnervingly liberating it was to speak to someone that way.

Keating had got hold of some thread of his being, and had walked away with it, and now, somehow, he had the sense that he was unraveling. He had no idea who or what would be left when this was done.

He'd lit a cheroot to have something to do, because she wasn't here. He had seen her dancing with Lord Vaughn as he went up the stairs.

They'd made a beautiful couple.

He closed his eyes, as if they were in front of him right now.

He aimed a stream of smoke at the ceiling and noticed, uneasily, how lonely it was to be alone now, when before it had only been a relief.

ON HIS WAY back to the ballroom, he veered past the refreshments table, aiming to join a few MPs over in the corner, when a splash of bold yellow color out of the corner of his eye stopped him short near an arrangement of ferns. His heart kicked.

But Keating wasn't hiding, thankfully; her expression was bright and alert, as though she was expecting someone to collect her for the next dance.

Despite himself, he was fiercely pleased that she seemed happy.

Before he could move swiftly on, she turned around as surely as though he'd tapped her on the shoulder.

And her face illuminated like a lamp.

"Lord Kirke! You're here! I didn't know you'd be here, too!" She sounded almost giddy.

He eyed her cautiously, as this was not the sort of reception he'd been expecting after their last conversation.

"Good evening, Keating," he said politely.

"I'm just waiting for Mr. . . ." She glanced at her dance card. "Barret. Mr. Barret and I will be dancing!"

He frowned faintly. If he was not mistaken, Keating was *un peu* foxed.

She beamed back at him. She *was* clutching a cup of ratafia.

"Excellent. Mr. Barret is a fine fellow. You're vivid tonight in that flattering shade of goldenrod." He knew he couldn't risk lingering here to speak to her.

"Golden*rrrro*d," she repeated, rolling her "r" extravagantly in a perfect imitation of his Welsh accent.

He blinked, taken aback.

"I wish my name was Rowena, or Rebecca," she said wistfully.

"How much ratafia have you had?"

"I wish my name was Ratafia," she replied, mournfully.

He stifled a laugh. "Quite a lot, apparently."

"Because your 'r's' are so pretty," she said, again wistfully. "They roll like the hills. Rrrrrollll like the hillllls."

"I'll just take that, shall I?" He divested her of her cup.

Whereupon she went very serious. "Say my name."

"Keating," he indulged.

"My name is Catherine."

"I recall."

"I know why you won't say my name."

And just like that he was rigidly wary. How about that. Drunk Keating was also dangerous.

Because an epiphany arrived like a slap: he suddenly realized why he wouldn't say it, too.

Damn her and her unnerving astuteness all cunningly disguised in beautiful softness.

He felt cornered.

"Say it now," she suggested softly. Insistently.

How ridiculous would it be if he refused? Or blustered and obfuscated? He was capable of arguing nearly anyone into the ground. He knew he wouldn't do it to her, however. He just hadn't it in him to lie to her.

After a moment he said, "Catherine."

He felt at once raw and exposed. Because they both heard it: the softness, bordering on shyness. It was how the word would sound if he murmured it to her while she was one pillow over. The way he would speak to a woman he knew intimately, and cared for, and desired.

Stripped of glibness or caution or formality. Purely himself.

He knew he would never be able to say it another way.

The casual, chummy "Keating" was a sort of wall he'd instinctively erected between them from the very first.

As if there had ever been any safety behind it for him.

She would have been entitled to do it, but she didn't raise her eyebrows.

But her expression was complicated: hurt and sympathetic, sorrowful and confused.

He felt as though his chest might crack in two. It ached from a sort of stifled, resentful fury at being stripped bare in a ballroom.

Finally, she said, "Horse Chestnut?" As she would turn to him and say, "Dominic?"

Drunk Keating was turning out to be one of his favorite things in the world. Also the most terrifying.

"Yes?" he said tersely.

"People fight when they're afraid, is that not so? Isn't that what you said?"

"That sounds like me."

"But . . . you fight all the time." She said it as though it had only just occurred to her.

He was speechless.

"What would happen if you didn't fight everything?" It sounded like a serious question.

He stared at her. He could not think of a single thing to say.

But she moved away from him swiftly when she saw her dancing partner heading toward her.

She put on a bright smile for the young man.

Kirke remained frozen for a time, for a moment, unseeing.

And for the next few minutes, out of the corner of his eye, everywhere in the ballroom, it seemed, was goldenrod. Like the sun always rising on the periphery of his vision.

Chapter Seventeen

cᴗᴗᴗᴗᴗ

Bᴇɴ Pɪᴋᴇ had just returned from a very satisfying errand involving haggling over—then purchasing for much lower than the original price—supplies he was going to use to repair a portion of the roof over the annex. He was quite proud of himself. From the moment he'd begun working at The Grand Palace on the Thames, Mrs. Hardy and Mrs. Durand had trusted his judgment and made him feel like an essential contributor to the happiness and comfort of everyone who lived there. Rather than like, for instance, furniture one could order around, which was how his erstwhile, dastardly employer the Earl of Brundage had treated his servants.

He *loved* his job at The Grand Palace on the Thames.

But every rose had its thorn.

He was on his way to the top of the stairs through the foyer to report the good news to Mrs. Durand and Mrs. Hardy, when he paused at the sight of the bane of his existence in the sitting room.

Dot appeared to be, of all things, caressing a lamp.

He watched, mystified, as she pawed at it.

Once.

Twice.

Three times.

Much the way one would stroke a cat.

Then she took a large step backward and stared

at it, hands held to her mouth in apparent excited expectation.

A few seconds later, she stepped forward and did the whole thing all over again.

What the *devil* . . . ?

Her face a picture of disappointment, she moved over to another lamp.

This time she tried a sort of twisting stroke that made the back of his neck feel uncomfortably hot.

She took a large step backward and stared at the lamp again, her posture tense with anticipation.

"What are you doing, Dot?"

She shot nearly straight up in the air and spun around. He watched with fascination as her face took on the exact shade of a tomato.

"Nothing important," she said. After a long silent moment during which she was clearly deciding how to reply.

"You were rubbing lamps," he noted, wickedly.

"If you could see what I was doing, why did you ask?"

"That's a fair question. I'll be more specific. Why were you rubbing the lamps?"

She studied him for a long, speculative time. "I will tell you, if you promise not to laugh."

"I promise." He might laugh later, alone in his room.

"In the sitting room at night, we're reading a book about a genie who emerges from a lamp when you rub it. He's a magic being. And he offers you wishes when he appears."

He took this in.

"I see. You thought perhaps genies lived in our lamps?"

"Wouldn't it be foolish not to find out if they do?"

He stared at her. He honestly had no idea how

to reply to that. He could not quite bring himself to say yes.

She had the most remarkable eyes, Dot. Sometimes they seemed almost vacant to him, other times all-seeing, as though she was privy to realms he couldn't possibly imagine. They were perfectly round, like saucers, and the palest blue. He found her absolutely, teeth-grindingly frustrating, and he wasn't even certain he liked her, yet she had begun to fascinate him almost relentlessly. The other maids seemed more sensible, if infinitely gigglier. But they were somehow far less interesting, too.

He was solid and shrewd and literal. He felt even more solid and shrewd and literal around Dot. He sensed she saw the world more vividly, more richly, than he ever could. And because he was proud and intelligent, he had begun to believe the way she experienced things was something he could never quite comprehend. This had begun to get under his skin.

"Well, it's brave of you to want to conjure a genie. But then again, you weren't afraid of ghosts, either, when you knocked me right down in the kitchen."

"Thank you. I suppose I might be a little brave. Although that is not a moment I am proud of, Mr. Pike, so perhaps you will consider not mentioning it so often," she said with great dignity.

He smiled at this. "Fair enough. Forgive me. It's just that it's one of the more memorable moments of my life so far."

This made her smile. She had two dimples, and her cheeks made charming little apples when she smiled.

"Have you ever considered," he ventured hesitantly, "that one of the main reasons I want to open the door at night is to keep you safe from harm? As well as everyone else?"

Her eyes flared.

"Oh," she breathed, thoughtfully. She paused. "I see." She cleared her throat. "Thank you."

He nodded once, shortly. Pressed his lips together. They regarded each other from across the foyer.

"What would you wish for, Dot, if you did find a genie?" he asked softly. It suddenly seemed important to know.

She tipped her head and studied him somberly. If he'd had a wish right now, he would have used it to learn what was going on behind those eyes.

"I'd wish . . . that The Grand Palace on the Thames had two front doors. So you could open one, and I could open the other."

He stared at her. "Oh, for *God's*—"

His head went back on a gusty sigh, and he spun on his heel away from her mischievous little smile to go to report to the infinitely more sensible Mrs. Hardy and Mrs. Durand.

CATHERINE SLOWLY ROTATED beneath the chandelier at The Grand Palace on the Thames, the crystals sprinkling tiny rainbows over her like a blessing while Mrs. Hardy, Mrs. Durand, and Mrs. Pariseau stood around her, hands clasped beneath their chins in admiration.

"You are just beautiful, my dear," Mrs. Pariseau assured her. "The dress was *meant* for you."

"You look like a princess!" Angelique exclaimed.

"A crown would be redundant," Delilah agreed.

But not one of those women envied Catherine, because they had each been in her place before. They didn't miss balls. They didn't miss husband hunting. They remembered the nerves, the uncertainty, the joy, the judgment, the hopes raised and crushed. They wished her the very best of luck from the bottom of their womanly hearts.

Lady Wisterberg and Lucy came to collect her, and they at last were off to the Shillingford ball.

PLUMLEY. SEACOMBE. LEFFINGWELL. Marbrooke. Vaughn. Holroyd. Gunston. Vaughn again.

Catherine had surrendered her dance card to Lady Wisterberg, who had examined it like a professor reviewing a pupil's exam, her eyes glinting.

"Vaughn twice! That young man is charmed," she declared. "*And* he at last responded to our invitation. He'll be attending our party! With his *parents*."

Catherine's heart gave a jump.

Privately, Catherine thought the young man—Lord Vaughn—sensed her ambivalence and found her a safe dancing partner. Like a cat who excels at finding the one person in the room who doesn't want a cat in their lap.

Or perhaps he had a sixth sense for detecting which females knew what it was like to have a man's clothed erection pressed against them in the dark of a carriage.

Tonight when footmen holding aloft lit torches led Catherine and Lucy and Lady Wisterberg into the Shillingford mansion on Grosvenor Square—a vast white marble edifice, featuring enormous columns and gilt and crystal glinting everywhere in the corners of her eyes—Catherine decided: *I would indeed enjoy this, if this was part of my regular life. I think I might take to being a countess. I could throw fancy parties, and insist all the ladies wear dresses that were two years old or older. Ha!*

If she nurtured this thought, really savored it, she could convince herself it was what she wanted. It was how habits were formed, after all.

And then perhaps it would, in fact, be *all* she wanted.

Only the cream of the ton was invited to this ball, or so Lady Wisterberg assured them. Lucy and Catherine were quite pleased to be considered cream, although there seemed to be a lot of people considered cream. The place was indeed brimming. She thought she never would forget the sounds of countless dancing slippers clicking across the spreading sea of gleaming marble as they funneled into the ballroom.

She was conscious of heads turning in her wake as she moved with Lady Wisterberg and Lucy into the ballroom, and she held her head high, her heart pounding. The blue dress, the most magical thing she'd ever owned, a dress to which she did not quite feel equal, conferred upon her a special glamour, and certainly was more at home in this mansion than she was.

Magic could be dangerous in the wrong hands, as she'd learned from *The Arabian Nights' Entertainments*.

The wonder and pride in the eyes of her first dancing partner for the evening set her aglow; she began to believe that this was no different from happiness.

Kirke was gathered with a clutch of MPs near an arrangement of Grecianesque statuary—marble blokes and maidens wearing togas and wreaths—on the periphery of the Shillingford ballroom. He'd always viewed this event as the sort of halfway point in the season; soon the social whirl would end and Parliament would adjourn and he'd move out of The Grand Palace on the Thames and back into his home.

"Looking forward to your usual rousing speech to

send Parliament out on an inspiring note, Kirke," Shillingford said. "I know your voters will count on it."

"Do you think it ought to be something like my Freedom Speech?" Kirke asked, expressionlessly.

"Yes!" Shillingford enthused with glee, as if Kirke had read his mind.

He hadn't yet written a damned word worth speaking aloud in front of a crowd of hundreds. Nor had he yet heard from Leo.

"My son will be dancing with that pretty girl in blue tonight. Miss Keating, I believe her name is." Lord Holroyd gestured with his brandy to the dancers. "He seems quite taken with her. Or, at least he's mentioned her twice, which is the most he's ever mentioned a girl. Does anyone know anything about her family?"

Kirke didn't answer. He suddenly couldn't speak, regardless.

He watched her, mesmerized, as she moved in the figures of the dance. Smiling, radiant.

The morning of the night he'd kissed Keating, he'd had his man of affairs send a note with a certain request to Madame Marceau, who had custody of a dress for which he'd already paid.

He had tried to sort out all the reasons why he shouldn't do it, which were legion, but they collapsed beneath his primary motive.

Which was why he frankly thought he'd be willing to watch his entire house burn down for the pleasure of seeing how happy Keating was to have that dress.

DURING A LULL between dances, Catherine fanned herself and demurely sipped her lemonade. After her night at the Coopersmiths', she doubted she would ever touch ratafia again. She had awakened the following morning with a headache that felt like someone wearing heavy boots was trying to kick her eyes right out of her skull.

It seemed impossible that a ball should become a crush in a house this vast, and yet between the dancing and the hundreds of bodies, she felt as though she was coated in a sheen of perspiration. She'd wanted a moment to chat with Lucy alone to giddily compare dancing partners, but unfortunately, Miss Seaver and Lady Hackworth had drifted over to join them.

"We're *so* looking forward to Lady Wisterberg's party in honor of you and Miss Morrow, Miss Keating. I understand everyone in London who matters will be there."

Good try, Miss Seaver, Catherine thought. She was too wise to fall into that particular little trap. "I'm honored and flattered that so many people are looking forward to joining us! We're going to have a fine little orchestra and other entertainments." She was tempted to add, "*And* we'll be singing a song with a clap in it instead of 'arse'!"

Regardless, she was increasingly excited about the party and she wondered if she returned to Madame Marceau if another beautiful dress wouldn't magically appear for the occasion.

"I've never seen so many pretty dresses as I have this evening," Catherine said to them.

"Indeed. Your dress, Miss Keating, is . . . splendid." It sounded as though it pained Miss Seaver to admit this. As if she hadn't thought Catherine capable of finally wearing something stylish. "It must have cost a fortune." She added this last bit lightly, but also a trifle suspiciously.

"Oh no. Not at all. It was after a fashion a gift," Catherine said airily.

Lady Hackworth's fan ceased moving. She fixed her eyes on Catherine, and a confusing, fleeting succession of expressions—wonderment and envy and astonishment—flickered across her features swiftly before—oddly—a sort of respect settled in.

Though her eyebrows remained knit.

"Interestingly, Miss Keating . . ." she said hesitantly. "I had my eye on that precise bolt of blue shot silk at the import shop near Fleet Street. But when I asked to purchase it, the clerk informed me it was . . . ah, already spoken for."

She stared piercingly into Catherine's eyes. As if she could read her thoughts.

How very peculiar. Catherine was nervous. She did *not* want to learn the provenance of her magical dress, lest it tarnish her pleasure. And she'd lost patience with Lady Hackworth's machinations.

"This color would look beautiful with your eyes," Catherine told her magnanimously, on the theory that she was the sort who could be distracted by a compliment.

Lady Hackworth merely looked more puzzled. Suddenly she turned her head and called over her shoulder, "Lady Pilcher. Here is the young lady you said you were curious to meet."

Catherine's heart jolted. Lucy had pointed out Lady Pilcher to her previously. She was a countess, and she was what people meant when they used the word "stunning." Both of these things made Catherine feel intensely shy. It seemed quite unreal that such a woman would specifically want to meet her.

Lady Pilcher drifted over gracefully. Her shiny, seal-dark hair was artfully curled and loosely piled atop her head, which was perched atop a swan-like neck, which was encircled with diamonds. *Her* dress was a confection of floating golden gauze and spangles and embroidery. More of what must be diamonds sparkled in her headpiece.

Catherine curtsied. "An honor to meet you, Lady Pilcher."

Breathlessly, she wondered if one day she would stand in a ballroom in front of another young woman from a small country town, who would address her as Lady Vaughn and feel shy because she was a countess. The notion plucked a strange, panicky note from her heart.

"And likewise, Miss Keating." Lady Pilcher inspected Catherine while wearing a soft little smile. Her golden-brown eyes tipped up at the corners, and the way her short top lip sat above her full bottom lip made her mouth look like a pink bow. "My dear, your dress, as I'm certain you know, is magnificent. And what a charming necklace. I have so many beautiful pearls, and yet it never occurred to me to wear only one at a time."

Cat eyed her in surprise. Perhaps it was true, and the wearing of one pearl was novel to Lady Pilcher.

Her instincts told her no: for some reason, the beautiful Lady Pilcher saw her as a threat.

This was disappointing and fascinating—and then she felt an odd spike of dizzy elation. This was perhaps why the people in the ton said and did such things—it was an attempt to taste this sensation of power again and again. Perhaps Lady Wisterberg felt something similar at the game table.

"Thank you, Lady Pilcher. So kind of you to say. It was a gift from my mother for my seventeenth birthday. It was once hers."

"And how old are you now?"

Did women normally ask this question of each other? "Twenty-two."

"Twenty-two. An important age." She leaned forward, alarmingly close, close enough to kiss her on the forehead, and, to Catherine's surprise, lifted the pearl on her fingertip. This seemed outrageously bold. "So many realizations at that age."

Catherine stiffened uneasily.

"Such a charming little birthmark, too," she murmured so very softly that likely no one but the two of them could hear. "Kirke has a darling freckle about that size on his hip."

The astonishing thing was that she'd looked Catherine full in the face when she'd said it. Such was her confidence in her supremacy, and her desire to perpetuate what she hoped was cruelty, a sword plunge, that she had no compunctions about meeting her eyes.

Catherine was so awestruck by the audacity it was nearly anesthetizing.

So there was a moment of respite before the searing, suffocating pain set in and nearly engulfed her.

"It's not always easy to see it when his hips are . . . moving . . . of course," Lady Pilcher added softly.

She drifted back into the crowd and never once looked back.

Chapter Eighteen

❧

"*I* SAY . . . MY partner for the next dance seems to have gone missing. I hope she's not unwell."

Young Lord Holroyd had paused next to his father, who was still standing with Dominic in his little clutch of Parliament members.

"Is she the young lady in blue?" his father asked.

Kirke was immediately alert.

"Indeed. The one I pointed out to you. She's a very amiable girl," Holroyd said wistfully.

Kirke stared at the boy, a decade his junior. No doubt he was the sort of "friendly" Catherine would appreciate.

"Perhaps she had a bit of a feminine emergency, m'boy," his father said. "They come in a wide variety. I speak from experience."

"Shall I go in search of her, or would that seem pathetic? I hope nought is amiss."

Kirke found it an odd sensation to both envy the boy and like him for caring enough to fuss.

"If you're wandering about looking for her, she won't be able to find you," his father said, practically. "Stay with us. She'll be easy to spot if she's just gone to the withdrawing room, or what have you."

But portent prickled at the back of Kirke's neck. He thought he knew where she was. And if she was where he thought she was, something was wrong.

A FEW MINUTES later, he began to think his assumption was incorrect. He'd wandered into the garden about fifteen feet, and it was getting darker with every step. And there was no sign of her.

He might never have seen her at all if not for the moon. It was the only illumination besides the scattering of flickering torches flanking the edges of the garden path.

It was blessedly quiet, and the air was cool and almost motionless.

The spangles on her sleeves caught his eyes. She was resting her arms on the edge of the rail surrounding a little gazebo.

He was very still, contemplating whether to approach her.

And then he did, slowly, and stood beside her.

She didn't turn her head. She in fact didn't move at all.

That's how he knew she'd known already it was him.

And that something was terribly wrong.

His heart felt like a hard boot-fall in his chest. His stomach did a slow, painful revolution. Was it her father? Had her father taken a turn for the worse?

"Winded?" he asked idly, finally.

"After a fashion." Her voice was very strange. It emerged dully, after delay.

"It's a lovely garden," he said carefully.

It might be. It was dark, and it smelled green, and the air was fresh, if London air could ever be said to be fresh. It was a thing to say, at least.

He might have said, "Any garden in which you're standing is a lovely one." He would have meant it, which was why he didn't dare say it.

"I'm a bit surprised you aren't dancing," he said, almost lightly.

"I am, too. Given that I'm apparently a success." Never had words sounded so ironic. "All thanks to you, it would appear."

He decided to be direct. "What are you doing out here instead of dancing, Keating?"

"I was just looking at the stars and thinking. About crocodiles." Another of those long pauses. "And something Lady Pilcher said."

He went rigid.

Bloody.

Fucking.

Hell.

Ice slowly spread in his gut.

He knew his long silence was incriminating.

"What did she say?" He said it resignedly. He didn't want to know. But he supposed he needed to hear how bad it was.

Keating swallowed. "She . . . she noticed that I had a little birthmark here, shaped like a heart. She called it charming." She pointed to her breast. "And then she said . . ." She took a breath, as if it hurt her. "Lord Kirke has a darling freckle on his hip about that size. And that it's hard to see when"—she cleared her throat—"your hips are moving."

He couldn't speak.

For a man accustomed to blazing ever forward in life, committed to progress, there wasn't much he wouldn't do to turn back time now to the point where he'd never met Lady Pilcher, had never made love to her, so that Keating would never need to hear that. He supposed he could turn the clock back to the point where he had never kissed Keating in the dark of a carriage, but he would need some memories to carry with him to hell when he went there for semiseducing an innocent twenty-two-year-old who trusted him.

"She had no business saying anything like that to you." His words sounded quiet in his own ears. But that could have been because there was suddenly a strange, high-pitched whining sound in them.

She made an irritated, dismissive sound.

"So you and Lady Pilcher were lovers." Her voice was so flat. "Or are lovers."

Needles driven beneath his nails. Manacles clamped to his ankles. A catharine wheel, splitting his bones apart. A rainfall of boiling oil. He could think of a dozen things he'd prefer experiencing than this conversation.

He was flailing in the dark in a windstorm. Furious and ungrounded accusations from jealous mistresses he could field. He'd never had a conversation quite like this.

So he'd never learned any strategies with which to maneuver it. That left him feeling naked and alone with the truth so that was what he gave her.

"Yes, we were for a time," he said. "Five years ago. Briefly."

She turned to him. He withstood her thoughtful, searching gaze. But the light had gone out of it. He could not feel it, and it terrified him.

"Well. You were certainly correct about the crocodiles," she said dryly. Remotely.

"Do you love her?"

"That never had anything to do with the nature of our relationship."

"Of course not," she said sardonically. Almost gently. "Silly me."

"Lady Pilcher," he began carefully, his voice scraped raw, "made an ambitious marriage that seems tremendously successful on the surface but was unhappy from the first. Which is a shame, but a common enough story. She and her husband essentially live separate lives. She is a lonely person. Tonight I suppose she saw you looking . . . radiant . . ." The word was soft. He couldn't help it. "Your future hopeful . . . and probably sought to retrieve a little of her power by diminishing yours. And I'm sorrier than I can adequately say if she used my name to hurt you, or to make you feel foolish."

And it was also troubling. He'd kept his distance from Keating in public since that waltz. But crocodiles knew how to lie in wait.

"I suppose I really am a success if the barbs have progressed beyond my sleeves."

He said nothing because it was regrettably true. True and perhaps inevitable.

He felt, for a moment, that he might actually be sinking into a hole in the ground.

She said, "Does that mean the whole of the ton knows about you and—"

"No. Because it's not a thing anyone is actually proud of, myself included. Lady Pilcher is usually much more discreet. Her husband doesn't mind what he doesn't hear about. He has his own affairs."

"I suppose it's what men do," she said dully.

"No. Not all men," he said at once. His voice was somewhat frayed. "Please do not think that of all men."

"So only men like you?"

Whatever that meant. She was trying to goad him. It was working. He could feel a furious defensiveness warring with guilt, neither of which he was obliged to feel. And yet. "When confronted with a need, with the desire, and the opportunity, some will. It's not uncommon in the ton. Among men or women."

"I expect it's the very height of worldliness," she said ironically. "Quite the done thing. Unlike sleeves with mancherons."

He didn't reply.

She cleared her throat. "So was I an 'opportunity'?"

It was an attempt at insouciance, but the question was shot all through with pain. She sounded as if she genuinely wanted to know.

He knew this was the question tormenting her. This was at the core of why she was out here in the dark alone.

It made him want to cut his own throat out of self-loathing.

"No." His voice was hoarse.

"Then why . . . why did you . . . why do you . . ."

He drew in a sharp breath. "Because you're beautiful. And your body is beautiful. The way you inhabit your skin, the sway of your hips, the set of your shoulders, the way your neck flows into your collarbone. Because your eyes are sky blue and when you look at me it's like that first sunny day after weeks of rain. Because your breasts fit perfectly into my palms, and I have imagined the sound you would make when I take them into my mouth. Because I know that you want me to."

It was a measured, articulate assault of raw, tortured truth. But it was only part of the truth.

Did he mean to frighten her away? Overwhelm her into keeping a safe distance?

Or did he simply take the opportunity to tell someone, anyone, something of what he'd been feeling?

She pulled in a sharp, audible breath.

But she didn't back away.

After a moment, she brought her hand up to her cheek, as if to soothe the heat flaring there.

Or to see if she could feel what he felt when he touched her. How she felt in light of how he experienced her.

She dropped it.

He didn't ask her why she desired him.

He was somehow afraid the answer to that would be "because you're you."

And she didn't look away from him. Not once. She faced things head-on, Keating did.

He liked that so bloody much.

"Desire is an appetite." His voice was a little steadier. "And sometimes . . . for whatever reason . . . it demands appeasing in no uncertain terms. Both for people married and unmarried."

He was lying through omission. He had only recently come to understand that desire was more than that. Desire could be a gift and a curse, especially when you traced it back to its origins, and realized it was less about a body shaped like it was designed to fit against him, as though it was the missing part of him. And about a laugh, and an inner light, and a smile that could cut a man in two with its sweetness, and a presence that was somehow both peaceful and crackling.

He didn't know if he forgot himself or remembered himself when he was with her.

Her expression told him that she knew there was a good deal he was leaving out.

"Before we met, believe it or not, I had some knowledge of what desire is or can be, though I have never acted on it. I'm not a child, *Dominic*. And now

I believe there is the kind of appetite which can be appeased, as you say. And then there is a sort of . . . craving. That just . . . it just never ebbs." She paused. "Is this different?"

Holy Mother of God.

It was more of a statement than a question.

For a moment he couldn't breathe for imagining her lying awake in the throes of wanting him. Of the two of them, in the rooms stacked one atop the other, staring at their ceilings, and wanting.

Mutely, he gave his head the slightest of slow nods. Resigned.

He wouldn't have her believing she was wrong. And his ego was such—and he loathed himself for it—that he wanted her to know that what they felt was incendiary. Extraordinary. He wanted her to believe there was no one else like him.

"So by your way of thinking, we can be lovers after I'm married."

"Christ," he exhaled on a gust, as though she'd rammed a plank right into his stomach.

"I won't, you know. Have lovers when I'm married."

"Good," he said evenly, when he could speak again. "You deserve to have everything you want from a marriage. And from a husband."

"If everyone can go about breaking their vows, what is the point of making them? Isn't that what gives marriage its meaning?"

"Life is long if you're lucky," he said shortly. "And people are complicated and flawed. And even saints are not immune to temptation, Keating."

She shrugged this obviousness away irritably with one shoulder.

Finally he said wearily, "But yes. People ought to be able to do hard things. You're not wrong."

"Why did your affair with Lady Pilcher end?"

Dear God, these silences: the weight of them between every question and every answer. Her pain. His discomfort.

"Because I had it wrong." His voice was thick; it was a struggle to put into words what he'd only instinctively felt, and his own sense of self-preservation fought him mightily. She was unraveling yet another layer. "And I don't suppose I felt any moral compunctions about it, so it's not that. Think of me what you will. It was just that it was wrong for me. There are reasons outside of purely baser impulses that people will seek out that kind of . . . let's call it companionship. Something in me wanted . . . easing . . . but when I soon realized it had nothing to do with Lady Pilcher and a bed, I ended it. I should like to cease discussing this now," he said abruptly.

She was quiet.

"Do you think Lord Vaughn is an excellent kisser?"

He froze. "I beg your ever-loving pardon?"

He'd thought *he* was a fighter. She was ruthless. She came out with knives whirling in her hands and one clenched between her teeth. A menace in silk, aiming straight for his weakness.

She was his weakness.

And even though he understood her tactics, he was shocked to find himself helpless against them. He could almost taste the jealousy, like blood in his throat. He was at once filled with ferocious admiration and fury, at both himself and her.

"I'm afraid I can offer no educated opinion on the matter, as I haven't kissed Lord Vaughn." His voice was cold.

"Is he the only person in London you haven't yet kissed?"

"Have a care, Keating," he warned quietly.

She fell silent at his tone.

"Would you like a list of them?" he added. "Because it's not very long. And I warn you, I will not lie."

They stared at each other.

"No. I don't think I would enjoy hearing it." She paused. "Would you like my list?"

"Yes."

"His name was Henry Thatcher. He was eighteen years old. He kissed my cheek after an assembly when I was eighteen years old."

There was a little silence.

"Lucky, lucky man," Dominic said softly. Fervently.

She exhaled a soft sound.

They stood side by side. Flickering torchlight competed with the waning moon to light her hair.

"Do you think someone like Lord Vaughn would know about . . . this spot here?" Without looking at him, she drew her fingers lightly up the downy hairs at the nape of her neck.

He stared. Absolutely clubbed speechless.

"Why there?" his voice was hoarse.

"Because . . . when you . . ." She swallowed. "I felt it everywhere in me," she whispered. "Everywhere in my body."

When had it become too late to walk away?

Five minutes ago? Three seconds ago? The moment he'd seen her standing alone?

He only knew he now couldn't move away from her if someone put a pistol to his temple.

From his head to his feet, lava replaced the blood in his veins. It became the very air he breathed.

"Or here," she whispered.

He followed with his eyes as she drew her finger from the nape of her neck to the lobe of her ear.

"Or here."

And he stared as her hand lowered, and she traced with a finger the curve of her breast.

"Or—"

"Here?" Dominic's voice, and then his lips, and then his tongue, were in her ear.

SHE HAD STEERED the both of them into this. She was furious and hurting and exultant and weak with want.

He gently took the lobe of her ear between his teeth, as one hand looped around her waist and the other traveled along her shoulder, glided down, across her chest, past the shape of a heart that had haunted him, and slid right into her bodice to cup her bare breast.

She gasped in shock.

He traced with a fingertip her ruched nipple, while his teeth ever so lightly teased the lobe of her ear.

Bliss forked through her so violently her knees nearly buckled. A choked moan rose from her.

And then she was suddenly rotating in the semi-dark, disoriented and lust-drunk, until her back was against the ivy-clad garden wall. Behind a thickly flowering shrub, Dominic's body pinned hers. And after his lips and tongue traveled her throat, her ear, sending hot, shivering trails of pleasure through her body, he found her lips and parted them with his own and their tongues reunited, twined, and teased. And his fingers were at her back, deftly flicking open the laces on her gown. Like a wanton, she slid her arms down to his hips and pulled him against her so she could feel the hard jut of his erection at the crook of her thighs. So she could feel that jolt of pleasure again and again.

And his hissed-in breath, his coarse whispered oath of pleasure, was as erotic as his hands on her body.

She felt terrified and powerful and eager. His matter-of-fact competence—as if it was a quadrille he'd performed a hundred times, with who truly knew how many people—was awful and erotic and mindlessly exciting. She wanted him to know what he was doing. She wanted to feel out of her depth, at his mercy. And she wanted to feel, wanted to know, in the wake of Lady Pilcher's ambush, how very much he wanted her. *Her* in particular. Because she sensed everything about the two of them together was incendiary.

She hadn't known that this degree of wildness lived in her. Some of it was anger and hurt and frustration. But all of it combined into need.

And while he drugged her with kisses, he slipped her sleeves from her shoulders, and gently dragged the bodice of that beautiful dress lower and lower until the only thing she was clothed in from the waist up was the night air.

And he filled his hands with her breasts, and stroked.

She moaned against his mouth. It was too good; how could it be borne?

He ducked to take her nipple into his mouth.

She stifled a cry by biting her lip. Her head whipped back and her fingers combed into his hair as he sucked then teased with his tongue and teeth her nipples, sending shocks of pleasure fanning through her again and again.

When she became aware of the air on the backs of her legs, she realized he had furled up her dress.

And he leaned forward.

"Look at me," he ordered on a whisper, as she felt his hand gliding along the inside of her thigh.

She stood, with her dress gathered to her waist, the air cold on the bare skin of her thighs. The toes of her slippers glinted in the filtered moonlight when she looked down.

When she looked back up, his eyes were like the night, deep and hot and relentlessly holding her gaze while his fingers slid between her legs. Without preamble, stroked.

She half gasped, half moaned.

"Tell me to stop and I'll stop," he whispered.

Rhythmically, his fingers stroked over her where she was hot and slick. And nothing mattered now except that this was clearly what she'd wanted all along, this was the secret to everything, and he knew it.

It was indescribably strange and incredible. A hidden glory she never would have anticipated. The terrible, terrible risk of being caught honed the relentlessly ramping pleasure to a blinding edge. It made a begging slave of her with shocking speed.

"Please don't stop. Promise me. *Promise* me." Her voice was a shred against his chest. Very nearly a sob. Her hips moved with his clever fingers, even faster now. She was frantically, shamelessly chasing something, or something was chasing her; she could not say what, only that it seemed to promise salvation.

"What is happening?" she whispered against his throat. "Dominic . . . ?"

His breath was in her ear. "I have you, sweetheart. It's safe. Let go."

The bliss called from corners of her being by his clever fingers built into a torrent that pressed against the very seams of her. Her breath was a roar. She whimpered, helplessly from it, against his chest. She was blind with need.

He knew.

And he knew when she shattered.

Because his hand fanned across the back of her head and he pressed her scream of ecstasy against his coat, as her body was whipped backward. She would have buckled; his arm was an iron band around her body, holding her upright as a violent bliss racked her.

She became aware of things in fragments: her own breath, a ragged roar; the chill of the air; his hard cock still pressed against her, and when she shifted against it he hissed in a breath.

She reached for his buttons and his hand clamped hers. "No."

"Let me touch you. Show me," she demanded on a whisper. "Show me how. Show me what you need."

He hesitated. For a heartbeat, he was in indecision. Then with deft, expert speed he opened the fall of his trousers and guided her hand beneath the miles of his shirt to his cock. "Hold me like this." He wrapped her fingers around his shaft.

Her breath hitched at the hot, thick primitive feel of it in her fist. Very like it had a life of its own. Which probably wasn't far from the truth.

He closed his hand over hers, and dragged it down and back again. "Like that. Fast. Hard. Hurry," he said tersely.

She obeyed. And at first he took her lips in a searching, carnal kiss as she moved her fist. But soon his head thrashed back from enduring the pleasure and the moonlight glanced off his glistening bare throat. She was *suffused* with the power of giving him that sort of pleasure. Of having him essentially at her command. His hands covered her bare breasts again and, God help her, she wanted him so badly.

Her moving fist and his hips were a quick frenzy, and then he went rigid, his body bowing back, his lip bit against a stifled groan. "Oh God. Oh Christ," he breathed.

She sucked in a shocked breath as he spilled into her hand, his body quaking as though struck by lightning.

And even though his chest was heaving from release he became efficient. Because every second they lingered they were in danger of being caught.

He found a handkerchief and gently, thoroughly cleaned her hands.

He folded it and tucked it back into his coat.

Wordlessly, he placed his hands on her shoulders and turned her around gently so he could lace up her dress.

She'd been undone, and now she was being done up again, and she submitted, still feeling pleasure-stunned and a bit removed from her own body, which rang from the aftermath of her release. It had felt as though she'd soared over London like a firework, as exploded particles of bliss and light. She had not yet fully reassembled.

Finally, gently, he pulled her into his arms again, and held her as if she was breakable. She could feel his heart thumping beneath her cheek. His breath against her temple.

Her heart felt too hot and too bright and too sore and too crowded with conflicting emotions, all enormous.

Well. She had asked for this. She was mortified

and exultant. Humbled and subdued and, in truth, thoroughly shocked. The dregs of the jealousy and hurt that had in part driven her to tempt him, to goad him, still simmered around the edges of her awareness.

But she understood now how someone could chase this feeling. How one could escape from the world through passion. How it needn't have anything to do with love at all. Indeed, until this moment in his arms, it hadn't seemed loving at all this time, for either of them. It had seemed a pure expression of anger and hurt and hunger. Primal and desperate.

But perhaps that was part of love, too. She couldn't possibly know. And though she'd naively pressed him for answers before, this was a question she didn't dare ask. She wasn't naive anymore.

He brushed his lips against her temple. Her brow. Her eyelids.

"Catherine," he said quietly, finally. "Have mercy."

He dropped his arms from her.

A moment later, thoroughly, unequivocally ravished this time and forever changed, she returned to the ball, and he remained in the dark.

Chapter Nineteen

❦

KIRKE WENT straight from the Shillingford ball back to the boardinghouse.

In bed before curfew with an arm draped across his eyes, he thought about the gigantic misshapen flower that bloomed once every few years.

Which made him think of his own misshapen heart, grown gnarled around the lightning-struck, hollowed-out, wounded part.

He exhaled roughly. His heart had not seemed to slow its speed since those moments in the garden.

When he dragged his hands down his face, he fancied he could still smell Catherine on his fingers. And desire lanced him so swiftly it tore the breath from him.

He growled and hurled the very fine pillow beneath his head across the room. It struck his desk chair, which wobbled.

He wished he could cut his heart out and throw it, too.

He didn't want to be in love.

He wanted to be left in peace. He'd survived love's devastation once, and he could not live through it again. He thought he'd arranged his life so that he would be safe from it.

Little by little, so gently, so subtly, so effortlessly she had peeled back layers of him until the green idiot he'd been at seventeen was exposed at the center of the man he thought he'd become.

And that boy was terrified.

It was the piss-yourself terror Delacorte described in the face of a genie.

It was the threat he'd felt shimmering on the edge of his awareness since he'd met her.

Seventeen. The age at which his heart had been destroyed.

The age at which he had forfeited his right to love and be loved ever again.

This was only just. And if he believed in anything, it was justice.

All these years since, he'd thought he had outfoxed love. Lived successfully on its outskirts. He was bemused to discover that all along he'd never had any say in it at all. The way a breeze will find a chink in armor, the way wildflowers will eventually carpet blood-soaked battlefields, it had overrun the stupid ruins of his heart anyway. He simply possessed no defenses against Catherine Keating. He'd wanted to be left alone, in peace, for the rest of his life, but love had no respect for the pain that had leveled him years ago.

For him, the notion of love was strangled by the prospect of terrible loss.

And thanks to Keating he saw other things clearly now, too. He'd called the brusqueness with which he'd ended his storied, succinct affairs over the years "honesty." This was utter shite.

He'd done it to protect himself from any whiff of pain. Because the whole of his life he'd been a walking wound. And no one ever suspected.

And Lady Pilcher had been able to hurt Keating,

no doubt at least in part because he'd been short
with Lady Pilcher when he'd ended things.

The shame of this realization was now caustic.

For there was no point to this love.

For how could Catherine Keating love him,
knowing what she knew about him? And when she
didn't fully know him at all?

What if you didn't fight everything? she'd asked him.

He'd suspected she meant the desire he'd kept
leashed. He ought to have fought it tonight, but it
was an unfamiliar foe, like a genie. He'd reacted instead, and he was ashamed. Oh God. But the feel of
her in his arms, and in his mouth . . .

The thing was, he was in love with her. And loving Catherine Keating meant telling her the whole
truth of him.

So she could be free of him and move on to the
life she deserved.

And perhaps then he would be free of her, too.

When he sat with this notion, he knew both profound relief and a terrible dark grief. But he didn't
suppose he would ever again be allowed to feel an
unfettered emotion. He had felt too many things in
one lifetime; there was not a single pain that didn't
touch the edge of a joy, and vice versa.

And so. He needed to tell her.

His chest felt nearly caved in with this realization. But like he'd told her, people should be able to
do hard things. And he could do this, too.

SHE'D APOLOGIZED TO young Lord Holroyd for
missing the dance, saying she'd been indisposed,
and she'd promised him a dance at the next assembly. He had countered by inviting her on a ride in

his high-flyer. And truthfully, she'd always wanted to ride in a high-flyer.

He'd been so kind. *You do look flushed*, he'd said worriedly *Almost feverish.* He'd brought her a lemonade.

She thought the taste of lemonade would, for the rest of her life, remind her of the first time she held a man's rhymes-with-clock in her fist.

She couldn't believe she'd found her way back to the ballroom from Kirke's arms, let alone danced even one more dance. She was amazed that no one seemed able to tell that she'd just silently screamed her first release into Lord Kirke's coat, and that he had spilled on her fingers. That she—Catherine Keating—had made the cords of his neck go taut from enduring an almost annihilating sort of pleasure.

She had come to London for new experiences, and this was her reward. Confirmation of her sensual power. Racking, unimaginable bliss. A few uncomfortable answers.

She understood *very* clearly now how powerful a motivating force lust could be. And how it might have nothing at all to do with love.

She'd wondered, as she twirled and clapped in a reel, if she should think of herself as one of the initiated. If what she'd just experienced was what Lady Hackworth had meant when she'd said she'd heard Lord Kirke was "good." She would not quibble with that. How many of his former lovers roamed the ballroom? He'd said there weren't many. She had little reason to believe him, but she did.

She thought of the hidden worlds—of lovers and mistresses, of unhappy marriages and secret affairs—braided through the visible ones. Contrasted with the happy ignorance of young men and young women participating in their first season.

Still, if she'd been able to choose only one moment to live again and again for the rest of her life, she thought she might choose this one: the smell of his coat, the sound of his voice murmuring *sweetheart*, his lips soft on her brow, his chest swaying against hers with their settling breathing. The moonlight pouring down on their sated bodies.

She hadn't seen Lord Kirke for the rest of the evening.

But she'd heard him, later, when she was in bed.

It sounded as though he'd thrown something across his room.

IT WAS TRADITION for the cream of London to stay in darkened rooms, cool cloths draped over their pounding heads, until well past noon the day after the Shillingford ball.

But Catherine awoke early and sober, after struggling to fall asleep. Her body was alive to too many realizations, both of the physical and existential sort. She drank several cups of healing coffee with sugar and devoured her morning scone.

And then she took a book—*The Ghost in the Attic*, because she wanted to see how it would end—out to visit the little garden in front of The Grand Palace on the Thames. She had settled onto the bench in the shelter of white blossoms when she heard the little click of the gate latch lifting.

She looked up swiftly.

It was Lord Kirke.

She stood at once. Heart in her throat. She had not expected to see him so soon, and she could feel the inevitable blush moving into her cheeks.

She examined his face.

From the looks of things, he hadn't slept particularly well, either. Those shadows were back beneath his eyes.

"Good morning," he said. "If I'm not intruding, Catherine, may I have a word?"

The way he said her name, with those lovely "r's," made the back of her neck buzz with sensual pleasure.

"Of course. Do you want to . . ." She gestured to the bench.

There was a bench opposite, but he sat alongside her, at as genteel of a distance as the length of the bench would allow.

"How are you this morning?" he asked after a moment.

The question didn't sound like a formality—it sounded like the sort of thing one would ask in the aftermath of a serious event, a catastrophe—so she gave it some proper thought.

"Enlightened," she decided to say. Gingerly.

This made the corners of his mouth lift, somewhat wryly. But his eyes were troubled. He seemed tremendously preoccupied.

"And you?" she inquired, carefully.

He didn't take this up. He audibly pulled in a breath, and released it.

And then another.

"I'd like to show you something." His voice was soft.

He extended his fist. She realized his fingers were closed around something in his palm.

She understood then that he was breathing to steady himself. He was nervous, she realized, astounded.

And now she was, too.

At last, he uncurled his fingers. She peered down and saw a miniature in his palm.

Her heart twinged sweetly.

It was a little painting of a boy who had lustrous dark eyes, a curly pile of black hair, and elegant bone structure.

The resemblance was unmistakable.

"Is this you when you were just a boy?"

He didn't reply.

He waited so long to speak that her heart began hammering and she knew.

She knew. She knew before he said it.

"He's my son."

The world teetered and flickered, such was her shock.

She couldn't yet look at Dominic. And she couldn't breathe. She was riveted by the sweet-faced boy looking up at her from her palm.

"But you . . . and you've . . . never been married." She managed to say it steadily.

"I've never been married," he confirmed. His voice quiet.

By-blow. The ugly word that Farquar had used. The rumor Lady Wisterberg had heard, too.

Well, then.

She breathed through this knowledge. In and out. In and out. Accommodating it. On the periphery of her awareness a fear shimmered. She knew she was about to learn something that might devastate her. And yet this was a feeling to which she knew she had no right.

Then she reminded herself forcefully: he didn't lie. He'd told her he had never been involved with more than one woman at a time. She believed him. He would *not* be ravishing her against ivy-covered walls at soirees if he was currently supporting another mistress.

But his voice. His posture. Whatever it was he needed to share was delicate, perhaps even volatile, to him.

Suddenly it was simple: nothing she might currently feel was as important as letting him know it was safe to tell her whatever he needed to say.

"He looks exactly like you." She looked up at him. "The poor sod," she added gently.

The corner of his mouth tipped, ruefully. Pleased with her.

"How old is he?"

"Seventeen years old." He seemed to be choosing one word at a time thoughtfully, gingerly, as though he was forging a path through unfamiliar terrain without armor, uncertain of his reception. Watching for her reaction.

He cleared his throat. "When I was seventeen, during my first year of university, I met a girl in a village in Scotland named Anna Jenkins. Brown eyes, black hair. I fell in love with her the way a boy of seventeen does. It wasn't so much falling as plummeting. Madly and recklessly and completely. And she was in love with me."

Cat held herself motionless, lest that sudden flare of spiked, acrid jealousy bump against her heart. Her breathing went shallow. Her head felt tight from imagining this controlled man a tender, ardent boy, helplessly in love.

And it was accompanied by the sore, paradoxical tenderness of picturing him as a boy, free and vulnerable, his feelings unbounded and reckless.

He swallowed. "Anna and I were . . . intimate. Just once. And she fell pregnant."

Catherine's breath left her in a sharp exhale.

He swallowed. "When she told me . . . we were both terrified. I was at university, would have ruined my life's plans, and yet . . . we became excited, too. It seemed a miracle. I wanted to marry her, of course."

Catherine was silent. Her breaths were shallow. Her arms were cold with nerves.

"And I suppose I ought to have taken her straight to Gretna Green, but like a fool I went the honorable route and paid a call on her father to ask for her hand. But her father had for some time been convinced I was worthless and held little hope of me becoming otherwise. To be fair, I was as unprepossessing a seventeen-year-old as ever existed. Skinny. Small. Had a temper. Full of myself. Had no notion of how I would support a wife and child at that age. But I would have found a way. No *matter* what it took. Believe me." He looked at her sharply.

"I believe you," Catherine said faintly.

"And right after that she disappeared. I called upon their house and her father aimed a rifle straight at my face and threatened to kill me if I ever came near him or her again. He had that musket cocked."

"Dominic . . ." she breathed. "Oh, Dominic."

Her heart was hammering. How ghastly, sick fear of the threat of death. His love and his child torn from him. She was nauseous from imagining the pain. Her chest felt tight.

"I *tried* to find her. No one who knew her would tell me a thing. I didn't know whether she was alive or dead. I didn't know if she'd survived childbirth, or if the baby did. I didn't know if I had a son or a daughter. I couldn't properly grieve and I couldn't forget. I never told another soul. And eventually I continued with school as my uncle offered, because what else could I do? I wrote letters to her that I could never send. And weeks became months became years and I suppose I got on with my life, but I never, ever forgot. It has *always* been a presence in my life. My life has been built around it. I simply didn't know where to look for her. Anna Jenkins. Do you know how many people in the whole of the British Isles are named Anna Jenkins?" He gave a short, dark, humorless laugh.

Catherine was motionless.

"I don't know quite how to describe the sort of . . . flailing, awful emptiness of someone vanishing like that. But I know you know what it's like to lose someone you love."

She took a breath, absorbing this. "I only know that for a time you absolutely lose your moorings in the world. Everything familiar is suddenly strange and almost frightening and new, and that's when you realize how much that person touched literally everything in your life."

His eyes were softer as he regarded her, kindling with warmth. He exhaled.

"That's precisely it."

"And I tortured myself imagining how alone and frightened Anna must have felt without me when she was sent away. Had she thought I'd abandoned her? I didn't know what she'd been told. It crushed me, Catherine. For that, I can never forgive her father."

She could feel it now: his suffocating desperation and grief. She could hardly breathe for imagining it.

"But you did learn what became of her?"

"I recently learned she was sent to an aunt in

Yorkshire, where Leo was born." He looked at her. "Leo is my middle name." His voice was frayed.

Dominic Leo Kirke. She hoarded this information like found treasure.

"When Leo was three years old Anna married a Yorkshire farmer by the name of Atwell. He was a widower. The man who raised him has always known the truth of his parentage, but raised him as his own. She has four children now. And as it turns out . . . Leo is the only troublesome one." He smiled faintly. "Because—and I know this will come as a shock to you—he's annoyingly clever and headstrong and beset with all manner of gifts. Which is why . . ." He turned to her. "When Anna saw my name in the newspaper in recent months, she wrote to me." He paused at length. "She hadn't been sure it was the same boy she'd known. But she knew she had to try."

She went airless, imagining the cataclysm in his life encompassed by his last two sentences.

The dam between him and his past finally breaking and the memories crashing through. The grief, the joy, the terror. The swooping relief of finally knowing. The renewed sense of crushing loss.

"It must have been a shock." The words felt inadequate.

He seemed to be considering what to say. "It was. And a relief. And tremendously awkward, as you may imagine. Then again, I've never shied away from awkward." He smiled with a hint of his usual wryness. "We met again for the first time in Yorkshire. Her father . . ." He cleared his throat. "Her father had told her I'd run away from her."

His voice was thick.

"Oh my *God*," Catherine breathed.

"Ah, but I came prepared. I had the letters I'd written to her. Years' worth of them. I asked her husband permission to give them to her. And he granted it. She"—he swallowed—"wept when she read them."

Catherine's own eyes burned with tears.

"She is still a lovely person. She says she harbors no resentment of any kind toward me. Age and contentment can do that. She's happy in her life, and claims she has no regrets. But she . . . she remembered being . . . afraid." His voice was arid. "And very alone. And that was my fault. *I* did that to her."

He drew in a steadying breath and exhaled again.

"Now . . . it's clear to me that we are almost nothing alike. All that drama, all that passion . . . funny, like an echo of a song once heard. I think . . . we all become more than one person throughout our lives, if we live long enough. We change. Who would we be if we'd stayed together? I do not know. I'll never know. I'm glad she found someone to care for her, and someone to care for."

For the first time in his harrowing conversation, the tightness in Catherine's chest eased.

"I cannot say that things are entirely easy between the four of us—Anna and her husband and Leo and me—but it is civilized, and I imagine it will get easier. Her husband knows about me, and I have met him. He's a good man. We all want to do right by Leo. And so I am helping to pay for my son's education, and I was able to get him admitted to the University of Edinburgh. They didn't ask me to intervene. But I knew it was a hope, and I offered, and I'm glad and grateful to be able to do it."

And *this*, Catherine realized, was likely the reason Lord Kirke had allegedly backed away from

enticing investment opportunities, as Lady Wisterberg had mentioned. He now had a significant
financial obligation to his son.

She was stunned, imagining the courage and humility it must have taken to meet Anna's husband.

For this proud, arrogant man to look his son and
Anna in the eyes, and somehow humbly attempt to
reckon with his past.

She closed her eyes briefly. She wondered if he
understood how brave he was.

"And you've met Leo?" she asked softly. Her own
voice was thick.

He nodded. "Just once. Very briefly. He doesn't
think much of me. He doesn't, in fact, like me at all."
He gave a soft laugh. He sounded uncertain, a word
she had never once associated with him. "Mainly
because he thinks I seduced and abandoned his
mother, regardless of what she tells him. He is exactly as pig-headed as I am. Filled with brilliance
and outraged morality. He'll go far," he said dryly.
"But I think he's a gentler boy than I ever was. The
main thing is, I can make introductions for him.
Pave his way. He may never like me. I can live with
that. I've lived with worse. He might be my age by
the time he comes to any understanding of what
happened between his mother and me. I am good at
waiting. I am good at playing a long game. He will
come to his own understanding, however he does."

"I'm certain he's remarkable," she said gently.

He cast her a wry, grateful look.

They sat for a moment. Silent but for the breeze
shaking branches near them.

"I like to think I would have been a good father,
Catherine. Or a good husband. But I don't know. I
wouldn't be who I am now, and so who is to say. I

know I likely would never have finished my education. More likely I would have become more and more myself, who I am now, without any direction for it, and I would have been even more insufferable and I would have made Anna miserable. But I didn't get to raise my son. And I wasn't able to help her, or comfort her. And that will *gut* me to the end of my days."

His voice was taut. She saw the raw emotion rush his skin, and how he braced against it.

The person the world saw when they looked at Dominic—the weapon-like eloquence, the warrior spirit, the fearlessness—was a fortress built around this person, who loved fiercely, tenderly, and permanently. Who could be—had been, and still was—mortally hurt. She had seen, she had sensed this person from nearly the moment she'd met him.

Whatever else he'd done, he was a man of integrity now.

She was certain he'd never lied to her.

"I'm so sorry," she said. She only hoped her voice conveyed how she felt better than the words.

He nodded, acknowledging this.

He was quiet a moment, apart from his breathing, which was still a bit unsteady.

"But here is the thing, Catherine . . . I think it would have been within her father's rights to shoot me when I went to him. Because even at seventeen I knew better. I wanted what I wanted when I wanted it. So did she, in the moment—I asked her if she was certain before I"—he closed his eyes briefly, and stopped himself—"but for God's sake, that is quite beside the point. It was up to *me* to stop it and I did not because I wanted it. It seemed impossible to deny myself at the time. I know now that's not true. I simply cannot forgive myself for that."

And this was the crux of it. What he was trying to convey to her.

Love and the loss of it had left a great smoking crater in his life many years ago.

It seemed clear now the very notion of love was entwined with terror and guilt and self-loathing. And desire, that powerful force which she now understood as one of the languages humans are given to express love, had been the thing that nearly destroyed him.

Could, in fact, still destroy the two of them even now.

He has affairs, dear. That's what Lady Wisterberg had said. She hadn't understood until now that the word missing from that sentence was "only." He *only* has affairs, dear.

He allowed himself these fleeting associations. What had he said about Lady Pilcher? *It wasn't right.* He was seeking something, and yet denying himself that very something at the same time.

"The man I am now is nothing like the boy I was. And I will *never* make that kind of mistake again."

She met his eyes.

She was silent. Too many thoughts and feelings, all enormous, excruciating, and beautiful, crowded around her heart, clogged her throat. She was impotently furious at the inadequacy of words and her own experience at that moment. She felt callow and young.

She understood now that everyone—Dominic, Lady Pilcher, Lady Wisterberg, her father, everyone at The Grand Palace on the Thames, even herself—struggled to always make sense of their lives, to manage and salve the blows and disappointments the best way they knew, to seize what pleasures they could in the time they had. Wisdom was seldom innate, she understood. It was hard-won. It was acquired through a process of elimination. Of learning from mistakes. Some people only ever lashed out, and thereby stole a little relief. Like Lady Pilcher.

"After a fashion, I suppose you've been fighting for Leo your whole life," she said slowly. "And against the injustice done to you and Anna. For the vulnerable."

He turned slowly and stared at her. Utterly still.

And she could see that this had never once occurred to him. That flicker of comprehension, then abstraction, in his eyes as he took this in. Considered it. A hint of reluctance, of wry appreciation. She loved the light in his eyes when she'd impressed him.

And maybe you've been fighting for yourself, too. Because no one else ever has, she thought.

She wondered if he also understood that he'd been punishing himself for it his entire life as well.

She wasn't brave enough to say any of that out loud. It seemed very close to the bone. Likely he would deny it.

"There are very few people who know I have an . . . illegitimate . . . son, but you're the only one who knows the entirety of the story. I have a feeling my erstwhile mistress somehow got a peek at my letter from Anna, which is how Farquar came to know of it. While I'm not proud of how it came about, I'm not ashamed of him, nor am I deliberately keeping him a secret. But for his sake, I want to protect him from gossip and speculation as much as I can, for as long as I can. I should be grateful if you would not share this information with anyone else."

"Of course. I'm honored that you trust me with it. I'm glad to know of him."

They sat in silence a moment.

Finally, some instinct made her gently thread her fingers through his. It was lovely just to touch his warm, strong hand, to twine with those surprisingly elegant fingers that had known her body so intimately. Her throat was tight. He would forever be the first man to ever touch her that way. Even now, when she thought about it, her body pulsed with longing.

Then she lifted his hand and brought it to her cheek. She held it next to her skin.

She felt him tense in surprise, perhaps, but she didn't release him. Presently, as surely as if the two of them were of a piece, she could feel the tension in him melt away. He took a long breath. Exhaled at length.

And she supposed this was why she'd instinctively done it. Somehow she'd hoped to transfer peace to him through her skin. Balm ancient aches. She hadn't anything else available to her to communicate how she felt.

But she also just wanted to feel him against her: The thrum of his ferocity and passion. His strength, his precious, irreplaceably unique, maddening spirit. He scared her so.

"*I* like you," she said quietly.

He smiled faintly. "There's no accounting for taste."

Tumbling about with all the other things she felt—aching pity and ferocious admiration and jealousy, the restless, consuming desire that stirred every time he was near—was guilt. Guilt about the relief she felt that her life was a relatively clean slate, empty as a blue summer sky. She could marry a nice young man who had plenty of money and no regrets or demons or guilt. Who wasn't a crusader or controversial. Who hadn't maddening complexities. Who hadn't yet been shot through like a battle flag by grief or terror or love or any other emotions to which all humans are subject, and from which they may never recover. She could grow up together with this nice young man, build a family, have a peaceful, cheerful life. This possibility remained to her and she turned toward it like it was an open window she could climb back into after taking a few steps out onto a tightrope.

This was why Dominic had told her about his son. So she would finally understand the depths of his struggle when she was near. The extent of their danger. And perhaps, too, the limitations of what he was able or willing to offer her.

He'd given her a taste of her own power and introduced her to the pleasures that could be had from her own body.

But he wanted to protect her the way he'd been unable to protect Anna.

And she wanted to protect him, too.

Which meant leaving him be. Walking away forever.

Have mercy, he'd begged. She could do that for him.

"Thank you for telling me," she said.

He nodded.

She gently released his hand.

He slid his fingers from hers in a slow caress.

He looked at her a moment, and then with a nod, he stood. He left her to hail a hack, striding off, she supposed, to find his next battle.

She watched him go, hating it still, because some part of her was taken away with him. The part of her he had forever changed. She stood, blinking and disoriented, as though she'd moved from the dark into the light or from the light into the dark. She didn't know which. Not yet. She only knew that somehow she would need to relearn how to be in the world. Almost as though she'd once again lost someone she loved.

Chapter Twenty

 •••

*N*OT SINCE his school days had he been required to report to a certain place at a certain time upon pain of expulsion. He'd always thought of himself as an unstoppable force.

But the more time he spent in it, the more he could almost feel this sitting room at The Grand Palace on the Thames subtly reshaping him. Like an excellent mattress might both make a spine creak into alignment while absorbing the weight of his day. Or the way an ocean lapped away at a cliff. In his arrogance, all his life he had not thought he could be changed without his permission. He'd traditionally resented any attempts to try.

He would leave here understanding that his life had long been missing all the rests and grace notes that transformed noise into a symphony.

And he ought to leave straightaway.

He should find another room in another hotel, one without rules, and without a beautiful girl always in the periphery of his vision, leaning as she was now toward Mrs. Pariseau, as if she could hardly wait to hear the next sentence of *The Arabian Nights' Entertainments.*

Or chatting happily at the dinner table about riding in Rotten Row in Lord Holroyd's high-flyer.

They kindly, carefully skirted each other as if they each were human bruises. No one else seemed

to notice. They passed gravy or jam as the case
might be at the dinner table. They did not exchange
words. This had gone on for a week and a half now,
and he'd begun to think he would be able to endure
it until he moved back into his home.

For his days were as full as ever, and his house repairs were coming along. The walls were restored;
the roof would take longer. It would be at least two
months, perhaps more, before it would be fully habitable again.

He wondered if Catherine would be engaged to
Lord Vaughn by then.

Another breathless gossip item had appeared in
the newspaper insinuating such an event might be
imminent. The newspapers seemed to be basing this
on very little more than a few dances, granted, but
this had never stopped them from printing anything.

"Kirke, I've something to ask you," Mr. Delacorte
said with great dignity. "It's a bit delicate."

One of his favorite things about The Grand Palace on the Thames was never knowing what might
emerge from Mr. Delacorte's mouth.

"Given what I've learned about you in the past
few weeks or so, I doubt very much that it's delicate,
Delacorte."

"Ha ha! How do you feel about donkeys?"

"Fine beasts," Kirke replied, as if this was an ordinary question to ask of anybody.

"I don't suppose I could interest you in attending
a donkey race with me?"

Kirke stared at him, eyebrows diving. "I don't
know if our relationship has progressed beyond
chess to the donkey race stage yet, Delacorte." He
was only half-jesting.

"Only one way to find out," Mr. Delacorte coaxed.

Kirke studied him thoughtfully.

Mr. Delacorte seemed to be holding his breath.

"What does this entail?" He couldn't help himself: he was curious. "This donkey race?"

"It involves loud cheering and wagers and donkeys running. And drinking. From what I understand you're loud when you want to be."

"I am at that." Kirke was amused.

"If we leave now, we can get a spot close to the finish line."

He had the sense that Mr. Delacorte was crossing his fingers for hope and luck beneath the game table.

Suddenly, leaving this room seemed the wisest thing he could do. Out of sight, out of mind, and all that. He flicked a glance at the back of Keating. For some ridiculous reason even the nape of her neck seemed poignant.

"I'll get my coat," he told Delacorte, who gave a delighted little hop.

IN THE WAKE of the Shillingford ball, Lady Wisterberg was consumed with the final preparations for their party, to be held within a week. She'd invited nearly seventy carefully curated (according to her standards) people. And all of them—all of them!—were coming.

Well, as of yesterday, all of them were coming save three, as three invitees had just regretfully informed Lady Wisterberg that they would not be able to attend, after all, and they were, to Catherine's relief, Miss Seaver and the Hackworths.

Oh, but that's to be expected with every party, Lady Wisterberg had said, airily. *We shouldn't receive more than that.*

Catherine had spent several mornings during the past week at Lady Wisterberg's town house with Lucy, pressed into helping to make decisions about flowers and menus and the order of dances, and whether they should hire someone to draw a fancy chalk design on the ballroom floor.

When the invitation to Lord Vaughn's friend's house party at last arrived—addressed to Catherine and Lucy—Lady Wisterberg had spent a moment speechless with glee and triumph, her hands clasped over her heart.

"Oh. My dear," she said, sounding subdued. Awestruck. "It's like a dream come true, isn't it?"

The young woman who had arrived in London a few short weeks ago would certainly have nodded in vigorous agreement.

Catherine knew what to do: she nodded. And she could, with a little effort, in fact muster a faint pang of genuine excitement, an echo of the enthusiasm with which she'd arrived in London. And given time, she might be able to fan it into a flame.

Surprisingly, no new invitations to balls or parties or picnics had yet arrived for her this week, but Lady Wisterberg wasn't concerned.

"Oh, it's probably just a lull, dear. After the Shillingford ball, everyone needs a bit of a rest," Lady Wisterberg said, comfortingly.

And now she lay stretched out on her bed, staring at the ceiling, waiting for sleep.

Now and again the floorboards above her creaked as he moved across the room.

Odd to think that she might never have another conversation with him. She had seen him only briefly this week. And there would come a day when she might not ever see him again.

He was impossible to forget. That was the trouble. But he was designed that way. And yet, perhaps it wasn't personal to her at all. The sun, after all, feels warm to everyone. She supposed that was the destiny of some people, to be felt far and wide.

Perhaps he was writing to his son.

She wondered if Anna, now married to another man, had thought about Dominic every day for seventeen years, even when she was in bed with her husband. Had she longed for him at night? Had she thought about him every time she looked at Leo? When and how had the longing for her first love ebbed, if circumstances were indeed as civilized as Dominic claimed? Had it at last felt merciful when the pain subsided, or had she been sad to realize the last of the old feeling was gone?

Had life seemed dull to Anna in the absence of that longing, or had she been relieved at last to be free of it, content with the life she'd made for herself? Had she truly managed to fall in love with the farmer she'd married?

Catherine couldn't quite shake the aching jealousy—perhaps it was more like envy?—she felt for Anna, who was the first and might be the last to ever have him. But it was undeniably tempered with compassion.

For how she must have suffered. Missing someone whom you know is gone forever was one thing. Missing someone while they still walked the earth was quite another.

And missing Lord Dominic Leo Kirke was something else altogether.

To know him when he was free and naive and passionate and open . . . who could have resisted him?

He had clearly never forgiven himself for a moment

of passionate selfishness that had ruptured lives. But she could not seem to muster anything like the total censure he seemed to feel he deserved. He'd been so young. And thanks to him, she now understood how passion could be a temporary madness. One could be lectured about its risks, but like love or death, there was no true way to comprehend how overwhelming desire could be until one experienced it. For instance, in a garden, in the moonlight, with one's skirts hiked up.

She thought about Leo, and how he must feel about discovering that he and the brothers and sisters with whom he'd been raised had different fathers. She wondered how his brothers and sisters might feel about it. Was there relief, or a new loneliness in this, too, to learn he was different? He'd thought he'd known who he was his entire life. And suddenly he was new to himself, and to them.

Just like she was. Changed forever as a result of Lord Dominic Kirke.

She wondered if he yet knew how lucky he was to have Dominic as a father. The man who raised him no doubt truly was a good man. But now he also had a father who would surely go to the ends of the earth for him, and do it with fiery flair, should the need arise.

She thought she'd heard Dominic curse—a staccato rap of a word—which made her smile. Perhaps he'd stubbed a toe, or read something outrageous, or spilled ink.

And then, at last, for quite some time, it was very quiet.

Perhaps he'd gone to sleep.

She listened to the silence for a time.

On a surely irrational impulse, she slid out of

her bed, and gently moved the little porcelain vase stuffed with blossoms from the desk to the floor.

And then she climbed up on the chair, gingerly. She spent a moment balancing, to make sure it could hold her weight. And then she took a step up onto the desk. Which brought her face just a little closer to the ceiling.

And she listened.

She just wanted to see if she could hear him breathing.

ONE COULD LEAD a horse to water but not compel it to drink; likewise, one could put a quill to paper, but not compel it to write. Kirke had inked up just the same, hoping tonight would be the night.

He moved the quill aimlessly in absent, wavy lines across the foolscap. Thinking, but not of his speech.

He'd never anticipated that he'd tell his oldest, darkest, most painful secret in broad daylight, in a sweetly blooming garden near the docks, to a clear-eyed girl more than a decade younger than he was. He'd felt a trifle unsteady since, a bit as though a fever had broken. He wasn't certain if he felt lighter, or freer, or just odd: it was a weight he'd borne so long, it almost felt as though it had affected his very posture. How would Atlas have felt if someone had lifted the world from his back? Grateful, or resentful of a loss of his purpose? Would he need to seek new meaning?

He'd told her in the spirit of honesty, to release the two of them from their feverish dalliance. To convey to her why it needed to end.

But he'd also told her because he wholly trusted her more than any other person he knew.

This realization shook him almost as much as telling her had.

He knew it was often impossible to trace an origin of a belief in something, whether it was in genies, ghosts, God, or the Whigs' chances of ever having a majority in Parliament. Was one born with a predisposition to a belief? Or was it shaped by circumstances? Instilled by upbringing? He'd told Keating that people's habits tend to mutate in unusual ways when they didn't have a useful occupation.

And maybe his useful mutation was just precisely what she'd suggested: the injustice done him—his lover and child and his right to be a father taken from him—had essentially forged him into what he was today. A justice seeker. A protector of innocents. That Catherine had indeed seen what happened to him as an injustice—that she hadn't looked at him with horror or judgment, but with compassion—had been a revelation, and he was reluctant to accept the unexpected grace of this. No part of him was yet willing to believe he deserved it.

She was giddy with plans for the party at Lady Wisterberg's; he'd overheard her discussing them in the sitting room. The party to which Lord Vaughn had also been invited. And now he realized part of the unsteadiness he felt was anticipation: soon enough some young man would claim her.

He had tried more than once to imagine what life would be like when that day came. But his mind encountered only blankness. As if the story of his life simply ended there.

He deliberately thought of it now, rehearsing for devastation. His heart obliged him, turning over hard in his chest. It felt like a jagged rock.

His quill screeched across the foolscap and he nearly fell out of his chair at the sound of an apocalyptic crash below.

CATHERINE YANKED OPEN her door at the sound of thumping.

Dominic's fearsome expression evolved into what looked like knee-buckling relief when she appeared. He flicked a swift inspecting gaze over her.

He was breathing like a bellows, and he looked ready to slay marauders.

"Dear God, did you break any bones?" he said.

"Oh—no—oh my goodness—I'm so sorry to disturb you."

He inspected her more closely, his eyes narrowed, to ascertain whether she was telling the truth.

And then there fell a little silence during which they stared at each other like awkward strangers.

Gradually, his eyes lit with amusement. "Were you cavorting again?"

She could feel herself flushing. "I was . . . standing on top of the desk."

There was something about being stared at by his dark eyes that compelled the truth out of her, no matter how mortifying.

"You were . . . standing on the desk," he repeated thoughtfully. "And then . . ."

"And then I slipped."

His eyebrows jabbed upward.

She cleared her throat. "And in order not to fall to the floor awkwardly, I was . . . I was compelled to take a sort of . . . a sort of great leap."

"A leap," he repeated, as if this was a fascinating, salient point.

"Whereupon I"—she swallowed—"landed. I skidded across the floor, and collided with the bedpost and then I . . ."

He gazed at her relentlessly.

". . . fell to the floor," she admitted.

A long moment ensued during which he studied her, his expression rather a fascinating blend of things, one of which was clearly hilarity.

"Exactly how I pictured it," he said.

She gave a little shout of laughter, covered with her hand.

They regarded each other in somewhat fraught silence, while she held her shoulder with one hand, where it stung from the collision with the bedpost.

"Why were you standing on the desk?"

He asked as if anything she'd just said had been at all reasonable.

It was a long moment before she could reply. She could feel her face scorching now, but she knew she was going to tell him.

"I wanted to know if I could hear you breathing." Her voice was hoarse.

Ironically, in that moment, he visibly stopped breathing. Almost as though he took the words like a blow.

His face blazed briefly with light she could feel in her chest.

His features were screened quickly with caution.

"Could you?" he said carefully.

There was a little silence.

"I can now," she whispered.

He pressed his lips together. His face was unreadable now. But then his eyes flicked to her arm and his face registered concern.

"Catherine . . . your shoulder. You're holding it. How badly is it hurt?"

"It's just a bump. It will . . . it will fade in time." Unlike whatever happened to her when he was near.

Too late, they both realized he'd reflexively reached out to lay his hand against her shoulder by way of comfort.

They both froze.

And as though he was Midas, just like that he transformed her blood: not to gold, but to lava. She could feel its slow, hot progress through her veins.

She tipped her head until it rested on his hand, and closed her eyes.

"It feels better now," she said. Her voice was cracked. "Thank you."

She could hear him breathing more swiftly.

"Tell me to leave, Catherine. So help me God. Tell me." His voice was a scorched whisper.

Have mercy, he'd said.

But what about her? Where was the mercy for her, when she wanted him so very badly, and he was standing right in front of her?

"Close the door," she whispered.

HE COULD INTERPRET that any way he pleased.

When she heard the soft click of the door closing behind her, and he hadn't moved his hand from her arm, her heart launched into her throat.

She opened her eyes to see his fixed upon her, burning.

His hand still on her shoulder, he steered her slowly into the room until her back was against the wall. And he stood inches away from her, staring down into her face.

His eyes were almost angry. Mesmerized. Help-less. For a moment she was certain he half hated her.

In this moment of madness she didn't care. In a way, she half hated him, too, for making her want him.

As long as he didn't leave.

Her heart was slamming now.

She wanted to tear off her night rail and hurl it across the room so she could feel his body on hers. She knew she didn't dare.

She would not have stopped him if he chose to tear it from her, however.

They were so close she could feel his hardening cock at the juncture of her legs. She moved deliber-ately against him and watched his eyes flare to black.

And then he lunged. He scooped his hands beneath her buttocks and brought her hard up against his cock, and he buried his face in her neck. He lightly bit the place it joined her shoulder.

She gasped as shocking pleasure forked through her. And when he dragged his lips then his tongue to her ear and gently scraped the stubble of his beard over her tender skin, a low moan rose in her throat as pleasure sparked everywhere in her body.

She braced her hands against his shoulders.

Their hot breaths met in a gust between them as they deliberately ground against each other. Their eyes never leaving each other's faces. They were each intent on a swift, animalistic release. His cock was so hard even through his trousers it nearly hurt her to move against him, but it felt indescribably good. She was already close. "*Yes*," she rasped.

She could see herself in his pupils, wanton, her lips parted with her gusting breath, her body rock-ing as they collided with each other.

"Oh Christ," he rasped. His forehead was sheened in sweat.

Within moments her release ripped through with a blinding white light behind her eyes.

Her body whipped upward and her head fell back on a long, near silent scream. She would have crumpled, but he held her fast, driving himself relentlessly to his own release. And with several swift thrusts he came apart, on a groan shaped like her name. It racked him; she could feel his body quake, against her gripping fingers.

Almost at once they took their hands from each other, as though burnt and stunned. Chests heaving with violent breaths.

She was grateful for the wall to hold her up. She could not have done it on her own.

Her entire body rang from bliss. But his eyes on her were almost like wounds. Amazed and tender, but a trifle hostile, too.

He fleetingly covered them with his hand, a gesture of almost despair. As if the very sight of her blinded and overwhelmed him.

"I'm *sorry*," she nearly said. She didn't know why. She almost wanted to hit him in frustration.

Finally he cupped her face gently, briefly in his hand. She turned her cheek to fit into his palm, as if it was its natural home.

And then without another word he left her, closing the door quietly.

Chapter Twenty-One

❦

CATHERINE KNEW something was amiss when a carriage was sent to bring her to Lady Wisterberg's town house *first* thing the following morning. A message had been brought in to her at breakfast by Mr. Pike. It read:

Dear Miss Keating,

You are wanted at once.

Yrs, Lady Wisterberg

Free of frills and exclamation points. Very unlike Lady Wisterberg.

Her stomach awash with icy foreboding, she boarded the waiting hack. She was already logy and subdued from her strange, swift, somewhat tawdry encounter with Lord Kirke the night before.

She was admitted to Lady Wisterberg's town house by another footman, whose expression was unnervingly grim, and led into the sitting room decorated in primarily green. It featured a gigantic portrait of the late Lord Wisterberg over the mantel.

Lucy and Lady Wisterberg sat side by side on a settee. Both were as pale as if there had been a death in the family.

Lucy looked up at Catherine with enormous eyes.

Terror nearly took the legs out from under Catherine. "S-something has happened. My aunt, my father? Are *you* sound? Please tell me what's happened!"

"No, dear. You may rest yourself on that account. Everyone is sound. But it seems we may have to, ah, postpone our party." Lady Wisterberg's voice was odd. Clipped.

And then Catherine realized it was because she was *furious*.

"We've just had a few more cancelations," she added. The word "cancelations" sounded ironically venomous.

Catherine's heart was now pounding painfully. "How many?" she asked weakly.

Lady Wisterberg closed her eyes. And said nothing.

So Lucy whispered it. "Thirty-two."

Catherine gasped.

"Lord Vaughn and his parents among them," Lucy said miserably.

Catherine's knees gave way and collapsed onto the settee.

They all stared at each other.

"But . . . how . . . . *why*?" Catherine's heart sickened her with its tempo.

"I don't know," Lady Wisterberg said tersely. "But I expect we will find out soon enough."

CATHERINE AND LUCY spent the morning helping Lady Wisterberg to write politely cheery notes to everyone invited to the party, regrettably canceling. It was a grim exercise in exquisite penmanship conducted in utter silence, unless one counted Lady Wisterberg's audibly incensed breathing.

According to the rules, she was required only to

spend four evenings per week in the sitting room at The Grand Palace on the Thames.

That evening she didn't feel she could bear to face anyone at all. She took dinner in her room, too.

And then she climbed beneath her blankets. She thought about how very odd it was that dread was an absorbing occupation, as consuming as plowing a field or reading a book. One could simply sit and dread. She imagined saying to Mrs. Pariseau, "I'm sorry, I cannot listen to the story tonight, I'll be dreading all evening."

She sat on the bed with her knees tucked up to her chest to make herself small, and because her chest felt as cold and hollow as a gorge. And she pondered.

An attack had been levied. Or at least that was how it felt. A message unequivocal in its nature had been sent.

There wasn't a thing she could conceive of that she might have done wrong, other than being herself. Surely no one had seen her in the Shillingford garden, in the ivy, her bodice half-off and her dress hiked up, with Lord Kirk? She had been quite certain they'd been hidden and alone.

But it seemed clear that some tacit, vociferous censure had taken place. She couldn't help but recall Lady Pilcher's beautiful, cruel face and Lady Hackworth's puzzled assessment of her dress. How had Lord Kirke put it the night she'd handed over her handkerchief? *Sometimes insults are more valuable than compliments, and sometimes what seems like kindness is a sort of a chess move.* Perhaps this censure was indeed a compliment: she was perceived as so powerful a threat to the women of the ton that she must be summarily removed, and they had found an excuse to do it.

Radiant, Kirke had called her. In a voice gone helplessly soft.

Remembering it even now made her skin warm. And then her warm feelings crested into frustration and something like fury.

He had warned her there would be consequences for dancing with him. Had these consequences finally descended?

It just seemed to her that nastiness was *inefficient*; it offended her sense of the practical. It was so unnecessary, when it was so much easier to be kind. And kindness was *not* tantamount to weakness. Kindness just meant recognizing the humanity in the other person. But she also knew it was easier to be kind when you solidly knew yourself. When you weren't buffeted by the whims of fashion, or dependent upon the approval of certain people. For this was what made one afraid and unsteady.

But perhaps this was more naivete on her part. Lord Kirke might have scoffed. His life was one of strategy, and he seemed to surf the vicissitudes of public mood like a gull.

He'd likely known from the first that she was destined to be crocodile food. One had to be born in the jungle to learn how to navigate it, it seemed.

She was no coward. She'd faced and survived difficult challenges, blood and illness and death among them. She had a healthy sense of competition, when it came to any sort of contest. She was unafraid of defending herself and perfectly willing to do it.

But this type of enemy was baffling and amorphous. It was like Lord Kirke's argument concerning why Lord Bolt would be less prepared to fight a genie than a pirate: she simply didn't understand, and couldn't anticipate, her enemies' powers. And she didn't think she could fight them with the ones she possessed. She felt, at the moment, like an entirely different species than they were.

For these reasons, she was frightened. She could feel the consequences of potential ruination howling like an abyss inches from her feet.

And how she felt told her how thoroughly she had come to count on her popularity. It had become a substitute for happiness. A sort of inebriation.

She could now too well imagine the loneliness that would follow. Her stomach churned. The possible years of skulking in the shadows as a companion to her aunt. Her father's disappointment and confusion when she returned home from a failed season. He would be hurt for her. She squeezed her eyes closed.

Perhaps she had indeed flown too close to the sun, and now she had only herself to blame.

Mrs. Pariseau, who was up before the birds the following morning, had gotten hold of her own copy of *The Times* before Dot could bring it in to read to the maids.

And she rushed with it into the kitchen as if it were a fire needing putting out.

"The horror!" was the way she announced her presence. She slapped the newspaper down onto the table and pointed.

Delilah and Angelique, who were sitting at the table discussing the day's menu with Helga, shot to their feet, hearts in their throats, and peered at the paragraph beneath Mrs. Pariseau's finger.

As so often happens in London, we have discovered the once-assumed-angelic Miss K has proven to have feet of clay—for we have it on good authority that she waltzed with an heir in an exquisite blue dress known to have been made especially for—you may wish to repair to your fainting couch before you read the next three words—Lord K's mistress! It's difficult not to draw the conclusion that "his mistress" and the allegedly angelic "Miss K" are one and the same.

Pass the smelling salts, s'il vous plaît. But what do we really know about the young lady, apart from her talent for bewitching? Don't worry, gentlemen. If Lord K's history is any indication, she'll be free again soon enough!

The words seemed to pulse with casual evil before their eyes.

"Oh dear God. The blue dress!" Delilah finally breathed. "Miss Keating's blue dress! Is *that* what this is referencing?"

"It's not true," Mrs. Pariseau said stoutly and immediately. "What a steaming, hateful pile of balderdash. What a terrible thing to do to a young woman! And to Lord Kirke! I was with her! I was with her when she tried it on! She refused to take the dress at first and Madame Marceau insisted she would look beautiful in it, and she did. I imagine that all of the women of the ton were jealous when they saw her. Awful, awful people who would perpetuate such poison. Pure invention."

She would get no argument from Angelique or Delilah about how awful the ton could be.

Angelique was pale with anger on Miss Keating's behalf. "Why? Why must they do it? Who *does* this sort of thing?"

They stood together in a certain wretched silence.

Delilah knew Angelique had once been devastated by a staggeringly unkind mention of her in the gossip sheets. She briefly covered Angelique's hand with hers and Angelique shot her a grateful look.

"But . . . how on earth did that dress come to be, Mrs. Pariseau?" Delilah asked. "Who originally had it made?"

It had to be asked.

Mrs. Pariseau was quiet for a time.

"I've no clues at all. I'm inclined to believe precisely what Madame Marceau said," she said slowly. "But I am *confident* that our Miss Keating is entirely innocent in the matter. And that is all I'm willing to surmise. Miss Keating fell in love with a dress she never would have been able to afford, she looked lovely in it, and it was being offered to her for no price at all. Who among us could have resisted?"

They could not argue with this: it was easy to fall in love with a dress.

Of greater concern was who might have fallen in love with Miss Keating.

And whether this meant she was ruined completely.

"Thank you, Mrs. Pariseau."

"We do have our share of dramas, don't we," Mrs. Pariseau said. Not without relish. "I will see you ladies at dinner!"

Despite the circumstances, Angelique and Delilah were touched by the "we."

The assumption that Mrs. Pariseau belonged to them and they to her; The Grand Palace on the Thames was home.

That they were in this together.

Behind them, Rose and Meggie, the maids, were

yawning and trying to look alert while Helga was patiently doling out the morning's chores.

Delilah pulled Angelique aside and lowered her voice.

"Angelique . . . Lord Kirke knew that Miss Keating and Mrs. Pariseau were going to visit the modiste. He was in the room when they planned it."

"I recalled that, too. But if he somehow had this dress made . . . *how*? He could hardly guess the girl's measurements precisely. I refuse to think even a rake has that kind of magical skill. What were his intentions, if so? What *are* his intentions? I thought the girl was being courted by Lord Vaughn."

Secretly, however, neither of them believed St. John was quite serious about getting married anytime soon. They had come to know him, and regarded him with a certain exasperated, impatient fondness.

"Maybe he had none, other than ensuring a lovely girl who wanted a dress got one? Maybe it *had* been made for his mistress. And for some reason was never given to her?"

Angelique was quiet. She'd been a mistress, too, long ago, in unhappier days. Such arrangements were seldom permanent, and seldom ended precisely as peacefully as either party would have desired.

Granted, those unhappier days had nevertheless led her to the life she was leading now, and had brought Delilah and The Grand Palace on the Thames and ultimately Lucien into her life.

"Do we dare ask him about it? Is there any call to do it?" Delilah ventured.

The notion was excruciating. Then again, they'd once called a duke to task for a transgression. But his transgression had been overt, and in front of witnesses. They could not see themselves confronting Kirke with an insinuation.

And there was another unspoken question: Would they need to ask him to leave, per the rules of The Grand Palace on the Thames? No proper gentleman would gift a young unmarried woman with a dress. It was just not done.

They were in uncertain territory, indeed.

"I think . . ." Angelique said carefully. "We must wait to see what happens next."

They'd also both learned that men who were utterly fearless, brilliant, and competent could behave as though they were lost in the wilderness without a compass when it came to matters of love.

It was the women who often had to guide them home.

IN CATHERINE'S ROOM Dot stood near her while Catherine stared at the paragraph in the newspaper.

As the words penetrated, it felt as though a sheet of ice moved over her skin. Until she couldn't feel her limbs at all.

Every one of her senses seemed to amplify. The pale morning light blinded. The very silence itself howled like a siren.

And then finally a sound penetrated her horror: above her, she heard a chair slide across the floor.

It might be a maid.

But it was very early, and Lord Kirke was still in his room.

"Miss Keating," Dot said quietly, finally. "Do you want me to throw it into the fire?"

"No, thank you, Dot." Her voice emerged almost as a croak. "But may I keep this for a little while before you bring it to the other guests?"

Dot nodded. "I'm so sorry if you are distressed. Should I have brought it to you?" she whispered.

"Yes. Thank you. Please do not worry. You did the right thing." Catherine could scarcely hear her own voice through the ringing in her ears.

Dot curtsied and scurried away.

The moment Dot vanished from view down the hall, Catherine did the formerly unthinkable.

She went upstairs with the newspaper and knocked on Kirke's door.

"CATHERINE." HIS VOICE was startled. Warm.

Then his expression went decidedly wary.

Because he'd registered her expression.

He was in shirtsleeves. His waistcoat cravat was looped around his neck. It was a strange echo of her first-ever glimpse of him.

"May I come in?" she said stiffly.

"I—" He stopped. He pressed his lips together.

After a hesitation. He stepped aside.

She closed the door.

Wordlessly, she immediately extended the newspaper to him.

He looked hard into her face. Then gingerly took the newspaper from her.

He glanced down. He seemed to instinctively know what to look for. God only knew, he'd allegedly appeared in the gossip pages often enough.

She saw the words enter him.

Because before her eyes, the blood drained from his face.

"Is this true?" she asked. "Was the blue dress made for your mistress? Did you arrange for me to have it?" She could hardly believe she was able to utter the words. They felt oddly foreign on her tongue.

He remained frozen and silent. His eyes fixed on the newspaper. But his breath was coming shorter now.

He looked very much like a man trapped, which was all the answer she needed. She could feel the storm of outrage stirring right outside the boundaries of her numb shock.

"Are you gathering your story, Lord Kirke?" Her temper was surging, rising in her body. It leaked into her words. "A yes or no will suffice."

He looked up at her at last. His eyes were stunned. As though he'd sustained a blow.

"Yes," he said simply.

The air went out of her.

"Oh my God." Her voice was a rasp. Her hand went up to her mouth. "But . . . how . . . how did you . . ."

"She ordered the dress without my knowledge, before she assaulted me and disappeared. I was sent the bill. I paid for the dress because I always pay my bills. I discreetly communicated my wishes to Madame Marceau via my man of affairs when I learned you would be visiting her establishment with Mrs. Pariseau. And the modiste . . . took care of the rest."

That beautiful dress. Every bit of it had been chosen by, and fitted upon, a woman to whom he'd made love. His mistress.

She didn't know why this should make her want to claw her skin away then and there. She could not rationalize away the scalding jealousy and outrage, all entangled as it was with embarrassment and shame that others knew. It held her in a vise. She could feel it in her throat. It boiled in her.

He was pale, and while his voice was quiet it was hatefully steady. "I knew Madame Marceau would never tell a soul, not if she ever wanted to take a commission from some duke in the ton who was trying to please his mistress, or anyone who cherished discretion. So the little item of gossip didn't come from her, I'm certain of it. It would mean the end of her business. I . . . have my suspicions."

"Lady Hackworth," she breathed suddenly. "She said she inquired after the bolt of silk and was told it was spoken for. Someone must have told her it was being held for *your mistress.*"

He squeezed his eyes closed. "Fucking. Hell. Tell me. Was I wrong about the Hackworths?" he said tautly.

She didn't even wince at the cursing, and he didn't apologize.

"How much did it cost? Dear God, the cost of a dress like that!"

"The cost is beside the point," he said almost coldly. "You were never meant to know it was I who paid for it, and you were certainly never meant to know the cost. You were simply meant to have the dress. I in fact entertained this possibility before you and I became in any way . . . significant . . . to each other. I knew it would make you happy and you would look spectacularly beautiful in it. And it did and you did."

She stared at him, still reeling. She gave a short, stunned laugh.

"Good God," she breathed in wonder. "You do think I'm an absolute idiot, a *bumpkin* of the first order. 'Clover,' indeed. Why else would you think I'd believe Madame Marceau would *just* give me such a dress. I feel like such a *fool.*"

His stance was wary and tense. "No one can make a fool of you if you don't allow them," he said tersely. "The gossip columns have not made a fool of you. You are not a fool, by any definition of the word. Why on earth should that dress go to waste when you could do it justice?"

"So it was by way of being practical, is what you're saying," she said sardonically, still light-headed from furious disbelief. "Like putting last night's leftover peas into tomorrow night's stew."

He dragged a hand over his face, as if he was about to lose the battle to maintain his composure, and his words were more clipped now.

"Believe it or not, Catherine, I took every bloody bit of this into consideration. I had no way of knowing whether you'd accept the dress, but I asked Madame Marceau to try. I considered your possible reaction, if you should ever discover it. I knew the chances were very slim—but not nonexistent—that anyone in the ton at large would know anything about the origins of your dress. And then . . ." He paused at length. Then gave a short, bitter, wondering laugh. "I did it anyway."

"But . . . *why?*"

He was silent for so long that she began to believe she was witnessing history: for the first time, Lord Kirke simply had no idea what to say.

His face remained leached of all color, which made his eyes look obsidian dark.

"You didn't see your face when you saw Mrs. Pariseau's new dress," he said quietly, finally. "But I did."

He sounded ever so faintly . . . not quite defeated. But resigned. As if he was confessing to a crime after years of running from the law.

What other words had he entertained and dismissed during that long hesitation?

But he said nothing more.

She froze, absolutely blank with astonishment. Uncertain and off-balance now.

Had the ache of wistful covetousness, the stab of pain she'd felt when she'd seen that dress been so obvious on her face? The notion made her feel raw and exposed and so terribly embarrassed.

But his strange composure and white face suggested to her that there was something else he was determinedly disguising. She could not quite bring it into view through her haze of furious, horrified mortification.

Her voice was hoarse and clipped. "I suppose none of that matters, anyway. Because here is the irony, Lord Kirke. You once claimed to have dreaded ruining me. And yet it seems I am now literally ruined. Lady Wisterberg informs me that *thirty-two* of the people who previously accepted an invitation to her party have now sent their regrets, canceling. We have canceled the party. My invitations to events have stopped completely. As far as the ton is concerned, I have clearly been cut dead. As though I never existed. My chances of a decent match *anywhere* in England are possibly over. My season certainly is. But I suppose you did warn me there would be consequences for dancing with you. I take responsibility for that." She said this bitterly.

She could hear the blood ringing in her ears in the silence that followed.

"I am sorrier than I can say to have caused you such distress," he said finally, so gently. "When I have valued our friendship more than I can say."

Friendship.

She didn't think she would ever forget how this room looked during this moment. The slant of the shadows. His coat slung over the chair. His papers strewn over the desk. How desperately she had wondered about the intimate details of his life. How she'd longed to know everything about him, as if in so doing she could finally know his heart. When this had always been impossible, because this broken man simply would not allow it to be known.

"I will find the person responsible for this little paragraph," he said calmly, "and I will destroy them."

She stared at him. She felt the little hairs prickling to attention at the back of her neck.

For the first time she understood how much of his eerie calm was merely skillfully contained fury.

"Will that make the fact that I wore your mistress's dress any less true?" she said bitterly.

"The object of the paragraph in *The Times* was to hurt you for entertainment purposes," he said slowly, laying the words down like bricks. "For the amusement of the masses. Do not think for one *moment* I will allow that to stand." His voice had escalated.

"Do not shoot anyone on my account, Lord Kirke. I'm certain the gossip columns will savor that, too, if you do. I will return home as soon as I can get the mail coach," she said, the words cracked and trembling now. "I can't . . . I can't stay in London any longer." Tears were gathering in the corners of her eyes.

Another of those pauses ensued while she could almost hear his formidable mind clearly working away. "I have a possible solution."

She waited.

He pulled in a breath and released it slowly.

And then another.

Still, his voice shook a little. "I am willing to marry you."

She stared at him. Her mind blanked in astonishment.

"*What?*" Her voice was cracked and threadbare, pitched flute-high with disbelief.

"It's what is normally done, isn't it?" His voice was still so very, very careful. "To salvage reputations in situations such as this. To provide a woman a modicum of freedom from judgment. To get the gossip to stop."

A fresh wave of nauseating shock swept through her.

"You . . . are . . . willing . . . to . . . marry . . . me," she repeated slowly. She moaned in near pain, and held her head in her hands. "I . . . it's . . . how *ghastly*. Do you hear it? Do you hear how that sounds? How martyred? As though I am some terrible problem that must be solved by throwing yourself on your sword? What kind of life would that be for you? What kind of life would that be for *me*? Everyone will believe I had been your mistress, and then no one will receive me, and we wouldn't have any friends. You would forever resent me for cornering you into this solution. No. *Never.* Never. Not if you were the last man on earth."

Her own torrent of furious words shocked her. Her capacity for blind rage and pain was a revelation. Her willingness to inflict it on him was another. She didn't know whether she even meant them. She only wanted to administer a killing blow, and they were the weapon at hand and so she used them.

She had learned an astonishing number of things about herself in London.

Kirke was as pale as if blood had never pumped through his veins. She could detect no movement at all. Not his breathing. Not a flicker of an eyelash.

"Maybe it's just you. Maybe you ruin everything you touch without trying," she added bitterly.

She could see these words land. She witnessed the breath literally leaving him. The pinched skin about his eyes. Which suddenly looked like dark bruises on his face.

The very air in the room seemed to sting her skin. Everything hurt intolerably.

"I will leave The Grand Palace on the Thames at once." His voice was uninflected.

She nodded shortly.

Then she turned her back so she wouldn't have to see what she'd done to him.

Chapter Twenty-Two

❧❧❧

$\mathcal{N}$OT MORE than an hour after Delilah and Angelique had read the little item in the newspaper, Dot came to them bearing an urgent request from Lord Kirke, who wished to speak with them at once in the reception room.

They scrambled out of their aprons to meet him there.

They had a feeling they had reached the "see what happens next" they'd been anticipating.

He stopped pacing before the fireplace when he saw them swiftly progressing across the marble foyer toward him.

Delilah discreetly closed the door of the room behind them.

"Thank you for attending me, Mrs. Hardy, Mrs. Durand," he said without preamble. "In light of the distress an item of gossip in the newspaper has caused Miss Keating, I feel it prudent that I take my leave of you at once, for the sake of appearances. I do not believe anyone knows that Miss Keating and I are currently living beneath your roof. I fear I am a veteran of the gossip sheets for many reasons, some perhaps warranted and some not, and can easily withstand the negative attention. She does not deserve it." He faltered almost infinitesimally here. "I am infuriated, and I will take action. I can state definitively that she is wholly innocent of the insinuation and I deeply regret that they feel they can somehow besmirch her name by associating it with mine."

He'd said all of this politely. Very nearly crisply. As though it was just a matter of business.

But the word "regret" was cracked in the middle.

They saw the tension tugging at his mouth, across his cheekbones.

His words might be polite.

But his eyes were shattered.

Angelique and Delilah thought they were witnessing a man coming apart. At the very least, in some terrible pain.

He'd arrived somewhat wild-eyed. He was leaving in a similar condition. And in between he'd looked as though he'd finally found a home.

Then again, this was a man who apparently did not live his life by halves.

What on *earth* had transpired?

They noticed he hadn't insisted the gossip item had no merit. Nor had he explained how he happened to know that Miss Keating was distressed.

Then again, perhaps he didn't owe them an explanation.

They had both learned that formidable men knew a thousand ways to disguise anything that might be construed as weakness.

"We are sorry for your distress, Lord Kirke, and we respect your wishes. We do wish all the best for you. I know Mr. Delacorte in particular will miss you. You are always welcome here," Delilah said gently. For this was true, for now.

He paused. "I have enjoyed my stay . . . more than I anticipated." He smiled faintly, realizing how that sounded. But his voice was rueful and wistful in a way that made both of their hearts contract with sympathy.

And then he smiled, and when he smiled it was so staggeringly clear how this challenging man could buckle any woman's knees.

"Please give my regards to your husbands and to Mr. Delacorte. Tell him if he practices hard enough, he might one day be as good as I am at chess."

With this last little bit of mischief fomented, he bowed, and then he and his portmanteau went out the door.

CATHERINE RETREATED TO her room and packed her belongings swiftly. Blindly. Punishingly, as if her two-year-old dresses were transgressors. Remembering how hopeful she had felt the last time she'd packed them.

How could she *ever* have been so foolish and naive? Thanks to Lord Kirke, naive was the last thing she was now.

She was still shaking violently from the storm of emotion and shock.

I am willing to marry you.

The *gall* of him. The bitter *shame* of it.

The ghastly, howling pain of it.

To be a problem to be *solved*, an albatross to be worn about his neck for the rest of his life.

Not a prize to be claimed.

Or a woman to be loved.

She sat down hard on the bed and dropped her face into her hands.

She was furious because she could see so clearly now that she had only herself to blame for all of this. What manner of madness had overtaken her? How had she ever thought she'd be equal to London? How had she thought herself equal to *him*?

No one can make a fool of you if you don't allow them, he'd said.

A stubborn echo of her usual common sense responded to those words. Because she was sensible, was she not? Because she knew what he'd meant. She subscribed to this philosophy, too.

And yet it also went some way toward absolving him of responsibility for what had happened.

He was a clever man, she'd grant him that, she thought bitterly. Quite the nimble thinker.

Nothing changed the fact that she had worn, on her own body, over her own skin, the dress meant for a woman to whom he'd made love as part of a business arrangement because he'd known she'd be gullible enough to take it from the modiste.

And she might never have known, if not for that gossip in the newspaper.

That the whole of the ton now seemed to know was unbearable. That they might actually believe she had all along been his mistress while masquerading as an innocent young woman made bile rise in her throat. That what had once been seen as charming and novel—her newness to the ton, the fact she was relatively unknown—was precisely the permission they needed to suspect her. She'd been like a shiny toy, batted aloft between them. She had reached the end of her usefulness, and the last bit of fun they could get out of her was tossing her away.

This embarrassment and shame had no precedence in her life; she was ill-equipped to bear it. It shuddered through her again and again. She didn't know how to ease the torment of it.

To think, she might never have known how muscular her pride was if some man hadn't dressed her in his mistress's clothing.

Surely embarrassment in and of itself wasn't fatal, her good sense chimed in weakly. *Do* these people truly matter? And it was just a dress?

She didn't want to listen to sense at the moment. Those people *might* have mattered if she'd had a future with someone like Lord Vaughn. Which she clearly no longer did.

She was finding great wells of strength in her outrage, which swelled into fear and back into outrage again. Because the possibility remained that she *was* forever ruined. And this was a reason indeed to panic.

She breathed into her hands. In and out, in and out.

She pulled them away wet with tears.

Then she gave herself a shake, dashed her palm across her eyes, and went to find Mrs. Durand and Mrs. Hardy.

MISS KEATING WAS *considerably* less composed than Lord Kirke.

She sat across from Delilah and Angelique on the pink settee, visibly shaking. Her eyes were pink-rimmed and swollen from tears.

"I am so terribly embarrassed by the gossip. It isn't true, I promise you! But I feel I must leave at once. It has become clear to me that my season is at an end."

Her voice was thick.

They gave her a handkerchief embroidered with the initials TGPOTT. They were always prepared.

"We do not believe all of the gossip, Miss Keating," Mrs. Hardy told her firmly, which was on the whole true. "And we do not believe it of Lord Kirke, either. We have loved having you here, and we very much hope to see you again. We're so terribly sorry your season has ended so unhappily. But we understand why you feel you must return home."

Miss Keating sat quietly for a moment. Simply breathing.

"Is he . . . has he gone, then?" Her eyes were suddenly wide in what looked like stunned realization.

"Lord Kirke? He departed a few hours ago," Angelique told her gently. "He's gone."

She went rigidly still. As if she was only now absorbing the ramifications of this. "He's really gone?" she almost whispered.

"Miss Keating . . ." Angelique said gently ". . . you must tell us at once if he behaved in any way inappropriately."

"No," she replied vehemently. "He has always been . . . he was always kind."

The last word was broken, and she buried it in her new handkerchief. She wept, her shoulders heaving.

Delilah patted her soothingly, while she and Angelique exchanged bewildered looks.

Miss Keating finally looked up abruptly.

"You have all been so very good to me." She hungrily swept with her eyes the sitting room, the chandelier, the Epithet Jar. Gathering it into her memory.

Catherine was so tired of saying goodbye to things she had come to love.

And yet, only a fool lingers at the scene of their devastation.

LADY WISTERBERG WAS generously paying for the royal mail coach so Catherine would have a swifter journey home, and she came to The Grand Palace on the Thames to collect her first thing the following morning to escort her to it.

"You know it isn't true?" Catherine said to her again. "You believe me? Please tell me you believe me."

Lady Wisterberg was both outraged and resigned. "Oh good heavens, my dear, I know it isn't true. You are a good girl and an innocent and the whole of the ton during the season are jackals." And yet Lady Wisterberg also sounded so matter-of-fact about it. She'd almost said it with a sort of bitter relish. It was clearly a milieu she understood in a way that Catherine never would. It was as though Catherine's season had been a game of five-card loo for Lady Wisterberg, and winning or losing had always been equal possibilities. She wondered at all of the things that Lady Wisterberg had seen throughout her life. And why she knew so much about everyone, and how she was able to get invitations for all those events in the first place. "I knew no good could come from associating with that man," the dowager muttered.

She hadn't known this at all, but Catherine didn't argue. That man was the only reason she'd had some semblance of a season at all.

It was also interesting to discover that her new lack of innocence wasn't at all apparent.

"I'll see what I can do to dispel that rumor," Lady Wisterberg continued. "I will contemptuously smash it like a fly if it buzzes up again. It should die down soon enough. But I do think leaving the ton is the wisest and only thing you can do. For your sake and for Lucy's sake, too, my dear."

Oh God! Poor Lucy! To have such a tainted friend!

But Lucy had been as perversely thrilled by the scandal as most humans would be, and impressed by the magnitude of ghastliness of it. She was also genuinely hurt and horrified for her. They had stopped at Lady Wisterberg's town house so they could say goodbye to each other.

No doubt she was also relieved that Catherine would likely never again turn Mr. Hargrove's head.

"I will visit you in the country," Lucy promised. "I'm so sorry about your season!"

"At least we have memories for a lifetime," Catherine said ironically. They both laughed a little. "I hope when you visit me you will be Mrs. Hargrove."

They had hugged each other goodbye, as though they'd been through a war together.

None of this had been Lucy's fault, either. And she was not at all certain whether she would see Lucy again.

"And do you know what else I heard?" Lady Wisterberg said, as the carriage carrying them to the mail coach reached the end of Barking Road. "It's a rumor, too, mind you. From a maid who is a friend of a maid who is having an affair with a footman at Lady Clayton's London town house. I learned that Kirke *paid footmen* to remind me to take you home from every ball before your curfew. At every single event. The cheek of the man!" Her own cheeks went rosy even as she said it.

Catherine's heart stopped.

"Lord Kirke did what?" she breathed.

"He paid footmen a *shilling* to remind me to take you home by curfew. At every ball. A shilling! To come and fetch me from the game room. And they did! Do you know how much a shilling means to a footman? As if I wouldn't remember my responsibility to you," she huffed.

But Catherine recalled how logy and resentful Lady Wisterberg had been in the carriage as she'd dutifully escorted her home. As if she'd been pulled from a trance. She began to imagine the scene that might have been caused by a footman attempting to get her up from a game in which she was deeply immersed and had no intention of leaving.

Her throat felt tight. She somehow hadn't even considered that Lady Wisterberg might simply forget about her. But of course that made sense. After all, Lucy, who was staying with Lady Wisterberg, had no curfew. All of the other adults in Catherine's life had always been responsible. Not a gambler or imbiber in the lot.

Dominic must have known how nearly drugged Lady Wisterberg was by gambling. After all, he knew the ton as well as Lady Wisterberg did.

He had looked after her from the first. From the very night he'd been hit in the face. He had seen to her safety. To the time he'd gone, against his will, to find her at the Hackworths' because she'd done a stubbornly reckless thing to get him to prove that he cared.

And he never would have told her about the footmen. She might never have known.

He'd done it because that was who he was. Her chest ached.

"Perhaps we'll never know who was responsible for the dress," Lady Wisterberg said. "But if you ask me, that man has taken an inordinate interest in you and you are safer in the country."

But Catherine was stunned.

You didn't see your face when you saw Mrs. Pariseau's new dress. But I did.

Of a certainty, he was a man who understood longing. And the suffering implicit in it.

Kirke had wanted her to have a beautiful dress, and he could hardly overtly buy one for her. So he'd done that, too.

Because he couldn't help himself. He'd wanted to ease her suffering.

She covered her eyes with her hands. They had begun to sting again.

He thought of his work as moving the world toward justice. But she saw now that what he really was doing was trying to move the world more toward love. Love seemed a fundamental part of him, however fiercely, indirectly expressed. Even as it had devastated his life years ago.

Perhaps this—these furtive gestures, this little secret safety net he had built for her, the acts of service he performed as part of his role as MP—was the only way he could love now.

What if she'd said yes to his proposal? Would he have been hers forever?

But it seemed to her there was a part of him that would not allow her to love him or himself to love her and she simply couldn't imagine a life lived that way. How empty it would be.

She'd once thought being married to him would be like yearning after something while it was clutched in your fist. Somehow she'd known from the first.

And surely a man who could speak so eloquently and at length about so many things could get out those three important little words if they were true?

Perhaps he hadn't said them because they simply weren't.

Perhaps he could only love once, and he had spent his love on Anna.

Because if he was willing to fight for everyone and everything else, why hadn't he fought for her?

He hadn't. Which must mean that he could do without her.

Leaving London was the right thing to do, she understood.

Still, in essence, she was ruined, in every sense of the word. She had been ruined even before the gossip item. Because she could not now imagine herself with any other man.

Yet practicalities demanded that one day she do exactly that.

Lady Wisterberg was undaunted. She gave Catherine a little thigh pat.

"There, there, dear," she soothed. "You'll be home soon. The gossip will stop—eventually. Your aunt and I will see about finding a landed country gentleman for you. Perhaps a nice widower who won't care about any silly rumors."

She handed Catherine a handkerchief, as the tears she could no longer contain spilled again.

HER FATHER AND Mrs. Cartwright were surprised and delighted when Catherine and her trunk appeared at the door of the home they all shared.

"I missed you both, and I missed the country. I had a wonderful time in London, and I made some nice friends, but this is where I want to be."

"Well, you're a sight for sore eyes and we're happy you are here," her father said comfortingly.

There was undeniable happiness in being the source of his happiness; her heart lifted a little.

"So are you, Papa!"

But to her alarm, he felt slighter in her arms when she hugged him. His white hair was longer and a little fluffier, as if he might drift away from her, like a cloud, at any moment.

But the most difficult part was that she could tell—by the way he'd studied her, eyebrows pitched together—that her father knew she was lying in some fashion about why she was home, because he was no fool. And because he knew what grief looked like. It soaked into one's bones, changed the way you walked and the rhythms of your speech. It hovered behind your expressions, no matter how much care you took to arrange your features in such a way as not to worry anyone else around you.

And if she hadn't already known that she loved Dominic all along, the grief would have told her. Grief was the price—the gift—of love.

Her father didn't press her for details. And she refused to say or do anything that would worry him.

And while she had local friends who were peacefully married; she could not imagine they could commiserate about London gossip, or tristes with a notorious baron in a carriage, or the garden of a mansion, or up against the wall of her cozy room.

The irony was that of all the confidants she could imagine, the only person with whom she could fully imagine discussing such a thing was with Lord Kirke.

So mainly she extolled the joys of The Grand Palace on the Thames, and she described in detail the fine houses at which all the balls took place, including the fact that all of them featured healthy potted plants.

She'd left the blue dress behind in her room at the boardinghouse.

In comparison to London, she found the quiet of the country somehow both deafening and as soothing as the coverlet at The Grand Palace on the Thames.

She'd arrived with her entire being ringing from a terrible blow, as if she had toppled from on high, from perhaps a desk. She let the familiar soft, green hills cool and comfort her until the tumult in her settled enough for something else to be clear:

Her country village was no longer enough for her.

The contours of her soul had changed in a short time, and she no longer fit it, like a dress she had outgrown.

What had Lord Kirke said in the sitting room that night: *We may not find precisely what we're looking for as we seek answers, but the search may reveal to us other useful or beautiful things about ourselves and our world.*

It was like wildflowers, she supposed: one never knew which ones might burst forth in the spring, having waited beneath the earth for just the right rain and warmth. London, and a certain beautiful, difficult, flawed man, had caused her soul to riotously bloom. She hadn't known passion or wildness or complexity or jealousy or daring were part of her. She hadn't known it was possible to be more fully, soaringly *herself* until she'd met him. She hadn't truly known the depths of her capacity for tenderness, or her need to express and receive it.

He was the cause of her suffering, but the notion that she might never have met him left her desolate. The idea that he could easily find a temporary lover to comfort and distract him scorched the breath from her if she dared entertain it for a moment. She'd grown up with such a fine, peaceful example of love. How had she managed to fall in love with a man who seemed unable to love her in return?

And at night, even the skim of her night rail over skin was a sensual torment. Because her skin remembered, and preferred, the skim of his fingertips.

She was more conscious than she'd ever been of how quiet it was in their house at night. She was

wistful for the merry sitting room of The Grand
Palace on the Thames, and the sound of cheerful
debate, and the clicking of knitting needles, and the
rustle of pages turning. For the little *pok* sound of
someone laying a chess piece decisively down on a
chessboard.

"I wonder if I could read a story aloud to you?"
she offered one night to her father.

He studied her, surprised.

"We haven't yet done that, have we? It sounds
lovely. Have you one in mind?"

It was one way to fill the room with other people:
by way of characters and stories.

How had brave Scheherazade managed to mine
her imagination for so many stories? As Lord Kirke
said, women were resourceful when the circumstances demanded it. And she knew she, too, would
find ways to survive.

HOTEL ROOMS WERE always scarce during the London season. Kirke finally found an unimpressive
one near the King's Theatre, where the poor madman shouted Hamlet soliloquies to an indifferent
audience.

He felt like his town house after the fire: still upright. Still looking more or less whole and normal
on the outside.

Inside, scorched to charcoal.

It seemed to him a blackly comic farce of Shake-
spearean grandeur that every time he truly loved
someone, he apparently destroyed them and shattered
his own life.

He tried, as one does, to trace it back to the beginning, back to the moment he'd taken her handkerchief from her, to see where he could have done

something differently. He did not see how he would have made different choices. He could rue them all now, but a different choice would mean he would never have held her in his arms, and this he knew he would never forego.

He was able, for a time, to function within a blessed shocked numbness. For a fortnight, he managed to allow in no feeling at all by working until he dropped into a black sleep at night. He was damned if his own stupidity and suffering would lead to more suffering for any of the people he'd been trying to help or the people he'd been elected to serve.

It was useful to have a sense of duty for a spine. To fill his days with meetings and appointments he would be required to attend. He reported to Parliament, and voted when needed.

But as one week became two weeks became three, his inner condition became outwardly apparent.

Because he scarcely ate.

He gave no speeches.

And he attended no balls.

He'd tried to attend one, and by his calm insouciance demonstrated that the rumors about him and an innocent girl who had merely visited London from the country for a few weeks were nonsense, as so many rumors were.

He knew—he heard—Lady Wisterberg had vigorously done her part to slap them down, too. She was convincingly scornful and indignant. Then again, if she had been just as forceful about protecting Keating's reputation from the first, Dominic would never have spent a moment alone with her.

So be it.

The ton gossips eventually gave up the outlandish notion of him taking the angelic young Miss K as a mistress, and stopped talking about her altogether, mainly because it was not as much fun to shun someone who wasn't present for the shunning. And because no oxygen was given to the flames.

But at the ball he'd attended, he found himself experiencing a nearly grotesque lurch of hope when he glanced at a collection of ferns in a corner of a ballroom.

After that, he found he simply couldn't go to another. That was it for him for the season.

And possibly for every season thereafter.

Chapter Twenty-Three

❧❧❧

IN THE absence of information about the notice-
ably thinner and paler Lord Dominic Kirke, more
rumors sprouted like mushrooms. About his health
and finances and love affairs and by-blows.

And even those who heretofore might have
gloated over the notion of Kirke becoming a shell of
a man were worried and disgruntled. Where would
they focus all of their rancor now? It was much
more fun when their opponent clearly held them in
contempt, too. Where was the sport in resenting a
clearly suffering man?

And there were those who rubbed their hands
together gleefully. Bertram Rowley, for instance.
"Kirke is a spent force," he declared to those who
would listen. "His debauchery has caught up to
him. Why would you want such a man representing
you in the Commons?"

Dominic had friends of the sort who would politely inquire after his health at White's but not pur-
sue the matter after he said, "I'm well, thank you, and
you?" Friends of the sort who enjoyed and sought his
company for a game of cards, or a good debate.

A determinedly friendly Mr. Delacorte tracked
him down through his man of affairs and issued invitations to come and play chess with him in a noisy
pub. He went. Paradoxically, the loud Mr. Delacorte
was surprisingly soothing company.

But he had no real confidants. No friends of the kind that Hardy and Bolt seemed to have in each other, for instance.

None whom he would trust with his current torment, if even he'd been able to articulate it.

As it turned out, this very realization was like the rope thrown into the deep, dark well he'd been down for weeks.

Thanks to Catherine, he realized now that it was because he'd long held himself apart from allowing himself to be fully known.

And in so doing, he had only hurt himself and others.

That in a lifelong commitment to protecting the vulnerable, it had never occurred to him that he was one of them.

That he had constructed his life in such a way to protect and disguise the grave damage of an old shame. If he'd let himself be known, it had seemed inevitable to him that people would eventually discover how contemptuous he really was.

It was a bloody unwelcome thought, and it joined the rest of the delightful torment stew he was currently enjoying.

Because he realized it was the source of all his problems.

And then it brought an epiphany: it might also be the source of all the answers.

She can't hurt me if she doesn't know me.

He mulled this again.

He was not convinced life-ruining was his vocation. God only knew worse things had been said to him and he'd survived it. But the accusation had been a spear to the ribs because she knew where to aim. It was the best and most unnerving thing about her. And he'd given her the ammunition.

He'd apparently done a stupid thing by arranging for her to have the dress. He realized now it was his way of saying "I love you" before he'd even known he did.

He'd insulted her with the world's most stunted marriage proposal, a craven, strategic attempt to keep her while still shielding himself from the threat of grave pain if she did not, in fact, love him. *Christ*. He sucked in a breath.

Still, he was blackly amused at himself. He couldn't fault a man for trying. His own instinct for survival was clearly pronounced. Because he simply had ceased being able to imagine a life without her.

Then again, most of the things he did were *not* stupid.

Gingerly, he ran his thoughts over the wounds and errors of his past, inspecting them honestly.

Anna was content in her life now, surrounded by her family. Leo was thriving.

And even though Keating knew the messy truth of him . . .

She'd still done a mad thing, and climbed up on a desk in the hopes she could hear him breathing.

Hope stirred and needled him.

He refused to allow himself to dodge away from the exquisite terror of hope. He sat with it, even as it unsettled his breathing. He allowed himself to imagine joy. To feel it fill his body, unfettered. Told himself he was not a fool to do it.

How long had it been since anyone had truly known him—and loved him anyway? So long he had gone blind to the signs, like a cave creature?

Because he'd forgotten how the minutest detail about a loved one became a treasure to gather.

She'd wanted to hear him breathe.

On the hotel ceiling was a stain shaped like Italy, and he lay on his back on the (lumpy) bed and stared up at it for a time as if it was an oracle.

What he wouldn't give right now to hear her breathing next to him.

Finally he closed his eyes, and lost himself to the memory of the unguarded tenderness with which Catherine's fingers had landed against his face. She had from the first looked at him, and spoken to him, and touched him, with the courage born of an innocence that hadn't yet been hobbled by heartbreak. He'd been almost unable to bear it. He'd not wanted to accept how desperately he'd needed it.

What if you didn't fight everything? she'd asked, the night she'd worn a goldenrod dress.

Had she seen what he could not? That he'd been fighting against the tide of his feelings for her?

Had she seen his fear? His pride recoiled from this notion.

And yet. She was the one person in the world he would trust with his fear.

Had she been trying to tell him then that he was free to love her, because she could love him, too?

He breathed as the impossible beauty of this possibility flowed through him like a sweet drug.

And yet. He wasn't certain she would even speak to him again.

It remained more than possible he'd botched things utterly.

But he saw very clearly now that the only chance he had of salvation was to lay himself bare. And in so doing, even if he never saw her again . . . he knew, somehow, he would at last be free.

His pillow at this hotel wasn't soft. It was no hardship to leave it, light a lamp, and settle in at the desk, which suffered from the absence of blossoms in a vase.

And he settled in to write a speech like no other he'd ever written.

It was time to let himself be known.

St. Stephens Chapel at the Palace of Westminster, where the House of Commons met, was stuffed cheek by jowl with members of Parliament from both the Lords and the Commons that day.

Word had spread that after weeks of silence, Lord Dominic Kirke was finally going to speak.

The speaker in question paced, as he always did before speeches, taking long deep draughts of the air breathed by centuries of MPs before him. His palms were damp. There was always a moment—and it was brief—where he felt almost lifted out of his body with unreality as he took in the hundreds of eyes fixed upon him. A euphoric sort of terror. The first words were always the hardest, but he gathered strength from each one he said, until speaking was as innate as breathing.

He knew his audience was expecting to be stirred. And usually he complied, with fire and passion.

Today, little did they know, they would be offered something completely new.

A love letter.

"When I was a boy, in Wales . . ." he began, conversationally, "I grew up in a tiny house of nine people. Yes, I had six brothers and sisters. I know what you're all thinking: thank God there are more Kirkes, because we cannot get enough of the one we have." He paused for scattered laughter, good-natured theatrical moans. "My childhood was chaos. Crying, screaming, arguments, laughter, wrestling, chasing, nothing but noise all day long. There was seldom enough to eat, and never a moment's peace, not even at night, when the whole of my family, parents and children, were all stuffed into two beds. The *snoring*. You could not hear your own thoughts, gentlemen. And I had a lot of them, as you can imagine."

Many faces were smiling; many remained impassive, or merely alert. But he had fully captured their attention now. He had never begun a speech quite like this.

"How did I survive? I had a secret." He paused, knowing the power of this word, and the power of silence, like a rest in a composition. "And my secret was this: I had a refuge. Whenever I wanted a moment alone, when the noise and bickering and babies became more than even a saint could tolerate—I am no saint"—he paused for a heartbeat to allow the chuckles to subside—"I would sneak out to a scrubby little hill near my house. It was as unprepossessing as a place could be. It had as its crowning feature: a large gray boulder, which obscured me from anyone who might be hunting for me.

"And this hillside was covered in the most heavenly carpet of clover."

He let the word linger in the air, like a caress.

"Like an embrace, that clover was. I never wanted to leave it. It was there, on that hillside, that I felt like my truest, freest, safest self. When I shuffle off this mortal coil, if I through some miracle make it past the gates, I'm certain heaven will look like that clover-covered hillside, scented with little purple blossoms. And instead of harps, I'll hear the hum of bees and the wind moving the long grass.

"So what does 'clover' mean to me? Refuge. Paradise. Peace. And I sometimes think that if anyone could peer at the contents of my heart—well, frankly, you'd find clover. And I will confess something, gentlemen. To this day, when I'm having difficulty falling asleep, I imagine I'm back on that hillside. It's my heart's true home."

It was absolutely silent. It was a silence created by motionlessness. Not a paper rustled. Not a bum shifted in a seat. Not a head turned away from him. He could not yet ascertain whether the quality of silence was uniformly rapt, or uneasy, or confused, or appalled by the spectacle of Lord Kirke ripping away the veil, so to speak, over the contents of his heart. They had never before heard him wax sentimental. But they were all enthralled because they wanted to see where this story was going. He suddenly felt like Scheherazade, waiting for her verdict.

He let the silence stretch a bit.

"And it's the English way, isn't it?" he said almost offhandedly. "When most of you were still small boys, I warrant, you were taken away from your homes and families and sent off to school. It will make a *man* of you, you were told. And you believed it because children believe what the adults we love and trust tell us. That is the nature of a child. What choice do we have?" He paused again, and his next words were almost intimate, a gentle question, as if they were all sitting across from each other at White's. "Do you remember that day? Think about it now. Did you wonder why your parents could so easily do without you? Did you long for home? You were only children. Small, innocent boys." He allowed this to settle in. "Did you feel . . . abandoned?"

And he could feel the emotional tenor of the place shift.

"How did you comfort yourself on those first long nights away from home? What did you think about? When did you begin to feel safe again? Some of us, in some fashion—well, I warrant, we never really felt safe again, knowing that life could take us from the things and people we love."

Finally a sound, the best sound of all under the circumstances: a stifled sob.

Oh yes. He would ever so softly break them, he thought, with a warm surge of triumph.

He saw a man passing a handkerchief to Farquar.

"So where did you go in your heart to feel safe when you were a child? What, to you, is your clover-covered hillside? Who were you, gentlemen, when you felt your best, your safest, your truest self, at peace with the world? How often do you feel that way now? Because I will tell you: the only way any living thing can bloom is if it's given the slightest chance to grow where the elements can't destroy it. Some measure, some shelter, some small moment of safety and peace. I would not be standing before you now if I had not found my own. Think of me what you will, but all of us, together, shape history."

And because his senses were so heightened, he saw it: tears shining in the eyes of the most cynical bloody men. He was speaking to some painful part of them that they had never dared visit or mention. That had been forgotten, abandoned, or buried. Laying himself bare and laid them bare, too, and they were all taken off guard.

"In the workhouse of Bethnal Green. In a dormitory attached to a textile mill. In orphanages. There are children who didn't ask to be born. Children who are as innocent as you or I were. Who began life as hopeful, and as trusting."

His voice rose and rose, subtly, gradually, until it was soaring. "Can you—CAN you—imagine the loneliness? The fear? The heartbreak? When a mill owner tricks them into signing a paper that says he essentially owns them for decades? The hope they felt, the joy, at finally belonging somewhere? A place of safety and refuge? And then to have that trust betrayed so brutally when the hours are inhumane, the food is inadequate, the conditions so often abusive.

"I think you can." He said it softly. Tenderly. Regretfully.

Ever so slightly accusingly.

He paused to allow this to settle in.

"We can be their refuge. And no—we might not be able to give all of them a clover-covered hill. But we can make them that much safer. We can create in their lives a space for peace and comfort and safety, so they can bloom. So one of them one day might stand before you and give a speech like this one. We owe it to them, we owe it to ourselves, we owe it to England, we owe it to the future of this great country. Together we can give that to them, gentlemen."

He went on to tell them how.

Through changes in laws. Through better enforcement of current laws. Through apprenticeship programs. And more. They listened to every single word because they were absolute captives now; they were *inhabitants* of the world of his speech.

He had often questioned why he'd been fortunate enough to be born with this gift, but today he felt he finally knew the answer: so that a doctor in Northumberland could read it aloud to his daughter at the breakfast table, and she would know that a man from Wales had given her his heart.

THE FOLLOWING DAY, Dot, Angelique, Delilah, and Mrs. Pariseau gathered in the kitchen around the newspaper and breathlessly listened while Angelique read the speech aloud.

They all sighed and murmured.

"My goodness. One of his finest," Mrs. Pariseau declared, brushing a tear from her eye.

The Times had, in fact, called it "ruthlessly sentimental, incisive, informative, personal, and moving—a tour de force."

"And to think he made Mr. Delacorte say 'defecate' out loud in our sitting room only recently," Delilah mused.

"Mr. Delacorte brings out the best in all of us," Angelique replied.

(Personally, they secretly thought this was true.)

Mr. Delacorte greatly missed Lord Kirke. "He's eloquent *and* a bit of a rude bastard," he'd mused admiringly, in the smoking room. "You wouldn't think those two things would go well together, but they do." He'd pressed Lord Bolt, who was a member of White's, to inquire about Kirke's man of affairs, and he'd tracked him down via a message. *"You can run but you can't hide, Kirke. I can still beat you in chess."*

"He called her Clover," Mrs. Pariseau said quietly. "In the sitting room."

They all exchanged glances.

Angelique extended her arm for them all to see. "Goose bumps."

They all knew who "she" was. The girl who wore

the beautiful blue dress. They all missed Catherine, too. She had fit in so happily at The Grand Palace on the Thames.

"I wonder if we'll learn what happens next," Delilah mused.

It was a fair question. Interestingly, the newspaper had printed an actual retraction of the spiteful gossip about the dress. This was unprecedented.

And not one scrap of gossip about Lord Kirke had been printed since.

DOMINIC'S SPEECH RESONATED throughout London, and the House of Lords—through all of England, eventually—for weeks thereafter. (It would, in time, be printed in history books.)

He did not yet know whether its echoes were felt in Northumberland. He did know it sometimes took weeks for the papers to arrive in the outer reaches of the countryside. And he didn't know if it would do anything to influence the immediate vote for limiting the working hours for children.

But in its immediate aftermath, he felt spent and almost peaceful. He had done what he felt he could. In light of this, he would accept his fate, whenever it was revealed to him.

Meanwhile, it bought him a measure of goodwill that manifested in surprising ways. He received invitations to events he had not anticipated. Cricket matches. Family dinners at colleagues' homes. More donkey races.

He went. He liked all of them much better than balls.

It brought him a fresh measure of resentment, too, because his political foes felt both reluctantly moved and sympathetic, and also foiled. As though he'd revealed yet another new weapon. He remained, as ever, the candidate they probably could never beat. Rowley looked like quite a fool for even considering a run against him.

And astonishingly, Farquar had sent to him an abject written apology for punching him in the face and for his underhanded dealings with Marie-Claude, and had made an enormous donation to an orphanage. Farquar clearly loved his wife. Even odious people could love and be loved, Dominic thought wryly.

But Farquar still owned his damned mill, however, staffed with children.

Dominic had assured him he would never, *ever* stop attempting to end this.

And then he received a letter he would cherish for the rest of his life:

Dear Lord Kirke,

I do not know yet what to call you. I contemplated Father Kirke, but it is the name of our very pious and judgmental vicar in Yorkshire and from what I understand the two of you have little in common. I hope you will forgive me if "Father" does not quite roll off the quill pen easily.

I should like to thank you for the books. I liked Rob Roy very much. The Ghost in the Attic is a trifle confusing, as the peril awaiting the heroine would seem to be in the title. I look forward to discovering how it ends. Mr. Miles Redmond has had an envious life, and I am enjoying his adventures, too.

I read your speech in the newspaper. My

*secret place is beneath an oak tree one mile
from the home in which I grew up. I hope one
day to visit your place in Wales.*

*I hope this letter finds you well, which is
perhaps how I should have begun it. I am well.*

Leo Jenkins Atwell (Kirke)

Sardonic and funny, polite and articulate, grateful and vulnerable.

That is indeed my boy, he thought, with a lump in his throat. God help the lad.

While all of London was introduced to the softer side of Kirke, some people in London had been reintroduced to . . . another side.

"While I'm conscious that a certain benefit to both of us occurs when my name appears in any capacity in your newspaper, whether the mention is flattering or not," he said very pleasantly to Mr. Barnes, *The Times* publisher, over drinks at White's, "I have decided to sue you into oblivion over the latest item. The public does not take kindly to the cavalier destruction of a young woman's reputation."

Barnes took this in thoughtfully and stared back at Kirke. He had an admirable game face.

Finally, he decided to adopt a wounded expression. "I thought we were friends, Kirke."

Kirke sighed heavily and tilted his head in a "come now, do better" gesture.

He waited in silence until Barnes was a little sweaty with nerves, then idly added, "I might be inclined to be more charitable if you tell me the source of the gossip."

Shortly thereafter, a retraction was printed. And every merchant in the ton ceased extending credit to the Hackworths, who had always lived on the teetering edge of ruin. Their furniture and carriage were repossessed, and two months later, their town house was seized by the bank. For Kirke had amassed plenty of credit in the form of support and goodwill of his own with merchants of the ton, and one subtle suggestion to a carriage maker about the likelihood of him ever recovering his money from the Hackworths spread to the others.

And as the builders steadily put his home back together, he stared at his hotel ceiling at night, and surrendered to, glutted on, in fact, the constant dull ache in his heart. Because that was all he currently had of Catherine.

All he might ever have of her.

"You'll have your memories," people liked to say about lost things.

And yet his memories were both bliss and torment.

But he would not yet go in pursuit of her. He simply could not be certain it wouldn't appall and distress her. He wanted to cause her no further suffering.

But he had sent out a signal. And if nothing else, whatever befell the two of them, at least hopefully she would know for the rest of her life that Dominic Kirke had loved her.

Chapter Twenty-Four

✦

"**M**RS. CARTWRIGHT, will you please pass the salt?"

"Of course, dear," she said absently. She didn't look away from the page of *The Times* she was reading as she pushed the salt dish over to Catherine, who sat opposite her father in the sunny morning kitchen. They were surrounded by a pleasant morning feast of eggs and toast and kippers and coffee.

Catherine sprinkled some salt over her eggs and scooped her fork into them.

She dropped the fork with a clatter when Mrs. Cartwright gasped theatrically.

"Good heavens, Mrs. Cartwright. What is it?"

"The news about Lord Kirke!"

Freezing dread roared through Catherine with such force she nearly toppled from her chair. She dug her fingertips into the edge of the table.

Her lips couldn't form the words "what news?" She merely made an inarticulate questioning sound. Almost a whimper.

"The beautiful speech he gave on the floor of the House of Commons a few weeks ago," Mrs. Cartwright expounded. "They're saying grown men were weeping. Weeping! Now, that must have been a sight. They're calling it 'The Clover Speech.'"

When Catherine said nothing for long seconds, Mrs. Cartwright looked up. "Catherine dear, you've gone pale."

Portent had sent tingles racing all along Catherine's arms and up the back of her neck.

She couldn't speak for the white-hot flare of hope in her chest.

"My dear. What's wrong? Something's wrong." Her father laid a hand on her arm.

Catherine could scarcely get the words out. "Did they print it? The speech?" Her voice shook.

"Of course."

"Will you read it to us, Papa?"

Mrs. Cartwright passed the paper to her father. "He does the voice so well, doesn't he?"

No. No one can do his voice justice, Catherine thought.

Her father cleared his throat and read it, in the stentorian voice he liked to adopt for Lord Kirke. "When I was a boy . . ."

When he was finished, Catherine brushed at her cheeks, surprised to discover they were wet.

"It is very moving, isn't it?" her father said gently. Deeply confused.

She nodded.

"I'll warrant he's a fine man," her father said, clearing his throat.

"The finest," she said fervently, thickly.

Her father and Mrs. Cartwright blinked.

Catherine found herself reflexively standing.

And then, without another word, she turned, walked out of the kitchen, and out of the house entirely.

Because some emotions were too big to be felt at a breakfast table. They required the whole of the blue sky and miles of unfurling green and movement.

Once out there she walked and walked. Faster, and faster. Until she was running. Because some great weight on her spirit had finally shifted and dissolved.

She wanted to cavort.

Perhaps roll down a clover-covered hill.

Finally she did twirl a little, arms straight out, for the pleasure of feeling the rush of country air sift through her fingertips.

He loved her.

He *did* love her.

And all along, she'd thought that he'd been willing to fight for everyone except her. When the truth was he was willing to fight for everyone except himself. He had tirelessly done all of his own fighting for so long, and that included battling his feelings for her.

How he must be suffering to call to her so in that speech. A speech the whole of England, in essence, had heard. How magnificently bloody clever of him.

With his marriage proposal he had tried to claim her in a way that protected his terribly wounded heart.

How had she not seen it?

She'd said *never* to him and he'd stood like a man killed. Her stomach turned in on itself as she relived the perpetration of such a cruelty.

But the fact that he had delivered that speech meant that he hadn't believed her. Not completely.

So she forgave herself. In the storm of emotion and pride and hurt feelings in the aftermath of the gossip, she had been unable to see *anything* clearly. She had no experience at all with this sort of thing, after all. And they *both* had botched things.

But how simple it all seemed now—if they loved each other, she knew there was nothing they couldn't face.

The winning is in the fighting, he'd said. He was a man who simply did not give up. He might not have fought for her a few months ago.

But he was fighting for her now.

And she could meet him halfway.

A LITTLE OVER a fortnight after he'd given the Clover Speech, Kirke encountered Pangborne on the street just as he was leaving a pub in which he'd taken lunch.

They greeted each other with genuine pleasure that surprised both of them.

And then Kirke took a sustaining breath to gather nerve. "I'm glad I saw you today. I've been wanting to thank you for your book recommendation. My son loves *Rob Roy*."

Pangborne went motionless. "Your son?"

To his credit, he managed not to inflect it with anything like shock. He said it almost gently.

"He's seventeen years old. We've met only lately. But I'm very proud of him. The feeling is not yet mutual," he said dryly.

Pangborne took this in silently for a second or two, during which Kirke's heartbeat ratcheted up in speed. Finally he said, "Take it from this parent: no matter what you do, it may never be, Kirke. And even if it is, he may not ever tell you."

It wasn't at *all* easy. It did not come naturally. But Kirke told him, very matter-of-factly and in just a few sentences, how Leo had come into the world: a youthful romance gone awry, a happy enough ending. And that the current relationships between all parties were civilized and congenial. He was paying for his son to attend college.

He was determined that thusly he would rob the gossip sheets of the air needed to kindle any more rumors. And anyone who bothered his son would need to answer to him.

"I am trying to protect him from gossip," he

added. "It may be futile. But I want the world to know I am not ashamed of him."

Pangborne nodded once. He paused a moment, reflecting. "Well, if he can tolerate your company for the duration of a house party, bring him grouse hunting at my estate in Kent in August." Pangborne sounded amused. "And . . . if he is unable to accompany you, just bring yourself."

Kirke couldn't speak for a moment. He endured a tiny pang of warm gratitude. "Thank you for the invitation. I hope we can join you."

And thus, little by little, his life, long held as jealously close to his vest as a hand of cards that could make or destroy his fortune, unfolded a bit more.

He left Pangborne and made for his favorite retreat spot, the pair of ugly lions flanking a bench in the park near the Commons, between which he could sit and glower and breathe in London in peace for a time before he dove back into the fray.

Ten feet away from his favorite bench he stopped abruptly.

It was already occupied.

By a woman.

And as comprehension settled in, his knees nearly gave way beneath him.

He found himself reluctant to move forward. Because if she was a hallucination, he didn't want it to ever end.

Finally, one cautious step at a time, he paced toward her. Slowly. To prolong the journey. To tease out the sweet miracle of it.

He stopped a few feet before her.

Her blue bonnet ribbons fluttered in the breeze while they regarded each other in a silence born of perfect, dumbfounding joy.

"I have looked behind every fern and every green thing I've seen for the last month," he said finally, quietly. "And every last one of them broke my heart, Catherine, because you weren't there."

She smiled tremulously. "I apologize if I'll be intruding on your meeting." She gestured to the lions.

He said nothing for a moment.

"Did you want to hear me breathing?"

She stared at him, and he could see her eyes welling with tears.

"Yes." The word was in shreds.

"I should think you'd be able to hear my heart beating right now, too."

She gave a soft little laugh. "I would stand but . . ." Her voice was faint. "I fear I do not trust my knees to hold me."

"May I sit down?" he asked gently.

She nodded.

He lowered himself next to her, carefully, at a discreet distance. "Please tell me you didn't come to London alone?"

She shook her head. "My aunt and I are staying with Lady Wisterberg. They are off gallivanting and won't be home until later this evening. She thinks I am having a leisurely day of reading."

He smiled slightly. "Your father—is he—"

"My father is well. He is still tired, but happy enough. He was glad to have me back."

"Very, very good." He paused at length. "And you?" he said tenderly. "Are you well?"

It was a long moment before she replied.

She swallowed. "I came to tell you something, Dominic. I thought I could do it. I am not as good at speaking as you are. I fear I am too nervous."

"Perhaps you wouldn't mind if I spoke?"

She shook her head.

He could hear his own breath gusting in and out in the silence, as if it were part of the weather. He could feel his own heart, his own precious heart, rising up from the ashes, thudding in his chest. Measuring out seconds before the courage gathered completely.

"Catherine . . . I am fatally in love with you."

His words seemed to echo in the absolute silence, like the toll of a bell. They hovered there, glistening. Nothing would ever be the same after.

"I think I fell in love with you the moment you handed your handkerchief to me. I love your wit, your kindness, your gentleness, your wisdom, your optimism, your eyes, your hair, your resilience, your mouth, and oh God, the way your body fits against mine. I could foresee no happiness for me unless you were happy, and yet I didn't think I could ever be what you wanted, or offer you the kind of life you wanted to live. And I tried—God how I tried—but I could not imagine the rest of my life without you in it. It was quite a predicament, Catherine. I have been wretched. I am confessing my wretchedness. How cruel of you to look so radiantly happy about it." Her face was, in fact, blindingly beautiful, a tiny sun. "And now you're smiling. All those white teeth. You monster."

She laughed delightedly and dashed her tears away with her hand.

One landed on the back of his hand, like a perfect diamond.

And that's when his own eyes began to burn in earnest.

"Bloody hell." The words were a soft, cracked laugh. "I like you better than anyone I've ever met."

Which only made her more radiant.

They gazed at each other, smiling, and no one

except a nearby bird said a thing for a good long while.

"I think I can speak now," she ventured, whispering.

He drew in a steadying breath, preparing.

"I came here to tell you that you have indeed ruined me," she said softly.

"Have I?" he said gently.

"Oh yes. For . . . polite people. For people who take the easy way. For men who have never had their hearts broken, who don't know what passion means, or what commitment means, or what forever means." Her words trembled with urgency. "If what you want is my happiness, you must accept that I love you and allow me to love you. I will do it so well, Dominic, I promise you, and I will never stop and I *will* not leave you. That's . . . that's what I came to tell you."

He nodded because he couldn't speak. She was blurry now, and he pressed a palm to his eyes to clear his tears.

"And . . ." She pulled in a breath. "I want to apologize for being so unkind and such a child and for hurting you. I didn't know . . . I wasn't sure . . . I didn't want to make you miserable by saddling you with a wife. Making you miserable while I loved you so is the worst thing I can imagine."

"Well," the word was graveled. "Don't apologize. I was a fool, and I deserved a thorough castigation. But I have never been more grateful to be an orator whose words are written in the newspaper. Because here you are. I summoned you. Like a genie from a lamp. Thank you for being brave when I could not be."

"No." She shook her head vehemently. "It was easy for me to be brave because I'd never before had my heart savagely broken. I think you are the bravest person I have ever met. So many people in England think so." She pulled in another breath. "And I have something else to say."

"Oh?"

"I came to tell you that I lied."

He went still.

"When I said the word 'never.'" Her lips tipped in a tremulous smile.

A gust of joy swept through him and took his breath with it.

It was a few moments before he could gather enough air to speak.

And when he spoke, his voice—the voice that rang out over the floor of the Commons, that stirred jaded grown men to tears, that little by little helped to move the mountains that stood between the vulnerable people of England and a safer, freer, more loving future—was textured like coarse velvet. And shook.

"Catherine. You are . . . you are my very heart. I am yours, forever, body and soul, no matter what happens after this day. I want only you, forever. If you would do me the honor of marrying me, the whole of my life will be devoted to loving you and our family. I think we would be so happy. I will *live* to make you happy."

She dashed her hands against her eyes again. Her words were tremulous.

"Yes. Yes, please. I want only you. I want to be your wife."

His head went back hard on an exhale and then he gathered her against him. They clung to each other tightly, wet cheek pressed against wet cheek, their bodies such a perfect fit it was hard to know whose hammering heart was whose.

He took her face in his hands, and laid his mouth on hers.

And between two scowling lions, he kissed her with such unrestrained longing that they were both in quite a state within seconds.

"I want you so," she whispered against his neck. "I cannot bear it any longer. I have wanted you so."

"We can be married inside a fortnight. I can obtain a special license." The words were rushed, staccato with need. "But I want to do this *properly*, Catherine. I want to speak to your father first. But . . ." He gave a short, humorless laugh. "Dear God, I want to make love to you."

"Your home," she said swiftly. "Is it fully rebuilt?"

"Very nearly. I've a chair." He paused. "And a mattress on the floor."

"Take me there now."

He closed his eyes. "Catherine."

"Please. What else am I going to do with this afternoon?" she added.

He gave a short, pained laugh.

"God help me," he said. "If something happens to me between now and the time, we're married . . ."

"It won't. I will not allow it. Even so, I would have made love to you. And then I might get to carry your child. And then I would still have you with me forever. And this is all I want. You forever. Don't you see? It's urgent we not waste another moment."

After a moment, he kissed her very softly and whispered, "So I see."

HE GRASPED HER bonnet ribbon and pulled gently until it came undone.

He lifted it from her, and set it aside.

She turned so he could undo the laces of her dress.

His fingers trembled.

His cravat tangled as he tried to drag it off; she helped him free it. He flung it aside.

He gently lifted her dress from her, and her arms went up to abet him.

He tore off his own shirt.

She reached for his trouser buttons, feeling the jut of his swelling cock against them, and freed it, working the buttons swiftly with shaking fingers.

Thusly they swiftly, almost ceremoniously, unwrapped each other. This methodical statement of intent ramped her desire unbearably, and her nerves, too.

For there would be no return from being entirely mutually naked.

Dominic was somehow much more primal and fearsome without his clothes. He was also almost too beautiful to be borne. She had not quite anticipated this. He seemed an entirely new person, or rather, an additional person, and this made her faint with a sort of erotic fear. The vast vertical line of his shoulders and the bulge of his biceps, the slant of his torso to his narrow hips, the legs that might well have been turned on lathes, much of all of this scattered liberally with dark hair, was the most shockingly carnal construction she could have imagined.

This weakness she felt at her knees—she wondered if it was a deliberate feature of their species: this impulse to crumple in the face of overwhelming strength and beauty and just be taken.

His eyes were black with fierce longing, his face tight with surging emotion, and that's how she knew he was undone, too.

She closed her eyes, shivering with nerves and desire.

He immediately clothed her in himself. Gathered her up into his naked body.

She found herself pressed against thighs so hard it seemed as though he could crush one of hers between them, the flats of his hands glided, feather soft, down either side of her spine, his fingers tracing the bumps of it; down, down, to scoop under her buttocks and urge her up against his swelling cock. And when he did, her head went back on a gasp as lust spiked her. And yes, she wanted to climb him.

His hands traveled back the way they came, and cradled her head, he laid his lips against her throat, where surely he could feel her pounding heart.

How glorious to have skin, so she could feel his against it. Hallelujah, her mind sang. She had never fully comprehended what a gift it was that it comprised nerve endings. Her nipples chafed against his hard chest, lightly furred in dark hair, arousing her nearly unbearably; she turned her cheek against it and rubbed shamelessly. His torso was cut into sections of muscle; he was constructed of furrows, planes, and hard curves. She kissed his nipple, like a wanton, like she knew anything at all about what she was doing. The little leap of his chest when his breath hitched, his arms tightening around her, told her, yes, she perhaps possessed an instinct or two.

She wrapped her arms around his vast back and set her hands free, finding the ditch made by muscles alongside his spine, the little indents in drum-tight buttocks made just for her hands. His skin was hot and smooth. And his cock curved up toward his belly, harder against her, and when she moved against him, his head went back on a hissed-in breath.

Their lips met, and his hands moved over her, long drugging kisses that made her desperate.

Suddenly she was falling, it seemed, or was she flying? But when she felt the mattress beneath her she understood she'd been lowered there, like a fainting maiden. For a moment, he stood, looking down like a conqueror, then he stretched out alongside her. She turned to him.

So odd that the sun was fully blazing into the room over their nude selves. She stroked his hair from his eyes.

"I hardly know where to touch you first." His voice was hoarse. "You are indescribably beautiful. Every bit of you."

"Everywhere," was her whispered suggestion. "Please. Don't miss even one spot." Her heart was hammering. He would be inside her soon, which was what they both desperately wanted. But she was, indeed, equally a little afraid, and consumed with need. She trembled with the surfeit of emotion.

He knew. He was so gentle, so purposeful. He set out to soothe, to arouse, ultimately to possess. Gently, he drew his fingers along the inside of her arm, lighting every one of those cells on fire, showing her a place she'd long taken for granted was a pleasure to touch, and could arouse her when touched.

He lowered his mouth to her breast, and pressed his lips softly against her little birthmark, then took her nipple into his mouth and gently sucked.

"God . . ." she breathed, and arched into his touch.

His hand roamed to her hip, traced the curve of her waist, and his lips were fellow travelers. She sighed when his lips skimmed her belly, while his hands slipped between her thighs, stroking so lightly the shockingly tender skin there, sending rivers of pleasure to the outer reaches of her body, until she was made of nothing but pleasure. It was everywhere in her. Rising, rising like a flood.

"Dominic . . . ?" she whispered frantically.

He knew what she needed. His lips returned to hers while his fingers lingered to twine through the curls between her legs, before sliding into her wet heat to take up a rhythmic stroking. She could feel his cock, hard, large, and impatient-feeling against her hip, and the swift gust of his breath against her throat as her head thrashed back, the pleasure building and building until her body whipped upward, a silent scream torn from her. He held her while bliss broke her into what felt like stardust.

He was shaking with need when he bridged her body. "Sweetheart . . ." His voice was shredded.

She slid her hands down his furred chest. "Don't be afraid," she whispered. "I love you. I want you so much. You won't hurt me."

But her heart was hammering as she shifted beneath him so he could guide himself into her.

The glorious strangeness, the joy of being filled by and completely joined with him, stole her breath.

His eyes were shining with unshed tears as he looked down at hers.

She kept her gaze locked with his, her heart nearly splitting apart from joy and wonder, which evolved quite steadily into a fresh wave of volcanic lust when she witnessed him lose himself completely in her. Saw him, little by little, go mindless with the pleasure of moving in her body. The muscles of his back quivered beneath her clinging fingers. She arched to meet the rhythmic, languid dive of his hips. And she felt everything he kept leashed. The cords of his neck taut. His eyes black and dazed. His breathing a tattered roar.

He closed his eyes. "Oh God. My love. I'm . . ." His breathing was bellows-ragged.

Her hands slid down to his buttocks and she arched against him.

"Faster, please. Dominic. Please. Oh *please*." She was chasing her own release now, too. That she might get yet another one was quite a miracle she hadn't anticipated.

In a mad, swift collision of bodies, of groans and sighs and gripping hands and oaths as pleasure built and built, they shattered together.

THE JOY SEEMED scarcely bearable. He thought it might crack him in two, but that was only because he was resisting it, as was his habit with any force greater than himself.

He breathed out and humbly surrendered. He felt as though he was indistinguishable from it.

She was curled up against him, her petal-soft curves tucked against his hard body, her eyes dreamy and sated, her arm draped over his belly. He possessively smoothed his hand over the pearly curve of her arse.

She rose up on her elbows to gaze down at him earnestly, gently stroking the hair away from his eyes. Her breasts now entirely filled his vision.

"Are you all right, love?" he said softly.

"Never better. Your eyes have gone very dark, suddenly."

"Because your breasts are *right* there and I love them," he said with grave sincerity.

She laughed, and like a wanton, dipped to brush her nipples across his lips, and he caught one, lightly, in his teeth. The sound she made, the little helpless gasp, went straight to his cock.

"It's just that I didn't know you would be so beautiful," she murmured. "It's quite overwhelming."

"You thought perhaps I was a minotaur under my clothes?"

"I'd *hoped* you were. This is even better."

He laughed quietly. Feeling almost shy.

"I didn't know there would be this lovely little road, for instance . . ." she said, and drew a finger lightly, slowly down the line of hair that divided his ribs, traveled down to his belly to his stirring cock. "Or that you would be composed of these distinct sections . . ." One at a time, softly, she kissed the six segments of hard muscle on his abdomen. "Or that there would be lovely fur here, and I could do this . . ." She dragged her fingers gently through the hair on his chest, back and forth over the hard rise of it, and closed her teeth lightly over his nipple.

"Christ," he half breathed, half moaned, *very* impressed and absolutely in thrall, as she discovered and seduced him all at once.

"Or that your thighs would be so *frighteningly* gorgeous and thick . . ." She drew her toes down one in a caress.

"And speaking of gorgeous and thick . . ." She shifted down and kissed his cock, which had leaped to attention and was now arched against his belly.

He made a guttural sound. "God . . . if you wouldn't mind terribly . . . doing that again . . ."

She laughed softly. "Like this?" She drew her tongue along it.

"Holy . . . Mother of God . . ." he breathed.

She quite rightly took this as a suggestion to continue what she was doing. And soon his chest was heaving with hoarse breaths, and he pulled up his knees, and his head thrashed back as he struggled to cope with the pleasure.

Finally he raised himself up on his elbows. "Catherine . . . please . . . come here . . ."

He opened his arms and gathered her, bringing her up close to him so she sat across his thighs. With a thrust he was inside her again. Her head fell back on a caught breath.

"Move with me," he whispered next to her ear. He gripped her hips and urged her in a rhythm guaranteed to drive them both to blissful madness, quickly. They locked eyes, and he knew a surge of triumph and gratitude from watching her eyes go hazed and dark, and feeling the frayed gusts of her breath against his lips, from how she shifted with him to find her own pleasure. He kissed her throat and felt her moan vibrate beneath his lips as they collided more swiftly.

"*Dominic* . . ." she gasped. She was close now. He loved the desperate, joyful way she said his name in the throes of passion. As if he were the key to the universe. As if he were her salvation. He would do anything for her, give her anything she wanted, lay down his life, slay dragons.

He held her tightly as release rocked her body and she screamed her pleasure to the echoing room, and when he came the pleasure nearly blinded him.

"I can't believe we're allowed to do this whenever we want for the rest of our lives," she murmured. His chest was her pillow. His arms were looped beneath her breasts. They might as well have been Adam and Eve lying there, naked in broad daylight on a mattress. "And as loudly as we like."

His laugh rumbled beneath her head. "And the *ways* in which we can do it, Catherine . . ."

Ways! Plural! This struck her as very promising, indeed.

Happiness was a consuming occupation, too, she thought. Nothing more seemed necessary ever than this man, this bed, the sun through the window drying the sweat on their well-loved bodies.

"What will the ton think when they discover we've married?" she wondered.

"I'll tell anyone who asks that we were introduced, I apologized for the distress the gossip may have caused you, and, subsequently, we fell in love. I will explain that we owe a debt of gratitude to whoever made the false insinuations, because they have made us the happiest humans alive. I'll make certain it's printed in *The Times*. All of those things are in essence true. And God, will it annoy a good portion of the ton."

"Clever," she said happily. "You are rather wily."

"Never with you," he said. "I never will be with you."

She was quiet a moment. "They can't hurt us if they don't know us," she said softly. Contentedly.

They were an "us" now; a new entity. There would be storms; he would always attract attention. Together they would always be the eye of any storm.

"If anyone ever tries to hurt you, I will end them," he said calmly. "One way or another."

"Likewise, Lord Kirke."

He smiled, and his chest rose and fell beneath her in a contented sigh.

She propped herself up on her elbows and gazed down at him. "Lady Wisterberg told me about . . . how you paid the footmen. She found out through a sort of chain of gossip."

She felt him go still. And then he gave a soft, rueful, not entirely amused laugh. "She is quite something, Lady Wisterberg is."

HER EYES WERE so soft. Her hair was coming down, the ends of it brushing his chin. The pleasure of it. She completely undid him. He felt incinerated by love and need. Humbled and made absolutely new. He was the bloody phoenix, rising right out of the ashes of a burned house.

To look at her was to crave her.

"I suppose," he said softly, his voice husky and careful, "it's because I loved you from the first."

She kissed his right eyebrow because he was hers, and because she could.

He'd long wondered whether he'd deserved to ever love or be loved again at all, but it seemed to him her love was proof that he was worth loving. That she loved him was a miracle, and yet he believed in it, while he didn't, for instance, believe in genies that lived in lamps, because he knew her heart was honest and true. It was simply who she was.

And if it seemed unlikely a beautiful young woman would choose a complicated life with a man like him, he understood that something in her craved those inhospitable crags and treacherous peaks that were part of his character, just as he craved the soft, green slopes and surprising, hidden, wild rivers in hers. They both were part light and part shadow and this had given their moments together a rare dimension from the first.

Love would be the new terrain they built their life on. They would have a lifetime to explore its perils and glories.

He noticed her gaze roving about the empty room, as if she was filling it with imaginary furniture.

"Do you know anything about decorating? Because I fear that I don't. As you may have noticed."

"Oh, I think we can make our house lovely and not spend a good deal of money at all," she said confidently and comfortingly. "And I think we should have blossoms in a vase in our room, don't you?"

Our house. *Our* room. He loved the word "our." He loved the word "we." He loved the word "wife." He decided he was going to use them with such obnoxious frequency that from now on this was what people would quote to him when he encountered them at balls and in sitting rooms.

"Precisely what I was thinking," he agreed, softly.

Epilogue

᠁᠁᠁

*H*IS BEARING was regal. His expression somber. His eyes were very intense, but then, they usually were.

His hand was cold in hers.

This was the only way anyone would have been able to tell that Lord Kirke was nervous. She knew the echoes of an old fear reverberated in him. She squeezed his hand.

"He will love you," she reassured quietly.

His mouth quirked at the corner. "Well, naturally. I'm easy to love."

She laughed softly. "*I* love you, and he's a lot like me. If all else fails, just use a lot of words with 'r's' in them, and he'll be too enchanted to say no."

He laughed.

He pulled in a steadying breath.

And so into her father's study he went to ask for her hand in marriage.

Dominic liked doctors, on the whole, because little impressed or shocked them. Few people understood better that humans were all the same underneath the skin. And, as Catherine had noted, doctors see a *lot*.

And so even when confronted by a somewhat legendary orator in the flesh, Mr. Keating eyed him with bemusement, amusement, and not a little surprise glinting in his blue eyes. His white hair gave him something of a saintly nimbus.

The study in which they sat was pleasantly lit by

shafts of pale sunlight through the windows, and stuffed full of books and papers. Dominic always felt instantly at home in such rooms.

"Well, Lord Kirke, sir. When my daughter informed me that we were going to have a distinguished visitor today, I confess your name did not spring at first to mind," he said dryly. "It is indeed an honor to meet you. I am an admirer."

"Thank you, sir. Likewise, in both respects. I have heard a good deal about you from Catherine."

Her first name, soft and so intimately familiar, rang between them. Her father's eyebrows went up.

They stared across at each other in mutual fascination and a bit of awkwardness. Given that the last time he'd done this someone had aimed a musket at his face, Dominic thought things were progressing well.

"To what do I owe the pleasure of this visit?" Mr. Keating asked finally.

Her father of course knew—Catherine had been all quivering, radiant happiness when she'd told him they were going to have a caller, even though she hadn't told him why—but he was complying with an unwritten, ancient script by asking.

"I have come to ask for your daughter's hand in marriage."

There was a pause.

"I see." He steepled his hands and tapped his fingers together. He narrowed his eyes and studied Dominic. "And Catherine has already accepted you?"

"I am indeed just that outlandishly fortunate," Kirke replied quietly. He suddenly felt raw and green again, and perilously like he might just—for the first time in two decades—blush. His heart had taken up a swift hammering.

Her father regarded him solemnly, furry white brows meeting at the bridge of his nose.

"Sir, she is . . ." Dominic cleared his throat. "Catherine is my heart."

He saw the words suffuse the man across from him with something like peace and light.

"Well, that much was clear, sir," Mr. Keating said. "You gave an entire speech about her, after all."

Dominic was stunned. "How did . . ."

"It was an easy surmise, son," he said gently. "I read the speech to her. I saw her face when I was finished." He paused at length, and then added, even more gently, "She wept."

Dominic breathed out carefully. The little hairs rose on the back of his neck, as he imagined her expression the moment she'd first heard that he loved her. Joy lit every cell of his body.

This man's gentle acceptance, his kind, matter-of-fact astuteness: how soft love could be. Like that sunbeam through the windows. He realized he'd lived his life somewhat like a feral animal, inching toward this sort of gentleness, unwilling to trust it. It was safe in this room to settle into it, he realized. This kind of love—Catherine's for him, and his for her—would be a feature of his life forever.

"You do know how lucky you are, Lord Kirke?" her father said somewhat absently, turning toward the window, as if studying the view. He gave his fingers a little drum on his desk.

"I do," he said gruffly. "I vow, sir, to keep Catherine forever safe and happy. I will endeavor the whole of my life to make her proud. She will always be comfortable. And never, ever bored."

Mr. Keating turned to him and his face split into a smile so like Catherine's.

"Of that I've no doubt. Just as I've no doubt she loves you. I am pleased and honored indeed to give the two of you my blessing." He extended his hand. "I wish you the same lifetime of joy I shared with her mother."

LADY WISTERBERG HAD, along with Catherine's aunt, first heard the news from the two of them when Dominic escorted Catherine back to Lady Wisterberg's town house the day he'd proposed.

Quite the panoply of emotions chased each other across her visage, while bewilderment and hope flickered across her aunt's. To Aunt Keating, Lord Kirke seemed a fine, famous figure of a man, after all. If somewhat notorious. She didn't regularly fill her cup at the spigot of ton gossip, like Lady Wisterberg.

Finally Lady Wisterberg sat back and sighed in a sort of surrender. Her bemused expression slowly evolved into something like thoughtful, wicked glee. She was clearly imagining the response of the ton when they got wind of this.

"Congratulations, Lord Kirke, on your exceptional good taste," she said with great dignity, finally. "And *well* done, Miss Keating. Congratulations on conquering your season of scandal."

Less than a fortnight later, Catherine and Dominic stood up before Reverend Bellingham at the church in Little Bramble and, in a quietly moving, private little ceremony attended by only her father, her aunt, and Mrs. Cartwright as witnesses, became husband and wife.

And while Lord and Lady Kirke longed to linger in Little Bramble with Catherine's father, duty required they return to London for the final few weeks of Parliament.

Catherine was perfectly game to sleep on a mattress in his London town house and make love like a pagan on the floor until they were able to fill the place with proper furniture, but Dominic wouldn't hear of his wife enduring such a thing when she could be cozily pampered at The Grand Palace on the Thames instead. Luckily, a suite had become available in the annex, despite the fact that the boardinghouse was now nearly full for the season. And as he'd never shied away from awkwardness, politely getting out the words "It's a pleasure to see you again, Mrs. Hardy and Mrs. Durand. We regret our previous dramatic exits. And by the way, Miss Keating is my wife now" posed no real challenge.

And he knew the proprietresses were rather unflappable.

"Oh, I confess we thought something like this might be afoot," Delilah said sagely. "We've some experience with the unpredictable progress of love. Congratulations. We are so happy for the two of you!"

Everyone there was delighted to have them back.

Catherine consulted with Angelique and Delilah about how to find gently used furniture and bargains on curtains, because she wanted their town house sitting room to be soothing and welcoming when Dominic returned home from a satisfying day of political skirmishes and speeches and irritating stodgy people.

They could easily make love like pagans while they were at the boardinghouse, after all.

And oh, did they.

Little Dominic Oliver Kirke (named for his father and grandfather) was born a year and a half after they were married, followed two years later by Serena Eleanor (named for Catherine's mother and grandmother), and then, at last, the handful that was baby Augustus Evander (named for the uncle who had sent Dominic to college). Each one was a uniquely delightful, clever, hilarious, heart-squeezing little terror, the light and bane of their parents' lives, the cause of gray hairs, tears, and hearts swollen with joy and gratitude. Catherine now had her merry racket at the dinner table—they took dinner all together whenever they could—and her chorus around the pianoforte.

When Parliament wasn't in session, the Kirke family often gamboled happily about Little Bramble, the little ones sometimes trailing their much older, very grown-up half brother, Leo, who visited occasionally and whom they worshipped. He, like his father, had entered Lincoln's Inn for law.

And her family had grown exponentially in all directions—she met some of Dominic's rather . . . er, singular brothers and sisters, which meant their children had a lot of cousins.

And eventually, she met Anna, too. Which hadn't been easy; Anna had been, of course, of nearly mythological import in her husband's life. But she was Leo's mother, and Catherine had come to love Leo. She came to appreciate Anna for loving Dominic at all, for giving him happiness when he was young, and for bravely raising that fine young man who was their son. What they had in common was love for their families, and in time they considered each other family, too.

And because they requested it, Dominic took Leo and Catherine to see his clover-covered refuge in Wales.

The three of them lay on their backs on clover and talked meanderingly of everything and nothing. Catherine was almost unbearably moved by so many things: By how the cadences of Leo's voice were so like Dominic's, even though he'd been raised in Yorkshire. By how patient Dominic was, and how he listened so intently to both of them—drinking in their words, asking questions, because they were precious to him. By how this modest little patch of grass and clover might as well be hallowed ground. For his penchant for seeking out quiet green places had indirectly brought Dominic to her.

After a time, she fell silent, and just held her husband's hand and listened to the two of them talking. And when Leo finally laughed with abandon at something witty Dominic said, she squeezed his hand with delight and he squeezed hers back.

And even when Lord Kirke was appointed lord chancellor and elevated by the king to Viscount Carlisle, a title which came with land and a house, it was to the house in Little Bramble they always returned.

In large part because it was where Catherine's parents were spending eternity side by side in the churchyard, and they could visit them. And sometimes when they visited the churchyard they stood together to watch the sunset in softly absorbed silence, his arms wrapped around her from behind.

Catherine's father lived long enough to see baby Dominic's first birthday. And both Catherine and Dominic were fiercely glad that his final years were ones of peace and joy.

As for nearly unflappable Lord St. John Vaughn, he was startled into several days of silent contemplation of the vicissitudes of life by the series of shocking developments—first the gossip about Miss Keating and Lord Kirke, which he'd fully believed to be nonsense, but which his parents had refused to allow him to chance, given the startling circumstances of his sister's marriage (to Hugh Cassidy! An American!).

And then by the news that Miss Keating and Lord Kirke had gone and gotten married.

He was shaken to have been wrong about the gossip. He was not heartbroken—he was, in truth, a bit disappointed yet relieved that the only woman he'd found interesting this season had been snapped up—but he felt mollified and somewhat vindicated that such a singular personage as Lord Kirke had done the snapping. It suggested that he had not been wrong when he'd seen something special in her.

That he'd never once had a clue about the direction of her affections suggested to him that perhaps he knew nothing about women at all, apart from how to get them to flutter their eyelashes (by merely looking at them, that was how). Like the violincello, this seemed something that might be worth learning.

And while over the years Lord Kirke's speeches continued to appear in the newspapers and to be quoted everywhere—and his work continued to stir up debate and controversy and progress, ire and fascination—the gossip columns lost interest in him, eventually, as the Kirkes were clearly blissfully happy, and this was less interesting. They were frequently seen out together, shopping at the Burlington Arcade, for instance, or at balls, always laughing and talking, as if they found each other the best imaginable company. Little by little they gathered around them friends who were good and interesting people, if not always *easy* people, from all walks of life. This suited them well.

Two of them were Mrs. Lucy Hargrove, and her

husband, Mr. Hargrove, who had learned to stop talking about himself constantly because he found his wife fascinating.

Over the years, every now and then when someone tried to stir trouble by bringing up old gossip about her husband, Catherine would field it with dry wit and feel compassion for how unhappy a person must be to feel such pain at the sight of someone else's happiness. *We all become more than one person throughout our lives, if we live long enough*, her husband had once said to her. Together, the two of them were inviolable. Together, they became who they were ultimately meant to be.

And soon everyone knew Lord Dominic Kirke as a man who always danced at balls.

But only with his wife.

"The two of you make sense," Delacorte told Kirke in the smoking room. "I knew she was a good one when she liked the song where you clap instead of saying 'arse.' She ought to be able to put up with you."

They had all, in fact, sung that wicked little song in the sitting room that evening to celebrate the wedding, and they'd all been given a little sherry.

"I'm touched, Delacorte." And Kirke meant it.

"I have begun to wonder if we ought to advertise as matchmakers," Angelique mused to Delilah at the top of the stairs a fortnight later. "Perhaps we should hold a lonely hearts ball in the ballroom and sell tickets."

Delilah laughed, then stopped and tipped her head, thoughtfully. "Hmmm. You know . . . it's not the worst idea."

"I was jesting, Delilah!" Angelique said hurriedly. "But perhaps it's time to have another concert or event. Think of how much fun we'll have planning the decorations!"

"Let's think about it when we have a little more time. But our secret seems to be serendipity, doesn't it? Can you imagine someone like Lord Kirke ever outright admitting his heart was lonely? I suspect he never thought he'd end this season with a wife."

The end of the season had been so satisfyingly busy at The Grand Palace on the Thames that Angelique and Delilah had scarcely had time for a frivolous conversation, or the sort of daydreaming out loud they liked to do in their room at the top of the stairs. The busy times made up for the inevitable lulls. The goodbyes were always poignant, and were seldom easy, but each one was a lesson in appreciating people while they were able.

But fueled in part by *The Arabian Nights' Entertainments*, everyone's dreams had lately been particularly colorful and lively—even, once or twice, lurid. Mrs. Pariseau had awakened with a start from a dream of strolling through an orangery, only to stumble across a naked Mr. Delacorte emerging from an enormous flower. She'd needed a shot of brandy to get back to sleep.

And scattered at very different points across England, a young woman was dreaming about the delightful way her life had been suddenly, improbably, upended. A formidable (some said terrifying) man with a title was mercifully dreaming of not much of anything, happily oblivious that he would soon be *furious* about the way his own would be upended. Another woman dreamed of escaping a way of life that confined her. And another man dreamed of his wicked past, which had been in many ways, great fun, but now he wished to outrun it.

None of them yet dreamed their paths would lead them to the door of a boardinghouse by the docks.

A door which remained under territorial dispute.

In his room, Ben Pike dreamed that a genie burst from a lamp had tried to kidnap Dot, and Ben had knocked him out with one blow. Whereupon Dot had gazed at him worshipfully.

Dot dreamed of a house made entirely of doors. When she finally chose one to open, she discovered Ben Pike standing there.

She'd been so startled she'd hit him again in the jaw.

THE PENNYROYAL GREEN SERIES